I0719744

# TITANS

## Volume One

Published by Acelette Press, 2018

# TABLE OF CONTENTS

**Novella**

Breathe

Book One

# A Nereid for the Titan

# PROLOGUE

Prometheus heard the thunderstorm that carried the chariot of the self-professed Father of Gods. Zeus was closing in.

Where was Pherusa?

She promised to meet him here at dusk. They couldn't hide from Zeus on land, but her father had Poseidon's ear and convinced him to offer them asylum underwater.

He looked around, though she wouldn't come to him from the land. The shore was empty as far as the eye could see.

They had to go now. Why wasn't she here?

Something glimmered in the darkness ahead, making the reflection of the moon ripple on the still waters.

"Pherusa?" Prometheus tried to keep his voice low, but hope and relief made it waver. He waded into the sea, toward her, ignoring the cold. He couldn't will himself to blink across the distance, since using his powers would catch Zeus' attention, but he didn't have to swim there, either. The motion he'd seen wasn't that far out, and even at this fraction of his full height, he was easily as tall as two human males.

Thinking of humans wrapped him in a veil of sadness. He and Epimetheus had such hopes for their creation. They'd teach them love and trust and honor and empathy. Now Prometheus' twin was dead, destroyed before his eyes by Kronos, and the humans had been used both to feed the Olympians' power and as meat shields in the gods' fight against the Titans.

Or rather, against Kronos. So many of the Titans refused to take Kronos' side, yet with him defeated, Zeus turned against them all. One after the other, he'd found them and sent them to the depths of Tartarus, while he'd left the Titanesses finish their lives as mortals.

Prometheus had watched from afar, hidden from Zeus, while his beloved Klymene grew old and perished. Tens of thousands of years had passed, yet he still remembered every line etched in her beautiful face.

He'd buried her and run from the Olympian, mourning his lost love. For eons he had nothing to live for, yet he persevered, unwilling to let Zeus beat him.

Until he met Pherusa—a Nereid as beautiful as Aphrodite herself.

Now he didn't want to run anymore. He ached to build a life with his Siren. A life that would begin tonight.

Where was his love? The water reached his waist now, but her head hadn't broken the surface.

"Pherusa?" he called out, a little more loudly this time.

Her tail sliced the water ahead of him. In the darkness, it seemed more gray than green. His little nymph wanted to play. Despite the direness of their situation, he found himself smiling. She was perfect, and would be all his tonight. Forever. With the approval of the god of the sea, he and Pherusa would be happy and safe together, beyond Zeus' reach. Poseidon was known for being territorial; even Zeus wouldn't dare attack someone his brother had granted asylum to.

Bubbles fizzled in front of him, and Prometheus plunged both hands in the water, meaning to close his palms around his Nereid's supple curves.

Something burned his wrists, and he pulled his hands up with a wince, to see a golden rope wound around them, searing the skin it touched.

Zeus' lightning whip.

Prometheus used his superhuman strength, trying to separate his wrists. To break free of his bonds. His hands could move mountains, but couldn't break Zeus' hold. All he got for his troubles was the smell of charred flesh, as the binds dug deeper. He lifted his arms over his head and roared his frustration—not that he'd been caught, but for Pherusa's betrayal.

She and her father were the only ones who knew Prometheus would be here tonight. She was supposed to take him under. Bring him to her father's underwater kingdom, and mate with him. Instead...

Pain speared his chest, and a bright blue light blinded him.

He didn't have to see, to know. Zeus had pierced him with his lightning.

Prometheus' arms were free now, but he couldn't move them. Or his legs. Or even his tongue, to give Zeus a piece of his mind, when the Olympian ruler floated in front of him.

He was frozen in place, and to add to his plight, his mind wasn't affected by the curse disabling his body.

"I'd take you to Olympus, to decorate my halls, next to Atlas and Hyperion, but I have enough statues there," Zeus said with a smug smirk. "Besides, I heard you wished to live out your long life in the sea, so I'll be magnanimous." His shrewd expression belied his words even before a snap of his fingers sent Prometheus tumbling into the black, cold waters.

It felt like an eternity before Prometheus' back hit the bottom of the sea, but his fall didn't end there. The ground shifted, sucking him into a crater, and earth covered his still form.

He wasn't doomed to Tartarus. He was buried alive, while inside he raged against the god who trapped him and the Nereid who betrayed him.

# CHAPTER ONE

Three thousand years since Pherusa lost the only male she ever loved, yet the way Prometheus looked when she first laid eyes on him was emblazoned into her memory.

He'd come to her father's kingdom, Vythos, to request asylum, and Pherusa was instantly smitten with his coal-black eyes that shone gold when he met her gaze.

Easily half a meter taller than Father, who was the tallest male she'd seen till then, he swam toward her with his dark mane swirling around his head. The humans' sense of propriety hadn't spread to Vythos yet, and he'd been naked and glorious. His body could have been chiseled into granite, from his wide chest, to his hard abs and strong legs.

But something else had caught Pherusa's hungry gaze.

Vythos didn't yet have the air bubbles that allowed her family and the merpeople to assume their human form, and while Pherusa had often visited the surface with her sisters, she'd never seen a disrobed human male. She was mesmerized by what hung from the thatch of hair between the Titan's legs.

Prometheus had caught her looking and smiled, and it was like dawn itself had forced its way into the bottom of the Mediterranean Sea and warmed her heart.

"Are you all right?" Palaemon asked, snapping her back to the present.

Father and the sea hag hid Vythos in the deepest region of the Mediterranean Sea the very day Prometheus was taken from her, to protect the merpeople from Zeus' wrath, if he decided to punish them for siding with a Titan. Nobody but the witch and sea daimons could travel between it and the surface unassisted since. Instead of a bespelled amulet, like Circe gave Father and Mother for that purpose, Pherusa had been assigned this sea daimon.

"I'm fine. Thank you for bringing me." She managed a smile for her old friend. Not his fault he was another painful reminder of Prometheus' demise.

*Not dead. In Tartarus.*

Same thing. He was lost to her and to the world, either way. And such a monumental loss it was—not only had her heart gone with him, but humans also suffered the lack of his guidance.

"Do you wish for me to wait?" Palaemon asked, same as every single time he brought her here. His eyes, blue like sapphires, glinted with pity she didn't care to acknowledge.

"No. Come back for me at dawn," she replied, like she always did. She knew what he'd say when he returned too. Not much changed in her life after her hope for a *happily ever after* was snuffed out by Zeus.

*May he and Poseidon and the rest of their ilk be lost in Lethe forever.* Though the last of the Olympians faded years ago, and she and her family were the only deities remaining in this world, she wouldn't voice her thought aloud.

Palaemon went under with a *splash*, and Pherusa turned toward the beach on which she'd once promised to meet her love. The waterline had receded through the years, and the persistent waves had worn the rocks into sand, but she still felt it as *their* place. Hers and Prometheus', even if he wouldn't set foot on it again.

She slapped the water with her tail, until she was close enough to shore for her scales to give way to smooth skin and her green tail to split into pale legs. She walked the rest of the distance to the sand, and there she dropped to her knees and wept.

Pain, raw and fresh as on the day he was taken from her, tore through her heart and made her stomach heave. It was a physical torment that squeezed her lungs like a vise and stole her breath. Hot tears spilled down her cheeks, until her eyes burned but could produce no more moisture, and her sobs were stolen by the wind.

She sat up and gathered her knees to her chest. The sand was still warm, though the sun had set, but it did nothing for the cold void between her ribs.

"I'm sorry," she whispered to the evening sky, although Prometheus wouldn't hear her. He wasn't up there. His gentle soul was locked up in the underworld, along with those of his brothers. And it was her fault. If she hadn't listened to Father that night, if she hadn't accepted his promise that the Ichthyocentaur Aphros would bring Prometheus to her...

And she was wasting her night, thinking of Prometheus' last day on earth, instead of their time together.

She lay on her back and studied the stars above, searching for a new one. Titans might be condemned to Hell, but there had been whispers in Vythos that the earth itself was nudging them awake. If any one of them could escape Tartarus, it would be Prometheus. He was always so creative and smart. He understood how things—and gods and animals and people— worked, just by looking at them.

And he was good with his hands, too. He'd had a wicked way of bypassing her defenses and making her ask for more. She'd beg him to caress her breasts, her belly, and lower...

Not a moment passed when she didn't begrudge herself the choice to wait until they had her parents' blessing as a couple, before she gave herself to him completely. If she'd done it sooner, she'd have memories of his sculpted body pressed to hers, to keep her warm when loneliness and sorrow chilled her to the bone.

She closed her eyes and spread her legs, for the lapping wave to reach the apex of her thighs.

Prometheus had convinced her to let him taste her *once*. Sadly, the sea foam couldn't come close to the sensations that had made her body tingle. Neither did her hand, when she slid her fingers through her short curls and along her slit. Nothing compared to him, and she'd forever be bereft.

The future looked bleak as her present, so Pherusa once more focused on her past with him.

Father didn't have the power to grant someone asylum within Poseidon's realm, but he'd offered the Titan a secret room, cloaked from the gods by the witch, so he could rest for a few weeks before he resumed running. Pherusa spent her free time trying to spot his hiding place.

Heat spread from her cheeks down to her chest, as she recalled the day she finally found it.

*He left the door ajar, disrupting the cloaking spell, and was on his bed, spread legs dangling over the edge. Pherusa watched through the opening as he fisted his hand around the flaccid member between his legs and tugged. She was intrigued by how his phallus grew long and thick with his strokes.*

*She barely breathed while he tortured himself, his beautiful face contorted in what she later found out was ecstasy. He turned and looked straight at her. "Like what you see, little Siren?" he asked in her head, the way sea creatures communicated underwater.*

*She liked it so much, she forgot she wasn't supposed to be there. Braveness or stupidity made her push the door open all the way, so he could see her nod.*

*Prometheus smiled that sinful smile of his and beckoned her closer. "Come inside, and I'll show you more."*

*She timidly swam a couple meters closer to his bed.*

*Sitting up with a wicked grin, he opened his mouth and inhaled, filling his lungs with water.*

*Immortals didn't drown, but Pherusa couldn't think, with his body turning hard again in front of her eyes. "Stop," she screamed in his head.*

*The oxygen bubble he blew out filled the room, displacing the water so fast, she barely had time to shift her position, so she didn't fall when her tail was replaced by legs. A flick of his wrist, and the door banged shut.*

*Before Pherusa could blink, he had her very human, very naked body pressed to the slick wood.  "I've seen you watching me, little Siren," he said against her cheek. His deep, smooth voice glided over her senses, adding to the ball of fire swirling in her belly. "Are you spying on me for your father, or is it curiosity, driving you?"*

*She hadn't felt desire this strong before. It took every ounce of willpower, for her to mutter, "My father has nothing to do with this."*

*Prometheus let out a growl that made her shiver, and crushed his mouth to hers. He ran his tongue along the seam of her lips, and at her gasp, thrust his tongue between them, to battle with hers. His teeth nipped at her mouth, as he swallowed her breaths.*

*Her body was on fire, and he hadn't even touched her. Yet.*

*When he broke away from the kiss, she met his gaze. "You said you'd show me."*

She cupped her sex now, on their beach, and circled her button with her index and middle fingers, pretending she was with him, in his room, more than three millennia ago, as he directed her hand first to please herself, and then to give him another climax.

She'd been trying to wrap her mind around this new power she'd discovered—to drive a Titan over the edge with just one hand—when he'd pushed her back onto the bed and covered her body with his.

If only she hadn't stopped him...

She moved her fingers faster, pressing down on her clitoris, while she pinched her nipple with her free hand. It wouldn't do. She'd chased after her orgasm before, but without him, it never worked.

Why hadn't she let him inside her body when he asked? She'd let him into her heart and mind and soul in the days that followed, but insisted they should wait for when they were officially mated. Father had given his blessing when she went to him in tears and begged him to ask Poseidon for help. But it was too late.

*"Let me see you."* Prometheus' words rattled in her brain, as vivid as if they'd been spoken aloud, and she spread her legs wider, in reality and in her fantasy. She stopped touching her mons and grazed her fingernails along her inner thigh, holding her breath as she served herself to the hungry gaze of her imaginary lover.

*"So beautiful. And all mine."*

She startled when she felt a heavy weight settle on top of her, but she didn't open her eyes. If her imagination offered her one single time with Prometheus, she'd do nothing to make it slip between her fingers.

"Look at me. I need to see your gorgeous eyes." The sea breeze caressing her cheek could be his breath, as if he whispered in her ear.

She shook her head. "If I open them, you'll disappear." It wouldn't be the first time he came to her in a vision, but she hadn't been awake before, and she wouldn't risk reality swooping in and taking him away now.

Something blunt nudged her mound, and in her mind's eye, Prometheus aligned his length with her entrance. "You haunt my dreams," he said. "Why do I love you in my dreams?"

Such a weird question, but Pherusa's body was humming with need, and deciphering a phantom's words would have to wait. "Take me," she whispered. "Please."

Rough fingers dug into her hips, the sensation so vivid, she hitched a surprised breath. Lips, warm and soft, yet demanding, closed over hers and swallowed her moan. When his tongue wedged its way into her mouth, to tangle with her own, Pherusa gasped at the intensity of his kiss. Her fantasy started fraying at the edges, and she tried to return her hand to her clitoris, needing the friction to help her hold on to the tattered images.

"No," Prometheus said. "That's mine." He pressed his thumb to her clitoris and twisted.

"Please," she cried to the heavens, squeezing her eyes shut harder. *"Please."*

His form solidified again behind her eyelids, and she focused on his eyes. She hadn't remembered how striking a gold they were when he called on his powers. She tangled her fingers in his long, dark hair, and the wet tresses felt so real, she half-expected him to be here, above her, if she dared look.

"Are you sure, little Siren?"

Oh, how she'd missed hearing him call her that. She nodded. "Yes. Make me yours."

She didn't expect the sharp jab of pain when he pushed inside her.

Her eyes flew open and teared up at the suddenness and force of the invasion. Her tight sex stretched around his girth as he thrust through her hymen. Her vision was blurry, but she wasn't mistaken. The man pressing her to the sand and plunging into her body was the one she thought she'd lost forever. *"Prometheus,"* she whispered

"Were you expecting someone else?" His smile was as bright as the sun, as he propped himself up on one arm so he could cup her breast with the other. "Play with yourself, little Siren. Like I taught you."

Pherusa didn't care how he was here or for how long. She was finally fully his. She rubbed furiously at her clitoris, while he devoured her mouth and then licked a trail down her throat. "So real," he murmured against her skin. "I can taste you."

He smelled of seawater and darkness and pure masculinity, his power crackling along her skin when he touched her. He closed his lips around her other nipple and sucked, his teeth and his callused hand sending jolts of pleasure to her core in time with his thrusts. Soon, the pain between her legs was muted into a dull throb that gradually gave way to white-hot pleasure.

And still he drove into her, making her writhe and moan, until stars burst behind her eyelids and her limbs trembled with the aftershocks of her release.

His shaft tightened and jerked inside her. He pulled out and pumped his length with his hand, until his spendings coated Pherusa's belly and thighs.

"My love?" She wrapped her arms around his neck, but Prometheus disentangled himself from her grip and stood.

His eyes were wild as he stepped away from her, but his gaze turned icy when he drew it down her body.

She resisted the urge to cover herself.

"Tell Nereus, this was only the beginning," Prometheus said, his mouth twisted in distaste. "Tonight, I took his daughter. Soon, I'll come for his kingdom."

# CHAPTER TWO

Pherusa sat up and reached for him. "My love, what are you saying? It's getting cold. Please hold me. Tell me what power returned you to me." Her tone was light, but he heard the slight tremble. What glistened on her eyelids wasn't saltwater; she was tearing up.

He put more distance between them. *Chaos.* This was supposed to make him feel better, not worse. Not the intercourse—that was as incredible as he'd hoped, back when he was truly alive and Pherusa fell asleep in his arms. As amazing as he dreamed it would be, those moments when he slipped into unconsciousness under the bottom of the sea, his mind tired of plotting against her.

He'd believed this to be a fantasy too at first, but being inside her was like coming home. His imagination couldn't summon the sensation of her slick body gripping him, her soft breasts pressed against him, or the taste of her mouth when he plundered it with his tongue.

Should he forget his schemes and take her in his arms? Make love to her again and again until they were too exhausted to move?

No. Claiming her might not have been part of his plan, but it would act as the first step toward settling their score.

"Prometheus, what's wrong?" She gasped and brought her hand to her mouth. "You're not him, if you're scorning me. *You can't be*. He'd never hurt me so. Who are you?"

She'd been the first thing on his mind when the earth shuddered and slid off his body. He'd felt warm blood rush in his veins and instinctively clenched his fists. He could move. He'd dug his way out of his watery grave and propelled himself through the waves, with her on his mind. He couldn't name what led him to *their* cove instead of Vythos, to surface in front of her naked form, spread out on the sand like a feast in his honor.

"Oh, it's me. Have no doubt." Prometheus tried to glare, but her sea-green eyes were filled with pain that tugged at his soul. He hated every traitorous cell in his body, for aching to wrap himself around her and make her feel secure and loved for eternity.

Throughout his imprisonment, he'd planned for the moment he'd cross paths with her again. He expected her to be shocked. Appalled that he'd returned. Scared about what that meant for her safety. She'd try to run, but he'd stop her. He'd never brought himself to fantasize about physically hurting her, but there were more ways to break someone. Like ravaging their kingdom and hurting those they loved. And he'd make her his slave for the rest of time.

Not a sex slave, of course. He'd never force himself on an unwilling female, even if she'd hurt him gravely.

*Chaos*, had he done so already? Had Pherusa been unwilling when he took her on the beach? She'd begged him to… Was it to placate him? But she'd seemed so happy to see him. And he'd been the first to push through her barrier.

"My love? Please?" Her plea made his knees weak.

What was wrong with him? He wasn't supposed to moon over her. That she welcomed him with open arms and offered herself to him was a pleasant surprise only because it made things easier, not because it allowed him to pretend for a moment that she really loved him.

Plucking her maidenhood should add to his satisfaction. She must have been saving herself for a male Nereus approved of, and Prometheus had destroyed every chance of that. He should be feeling victorious. Instead, he felt colder than when he was covered by tons of earth and water.

Not trusting himself to speak or move without yielding to her pull, he concentrated on the cavern that had been his home, and willed his essence to its entrance. The beach and Pherusa faded from view, to be replaced by a different seaside scape. It took him a heartbeat to recognize it. Trees he'd never laid eyes on cast their shadow on rocks smoothened by the tide, and new structures lined the shore to his right that was much more expansive than it used to be, but his senses marked the place as *his*.

Like Pherusa was his.

He shook away the thought and turned to his cave. Its mouth was littered with odd-shaped objects. Offerings? They were unlike anything he'd seen before. The materials were odd, and the colors brighter than he'd encountered in nature.

He treaded over them, careful not to disturb them and make his presence known, and looked around. Rocks blocked the entrance to the lower level. Hopefully, that meant it remained undisturbed. Not that he'd mind finding a beast had claimed the place as its own. A fight might help fill the void that spread in his gut at the memory of the pain etched on Pherusa's gaze when he left her. He could still hear her cries for him to stay, though he'd put miles between them.

No. He didn't care about her pain. She'd betrayed him. She deserved everything she got.

But she'd remained untouched while he was away.

Unwilling to linger on that, he blinked to the depths of the cave and reached out with his senses, to ensure he was alone. His eyes had yet to adjust, but he heard no heartbeat or breathing, and smelled nothing but dank, stale air. He waved his fingers and willed light to spill out of them and tear through the darkness. His private space wasn't marred by anything but time.

Not that anyone could tell the space had been occupied before; there was no furniture or clothes. Prometheus shaped the earth to suit his every need as that arose, and he had no need for loincloths, which were an invention of the Olympians. But there, in the corner, the floor was raised in a circle, where he rested his body the last night it was his to rest.

How long since he last slept here?

How long since he last laid eyes on her?

He had no way of tracing the passage of Helios's chariot across the skies while he was in stasis, but it hadn't been long enough for Pherusa's lovely heart-shaped face, sea-green eyes, long golden locks, and full lips, or the curves of her supple body to fade from his memory.

He slammed his fist into the stone wall, and cursed when it gave way instead of hurting him.

"Feeling more manly, now that's out of your system?"

Prometheus spun around at the sound of the male voice, but he was still alone, except for Pherusa's sobs echoing in his head.

"Show yourself, god," he ordered.

"Not until you promise to behave. I saw what you did to that poor Nereid. You broke her heart."

Prometheus' gut twisted. "It was nothing she didn't deserve." Did he still have feelings for her? How, after what she'd done? Her tear-streaked face flashed before his eyes, and he hated himself. For making her hurt. For caring that he did. "And how is what I do any concern of yours?" he asked.

"I'm trying to figure out if you're the man my mother told me you are, or this asshole who fucks women on the sand and leaves them in a crying heap."

Half the words in that sentence meant nothing to Prometheus, but he got the gist of it, and he didn't like how it made his chest constrict. "Avoiding derogatory remarks might be wise, if you wish to ensure your safety." He had to keep talking, to locate the god's position.

"You'll excuse me for not taking advice from you when it comes to manners. I'm not the one who left his woman bawling her eyes out on the beach after he took her virginity." Like a dog with a bone, this one.

Prometheus roared and swung his fists in the air. Not his fault. *Not his woman.*

"Relax, man. I'm here to help, not get my ass handed to me."

What was he talking about? "Why would I want to hand you anything?" And what was an ass?

"I really can help you. Say you won't hurt me."

Prometheus swallowed back his irritation. "I won't unless I'm forced to." Which he probably would be, the way the god was going, and that was a good thing. A god could hurt a Titan, and if Prometheus was in physical pain, he might forget the agony of having his heart torn from his chest by Pherusa.

A male form shimmered into existence in front of Prometheus' eyes. He wasn't one of the Olympians, but that didn't make him a friend.

"I am Eros, the god of love." The god gave him a sweeping bow. "At your service."

Prometheus studied him with narrowed eyes. Could he be Zeus transformed? No. He didn't give off that sense of infinite power. "You're not an Olympian?"

The god shook his head. "My mother was Aphrodite."

That saved him from being pummeled. Aphrodite had won a spot in Prometheus' heart, with her charming, easygoing nature. Prometheus could see the resemblance now. Eros had his mother's pale-blue eyes, dimpled chin, and golden hair. But—
"She *was*? Did something happen to her?"

Eros' expression fell. "She was the last of the Olympians to fade from existence as the world moved on without them."

The world moved on? The Olympians were gone? So Zeus was gone too? Prometheus wouldn't be able to torture him like he deserved. Fresh fury clawed at his insides, but he stifled it. "Your mother was kind and gracious. I am sorry to hear of her demise. Who rules the world now?"

Eros shrugged. "Technology. Money. Greed. The internet."

"New gods? Were they the ones who freed me? And what about my brothers?"

Leaning back against the cave's wall, Eros said, "You were the first to break stasis. We aren't sure if you were awakened by human action, but whatever caused it, you may want to treat Pherusa better from now on."

"You are here to plead her case?" Prometheus roared. The cave rattled around them, and small rocks came loose to clatter to his feet. Good. He ought to transform to his full size and let the cave collapse. They'd survive it, but it would shut the insolent mini-god up for a while.

"See this?" Eros pointed to a crack on the wall. "This is gonna happen to you, if you're not careful. The way Zeus formed the curse he hit you with, if you were ever free, you'd have to bond with your soulmate, to keep from unraveling."

Prometheus arched his eyebrow. "The words you sling my way hold no meaning."

Eros blew a blond curl out of his eyes. "I was afraid of that. Give me your hand."

The underworld would be turned into a flower garden before Prometheus willingly let a god touch him.

Eros must have known, because in the blink of an eye, he had his palm pressed to Prometheus'.

Prometheus tried to break the contact, but the god said, "Let me show you," and all resistance melted away, as images and sounds and smells flooded Prometheus' senses. He searched the instances for glimpses of Pherusa and hated himself for it, but she was nowhere to be seen. Because this wasn't about her.

*Civilizations, rising and falling. Mortals, killing each other and bringing forth new life. Creation and disaster. Nature, yielding and pushing back. New languages. Old passions. New gods—some benevolent, some calling for blood—and humans leaving those behind too. Pain and pleasure and knowledge and idiocy and a million ways of disseminating information.*

Also, Eros was more widely known as *Cupid*. Which was Latin. And Prometheus could speak and understand it, along with every language invented since he last walked the earth—including those forgotten.

His head throbbed, as he absorbed millennia of knowledge and experience. *Millennia.*

Eros let go and stepped back. "Now you're all caught up, I need to talk to you about Pherusa."

Prometheus growled and blinked out of there.

He'd been trapped under the seabed for three thousand years, kept from this new, human world.

He'd tried to save it. Now it was time to tame it. And he'd start with the sea.

# CHAPTER THREE

It must have been a dream. That, or a cruel joke by a shape-shifting being. But who would do such a thing?

Palaemon and Delphinos could change forms at will, like all sea daimons.

No. Neither Pherusa's old friend nor her sister's mate would lie with her as a joke, and the rest of the daimons wouldn't dare as much as touch her hand without her explicit permission.

The man who'd... *fucked* her, as some of Mother's favorite reads called mating, didn't only look like her Titan, he also felt and smelled like him. His scent lingered in her nostrils. She tasted him when she licked her lips—Prometheus and the saltiness of the tears gliding down her cheeks.

*"Tonight, I took his daughter."*

Why would he be so cruel? For centuries, Pherusa wished she could have touched him once more. Kissed him once more. And now he came to her and completed her—showed her what true ecstasy meant—only to cast her aside?

It had to be a dream.

Pherusa looked down at herself. The seawater had washed away his spendings and the blood of her maidenhead, but she was sore between her legs, and his palm had left red marks on her breast and hip.

It had been him. Somehow, Prometheus was returned to her. She still felt him inside, and she wanted nothing more than to make it a happy memory, to last her the rest of her eternal existence.

But she couldn't forget his look when he turned her away, or how it shattered the remains of her broken heart.

Prometheus wouldn't hurt her like that. His imprisonment was messing with him.

*Why do I love you in my dreams?*

Or an unseen power was messing with them both. He might believe he was dreaming too, and that she hadn't truly been there with him.

She stood on shaky legs, to look around. "Prometheus?" she called out. The beach was empty at this hour, but she wouldn't care if someone heard.

She turned one way, then the other, seeking the outline of his body against the city lights in the horizon. "Prometheus, where are you? Talk to me. I love you." But did he still love her? The look he'd given her was one of hatred. And his words...

*Soon, I'll come for his kingdom.*

He'd coupled with her to prove a point? Something was wrong. The Prometheus she knew and loved had nothing but love for her and respect for her father. Could the ages he spent in Tartarus have warped his mind?

"Prometheus?" she called out again. She'd gladly search for him, naked as the day she was born, but she had no idea where to start. "My love?" Her voice broke, but she kept calling for him until her throat was sore and her eyes burned.

A head appeared in the distance, and then wide shoulders, as an obviously male form slid through the water toward her. Hew heart skipped a bit. Was he back?

The male waved and called her name in a voice she knew well. It wasn't her Titan. Palaemon had arrived, to deliver her back to the palace that hadn't felt like home in forever.

But she still had a couple hours till dawn.

She stood and splashed toward him until the water was as high as her hipbone, then dove under the surface. Her legs gave way to her tail, and she swished it from side to side, propelling herself forward.

She ducked her head in the water, to wash away any signs she'd been crying, and then surfaced to meet Palaemon. "Why are you here?" It came out snappier than she meant for it to.

"Your father sent me. The sea hag said one of the Titans awoke, not far from here, and the palace is on high alert." As the last remnants of the old world, Nereus and his people's survival hinged on keeping their existence secret, and it'd be very difficult to do so if Titans were running loose. Plus Father was worried that, if the Titans returned and found no Olympians to take their wrath out on, they'd redirect it to Vythos.

Was he right? Was that what Prometheus was going to do?

*Soon, I'll come for his kingdom.*

She placed her hand on Palaemon's shoulder. "Let's go."

Pherusa barely paid any attention to how the waters changed around them, until her father's kingdom spread out beneath them, awash in the pale-golden glow that replaced both the rays of the sun and the moonlight down here.

Palaemon helped her in the bubble and averted his gaze when she regained her human form. "Call me if you need me," he said, as Pherusa was wrapping a seaweed robe around her bare body.

She entered the palace and made her way to her room. She'd say nothing. What happened was between her and Prometheus. She'd shower and lie in her cool sheets and only recall the parts of tonight that made her happy.

*Drat.* Halie was waiting outside Pherusa's door. For an achingly long moment, Pherusa wanted to slap away the smile that hadn't left Halie's face since she and Delphinos got together.

Shame over her pettiness was added to the swirl of emotions tugging at Pherusa's chest. She should be happy for her younger sister.

She tried to return Halie's smile, but her cheeks hurt, and her eyes stung, and her heart was breaking all over again. "Sister. What brings you here at this time of night?"

Halie buzzed with barely concealed excitement. She always was a ball of energy, but her hazel eyes never shone this bright before she bonded with her sea daimon. "Didn't you hear? One of the Titans is up, and I heard mutterings among the fish that it's"—she lowered her voice—"Prometheus."

Pherusa tried to swallow down the fresh bout of tears, but her throat was clogged with emotion.

Halie grabbed both Pherusa's hands and bounced on the balls of her feet. "This is your chance. You could be with the man you love. Don't you see?"

How did Halie know she still loved him? Halie wasn't born yet when Zeus took him away, and Pherusa'd only mentioned him once, in passing.

"*Pherusa*, I'm telling you your man may be back. This is good news, no matter what Father says."

Pherusa leaned against the wall, letting the cool seep through the thin robe and into her skin, to soothe her nerves. "What *does* Father say?"

Halie flicked her wrist in a dismissive gesture and tucked her red hair behind one ear. "Oh, you know. That any Titan who returned from Tartarus will probably be mad after all this time, and that we should be ready for an attack or something."

The cool was no longer soothing. It felt clammy. Pherusa wanted to shed her robe and her skin and everything Prometheus ever touched. He hadn't made love to her; he'd conquered her. And he planned to do the same to Vythos.

"Father is right," she whispered and forced herself to tell Halie how Prometheus came to her and made her his before spitting out a threat and disappearing.

Halie's expression fell, and her eyes darkened with rage. "That *asshole*," she spat.

Pherusa winced. She didn't recognize the word, but she got its meaning. "For years, I blamed Father for Prometheus' imprisonment. Maybe Prometheus does too." But why take it out on her? Didn't he know she loved him?

"That doesn't excuse his behavior." Halie's scowl deepened. "Though I guess it would explain it. You have to tell Father."

Pherusa felt the blood drain from her head. "I can't—"

"Not about the sex, obviously. About Prometheus' coming after Vythos. We have to be prepared."

How? What could they do against a Titan set on destruction? Maybe the witch knew a spell to hold him in place long enough for Pherusa to talk to him. Pherusa nodded. "Will you come with me?"

Halie pulled her into a hug. "Wild seahorses couldn't stop me."

The contact was more than Pherusa had allowed any of her sisters in a long while. She and Halie were never close, and accepting her support was odd, but she couldn't help feeling grateful as her sister led her to the council room.

Halie knocked, and a servant answered the door.

"We are here to see our father," Halie said.

The man seemed uncomfortable. "King Nereus is meeting with his generals. I will tell him you asked—"

"*Father.*" Halie pushed the door open and strode inside, pulling Pherusa along. "You need to hear this."

The room erupted in objections, but Delphinos was at their side in the blink of an eye. "*Silence,*" he yelled, and the other generals quieted down. As the king's son in law, he commanded more respect than when he was only their peer.

Father stood. "I will need a moment alone with my daughters. We will reconvene afterward." Even before he knew what this was about, he prioritized family. How could Pherusa ever suspect this man would jeopardize her happiness by handing her beloved over to Zeus?

"No. They should stay." Pherusa's voice came out a croak. She looked at the seven sea daimons in the room. They needed to hear this. She only wished the witch weren't here. The woman's haggard visage always unnerved her, and her blind eyes seemed focused on her. But Father trusted her, and the witch never steered him wrong.

Pherusa squeezed Halie's hand in a gesture meant to reassure, and then stepped to the middle of the gilded room. "Prometheus is back."

Nereus' smile made her cringe. "He was the one awakened? That is such good news, daughter."

Pherusa shook her head. "He's not who he used to be. He said he's coming for your kingdom, Father," she said loud enough for everyone to hear, though her gaze was locked with her father's.

Shocked gasps filled the air, as Father fell back in his coral throne with a huff. "You must be mistaken. Please, tell me exactly what happened."

Parts of the night were to be hers alone, but she'd share what she could. "Tonight was the anniversary of… his capture. I went to the beach where I was supposed to meet him that night. I don't know where he came from. One moment I was alone, and the next he stood above me—"

*He lay on top of her. Thrust into her. Made her come until she couldn't contain more pleasure.*

"—and said to tell you he was coming for your kingdom."

*Next.* He was coming for Vythos next, because first he'd taken her.

Whispers rose around her but were silenced. All gazes were trained to somewhere behind her. She spun to see Prometheus, huge and naked, with wild hair and even wilder eyes.

"Why don't you tell your father the whole truth, little Siren?" he boomed, staring her down.

# CHAPTER FOUR

Pherusa blanched and stumbled backward, but Prometheus squelched the voice that told him to run to her and never hurt her again. Only her pride was wounded, for now everyone knew the Titan she'd deceived had found his way between those shapely, pale legs. Nothing like the pain she caused him when he realized the female he planned a life with had sold him out to the Olympians.

But she was so beautiful to look at.

The puffiness around her eyes brought out the green in her irises, and her golden tresses—tangled from their time on the sand—called for him to run his fingers through them. Was she a witch, to still have such a hold over him?

Nereus' seven generals stepped forward, swords and lances at the ready. Prometheus had broken bread with more than a couple of them and would hate to end them, but he would if he had to.

"Stand down," King Nereus called out to them. They lowered their weapons but didn't sheathe them, and their tense posture, shoulders hunched and legs slightly bent, said they were ready to pounce.

Prometheus smirked at Pherusa. "Why don't you tell your father you begged me to—"

"Say no more." Nereus' voice reverberated off the walls. "Though we all know of the fondness between you and my daughter, private matters should be kept private."

Prometheus spared Pherusa a glance he hoped spoke of his disdain, and not of worry that she seemed to use the woman next to her as a support to remain upright. "Funny you and your daughter didn't give privacy a second thought when you told Zeus exactly where to find me."

A squeak came from Pherusa, and when he looked, shock and pain were etched on the widening of her eyes and the roundness of her mouth. Such a good actress, staying true to her role even after all these centuries.

"Save your theatrics, little Siren. You and Nereus were the only ones who knew where I'd be."

"I swear to you, it wasn't us. I loved you with all my heart. How could you not know that?"

Pherusa's cry tore at his heart as much as her use of the past tense did, but he wouldn't allow himself the weakness. He turned back to Nereus, unable to watch the tears rolling down her cheeks. "And you—"

"How dare you?" Nereus closed the distance between them and glowered at Prometheus, impossibly imposing for a man half a meter shorter than him. "I grieved for you like I would for my own blood. My daughter mourned for you every day you were away. She became a recluse. No one has heard her laugh in three thousand years, and you think she'd betray you?"

Something skittered in Prometheus' chest, but he paid it little heed. His rage was too potent, too consuming, for it to allow room for other feelings. "Was it you then, *old friend*?"

Nereus backhanded him.

Prometheus thought he was done being surprised, but this minor deity's laying a hand on a Titan stunned him long enough for Nereus to say, "I understand you need a target for your wrath, but you won't blink into my castle, inside my kingdom, to hurl unfounded accusations and make my daughter weep."

Prometheus should smite the man, but that might not hurt enough. "Oh, you should see how I made her weep on that beach, when I—"

"*Stop*," Pherusa pulled him back from her father. "Look at me. I swear to you, on everything I hold dear, that neither Father nor I had anything to do with your capture."

It took everything he had to withdraw from her warm touch that made his skin tingle. "*My capture?* I was in stasis, buried alive beneath the bottom of the sea, for ages."

"Three thousand years, yesterday. I counted them," she whispered.

Had she? Could he be wrong? Could his imprisonment have cost her as much as it did him? *No.* He'd been the one trapped in darkness. Alone. "You also swore you loved me and would help me hide from Zeus, and I believed you. You think your oaths hold any weight now?"

"It wasn't me. Father was worried that night, and he implored with me to stay here and let Aphros bring you to me. I shouldn't have listened, but I would never knowingly hurt you. You have to believe me." She took a step back, her gaze pleading with him, but it wouldn't work. She'd once convinced him he was her everything. Now, he knew better.

"Every time you open your mouth, more lies come out. No matter. I'm not here for you; I'm here for your father. " To Nereus, he said, "You have a day to hand me your kingdom, before I destroy it."

A sea daimon with green hair, whom Prometheus didn't recognize, stepped up. His hands were bare, but sea daimons could change form at will, so being weaponless made him no less dangerous. "King Nereus, let us detain him. He may be more reasonable after a few hours locked away."

Prometheus laughed. "I was *locked away* longer than you've been alive, little man. See what it did to my reason? Make a move, and I'll show you my true form before I bring this palace down on all of us. I have nothing to lose."

"No blood will be spilled because of me," Nereus said. "But I cannot hand you—"

The old crone behind Nereus put a skeletal arm on the king's shoulder and whispered something in his ear.

He shook his head, never looking away from Prometheus. "Titan, know you are making a mistake. You had nothing but allies in this room until you chose to lose us. I will not yield to your threats, and neither will my kingdom. Make such a demand again, and prepare for war."

Prometheus glanced at Pherusa. Her arms were wrapped around her midriff, and her eyes looked haunted. Her heaving bosom had one perfect breast pushing through the opening of her robes. He'd seen this breast before. Held it in his hand. Nibbled on it. It obviously hadn't been enough, since he couldn't look away from the pale flesh now.

With a lewd smile, he said, "War, huh? Then I guess I'll have to take my spoils and leave."

"Let's not make any rash decisions here. Titan, why don't you put some clothes on, and we'll talk like civilized men?" the daimon said.

Prometheus chuckled. He wouldn't get caught dead in the seaweed robes they all had on. "Like humans, you mean. But we're *not* human, are we?"

Nereus said something, but Prometheus wasn't listening. He wrapped his fingers around Pherusa's wrist and blinked with her to his cave.

# CHAPTER FIVE

Why take her, if he hated her?

Pherusa tried to get her eyes to adjust to the sudden darkness.

Prometheus' grasp on her wrist was the only thing holding her upright. She wanted to collapse and sleep, and wake up to a world where her love was back but didn't hate her. Didn't consider her a consolation prize.

A dank scent mingled with that of sea air, and she knew where they were even before Prometheus muttered something and a glow illuminated the inside of his cave. This place belonged to Poseidon's realm since before her time, back when the area was submerged under water, and had been Prometheus' secret home before he asked Father for help.

Prometheus and Pherusa stole moments here together when the scrutiny of the palace was too much, and he'd spent the last couple nights before his capture here. It had been Father's idea, so Poseidon wouldn't realize Prometheus was already living in the palace when Nereus pleaded his case.

Pherusa had tried to locate the cave after he was gone, but he'd always blinked her inside, and she could never find the entrance.

Anger and pain tore her insides to shreds. *Father.* Both times he tried to protect her, he'd failed her and her love. If he hadn't insisted on propriety—if she hadn't listened—Prometheus would have spent the last few millennia by her side. He could have been happy. She would have been complete.

She squeezed the thought into no more than a tiny niggling at the back of her head. The past couldn't change.

She took in Prometheus' chiseled profile. His brow was furrowed, his lips a grim line. But somewhere inside this hurt, angry Titan was the soul of the immortal who braved the gods' wrath, to give humans fire, so they'd protect themselves. Who was creative and smart and funny. Who loved her.

And she should forget he ever existed. Fate had cruelly returned him to her, only to keep him out of her reach.

Pherusa leaned on the cold stone wall and pressed the side of her face to it, not caring about the dirt. Being in here again, this close to him, and feeling his touch set her on fire, and she needed to cool down. To think.

Why did he take her, if he hated her?

"Sit," Prometheus barked, pointing to the raised plateau in the corner.

They'd lain together on the double bed before, while he taught her ways to pleasure both him and herself. He'd held her there, while she slept, on the few nights she managed to stay out of the palace till dawn without one of her sisters coming to look for her at Father's orders.

Now, it was to be her prison.

"Why take me from Vythos? What will you do to me?" She hated how her voice trembled. He'd once loved her. Surely he'd never hurt her.

The memory of his cold gaze when he left her debauched and crying on the sand made no such promise.

Prometheus snorted. "Feed you, for starters. We wouldn't want you to starve. Then... we'll see."

"Feed me?" That didn't sound threatening, unless he meant to feed her to a larger beast. Had she heard him wrong?

He grunted something that sounded like a *yes* and disappeared, taking the light with him.

Pherusa made her way to the makeshift bed, using the wall for guidance. She sat on the edge and dropped her head in her palms. Did he mean to keep her here for as long as he'd been in stasis? *Gods.* At least he'd bring her food. As a Nereid, she wouldn't waste away without nourishment, but she'd weaken. She was only a minor deity; she needed *some* sustenance. And she needed the sea. After a month out of the water, she'd forget who she was and all about Vythos. Would he release her then, with no memory and no way of getting back home?

Light made it to her lids through her fingers, and she looked up to see him frowning. "I don't know where to get you food. There are buildings where there once were orchards. Eros showed me the humans now have"—he moved his lips, like he tasted the word before forming it—"*restaurants*, but I need to make payment for goods and services, and I do not have... moneys."

He looked adorable, fumbling through modern speech, and for a moment, she allowed herself to forget that he hated her. "I can come with you. There should be shops around here. If you cast an illusion to hide"—her gaze fell to his member, half erect as always, and so very big—"your nakedness from the mortals, we can get food, and you can convince them that you paid."

His chuckle was bitter. "You'll have me influence the minds of innocents so easily? I supposed I should expect that, after...?" He trailed off, and Pherusa felt righteous anger shoving aside her guilt and pain, to claw up her throat.

"I. Did *not*. Betray you. Father thought it unsafe for me to come to the surface when Zeus was closing in. He asked Aphros to find you and escort you below. Aphros never returned to Vythos, and we're sure he was the one who told Zeus where you'd be, but it had nothing to do with us." Whether of the land or the sea, centaurs were devious creatures.

"If you knew nothing about that betrayal, then Nereus must have."

"Father swore on his eternity that he played no part in it, and I believe him." Though she still blamed him for trusting Aphros with her secret.

Prometheus closed the distance between them and glowered down at her. "Why else would he keep you in Vythos and send the Ichthyocentaur in your stead?"

"*Ugh.* I just now told you." Pherusa tried to return his glare, but his penis bobbing in front of her face made it hard to focus on her fury that he wouldn't believe her. She hopped to her feet and climbed on the bed on tiptoe, to get as close to eye-level with him as she could, though he still towered over her one meter sixty.

Prometheus huffed, and the intensity of his gaze burned her to the core. "Why should I believe you?" he growled.

She ignored the hardness pushing into her stomach and narrowed her eyes. "Because I have no reason to lie. I'm not asking for mercy; I'm telling you the truth. But you don't care, do you? You've made up your mind, and I'm your prisoner. So what's my punishment?"

He raised his fists, clenched so tight his knuckles were white, and Pherusa flinched. *Her* Prometheus wouldn't hurt her in a million years, but this Titan who wore his face oozed fury, and there was no telling how he'd treat her.

Let him. His touch made her feel alive for the first time in forever. If she were to die, she might as well go by his hand.

Prometheus cupped the back of her head and attacked her mouth with a ferocity that left her breathless. His free hand tore at her robe, until his palm closed over one bare buttock.

Pherusa melted into his touch and let him lead her, until she was pressed between him and the cave's wall. She wrapped her leg around his, trying to climb his body. To feel more of his rough skin on hers. The hairs of his legs scratched her inner thigh, and she tingled at the contact.

Whether he loved or despised her, the passion in his kiss was undeniable. He moaned in her mouth like a starving man offered ambrosia, and she slanted her hips, to rub her center against his leg.

Prometheus growled and used his hold on her bottom to lift her.  Her robe got snagged on the stone wall and left her upper back and breasts bare.

He was so big, he was easily pinning her in place with one hand and his thigh.  And she wanted more.

She wrapped her legs around his hips and caressed his breastbone, his shoulder, his arm. Every muscle in his body hummed with tension. She wanted to absorb that tension. Absorb the pain of the years they spent apart. Absorb everything negative that darkened his gaze.

Moisture pooled at the apex of her thighs, as his erection slid between them, as hard as the rock he pressed her into.

Pherusa grabbed a fistful of his hair and tugged until his lips left hers and found her neck instead. He sucked on the tender flesh, sending jolts of pleasure straight to her core. She tilted her hips and wedged one hand between them, to position his shaft at her entrance.

He wanted her. He loved her. A bubble of happiness made Pherusa feel weightless. If this was her punishment, she'd survive it.

The tip of his erection brushed against her, but never entered her. Prometheus disentangled himself from her legs, and though he still held her buttock, he let her slide down the wall till her feet were flat on the ground. "No." He shook his head.

"What…?"

He disappeared.

Blasted Titans and their ability to transport around the globe in the blink of an eye.

She screamed, and her frustration bounced off the walls to reach her ears magnified.

Was this how he'd pay her back for what he thought she'd done? Drive her insane with desire and then refuse her?

She used her ripped robe as a sheet on the stone bed and climbed on top of it, then lay in the fetal position. Her body begged for release, her head was light with unquenched desire, and her heart was heavy and aching.

Prometheus was back, but he hated her. He'd only made love to her—*fucked her*—to hurt her. Her eyes burned, but she had no more tears to shed. She curled into a tighter ball and wished Morpheus hadn't faded with the rest of the gods, because she could do with a few hours of dreamless sleep.

# CHAPTER SIX

The sun peeked above the horizon, and an orange glow spread across the sky, licking at the mountains in the distance.

Pherusa would look gorgeous in this light. Her pale skin would look golden, and her eyes would shine like precious stones, framed by the spun gold of her hair.

Prometheus roared at the water, and the waves roiled back until the handful of rocks he stood on in the middle of the Aegean turned into a small island for a split second. She thought he meant to… *fuck* her—the word flashed at the forefront of his mind, courtesy of his speed-learning course by Eros—as punishment?

Taking her was foolish. Besides, it wasn't the plan. He was supposed to seize Vythos and enslave her and her family for the rest of eternity. It'd hurt her more than any physical pain he could bring himself to dole out.

"Who goes there?" asked a voice in Turkish. A light shone in Prometheus' eyes, as the rumble of a motor reached his ears. *Nice.* He'd alerted the Turkish coastguard.

He blinked right outside his cave, still shaking with anger. Seeing a group of teens drinking beer around a campfire on *his* beach didn't help his mood. "Leave and never come back," he bellowed, letting compulsion seep into his voice. The kids scattered, and he stomped out the fire with his bare feet. Normal flames couldn't burn him.

But his soul *was* on fire.

Claiming Pherusa last night had been a slip of his focus, and at the moment, he'd been certain she wanted him. Like he was certain moments ago. Only, she didn't. She thought sleeping with him was something she had to endure. Her punishment.

Which shouldn't bother him. For thousands of years, when he fantasized about having her under his control, he dreamed of breaking her and leaving her an empty shell, like he was without her love. He just didn't want to do it this way. The idea of hurting her physically brought bile up his throat. Even in his angriest imaginings, he never saw himself roughing her up—only yelling threats, while she cried and begged him for mercy.

"*Fuck.*" It felt good to scream it. Better when a handholding couple heading toward him turned around and scurried away.

Why did he love terrorizing these random humans but hated the idea of scaring Pherusa even now? After everything?

He'd gone searching for food for her because she hadn't eaten for hours and looked pale and drained. *Not* because he cared. She'd betrayed him, and she meant less than nothing to him now. But then, when she proclaimed her innocence, gaze blazing, he'd almost believed her.

His body obviously had. He'd been unable to resist the fire that burned in him and matched the one in her green eyes. He shouldn't have kissed her, but he'd been helpless in the face of her anger and her desire.

She'd melted like putty in his hands and returned his kiss with a hunger that scared him as much as it spurred him on. He was about to bury himself inside her and was convinced it was what she wanted too, when she'd said those words that sent ice slicing through his veins.

*If this is my punishment, I'll survive it.*

No. *Tartarus,* no.

What was worse? That she considered him capable of such a thing, or that that her resignation broke his heart all over again?

"Feeling more chatty today?"

Prometheus swung at the direction of the voice.

Eros barely ducked under the fist flying his way. "Woah. You really need an outlet for this aggression. I can hook you up with my personal trainer."

"What do you want?" Prometheus had no patience for the god's antics.

Eros raised both arms, expression serious. "I'm only here to talk. About Pherusa."

"I'd rather punch you." Prometheus tried again, and once more Eros evaded his assault, hopping aside like a mountain goat.

"What is your damage? Just hear me out for two minutes, and then you can go back to your caveman shtick."

Prometheus leaned back against the outer wall of the cavern, the fight sapped out of him. "Nothing you have to say interests me, brat."

"Right. Because you're a cold slab of stone now, and have no feelings, right? My mother used to call you the heart of the Titans. Guess Zeus managed to defeat you after all."

Prometheus growled and lunged for him. And plummeted into the sand, head first.

"Okay. I didn't want to do this, but you left me no choice," Eros said from behind him.

Prometheus propped himself on his arms and tried to roll on his back, but his body wouldn't obey him. "What did you do?" he asked, his jaw clenched so tight it ached.

"It's only temporary. Will fade in a couple minutes." Eros' bare feet appeared in Prometheus' line of sight, and then Eros sat cross legged in front of him. "So now you have the Nereid of your nightmares. What are you gonna do with her?"

Prometheus kept his mouth shut and tried every single muscle of his body. None moved, but they soon would, and then

Eros would share the fate of the Olympians. Or its messier, bloodier version.

Water pooled around Eros, who twirled the fingers of one hand in it. "The waves shouldn't come this far up the beach," he said.

Prometheus' hand trembled, and the water lapped up Eros' calves and thighs. Around them, the wind picked up, spraying them with droplets and sand. "What are you doing?" Prometheus hissed.

Eros moved his lips, but voices rose to drown his out. Were people heading their way?

No. The voices were inside Prometheus' head.

*His brothers.* They raged and thrashed against their binds. Cursed Zeus. Called for Prometheus to help them.

He had a clear vision of Hyperion in a large room, watching life pass him by and praying to Helios and Selene for release. And Atlas, crouched as if he still supported the world, and surrounded by rubble. The remains of a temple? Was he free?

Atlas' bloodcurdling scream threatened to split Prometheus' head. Not free. Frozen. In stasis. And not the only one.

A deep sense of shame battled the chaos in Prometheus' mind, and spikes of pain pierced him ruthlessly. He should have been searching for Hyperion and Atlas, instead of thinking only of himself and his vengeance.

"Why are you doing this to me?" he asked Eros when the agony subsided enough for him to draw breath.

Eros' blue eyes were filled with sorrow. "It's not me. It's you. You're unraveling." He seemed to want to say more, but he bit his lip.

"And what the fuck does that mean?"

"If you weren't so stubborn and would just listen, we'd have been over this hours ago." He clapped his hands once, and then rubbed them together. "Let's try this again, now that you're more inclined to follow the conversation. Thanks to your nephew, Zeus, once you're awakened from stasis, you only have a limited time frame to find your soulmate and bond with her before you spin out of control. Now, I'm pretty certain Pherusa is your soulmate, which means you don't have to keep looking, but you'd better get a move on, or it's buh-bye universe, before you yourself burst into stardust."

Pherusa, his *soulmate*? And saving the world required bonding with her? The possibility of sinking into her supple body again made Prometheus' heart soar for the briefest of moments, before he squelched away the remnants of his affection for her. "Then you'd better start kissing your loved ones *goodbye*." Because he'd never again love the Nereid who'd wronged him, and if he couldn't have her, the universe might as well burn.

A wave rose like a wall and crashed down on where Eros sat moments ago.

Prometheus climbed to his feet, as a tremor shook the earth.

*Pherusa.* She was trapped in the cave. If its walls collapsed, she'd be hurt, even if nothing of this world would harm a Nereid gravely.

He focused on her and blinked back inside the cave.

Things were quiet in here, and Pherusa was asleep on his makeshift bed. He waved his fingers and ordered grass blades to brave the barren earth and spread beneath her. He wasn't thinking of her comfort; this corner had the perfect temperature, so he was going to share the space.

He stretched out on his back next to her and folded one arm under his head. The warmth of her body was as alluring as her nakedness, but he wouldn't touch her again. He'd just stay here and study the cave ceiling and wait for creation to run out of time.

# CHAPTER SEVEN

Pherusa tried to roll onto her back, but she bumped against something hard.

No. Not something. Someone.

Last night came back to her in vivid detail, as did this morning. Prometheus made love to her, then broke her heart. He accused her of the ultimate betrayal, then took her to his cave.

He kissed her against the wall, before disappearing.

Yet here he was, in bed with her.

His arm came up around her waist, his fingers grazing her breast as he pulled her into the curve of his body. The contact sent a bolt of lust straight to her core and hardened her nipples. If only her body would stop reacting to him… But he'd awoken in her a hunger so potent, she couldn't fathom never having him inside her again.

He bent his legs beneath hers, and if she kept her eyes closed, she could pretend they were lovers, resting before their bodies merged again. She could pretend he loved her.

Though really, *she* should hate *him*. He blamed her, hurt her, and tore her away from her family. And he used her lust for him to manipulate her.

She nudged him on his back and scooted aside, to put some distance between them, but his other arm sneaked between her body and the grass mattress they lay on, and tucked her flush against him. Her head was on his shoulder, her face centimeters from his. She should wake him and tell him to keep his hands to himself—she was done being toyed with—but she didn't know what mood he'd be in, and was in no hurry to engage a Titan who could mold and shape the earth.

So she lay still, her pulse thudding in her ears, and looked up at him through her eyelashes. He frowned, even in his sleep.

Her fingers tingled with the urge to smoothen out the crease between his eyebrows and kiss away the tightness of his mouth.

No. She wasn't his lover; she was his prisoner.

She placed her hand on his chest, meaning to push away. He was warm under her palm, his heart beating as fast as hers. "I don't care if you believe me," she whispered, "but I didn't—wouldn't—betray you." And she'd never stopped loving him.

His eyelids didn't flutter as he covered her hand with his. Did he hear her?

Pherusa let him lead her palm down his torso, thrilling at the sensation of smooth skin breaking into goose bumps under her touch. She reached the line of short hair beneath his navel and circled her fingertips through them. She wanted to follow her hand's path with her lips, but she was too busy watching Prometheus' face for a reaction.

He was expressionless, and she almost withdrew her touch, before he nudged her hand lower.

Perhaps he was reacting in his sleep, starved for someone's touch, after this long in solitude.

She wouldn't be any *someone*.

When she made to withdraw, his grip turned to steel. He wanted this.

Under his guidance, she ran her fingers through the coarse short curls, to wrap them around his manhood.

He was erect and long and thick, and her hand wouldn't encircle his girth, but his hand over hers guided her to twist her grip as she stroked from tip to bottom, like when he'd first taught her to pleasure him.

"Pherusa…" he muttered, his lips barely moving.

"Yes?" She stretched her neck, so her lips were a hairsbreadth from his. Would he kiss her? Did she want him to?

He didn't. His breaths turned shorter, more urgent, as he squeezed his fist over hers, tightening her hold on him on every upstroke.

Pherusa glided her thumb across the tip, and he groaned. He claimed her mouth and she sucked on his tongue in tandem with tugging on his erection.

He was close. She could tell by his panted breath and the way he pumped his hips against her fist. She broke away from the kiss to watch the corded muscles in his neck stretch and the line of his jaw harden, as he approached his release, and then relax as he coated her hand with his seed.

When he opened his eyes, they were wild. Angry. Not glazed in post-orgasmic bliss. "On your back," he rasped.

The ache between her legs begged her to comply, but she held his gaze. "Why?"

"Because I owe you a release, and I don't like debts."

She shook her head, as his words ripped her heart to confetti. He didn't like debts. Bastard. Did he plan on paying her back for every moment he believed she stole from him?

"Suit yourself." He stood too fast, jarring her, and walked to the farthest corner. He twirled his fingers, and water sprung from above, to hit his head and shoulders. Wet like this, he looked like the first time she'd seen him. Only his gaze had lost its playfulness, and his full lips looked incapable of smiling.

She tried to hide her interest, as she stole glances of him showering his large, perfect body. Muscles bulged on his wide shoulders and arms, and rippled on his chest and down his stomach, making her palms tingle with the urge to trace every curve. But it was his long, thick, strong legs she loved the most.

She wanted nothing more than to join him under the water jet, straddle his thigh and kiss him, but he wouldn't appreciate her company.

When the water stopped running, he blinked away, thankfully not taking the light with him this time.

Pherusa about had it with the hot-and-cold treatment. What had been done to him was horrible. He believed her responsible, and though she might not have alerted Zeus to his presence, she did feel guilty for not making it her eternity's purpose to find him. She would accept his indifference or even his hate, but she couldn't handle the dissonance between his desire and the cold detachment with which he looked at her.

"*Prometheus?*" she called out. "You need to stop doing this."

He reappeared, holding two brightly colored towels. "These are all I could find in the vicinity." He tossed one to her and wrapped the other around his waist.

Pherusa didn't move, letting the towel fall on her crossed legs.

She'd seen a giant jungle cat on the prowl, one time Father sent her and Galene to the Amazon rain forest, to gather some plants for the sea witch. Prometheus looked every bit as feral and dangerous, as he approached to loom over her. "Cover yourself."

The menace in his voice made her feel small. If only she could disappear as easily as he did. Instead, she made herself stand, put her fists on her hips, and stare at him as fiercely as she could. "Why?"

"Because I won't take kindly to rejection again, if you keep making yourself so readily available."

That stung. "*I'm* readily available? *You*"—she poked his chest—"brought me here against my will. *You* lay next to *me. You* used my hand like… like a prop."

He huffed. "I will not be repeating that mistake."

"Why? Because I turned you down? Did that hurt your fragile male ego?" she asked with a sneer.

His icy laugh made her skin crawl. "My ego can take it, Pherusa." Her name dropped from his lips like a curse. "But unless you cover yourself and keep your distance, I'll spread your thighs and fuck you against the nearest surface. Take my pleasure from you and leave you weeping. Again." He spread one palm across her hipbone, his thumb brushing her mons. "Do you want to risk that?"

Her arousal coated her inner thighs. Couldn't he see how her body yielded to him? She bit her lip, to keep from begging him to touch her.

With a wicked grin, Prometheus ran his thumb along her slit. "Do you?"

She held his gaze, one eyebrow arched in challenge, as he replaced his thumb with two fingers, to rub between her sleek folds.

He groaned. "You're so wet."

Only for him. She hadn't been touched by another man in three thousand years. But she wouldn't tell him that.

Her hips jerked forward as he wedged his fingers inside her and pressed his thumb to her clitoris. Losing her composure, she dug her nails in his shoulder.

"So I've been thinking you can't stay cooped up here all the time, and if you want to go for a stroll on the beach, clothes might be good." The male voice came from a ball of light behind Prometheus.

A young man materialized, as if spilling out of the light.

Pherusa squeaked, and Prometheus let go and spun toward the intruder. "You again?" he snarled.

The man—god, judging by his entrance, though not one of the Olympians—held out a palm, his other arm laden with folded clothes. "Don't let me interrupt."

"Too late for that," Prometheus said, as Pherusa asked, bewildered. "Who are you?"

"Eros," Prometheus whispered. "Aphrodite's kid. God of love, and annoying pest who won't leave me alone."

"Sticks and stones… Anyway, I'll just leave these…" Eros looked around and scrunched his nose. "Prometheus, dude, not even a chair? Seriously."

Prometheus flicked his wrist, and a section of wall folded outward, to form a sort of shelf.

"Yeah, okay. That'll do." Eros placed the armful of clothes on there and snapped the fingers of one hand. A flat rectangular thing appeared in his grasp. "This is for money. A credit card in the name *Prometheus Titanas*. Prometheus, if you scroll through the memories I gave you, you'll know what to do with it. It's practically limitless, so you could upgrade your digs too. Maybe buy your lady something pretty."

Prometheus mumbled, "Not my lady," but it sounded halfhearted, and Eros had flickered out anyway.

Pherusa had many, *many* questions about what just happened, but she also had two of Prometheus' fingers inside her, and she'd rather focus on them.

There was a flash of regret in Prometheus' eyes as he pulled away. He went to what Eros had left them, and rummaged through the stack until he pulled out something white with bright flowers painted on it. He balled it up and tossed it to her. "Get dressed. You need to eat something, and a little fresh air might do us both some good."

Food was the furthest thing from her mind, but the moment had passed.

The dress he'd selected for her was cut like the robes they had at the palace, and she easily wrapped it around her body and tied it at the waist. She looked down at her bare feet. "We can't go too far. We have no shoes."

Prometheus fumbled with the button of his short trousers. "There are eateries along the beach." He slid the credit card in his pocket and held out his hand.

She took it. His large palm clasped around her smaller one felt natural. Right. Perfect.

Blackness closed around her, and then the bright early-afternoon sun made her squint. None of the people around paid them any notice, as Prometheus tugged her along. He had to be doing his compulsion thing, planting in their minds the suggestion to look away.

The sand was warm under Pherusa's feet, and the sea called to her. If she broke free, she could have her tail back in no time.

But Prometheus' pull was about more than his hold on her hand. She was drawn to him, body, mind, and soul, and didn't want to leave his side.

As if he read her mind, he said, "If I let go, will you run away?"

"Probably." She bit back a grin when he tangled his fingers through hers. Now they looked like yet another couple strolling along the shore.

Prometheus led her into the first establishment they came upon, a stark-white building with blue tables spread out in a yard under a canopy. He pulled out a chair, and when she sat, made himself comfortable across the table from her, then called the waitress over and asked her for the day's specials, like he'd done this a million times.

"No seafood," he said. "My… companion is allergic."

Pherusa smiled. That was nice of him, not making her see cooked sea creatures.

He ordered for the both of them, and the waitress left. She returned with a glass jug of wine and served Pherusa first.

"Let's see what modern Greeks have done with wine," Prometheus said.

The waitress gave him an odd look, and he laughed. It was his real laugh—the one that made Pherusa's legs weak and her heart speed up. It must have a similar effect on the waitress, who blushed and let her hand linger on his shoulder as she told him to call her if he needed *anything.*

There was something weird about the exchange, and it wasn't the woman's flirtiness. Pherusa figured it out as the waitress walked away. "You speak modern Greek," she said to Prometheus.

He nodded. "Eros gave me a quick lesson on… well… everything I've missed." He brought his glass to his lips and made an appreciative sound. "Delicious."

The word flipped in her belly, and warmth sped through her. She sipped her own wine, but it did nothing to put out the fire Prometheus lit inside her. *Focus, woman.* She met his gaze. "If you've seen everything, then you saw me cry for you. You *know* how I—"

His black eyes hardened, and he turned toward the sea. "He showed me the big picture. Teutonic plates shifting. Populations emigrating. War. Famine. Technological progress. And he taught me a few dozen languages."

"I see." She could think of nothing else to say.

Thankfully the waitress showed up with their salad, along with an incredible thing called *feta* and something like a thick savory cloud with a crunchy crust called a *bread*, and their mouths were too busy for conversation anyway.

Pherusa paced herself until a platter of what was impossibly tasty fried earth apples arrived. Finally full, she sat back and watched Prometheus work his way through the rest of the dishes.

A small smile curved one corner of his lips even as he buried his teeth in a meatball and chewed. He was enjoying this, and for the first time since he was returned to her, he appeared relaxed.

She envied the food for making him so happy, but he might be easier to talk to now. "What do you plan to do with me? Will you keep me on land until I forget Vythos?" She was proud of herself for keeping her voice steady, but honestly, the prospect wasn't as terrifying when he was this close.

Prometheus swallowed the bite in his mouth and shrugged. "I haven't thought that far ahead."

"Then why take me?" She held her breath, waiting for his answer.

He arched an eyebrow and patted his lips with his napkin. "I wanted your father's crown and trident. He wouldn't relinquish them. I thought losing you instead would hurt him more."

She gulped down the rest of her wine, to hide her wince. Its aroma was muted by the bile in her throat, but the burning down her gullet was a welcome distraction.

She'd spent more time than she cared to recall, drifting through one day after the next and pretending to be present in her life, while after nightfall she cried into her pillow for her Titan and what might have been. Now she was no more than a trophy, close to him, and at the same time unable to touch his soul.

# CHAPTER EIGHT

He was still in love with Pherusa.

He chewed on the bread that had lost its flavor, and he was in love with her.

He looked at the sun dipping lower on the horizon, and he was in love with her.

He winked at the waitress when he told her everything was delicious, and he was still. In love. With Pherusa.

He might hate the idea of loving her, but he didn't hate *her*, and when her expression fell at his brushoff, he almost blurted out as much.

But no. No matter what was in his heart, his head set the rules for this game, and it said he'd keep her ashore and enjoy her company until she forgot who she was—if there was time for that before he unraveled.

The table between them shook, and her glass trembled in her hand. The waitress hurried to lean against the threshold that lead inside. Silly girl. They were safe from earthquakes out here.

A sound like a hard slap made him turn in his seat. A wave crashed against the short white wall surrounding the yard. Down the beach, people screamed, as the water swelled over the shore and pulled them and their belongings into the sea.

"Is your father doing this?" he asked Pherusa.

Her face was drawn. "No. He wouldn't put humans at risk." She bit her bottom lip. "I... I think it's you. Your eyes are gold, and…" She slid further back in her chair and indicated his hands with a tilt of her head.

Prometheus looked down to see them shaking. He stood and slammed his palms onto the table, making it creak. "*Chaos.* Come." He reached for her, but she pulled back so hard her chair topped over.

"Where?" she asked.

"Back to the cave. Come on."

She took a step toward him, when her name was carried to them by the wind.

"*Pherusa.*" It was a man's voice.

Prometheus spun toward the sea. "It *is* your father. Or someone working for him." He raised his arms, and the waves followed his motion, arching higher than their heads. He couldn't drown a sea deity, and Nereus would assume control of the waters in no time, but Prometheus needed to cause a distraction until he grabbed Pherusa and blinked away.

"Wait," Pherusa yelled. "He's a friend. Let me talk to him, and I give you my word I'll be right back."

Prometheus stood between her and the waves, swallowing the bitter taste of jealousy. Whoever the male was, Pherusa belonged to Prometheus now. "Your word means nothing to me," he spat.

She narrowed her eyes and her nostrils flared. "That is a pity." Before he could stop her, she ran past him and jumped into the water.

Prometheus ordered the waves to toss her back out, but they didn't obey. His hands still trembled, and people still screamed, and now gray slates tore out of the floor beneath his feet and spun wildly before crushing into the restaurant walls and marring their perfect white.

*Was* he causing this? Was he unraveling, like Eros warned?

His head throbbed, as Atlas' roar bounced inside his mind. Prometheus felt Hyperion mentally slam against the marble he was locked into. Another, primal echo overrode everything, threatening to destroy him with its intensity.

Prometheus took a long breath and focused on letting it out slowly. He wouldn't hear his brothers, because they weren't here. This was his mind, playing tricks on him. His emotions, getting the better of him. He wouldn't be jealous of Pherusa's daimon, because Pherusa was his now, whether she wanted to be or not. He wouldn't be angry at himself for loving her, because love couldn't be reasoned with.

But he *was* still jealous, and he *was* still angry, and he was *still*. Fucking. In love with her.

"*Fuck*," he called out, to the darkening sky. Lovely word. So versatile.

*Fuck* the daimon and *fuck* Pherusa and *fuck* this entire world. Prometheus would let earth split in half if it came to it. He had nothing to lose.

He strode to the edge of the yard, above a three-meter drop that ended in glistening dark rocks, and tried to make out Pherusa's form in the water. Her green tail broke the surface beside a blue one, and then she was gliding over the waves, hanging onto a dolphin's back. The wind dropped as suddenly as it had picked up, and the beach goers quieted, but they were pointing these… things toward Pherusa. *Cell phones.* And cell phones had cameras that could capture Pherusa's tail and the moment it gave way to legs, and get her and all remaining immortals into trouble.

Prometheus called on the electrons in the atmosphere, and static crackled throughout the air. This would wipe the phones' memories, if he got it right. Humans weren't ready to know about Vythos and its creatures.

Which didn't matter. Because he'd soon be ending creation.

The waitress braved the weather, and in a shaky voice approached him and asked him to pay.

He gave her his credit card and told her to keep a tip of twenty percent—more than her usual, judging by her dazzling smile. When she returned, he flattened the flapping piece of paper she held out to him on his knee, and used the pen she offered to scratch his name on it.  He knew how to use a pen, like he knew how to handle himself with the rest of this modern world—thanks to Eros—but it felt fragile and awkward between his fingers, and it snapped in two when he got to the *s* in *Titanas*.

The waitress recoiled, but her smile remained in place. "Thank you." She took the paper back but left him the broken pen. "And this is your receipt." She handed it to him and scurried off to the relative safety of inside.

Prometheus pocketed the card and receipt. It was surreal, this bit of normalcy he'd never before experienced, in the midst of the chaos.

He returned his gaze to the sea, just as the dolphin approached with Pherusa holding onto his back.

It shifted into a blue-haired man, who helped her find her footing on the rocks that lay at the bottom of the outer wall.

Prometheus leaned down and held out a hand for her before he realized he was about to. As soon as Pherusa clasped it, he blinked back to his cave.

He made sure she had her balance, and then conjured a soft glow that resembled that of the evening sun. "You came back."

"I told you I would." She didn't let go of his hand.

"Why didn't you look for me when I was away?" And where did that come from? If he was right all along, she'd wanted him gone. Were her lies getting to him, or did his heart see past his anger and recognize what his mind refused to?

Her red-rimmed eyes pierced holes into his soul. She licked her lips. "I didn't know I could. Zeus told Father you were gone—in Tartarus. I considered taking my life, but even then we wouldn't be together, since death would deliver me to the Elysian Fields." Those deemed *worthy* by Hades were allocated there after their passing, and minor deities had sort of a standing reservation at the place.

Would she have really died for him?

Irrelevant.

He should focus on current matters. "What did the daimon want?" he asked.

Pherusa's shoulders sagged. "Palaemon said two of your brothers are stirring."

The feeling spilling through his veins took a moment to recognize. *Relief.* His brothers would soon join him on earth, and then maybe the world wouldn't have to end, and he wouldn't be alone anymore.

"The sea witch doesn't know which ones"—Pherusa grimaced—"but she's afraid one of them might be Kronos."

*Well, fuck.*

# CHAPTER NINE

Prometheus was quiet for so long, Pherusa wasn't sure he heard her. "What if it *is* him?" she asked.

He absentmindedly caressed her wrist with his thumb, sending a wave of warmth up her arm and across her chest. "What if it is?"

"He might want to pick up where he left off." Kronos had ruled the world before Zeus overthrew him, and had fought hard to remain in control. Pherusa was born after the Titan's reign, but she'd heard horror stories about the Titanomachy—the battle that decided all Titans' fate. "The witch and my father are worried he may come after the remaining deities, to establish his dominion. A war could be devastating for Vythos and the mortal realm alike." The prospect was terrifying. If only she could burrow in the safety of Prometheus' arms...

He had no reason to want to comfort her.

He tightened his grip on her hand for a second, before letting go and stepping away. "Did your daimon friend come to ask you to recruit me on Nereus' behalf?" His eyes blazed in the dim light, and the muscle in his jaw ticked as he clenched his teeth.

"Would it be so bad if he did? You may hate me and Father, but the humans? You created them. You can't tell me you don't care that they'll be sacrificed in the altar of your brother's ego." She snapped her mouth shut before she added *again*.

Prometheus let out a bitter chuckle. "You don't know me anymore, little Siren. Don't act like you do."

She should be more understanding, after what he'd been through, but fury—white hot and all consuming—shoved aside her sympathy and guilt. "I know the man I used to love would never do that." Her voice boomed in the confined space. "I know he was good and fair, and he wouldn't support a murderous, power-mad proto-god, even if he was his own blood."

He shook his head, and tension rolled off him in waves, thick enough it tightened around Pherusa's chest. "I didn't stand by my brother last time, and you saw what it got me. I shared his fate, even after all I did for Zeus. Maybe this time I'll pick the right side."

"*The right side*?" She snorted. "What can possibly be right about Kronos? He was insane before he was ever put in stasis. Can you imagine his state of mind if he's released? He'll wreak havoc. He'll—"

"He'll unravel," Prometheus said in a flat tone. "And the world will follow him into demise."

She couldn't believe what she was hearing. "And you're fine with that?"

He shrugged. "Why not? Eros showed me what humans have done with the life I gave them. They kill each other in the name of religion as easily as they do over petty cash. They pillage and rape and torture. They destroy without second thought. What about them is so special that I should fight my brother to protect them?"

It broke her heart to see him so jaded, as much as it incensed her that he'd given up on all that was good. She tried to reason with him. "What about love? And children? And... and puppies? Yes, there is bad in humans, but there's good in them too. They save each other on a daily basis. They grow and learn and discover and evolve. You cannot support their destruction because they've disappointed you."

"Watch me," he said. His eyes glowed gold, before he squeezed them shut. When he opened them again, they were black like tar, and his face was relaxed. Impassive. "I'm tired. I need to rest. If you wish to go outside and play with your daimon friend—"

"His name is *Palaemon*." It was the second or third time Prometheus referred to him as *your daimon friend*, and it grated on her nerves along with his dismissive attitude. "And if you're implying he and I are anything more than friends, you couldn't be more wrong."

He closed in on her, like a shark circling its prey. "I didn't ask. And I couldn't care less if he bent you over a rock and plowed you, now that I've opened the way. But whatever you do with him, make sure to be outside this cave at dawn, or I'll come looking for you. And if I do, *your daimon friend* will perish."

She slapped him. She didn't realize she was going to, until her palm made hard contact with his cheek. The red mark that blossomed on his skin—bronzed, though the sun hadn't seen him in forever—almost smudged out her ire. *Almost.* "How dare you imply that I..." She huffed. "I mean, that you'd think I'd..." Forming a coherent accusation eluded her, so she raised her hand for another blow.

Prometheus snatched her wrist midair and drove her back with his body so hard, the air whooshed out of her lungs as he pressed her against the wall. "Consider this your final warning. Next time you touch me, I won't stop myself," he whispered in her ear.

He wanted her, despite himself. He'd said so, and his erection against her belly proved it. His breath, hot against her neck, made her shiver in anticipation. She licked her lips, trying to calm her racing pulse. Part of her wanted to touch him and make him lose control, but should she? What good could come out of it? He'd still resent her—possibly more if they made love again.

*Sex.* It was sex. Better yet, a quick romp, devoid of emotion.

He lifted his head, to look her in the eye. "That's what I thought. So you'd better think twice before laying a hand on me ag—"

She slapped him again.

His stunned expression would be funny, if raw desire didn't singe her senses at the hunger in his gaze. "You—"

"Touched you."

His grin was beautiful and scary, and she shivered when he ducked to tug her earlobe between his teeth. "Then I suppose now is my turn."

It was all the warning she got, before the wall stretched out behind and under her, until she lay on it with her legs dangling off the edge and Prometheus between them.

Her dress had ridden high, and her thighs weren't the only part of her exposed. As a rule, Nereids didn't wear undergarments. Underwear wasn't of much use under the sea, when their legs gave way to a tail, and there was seldom reason to bother with them on their short jaunts ashore.

Prometheus trailed his fingers up her inner thigh, barely making contact. She wanted to scoot closer, rush him to where she needed him the most, but his focus on her face was so intense, he might as well be holding her in place.

He reached her mound and traced her slit with a feather-light caress. "Is this what you want me to touch?"

*Gods*, yes.

# CHAPTER TEN

How could this female, trembling at his slightest touch, have sold him out to Zeus?

*The man I used to love*, she'd said. Like she didn't anymore.

But she wanted him?

He was giving this too much thought, when her divine pussy dripped against his fingertips like a ripe peach, begging him to bury his teeth in its flesh. No reason to hold back, when she was obviously a willing participant.

But he could make it more about his pleasure than hers.

"No," he said and watched her thighs tense.

She whimpered. "No?"

"Drop down to your knees and take me in your mouth first. Make it good, and I'll reward you." He could tell himself this was about exerting power, but in truth, he ached to see if her desire matched his.

Pherusa covered herself with her dress. Was she going to turn him down?

A smile played on her lips as she slid down from the parapet he'd forged and lifted the hem of his shirt to skate her palms up his chest.

"I said—"

"You said to make it good." She placed an open-mouthed kiss over his heart and blew a puff of cool air on it.

He'd taught her this, on a starry night, back when there was hope and love in his heart.

No. No… trip down memory lane—yes, that was what they called it. He might not have her heart, but he'd enjoy her body on what few moments like this they had left before he imploded and took this planet with him.

Pherusa kissed down his abs and licked a trail along his hip bone, just above his confining pants, before sinking onto her knees. He wanted to tangle his fingers in her golden locks and push her lower, but every square centimeter of skin her lips touched was on fire, and he enjoyed the exquisite torment.

She undid the button on his shorts and pulled down that metallic contraption called a *zipper*, and cool air caressed his hard cock.

Pherusa took her time, edging her fingers inside his waistband and dragging the garment lower, then scratching her nails down his ass and the backs of his legs.

He pumped his hips, and his shaft tapped her cheek, but she paid it no attention, as she brought her hands around front and scraped them upward, her thumbs digging into the muscles of his thighs.

When she turned her green eyes up at him with undisguised lust, it took all he had not to grab her head and thrust himself between her rosy lips. Still, he raised the ground beneath her shins enough that she was at the perfect height, eye-level with his cock.

Pherusa flicked her tongue over the tip and hummed appreciatively, before stretching her lips around his girth. *Gaia.* She felt incredible, but it was her expression—eager and satisfied, eyelids fluttering—that made him groan.

Prometheus fisted his hands at his sides and focused on remaining still, while she sucked him in, centimeter by agonizing centimeter. With half of his length ensconced in the scorching heat of her mouth, he couldn't refrain from rocking against her, but Pherusa wouldn't be hurried.

Digging the nails of one hand into his ass, she cupped his balls with the other and tugged lightly. So very, *very* slowly, she glided up his shaft until only the head of his cock was still in her mouth, and then circled it with her tongue, before sucking him in again.

Unable to hold back any longer, Prometheus knotted his hands in her hair and used his grip to guide her up and down his cock faster.

She let him dictate the rhythm, slurping at him when he allowed her tongue room to move, and moaning around him as he bottomed out.

Prometheus throbbed with the need for release, and he wouldn't deny himself. His Titan constitution meant he could achieve an erection again seconds after he came, so he wasn't lying when he promised her he'd make it worth her while.

"I'm close." He loosened his hold, so she could pull away, but Pherusa let go of his sack to pump him with her hand while she sucked him harder.

Didn't she hear him? She always stopped at this point.

"Pherusa, I'm going to come," he said through gritted teeth.

She gave him a half-shrug and took him down her throat, as she tugged faster at the base of his shaft.

Prometheus spilled inside her, his skull tingling with the force of his orgasm. His strength sapped out of him with every string of cum that shot out of his cock, and she kept sucking and swallowing. All he was, all he saw, all he felt was bliss.

He shivered and pulled her up by the hair for a fierce kiss.

"Good?" she mumbled against his mouth. She tasted of the sea and the sun and him.

It wasn't good. It was amazing.

He blinked them across the cave, to their bed. He laid her on her back and knelt between her spread thighs. "Your turn." Instead of burying his face in her pussy and feasting on her, like he yearned to, he lifted one leg and placed a chaste kiss over her ankle.

She giggled, and for a split second, the years hadn't gone by. He hadn't been cursed by Zeus. She hadn't broken his heart.

He shook away the nostalgia and nuzzled her calf, grazing the soft skin with his stubble, then licked the underside of her knee.

She tensed. "Higher. Please."

He lifted his head to mock-glower at her. "I am calling the shots, little Siren. You don't tell me what to do."

The perplexed look she gave him couldn't have been faked. "I didn't speak."

"Right." He bit her inner thigh as punishment for lying, and when she *eeped*, laved the spot with his tongue until she moaned and pushed down against him.

"More… Your fingers." There was something odd about her voice.

No echo.

Prometheus glanced up. Her head was thrown back, her eyes closed. He rose on his knees and watched her face as he slid his palm up her thigh and stomach, to where her dress was held in place around her waist.

"Touch me. Touch all of me," she said.

But she *didn't* say it. Her lips didn't move. He'd picked up her thought, like he would if she projected it at him underwater. And yet they were very much on dry land.

Titans could read mortals' minds, but not the thoughts of gods, and Nereids were gods, if minor ones. How was this possible?

He undid her sash and used both palms to uncover her perfect breasts. Her creamy flesh made the perfect contrast against his bronzed skin. He squeezed one breast and watched transfixed, as red marks appeared under the pressure of his fingers, only to fade in a heartbeat. He did it again, and then pinched and twisted her nipple, which rose and hardened under his attentions.

"*Gods*, yes. I love this."

So he did it again, this time closing his mouth around the other nipple and swirling his tongue over it.

Pherusa arched her back, and Prometheus' cock, erect again, demanded to be inside her. But Titan Junior would have to wait.

Prometheus licked his way down the valley between her breasts and grazed his teeth down her stomach, before dipping his tongue into her belly button.

"Hey. That tickles." Her words carried the echo of having been spoken aloud, but the next ones didn't. "Need you. Lower."

He sat back and drove two fingers inside her. "What was that?"

She opened her eyes and bit her lip. "Nothing." But inside his head, she cried, "Yes. More."

Incredible. He tried projecting a thought to her. "Lift your knees to your chest."

Pherusa furrowed her brow, flicking her gaze between his eyes and his lips. "How…?"

This wasn't the time for questions. "Do it," he said.

She complied, and he grasped a buttock in each hand to push her further up before ordering the earth beneath her to raise her so her gorgeous pussy was offered to him as if on a platter. Her juices glistened on the soft curls covering her mound. He sleeked his thumbs along her slit and spread her open, so he could push his tongue inside her. She'd only agreed to this once before, but he never forgot her flavor on his taste buds. She tasted of life.

He trailed his tongue higher, to find the pearl between her folds, and circled it while he slowly edged three fingers inside her. She bucked her hips under his intrusion, and he nibbled on her clitoris, pushing his fingers deeper.

"Not enough. Need…"

He should take his time with her, but her next thought slammed into him with more force than Zeus' lightning bolt.

"Need you. Now."

Prometheus begrudgingly abandoned her clitoris with one last long swipe of his tongue, and stood. He tore his shirt in two, too impatient to take the time to peel it off. His body overrode his mind, demanding he enter her *now*. He closed his fingers around her slender ankles and placed her feet flat on his chest. Then he lifted her hips and slid his cock along her cleft, wetting it in her juices, before thrusting inside her to the hilt.

Pherusa's groans filled the cave as he slammed inside her again and again. "More. Faster," she screamed in his head, incoherent sounds spilling from her lips when he upped the tempo.

He hammered into her until her thoughts reached him fragmented and her legs flopped over his arms and her face was contorted in ecstasy.

When he finally allowed himself to follow her over the edge, he spilled inside her. Not worrying about an unwanted pregnancy was among the perks of bedding a Titan. His seed would only be potent when he willed it to, and this was not the right time to father a child.

Pherusa was putty in his hands, as he cradled her to him, lowered the ground beneath them, and filled it with daisies, so she didn't have to smell the dank earth in her sleep tonight. Then he laid her back down and curled around her outstretched form.

"I still feel you inside me," Pherusa said sleepily. "I like it."

He had to kiss the smile on her lips. "Give me a few, and I can make sure you feel me for a week." His heart clenched. Did they have a week?

She turned in his arms and draped a leg over his. "I'll need more than a few." She yawned and hid her face in the crook of his neck. "I could stay like this forever."

Did she say that or think it?

# CHAPTER ELEVEN

Waking up with her bare body pressed against Prometheus' wasn't disorienting this morning. She had an arm flung over his chest and a leg across his hips, and his arm was folded around her waist, his palm cupping her bottom. He was hard again. Or still.

Should she climb on top of him and ride him? Better not while she was sore from last night's romps—plural. Prometheus had woken her up in the middle of the night and made slow, sweet love to her until she couldn't move a muscle.

She withdrew from his embrace, careful not to wake him, and propped herself up on her elbow, to study his face. His expression wasn't tense today, his mouth relaxed in slumber, and no lines creasing his forehead.

Pherusa traced one of his brows with her fingertips, then ran her fingers through his long, black hair. He was gorgeous, and last night he'd been the same man she fell in love with. He'd let go of his anger. He still loved her. He couldn't have looked in her eyes with so much tenderness when he was inside her if he didn't. They could be together for real.

Her happiness was marred by reality splashing across her body like a bucket of ice-cold water.

How could she stay with him, when every day she remained ashore was one day closer to forgetting her past?

Her heart constricted in her chest. Would she choose Prometheus over anything else, even if it meant forever losing her family and the only home she'd ever known? Would she get a choice?

Did it matter?

She trailed one finger down his jaw, then laid her head on his chest, to let his heartbeat soothe her. The love she felt for him hadn't diminished in his absence, and now that he'd claimed her in the name of something other than vengeance, she couldn't fathom ever bedding another male. If she had a soulmate in this world, it had to be Prometheus.

The witch would know. She'd given Father a mating prophecy for each of his fifty daughters, and every Nereid had a century to fulfill hers once her turn was up, or the merpeople of Vythos would be barren for three hundred years.

Pherusa doubted Prometheus would permit her to visit Circe's island and ask if he was Pherusa's destiny. Besides, it wasn't her time. Father hadn't revealed the prophecy that pertained to her, and her next sister to mate was Callianassa—who had a hundred years or so, since Halie'd just bonded with her own mate.

Then again, Circe had given Halie a jagged prophecy that made her seek true love among the mortals, when Delphinos had always been within her grasp. Perhaps she knew something about Pherusa's destiny that she hadn't shared.

Pherusa willed her thoughts back to the present. Her fate wouldn't be decided by the sea witch, but by Pherusa herself. Prometheus held all the power, and if he wanted her, she was his.

She stretched her neck to reach his lips, but a bright light behind her made her roll onto her back and pull her discarded dress over her naked form.

Beside her, Prometheus sat up, not bothering to cover himself. "Eros?" he called out. "You're not welcome. Try again later."

What did Eros want this time?

"There won't be a *later* for much longer, unless you took care of business." Eros' form was transparent, but his voice was loud and clear.

"What business?" Pherusa asked.

Prometheus wrapped an arm around her and gathered her close. "Nothing. Ignore him, and he'll go away."

Eros smirked and leaned against the wall, color filling in his features until the rocks were no longer visible through him. "I wouldn't count on that." He sniffed the air, and his lips stretched into a toothy grin. "The two of you mated."

"No." Prometheus's word snapped through the air like a whip.

Pherusa flinched. "What would you call what we did most of the night?" And why was it important to her that he admit it?

"*Intercourse. Sex. Fucking.* But we didn't mate." He caressed her arm, but his warm touch did nothing for the chill creeping up her spine.

"*Fucking*?" That was what he called the most intimate, soul-baring experience of her life?

"It was *one* of the words I used. I'm only saying we're not mated."

Eros tutted. "The clock is ticking, Titan. Get your shit together, or you know what will happen."

"Don't you threaten me, godling, and get the fuck out of here," Prometheus yelled, and Eros disappeared in yet another ball of light.

Pherusa's jaw hurt with tension. She relaxed it and pierced Prometheus with her gaze. "So last night you *fucked* me?" In her head, she screamed, *again?* How cruel was he, to make her think he'd mellowed toward her—might even start having feelings for her once more—only to destroy her hopes for a second time?

"Don't get hung up on that. It's a word that describes sex. I just meant to explain to Eros that we're not... bonded in some way."

Pherusa stood and pushed her arms into the sleeves of her dress. It was caked with dirt and dead flower petals, but being bare felt more vulnerable than she cared to be. She wrapped the dress around her and tied the sash so tight, she could barely breathe.

Or it was the pain of his casual dismissal that crushed her lungs.

She needed to busy herself with something. Looking at him hurt, but she wouldn't avert her gaze like a coward. The stack of clothes was where Eros had left it—minus what she wore and Prometheus' torn shirt and abandoned shorts—but it didn't look as neat, after Prometheus' rummaging through it. She selected the shirt that lay on the top, shook it out, refolded it, and placed it next to the initial bundle.

"Why did you have to tell Eros anything?" she asked in as uninflected a tone as she could muster. "What did he mean about getting your shit together?"

"I told you, it was nothing. Come back to bed. I need more sleep. Don't you?" He lay back and folded an arm behind his head. When she glanced his way, his eyes were closed.

She returned to her task, folding a too-short skirt in two and placing it over the shirt. She'd let the matter lie, if he wasn't going to be honest with her.

Only it ate her up inside. Garments forgotten, she closed the distance to the bed and glowered down at him. "Tell me the truth."

Prometheus frowned but didn't open his eyes. "I can't."

The knot in her throat tasted like tears, but she wouldn't shed them. She'd cried enough over him. "Then you and I are through. You may keep me here until my memory of the sea world is gone, and you can take my body by force, but I'll no longer willingly share your bed." Every word scratched her throat and burned her tongue, but she'd caught a glimpse of the heavens and would settle for nothing less.

He snatched her wrist and pulled her on top of him before she registered him moving.

"That's no longer your call, little Siren. Now you belong to me."

# CHAPTER TWELVE

What was he saying? Making love to Pherusa, sleeping with her tucked snuggly against his body, and waking up next to her had been a revelation. There'd been no speck of resentment in what he gleaned from her thoughts. She'd given herself to him wholly.

But he couldn't tell her of Eros' reveal. For the bonding to work, she should be willing to give Prometheus her heart, and knowing what was at stake would take away her choice.

Besides, however much she wanted him, Pherusa didn't love him any longer. *The man I used to love*, she'd said.

He wouldn't burden her with his unraveling. He'd send her home to her family, and blink himself to the other side of earth—to another planet, even—to make sure she wasn't harmed when he lost control.

Of course he'd have to explain why he gave her her freedom after he'd just declared that he owned her.

He cracked an eyelid and glanced at her face. Her lips were pursed, and her eyes blazed. She looked as fierce as a Titaness—Klymene herself—despite her diminutive stature.

*Chaos*, he loved her. How did he ever think otherwise?

"Forgive me," he said. "I didn't mean that. I don't see you as a conquest, and I've told you already I'd never force you. For that, I cannot share why I answered Eros the way I did." He held out a hand, and her expression softened. Would she drop the subject?

Then she curled her hand in a fist and shook her head. "I cannot trust you anymore. Your words don't match your actions, and I won't let you play with my—"

A deafening crash made him jump to his feet. It came from the other end of the cave. He placed his body in front of Pherusa, ready to face any threat, and called out, "Eros? This has gone too far." It could be no one else. Nobody but Prometheus, Pherusa, and the annoying god knew this cave even existed, let alone where it was located.

The sound came again, rattling the rocks around them.

Pherusa touched his shoulder. "Are you doing this?"

He looked at his hands. No tremors. He shook his head. "Whoever this is, you'd better leave while you still can," he bellowed.

When the wall in front of them collapsed, he flinched but stood his ground. He'd pummel the little shit to the ground for this.

It wasn't Eros glaring at him from the other side, though. Nereus hovered there, the long white braids in his hair and beard floating around his head. It took Prometheus a second to realize his cave had somehow opened *inside Vythos*, an invisible wall keeping the water out. Nereus' torso was covered by an armor of pure gold that matched the color of his swishing tail. Flanking him were the two sea daimons Prometheus saw before, Pherusa's *friend* and the green-haired one, garbed in a similar manner, though their breastplates were silver, not gold. Mermen filled the waters behind them, as far as the eye could see, but Prometheus wasn't bothered by Nereus' show of strength.

What bothered him—what cut him to the core and made breathing a chore—was that Pherusa had told her blasted father where Prometheus' inner sanctum could be found.

The withered crone who had the king's ear pushed by the green-haired daimon and hovered to the front, swathed in dark-gray robes. Her eyes were milky white, and her thin, lined lips formed words that never reached Prometheus' ears. He didn't have to know what she was saying, though. She was maintaining the spell that had brought the sea to his front door. If he killed her, would the magic die?

Pherusa wrapped both her arms around one of his. "Please don't attack. Hear father out, and then you can blink us anywhere you'd like."

It was that tiny word—*us*—that kept Prometheus from lunging at those who dared invade his home. "King Nereus, what brings you and your pitiful army to my doorstep?" Hey, he was calm. He didn't have to be polite too.

"I've come for my daughter," Nereus thought at him.

The laws of the sea world apparently applied in their situation, though Prometheus and Pherusa weren't underwater. Was this why Prometheus had heard her thoughts last night? Had the sea witch already started on her magic without them realizing?

"Father, no," Pherusa said loud and clear. She pushed in front of Prometheus, her voice pleading. "He's not holding me against my wishes. I want to be here. With him."

Nereus' narrow-eyed gaze slid from her to Prometheus and back again. "You may still have feelings for who he used to be"—he didn't keep his thought private, but broadcast it for all of them to hear—"but he no longer returns those feelings. Your place is in Vythos, with us."

Palaemon motioned for her to approach, and Prometheus' decision to send her away before he unraveled shattered under the primal urge to protect what was his. "Pherusa stays with me," he roared. He willed his body to grow until his head was a couple centimeters shy from the cave's ceiling. It wasn't his full size, but he was twice as big as any other male in the vicinity, and those tails of theirs were *long*.

"I wish to stay." Pherusa planted her fists on her hips. She could have said she loved him, but this would have to do.

Prometheus folded his arms over his chest, giving Nereus a triumphant look. "You heard the lady. Go."

Palaemon squared his shoulders and looked at Pherusa. "If he's threatening you somehow, you don't have to fear him." Like Nereus, he projected his thought. Why not talk to her privately? Why did they want Prometheus to hear this? Or did the magic not allow their thoughts to reach only a single recipient?

When Pherusa didn't speak, the daimon continued. "He caught us unawares last time, but Delphinos and I can shift into monsters the world hasn't seen in millennia. We can overpower him if need be."

Pfft. The world hadn't seen a full-sized Titan in millennia either.

"Stand down, *boy*. You know nothing of my power. I was here for the creation of the world. I've fought Chaos. I've had"—Prometheus rifled through the knowledge of history Eros bestowed on him, till he found a name for the enormous scaly beasts—"Tyrannosauri Rex as pets. I've survived Zeus. Nothing scares me." Except the possibility of losing Pherusa again, forever.

The sea witch tilted her head, and Prometheus swore her blind eyes saw right through him. A terrible smile stretched her lips, baring rotting teeth, as she pointed at Pherusa.

When the witch opened her mouth to speak, there was no doubt in his mind she'd do something to Pherusa. Unbidden images of his Siren writhing in pain filled his head, even though the crone was supposed to be on Nereus' side and shouldn't wish to endanger a Nereid.

The witch formed a word, and Prometheus' instinct took over.

"*No.*" He shoved Pherusa out of the way.

The witch's cackle came at him from every direction, as Pherusa slammed against the wall and fell.

"*Pherusa.*" He dropped to his knees by her side.

She rolled on her back and blinked slowly at him. "Ouch." One sleeve of her dress was torn, revealing bloody welts on her shoulder, and blood oozed from a wound on her head.

*Chaos*. Nereids didn't age beyond maturity and couldn't perish by mortal means, but Titans preceded them. He had the power to harm her, and he hadn't reined it in. He'd hurt the woman he loved. Her eyes held no blame, but he couldn't forgive himself. What if he'd done worse than a bump to her head? What if he'd unraveled and ended her?

He should leave, but then she'd think he abandoned her.

The background sounds he'd blocked out when he saw her crumble to the ground rushed back in. Nereus was yelling at the witch to let him get his daughter *now*. Someone growled. Probably the daimons, assuming beastly forms, but Prometheus wouldn't stick around to see what those were.

He gathered Pherusa to his chest, and his heart skipped a beat when she looped her arms around his neck. "Hold on, little Siren." He nuzzled her cheek and blinked them to the last place anyone would think to look for a Titan.

Mount Olympus.

The Pantheon—meaning *All Gods*—at the very top held no remnants of the gods who once convened here. The rocky terrain, high altitude, and steep drops made it virtually uninhabitable, so he and Pherusa ran little danger of being seen as they appeared out of thin air. If a hiker happened to notice, Prometheus could make them forget.

He gently placed Pherusa on the ground and resumed his human size. "Wait here. Your father and his army won't find us for a while. I sense running water nearby. I'll get some to clean your cuts." He could use his powers to bring the water to them, but he needed some time to clear his head. If he'd shoved her aside with more force, he could have lost her for good.

"Don't leave," she muttered. "I'll heal within minutes, anyway. Siren constitution, you know?" Her smile was weak, but it made his heart soar. She didn't begrudge him his mistake. She wanted him close. Could she still love him?

He lay down facing her and tucked a golden lock behind her ear. Her hair was matted with blood, but the wound was already closing.

"In that case, I'm not going anywhere," he said. He didn't mean now. He would claim her, pledge his heart to her, and make the bond work.

"Where are we?" Pherusa asked.

Prometheus indicated the area around them with a sweeping gesture. "This used to be where Zeus held court."

"Really?" She sat up and looked from one side to the other. "His throne room? Right here?"

"Uh huh." He pulled her on top of him, careful not to touch her shoulder, though the skin he glimpsed through the ripped fabric wasn't scratched anymore.

"What would he think of us desecrating it?" She touched her lips to his, and sucked on his tongue when he slid it between them.

Not mad at him anymore, then. Good. He couldn't imagine not having her again, like she'd threatened before her father barged in on them, without unraveling ahead of schedule.

And he shouldn't be thinking of *that* when she was rubbing against his body.

He poured himself into the kiss, gliding his palms up Pherusa's belly to cup her breasts.

Naturally, that was when Eros dropped in on them. Again.

# CHAPTER THIRTEEN

"You know, your foreplay is a little too bloody for my tastes, but to each their own." Eros looked down on them reproachfully.

"What is the matter with you, sneaking up on us all the time?" Pherusa glared at him.

Prometheus dropped his hands and growled. "You have the worst sense of timing."

Crossing his arms, Eros tapped his foot on the dirt. The crunching of rocks was disproportionally loud in the quiet. "*I* have the worst sense of timing? You have Nereus' army after you, and you come *here* of all places, for nookie time? Did you at least decide to bond?"

*Bond?* Like with a soulmate? Pherusa's heart fluttered in her chest. She looked to Prometheus for an explanation, but he let out a disgruntled huff and gripped her by the waist, to lower her to the ground beside him.

"We might, if you left us alone long enough," he said. "Besides, I don't know if she wants to."

Would someone ask her, or was her value ornamental? She opened her mouth to speak up, but Prometheus stood and dusted dirt from his immaculate behind, and her attention diverted to his buttocks.

Eros cleared his throat, and Pherusa snapped her gaze to his face in time to catch him rolling his eyes. "Yeah, she obviously can't stand the sight of you," he said. "You can tell by how the two of you are all over each other whenever I happen by."

Prometheus harrumphed. "*Happen by*? You're constantly nagging at me."

"Why is that?" Pherusa asked.

The males ignored her, staring each other down.

"Well, excuse me, for wanting to protect creation," Eros said.

Prometheus' eyes strayed her way for a split second, before he looked back to the god. "That will not be an issue. I'll leave if it doesn't work."

The bottom of Pherusa's stomach plummeted to her feet. "Go where?" And if *what* didn't work?

The crease between Eros' brows deepened. "No place on Earth is far enough."

"A different planet, then," Prometheus said defiantly. "Another solar system. A random rock in space. I'll unravel there, and this world will have nothing to fear."

Eros studied the ground around his feet. Lightning fast, he picked up a small stone and hurled it at Prometheus's chest.

"What are you doing?" The befuddlement in Prometheus' expression would be funny if his promise to leave the planet hadn't broken Pherusa's sense of humor.

"Trying to snap you out of your self-doubt," Eros said.

Prometheus' eyes widened further. "By annoying me?"

Eros shrugged. "How else?"

"Maybe by leaving us alone? I'd have known by now, if you'd given us half an hour." Prometheus pursed his lips and arched a dark brow. "Make that a couple hours."

Even if Pherusa didn't hate being unable to follow the conversation, she'd be fed up with this posturing. She stepped between the two infuriating males and placed one palm on each man's chest. "Stop, right this minute." She turned to Eros. "You. Explain."

The muscles on Prometheus' chest stretched under her fingers, as if he drew breath to speak.

She snapped her head his way. "And you, don't say a word till he's done." Her skull throbbed at the abrupt movement. It'd be great if they could have this discussion in the sea, where she'd heal faster, but she didn't trust them to remain civil long enough to get there. Plus, Father's forces would be on alert, and she'd rather not have to watch those she loved fight among themselves if she could avoid it.

Eros stepped back and sat, as if on a chair, though there was nothing but thin air supporting him. He crossed his legs and blew a blond curl off his forehead. "Better make yourselves comfortable, kiddies. This is a long story."

"Condense it." Prometheus' dry tone brooked no argument, but with a wiggle of his fingers, he fashioned himself and Pherusa a seat out of the earth and covered it in fresh grass.

"As you wish." Eros steepled his fingers. "When Zeus put the Titans in stasis, he meant for it to be eternal. Mother, Hephaestus, and Hestia insisted that was too cruel, and eventually convinced him to add a clause, so you could be awakened after all the Olympians were gone, but only by your soulmate."

"Awakened, how?" Could her pining for Prometheus have brought him back? Was she his soulmate?

"Technically, their soulmates would have to be within touching distance." Eros' words snuffed Pherusa's hope, but he went on. "I wasn't around at the time, but from what Mother had heard from Zeus—who also didn't witness this for himself—Titans and Titanesses were created in twos, each pair supposed to share a soul."

"That's why Zeus turned the Titanesses human," Prometheus muttered.

So his true mate had died long before Pherusa was born? Sadness spilled in her veins like poison, making every nerve in her body feel raw. It hurt that she and Prometheus weren't two parts of a whole, but what cut her to the core was that he'd lost the one he was destined for. If Pherusa's life had no meaning without him, how did he feel with half his soul torn away?

She reached for his hand and squeezed. "I'm so sorry."

His gaze was startled, rather than pained, when he met hers. "Klymene has been but a memory since—"

Eros snapped his fingers. "*Children.* You're missing the point."

"Stop calling me a *child*, you infant," Prometheus growled. "I'm eternal. You are but a speck in history."

Eros buffed his fingernails on his very short loincloth, blew on them, and studied them, an infuriating smirk in place. "Yet I'm much more relevant than you, old man."

The tension in Prometheus' body warned of violence.

Pherusa cupped his cheek and forced him to look at her. "Let him finish."

"I know what he'll say."

"I don't, and I want to hear it."

The feather-light touch of her thumb on his lips seemed to placate him. His shoulders relaxed, and he clasped her hand so he could lay a kiss on the inside of her palm. "It's your choice," he said against her skin.

But his lips didn't move.

"Where was I? Ah yes." Eros looked extra smug, even for him. "Zeus was wrong, both about what could free you and about soulmates, because..." He made a weird jerky motion with both fists and a rolling sound with his tongue. "Drum roll? Nothing? You're a tough audience."

"Finish," Prometheus barked so loud, a flock of birds behind Eros took flight.

"All right. So working theory is that the oil drills in the Aegean ended your stasis, and the fact that you zeroed in on

Pherusa as soon as you were awake indicates she may be your soulmate."

Glee bubbled up inside Pherusa, stealing her breath and threatening to come out in an undignified squeal. If this was true, she could be with Prometheus forever, without giving up Vythos. And with him on their side, Father wouldn't have to fear Kronos' awakening.

Unless Prometheus didn't want her.

Prometheus hung his head, staring at the ground, his expression dark. "How can you think that?"

Her insides tightened. He didn't even consider the possibility she was his soulmate?

"That's not what I'm saying." His voice rolled down the hill and felt as if it came from everywhere at the same time.

"Who are you talking to?" Eros tilted his head at Prometheus.

"Pherusa. I don't know how she can think I don't want her, after everything."

Eros waggled his eyebrows. "She can *think* whatever she pleases."

Prometheus jumped upright and closed in on the god. "Yeah, well, I don't like hearing it."

Huh?

Eros appeared right behind him. "Which may be why she didn't say it," he said, smacking Prometheus upside the head.

Prometheus spun so fast, Pherusa almost missed the moment he closed his hand around Eros' throat. "No more games." His whisper was menacing.

Eros pulled at Prometheus' fingers but couldn't pry off his grip. "All right. I know for a fact Pherusa is your soulmate, and unless the two of you bond by nightfall, you'll unravel."

Fear for Prometheus joined the jumble of happiness, hope, and hurt knotted in Pherusa's stomach. She tugged at the most recent thread. "Unravel?" Like he'd said Kronos would?

Eros gave her a sorrowful look. "His powers will take over, and he'll cause one natural catastrophe after the other, before he self-destructs."

Prometheus knew the danger. Was that why he tried to shoo Eros away? So she wouldn't know he'd bond with her solely to save his precious humans?

The mountain shook beneath them, and dark clouds swarmed the skies above.

"No," Prometheus said. "I'd bond with you because I'm done pretending I hate you."

Hands on hips, she narrowed her eyes at him. "That's a long way from *you and your father betrayed me. Aaargh. I'll punish you.*" Just as long a way from *I love you.* To Eros, she said, "Isn't there another option?" She'd love Prometheus forever, come what may, but she wouldn't bond with him out of self-sacrifice. He'd have to love her back, wholeheartedly.

"The only workaround we've found is for the sea witch to turn him back into stone," Eros croaked.

Pherusa's chest hurt at the thought of losing him again.

"The sea witch? You mean Nereus' crone?" Prometheus asked.

Because *that* was the important thing. *Males.*

Eros winced. "Circe."

"Call her, then. If Pherusa won't be mine, there can be no bonding." Prometheus' eyes had turned golden and blazed like twin fires.

"You'd turn to stone rather than be with me?" Pherusa stood, ordering her legs to stop trembling, though the ground still rippled with tremors.

Prometheus snorted. "I'd mate you where you stand, while he watches"—he clenched his jaw, his gaze unreadable— "but you don't love me."

Was he saying whether they bonded or not was up to her? She closed the distance to the men and placed her hand gently on Prometheus' wrist. "Do *you* love *me*?"

"That's irrelevant." The stubborn fool would return to stasis, rather than say the words?

A boulder behind him was dislodged from the mountain and flung aside by an unseen hand.

By his power.

A strange calm unfurled in her belly, despite the chaos raging around her. "Tell me."

"I do, Chaos damn it. I love you with everything I am." He screamed the words.

In her head.

She could hear his thoughts.

Had he heard hers before? Was that why his responses to Eros made no sense?

She probed his mind and saw his love for her, clear as day—it was bound inside fear and pain, but it shone brighter than Helios himself.

Focusing on where her skin met his, she projected a mental image of herself peeling away the layers of darkness around his heart. "I love you," she thought at him. Aloud, she added, "I never stopped. It's on you that we're not already bonded, because I gave my heart to you the moment we met."

Eros flickered, and then disappeared, Prometheus' grip on him not that confining after all.

Prometheus stumbled but righted himself. "Say that again," he ordered her mentally.

"I love you," she said inside her head and out. "You are my soul. You have my heart."

The earth heaved beneath her, throwing her into his arms, and Eros' disembodied voice said, "You'd better continue this elsewhere. If Circe is right, Kronos is buried inside Olympus, and what you're doing is bringing him closer to consciousness."

# CHAPTER FOURTEEN

Even before the echo of Eros' words faded, a splitting headache ripped through Prometheus' skull. This must be how Zeus felt when Athena was born, only no goddess was tearing her way out of Prometheus' head. It was his brothers' screams, clanging against his brain.

He saw Hyperion again, frozen with his arms over his head and at the same time thrashing inside his own body. Atlas, kneeling behind a glass pane, roared so loud, Prometheus grinded his teeth to bite back his own agonized scream.

And once more, Kronos' wrathful bellows overtook everything else.

Prometheus willed the voices and images away. His head grew quiet, but the brewing storm above didn't relent. He brushed a quick kiss over Pherusa's lips and grabbed her hand. "Come on." If it was up to him, Kronos would never walk this earth again.

"Where are we going?" Her cheeks were flushed, and her green eyes shone feverishly with desire. She bit her lip, and Prometheus wanted to bond with her right here, this very moment, even if it brought Kronos back to life.

But this time they'd do things right.

"You love me," he said. He'd never get tired of hearing it.

Her expression turned somber. "With all my heart. Always have."

"And you and your father had nothing to do with Zeus' capturing me." It was a statement, not a question.

She flinched, but her voice was steady as she said, "Nothing whatsoever." She pursed her lips, then added, "I know you can read my mind. Why not see for yourself, if you still doubt my words?"

He was as tempted as he was surprised she'd figured out he could glean her thoughts uninvited, but love came with inherent risks, and he'd have to risk trusting her on this if they were to have a future. "I believe you. Let's go." He realized he was yelling. The wind had picked up and howled in his ears, the air filled with the smell of rain. They were cutting it close.

Pherusa raised her gaze to the darkening sky. "You still haven't told me where."

He grinned. "To Vythos. I need to patch things up with your father, and ask for his and your mother's blessing to become your bonded mate." Not that he wouldn't bond with her anyway, but it would make Pherusa happy to have her parents on her side, so he'd extend this olive branch.

A crack formed on the earth beside them. It was small, but he didn't plan on sticking around till it widened. He tugged on Pherusa's hand and blinked them right outside Nereus and Doris' bedroom. He was surprised not to see a guard outside the door, when a Titan—he—was on the loose.

Maybe the royal couple weren't afraid of him.

The thought pissed him off a little, but mostly it warmed him up inside. They didn't see him as a threat, because they knew deep down he still cared. Like they did.

Pherusa frowned. "Why not the throne room? Or the council room? Father should be there now, regrouping his forces."

"If he's not here, we'll wait. He'll have to go to bed at some point, and I'd rather we talked to him and Doris without dozens of armed mermen vying for my blood."

She tapped his shoulder playfully. "Yeah, because they scared you so much, Mr. I've-had-a-Dinosaur-for-a-Pet."

He snatched her hand and laid it flat over his heart. "Not *any* dinosaur. It was a Tyrannosaurus Rex."

"Sure. Gods forbid it be a *plain* dinosaur." She laughed, but there were thin lines of tension at the outer corners of her eyes. She was stressed about how this would go.

"Before we talk to your parents, I need to apologize to you," he said. "For hurting you."

Her fingers flew to the blood on her head, where the skin had knitted itself back together. "It was a tiny cut. It's healed."

Prometheus shook his head. "Not now. When I first awoke. I would have been gentler, if I knew... I thought you were a dream, and then... I wasn't thinking with my head."

"I forgive you." The words felt like a caress that broke the last of the chains binding him to the past.

He wrapped an arm around her shoulders and rapped the knuckles of his free hand on the door.

Nothing.

He raised his hand to knock again, when Doris' voice reached his ears.

"Come in." The queen sounded tired.

Pherusa turned the door handle and pushed.

Prometheus was close enough behind her to see Doris' eyes light up when her daughter entered. To his relief, Doris didn't scowl when she spotted him.

Doris opened her arms, and Pherusa burrowed into them. "I knew you'd bring her back," Doris said. She had more faith in him than he deserved. A smile blossomed on her young face, making her look so much like Pherusa. She motioned him closer and patted his arm. "You didn't stop loving her." It wasn't a question.

"Yeah, well, he had me fooled for a while." Pherusa sniffed indignantly and stepped out of her mother's embrace, immediately seeking out Prometheus' hand.

He tangled his fingers through hers, letting the contact ground him. "My rage wouldn't let me see straight. Now my head is clear, I know better."

"Good." To Pherusa, Doris said, "Have you told your father yet?"

Pherusa shook her head. "Prometheus thought we should wait for him here."

"Wait? And let him go mad with worry?" Doris tutted and went to an old armoire, made of driftwood and coral, like most of the furniture in the palace. She opened the first drawer, retrieved a small, sculpted horn, and brought it to her lips. No sound reached Prometheus' ears, but Doris nodded to herself and returned the horn to its place. "He'll be here shortly."

She led them to a sofa and two mismatched armchairs, and motioned for them to sit. "He'll be better behaved if he doesn't perceive you as a threat," she told Prometheus. "Though you might want to cover yourself. The palace is not *clothing optional* these days."

Prometheus wasn't embarrassed by his nudity, but he'd come here as a friend and would follow the rules. "I am afraid I have nothing to wear," he said.

Doris left the room and returned shortly with a seaweed robe. "It will be a snug fit, but he'll see you made an effort."

A couple days ago, Prometheus would give up his life before he was forced to put on one of these things. Now he thanked Doris, pulled on the robe, and sat on the sofa, careful to keep it closed over his groin.

Pherusa made herself comfortable next to him, one hand on his thigh.

He hadn't realized he was nervous until a sense of calm spread through him at her touch.

Opposite them, Doris folded her lithe frame in a chair. "So what have you two crazy kids been up to?"

Images from their lovemaking the past couple days flitted through Prometheus' mind, and he ducked his head as if the queen could read them in his eyes.

Pherusa gave him a light squeeze. "Not much. Rediscovering each other."

Doris smirked. "Can't say I blame you."

The main door to the bedroom opened so fast, it slammed against the wall behind it, and Nereus strode in. "You called, my love?" He was still in his fighting gear, though the tail had been replaced by legs. When he saw Prometheus, his hand flew to the hilt of his sword.

"You don't need that," Doris said. "There is no threat here."

Prometheus instinctively half-leaned in front of Pherusa, though her father posed no threat to her. "King Nereus." He stood and gave a small bow, hoping this was enough to show he wasn't here for a fight.

The thin line Nereus' lips formed indicated he didn't see it that way. "Prometheus. Are you here to return my daughter, or to demand my throne again?" His voice was so loud, Prometheus wouldn't be surprised if guards barged in any moment now.

"Neither," he said. "I'm here to do something truly difficult—apologize for not accepting your word to begin with, old friend. I should have believed you and Pherusa. I should have known..."

"And now you do?" Nereus asked. His tone was guarded, but he crossed his arms, no longer poised to attack.

Prometheus nodded. "I wish to ask for your blessing to be mated to your daughter." Out of the corner of his eye, he saw Doris arch an eyebrow. "Yours too, Queen Doris," he added hastily. "As a show of good faith, I promise to side with you, should Kronos arise, and I'll do my best to ensure all other Titans who awaken join us."

Nereus flared his nostrils. "You put us through a lot. My wife has not slept in two nights—"

"Only because of your incessant grumbling and pacing, husband." Doris rolled her eyes. "I never feared he would harm her. Even Circe told you they are soulmates, but you only listen to her when it suits you."

Nereus gave her a dirty look and then glared at Prometheus. "Hurt my daughter, and Zeus' wrath will be nothing compared to what I will do to you."

Prometheus could point out that he was more powerful than the king and his army combined, but he put aside his ego and kept his mouth shut.

"Good boy," Pherusa said in his head.

"You like me better when I'm bad," he replied in the same manner.

Doris glanced from one to the other, then slid her gaze to Nereus and smiled.

Nereus shook his head. "If my wife is correct—"

"Which I always am."

"—you are already mentally linked. Far be it from me to keep my daughter from a happiness long due. You have my blessing. Both of you."

Pherusa's face glowed with happiness. "Mother?"

"Let me think about it." Doris scratched her chin.

"*Mother*."

"All right, *daughter*. You and your beloved have my blessing. May your eternity be filled with love."

"And sex," Prometheus thought at Pherusa.

Her pale skin turned rosy with the most beautiful blush. "Then, if you'll excuse us, we'll be in my room," she said with a giggle.

Nereus covered his face with his palm. "And I will be far, far away," he mumbled. "The Atlantic is nice, this time of the year."

Prometheus didn't hear what Doris said, because he was too busy blinking Pherusa and himself to her bedroom, on the other side of this floor of the palace.

He took in the room before him. He'd been here a couple of times, in another lifetime, and it hit him hard how unchanged it remained. Time had frozen for the girl—woman—who lived here.

The curved single bed, forged out of pink coral, was adorned with white sheets and a dozen of fluffy pillows, picked up from shipwrecks through the years. Their colors had barely faded, the magical light of Vythos nowhere near as destructive as the rays of the sun.

The nightstands were littered with pieces of colored glass, smoothened by the waves, and shells in all shapes, hues, and sizes. Even the pale golden glow of Vythos was filtered through red-tinted glass, washing the room in pink hues.

A vaguely humanoid shape caught his eye at the far left corner. Was someone else in the room?

He spun, pushing Pherusa behind him, and blinked in disbelief. A statue of himself in bronze stood there, smirking at him. The resemblance was uncanny. He turned to face Pherusa, who was blushing. "How...?"

Her lips twitched. "From memory."

The level of detail was astonishing. "You made this?"

"I had help, but mostly yes. Took me a few hundred tries to get it right. I needed to see you, so I forged you."

How had he ever doubted this woman's loyalty and love? He slanted his mouth over hers and poured everything he felt— his every hope and fear and all his love—into this kiss.

She pushed gently on his chest and whispered against his lips, "We're filthy."

What?

Oh, she meant it literally. Sprigs clung to their hair, her dress was matted with mud, and his ass had a coating of dirt. Shower sex could be fun, but he wanted to bond with her in her bed. "I have an idea," he said.

"What?" she asked in his head.

He blinked them to the ocean, for the water to clean them. Pherusa's legs melded into a gorgeous green tail that she flapped from side to side, as she glared at him. "You could have given me a moment's warning," she thought at him.

Prometheus laughed, not minding the water rushing in his mouth and down his throat. Titans couldn't drown, after all.

"We can't blink back to my room like this. Everything will get wet," she sent him.

The mental image of her divine pussy accompanied her words, and he was painfully hard in a heartbeat. But he'd do things the way his Siren wanted. He focused on the top of the castle, just inside the bubble, and in a split second, they materialized on the soft pillows there. Pherusa stood and discarded her soggy dress, and he took off his robe in favor of a dry one she handed him from beside the door.

"Thetis made sure these are on all of the entrances to the palace, so nobody's sensibilities are offended," she said with a smirk as she wore one too. She twisted the water from her long, golden locks and held the door open. "Shall we?"

# CHAPTER FIFTEEN

Pherusa was thankful they ran into none of her siblings or any of the palace staff on their way to her room. Nothing should delay their lovemaking.

The moment her door was closed behind them, though, butterflies fluttered in her stomach. Why was she so nervous?

Perhaps because she'd dreamed of this moment so often but never expected to experience it. Now it seemed her long life had always been leading to this.

Prometheus was about to make love to her in her virginal bed—the same bed in which she'd fantasized about him a million times while she pleasured herself, never reaching the peaks he took her to.

She stood on her tiptoes, to lay a soft kiss on his lips, then held out a hand to him.

He gazed at it reverently, before closing his large palm around hers and letting her lead him to her bed.

Her fingers trembled as she undid the sash of his robe, as if she hadn't touched his body mere hours ago.

He stopped her and tilted her chin up, so she'd meet his eyes. "There is no need to rush this."

Right. Because the world *wasn't* hanging on the balance. She forced a smile that turned real when she saw the laugh lines around his gorgeous black eyes.

"Let me," Prometheus said, and she sat on the bed, waiting for him to undo his robe.

Instead, he gently nudged her to lie back and stretched beside her on her narrow mattress. "Are you sure about this?" he asked.

What? Making love?

He sombered, studying her face. "I understand if you don't want to bind yourself to me for—"

"I do." Did she sound too eager? Who cared? "It's all I want. Please make love to me, my Titan."

His smile was dazzling. He buried his face in the crook of her neck and inhaled deeply. "You smell of home. Of the ocean and the dawn and creation itself."

His new beard tickled her sensitive skin, yet her giggle wasn't a reaction to that but an expression of pure happiness.

Prometheus' agile fingertips found the neckline of her robe and slipped underneath it, to trace the valley between her breasts and skim down to her navel. "I love touching you," he whispered and nibbled on her earlobe. "Your body is so responsive." He undid the belt keeping her robe in place and continued his trail down her belly and then her thigh, uncovering a strip of skin a couple centimeters wide.

Pherusa wanted the stupid robe to disappear, so he could touch more of her.

Prometheus licked along her collar bone and shoved aside the fabric covering one breast. He teased the nipple with his palm, barely touching the sensitive peak that puckered and tingled with the need for more attention. "See how inviting your breasts are? How can I resist?"

"Who says you have to?" she muttered, tangling her fingers in his hair to bring his head lower until he grazed her nipple with his teeth.

The sharp sensation was replaced by the warmth of his mouth, as he closed his lips around the tender flesh and sucked, sending a jolt of pleasure to her womb.

He skated his palm down her stomach, caressed her hipbone, dragged his fingers up her thigh, and kept sucking on her breast.

Pherusa spread her legs, moisture pooling at her core. "Take your time with me later. Now I need you inside me."

He raised his gaze to her face. "I didn't prepare you." His hand slipped between her legs, and his expression turned hungry when he dipped a finger inside. "Seems I don't have to."

She shook her head. "In me. Now."

He laughed as he rolled his body over hers, and kept laughing as he slowly entered her.

It did delightful things to her nether region, but mostly, it made her heart expand. He was relaxed and carefree and with her. Really with her. This coupling held no trace of urgency or resentment. No fear that he'd cast her aside when they were done.

With every thrust of his hips, Prometheus declared his love for her through their mental link. His eyes blazed gold with desire as he drove in and out of her body, pulling tiny mewls and moans from her lips. "Who do you belong to, Pherusa?" he asked, withdrawing until only the tip of his erection remained in her.

Pherusa tilted her hips. "You. I belong to you. My heart is yours." In his head, she added, "Forever."

Prometheus tensed, every muscle in his body coiled. He squeezed his eyes shut and shook his head, his expression pained.

Was he having second thoughts?

"Never." His answer rang in her head, and he opened his eyes again, to look at her with a near-tangible intensity. He inched back inside so agonizingly slowly, she buried her nails in his wide shoulders and pushed her heels into his buttocks. When he was seated all the way inside, he said, "My heart is yours. Forever."

Nothing snapped in place. No supernatural string sprung between them. But Pherusa knew the bonding was successful, because of the sense of completeness that spread throughout her body. She was where she was meant to be.

With Prometheus. Forever.

She caressed his mind with her thoughts and was filled with wonder. Even now, he was amazed she was his.

She pumped her hips and urged him on. They'd done their service to the world. Now they were going to have fun.

Prometheus gave her a feral grin and dug his fingers in her hips. He knelt on one leg, the other planted firmly on the floor, the adjusted position both changing the angle of his strokes and adding to his momentum.

Her body bowed the way he held her hips, Pherusa's pulse thudded in her ears as he drove inside her in a steady, measured tempo, stoking the ball of fire in her belly. Her head was light. She tried to bring her hand to her mound, to touch her clitoris and add the friction she needed to orgasm, but her limbs wouldn't follow orders. "Need..."

Without slowing his thrusts, Prometheus splayed his hand over her belly and dragged it down her body, to where they were joined. "I love seeing you like this, wild and ravenous for me." He drew his thumb along her lower lips and to her clitoris, to circle the sensitive button in ever tightening loops. As he added pressure to his touch, he slammed inside her harder, without changing his rhythm. He kept her on a plateau of pleasure, not letting her fall over the edge.

"Say *please*." He pinched her clitoris between index and middle finger, making her groan.

"Please. *Now*."

Her eyelids were heavy, but she kept them open long enough to see his satisfied smirk, as he thrust inside her in a frantic pace, twisting his thumb on her clitoris. The combination of sensations made her feel like she was the one unraveling, pleasure splitting her open for the fire inside to consume the world.

Prometheus kept pistoning into her, until he reached completion with a roar that made the room shake and a fresh rush of heat spread up her neck to her cheeks. Everyone in the palace must have heard that.

She tugged on his hand and used her tongue to lick his fingers clean, feeling him harden inside her once more.

Pherusa was sated and pleasantly sore, and wouldn't say *no* to a couple hours of sleep, but when Prometheus waggled his eyebrows, she decided rest could wait.

Eros obviously couldn't.

She saw his head appear behind Prometheus' shoulder.

"About time, people," he said and clapped his hands.

"This time, I'll fucking kill him," Prometheus roared. He blinked behind the god and was fast enough to get him in a choke hold. Prometheus' gaze zeroed in to between Pherusa's legs, and he scowled.

*Gods*, she was exposed for Eros to look his fill. Nereids weren't inherently shy, but this was a private moment, and Eros was intruding. She crossed her legs and scooted higher on the bed, covering herself with her robe.

"Speak your piece and take your chances, godling," Prometheus growled.

"You're not the thankful sort, are you?" Eros harrumphed. "I'm here to congratulate you on your bonding and let you know Hyperion is up and running. Naked. In a hotel somewhere."

Prometheus adjusted his grip, glaring daggers at Eros. "Has he found his mate?"

"She's who he's running after," Eros said with an exaggerated sigh. "Let's just say he'll need less prompting than you did."

Looking at Pherusa, Prometheus said, "I should go to him. Help him—"

"You'll do no such thing." Eros' voice was so amplified, Pherusa winced and covered her ears, though she still heard what he said next. "Unbonded Titans are unstable, and the proximity of their siblings can exacerbate their unraveling. I'll bring him to you when it's safe."

# CHAPTER SIXTEEN

Bring Hyperion where, though? Would Prometheus and Pherusa live in the palace?

She must have read his mind, because she said, "I'd be as happy in your cave as I'd be here, as long as I'm with you."

Could he possibly love her more?

Eros *aww*'ed. "That's adorable, but Big Guy can afford a mansion to house your love now. The credit card I gave him?"

Prometheus nodded. It was in the pocket of his shorts, somewhere on the floor of his cave.

Eros went on. "I told you it has no limit. It's linked to a rather hefty bank account, and everything else you need is here." He somehow slipped from Prometheus' grasp. When he snapped his fingers, a large brown envelop slapped the floor by Prometheus' feet.

As Prometheus reached for it, the god said, "We'll be in touch," and disappeared in a cloud of sparks.

Prometheus flicked through the envelope. Birth certificate, ID card, driver's license, passport, and a handful more credit cards, as well as a cell phone.

"What's in it?" Pherusa asked.

He tossed the envelope on her dresser and crawled into bed next to her. It was a tight fit, but it'd do till they found the perfect place. "Nothing important," he said. "All that matters is in this bed with me."

She turned in his arms and draped a leg over his, her wet center pressed against his cock. "I believe we were in the middle of something."

He claimed her mouth and pushed inside her slowly, until he was fully sheathed.

Pherusa sighed. "I like this."

"Good, because it's going to be happening a lot." He rocked against her, holding her gaze. "I was thinking we should get a big place. Many bedrooms."

"For visitors?" She bit her lip as he twisted his hips.

"Or children." He watched her face for any signs of distress. They'd never talked about this before, but there was no rush.

The smile that blossomed on her lips made his heart race. "Sounds good."

They made love until Pherusa's eyes drifted shut. He curved his body around hers, without withdrawing from inside her. This was what he wanted for eternity.

He ached to follow her into slumber, but the image that had flashed through his mind the moment of their bonding wouldn't let him. Glimpsing the face he thought he'd never see again had chilled him to the bone. *Epimetheus.* Prometheus believed his twin dead, not trapped. He'd seen him turned to dust by Kronos, before the Titanomachy. Was there hope for him yet?

He touched his lips to Pherusa's temple and watched her sleep. He had his soulmate, and now his brother might be returned to him too. He wouldn't tell her anything, but once they'd settled in a place of their own, he'd talk to Eros. The thought soured in his gut. He hated admitting it, but he already owed the little god more than he was comfortable with.

Call it restitution for what the Olympians had done to him and his brothers.

He kissed the tip of Pherusa's nose and closed his eyes.

He awoke to something pressing down on him. Was he still under the seabed? Had the past couple days been a dream? Panic sliced through him at the thought he was still in stasis. But no, this wasn't cold mud covering his body. It was the supple form of his little Siren.

Prometheus blinked away the last dregs of his sleep and folded his arms under his head. "You feel like going for a ride?" He pumped his hips.

Pherusa wiggled and planted her hands on his shoulders, her face centimeters from his. "I just wanted to take a good look at you." When she sat back, her heat was pressed to his shaft, but she made no effort to take him inside, and he was happy to lie here, gazing into her adoring eyes.

"Talk to me," she said. "What was it like, where you were?"

He rolled back his head and brought his hand to her thigh, to caress the silky skin. "Dark. Wet. Cold. I could feel the pressure and the cold, but nothing else."

She swallowed audibly. "Did you... Were you aware, the entire time?"

Was he? He drew circles with his fingers on her bare back. "I'm not sure. I think I swam in and out of consciousness. Dreamed of you a lot—or it was fantasies. Might have been part of Zeus' curse. Sometimes we had this. Others..." Others, he made her pay for betraying him. He made her cry.

Pherusa sprawled on top of him, her fingers idly playing with the hairs in his armpit. "You were living but dead. Like..." From her mind, he picked up the rest of that thought. "Like me."

His first instinct was to protest the belittling of his ordeal—she'd been at home with her family and friends—but moisture gathered where her cheek lay on his chest. He'd made her cry again.

She pressed her lips to his skin, over his heart. "I breathed and moved freely, but inside, I was in stasis, with you. I drifted through the days, looking forward to bedtime, when I'd hopefully see you in my dreams."

Prometheus wanted to tell her it was all right, that he was here now, but he felt her need to talk about her pain and exorcise the ghost of their forced separation.

"When you... came to me on the beach, I thought my dreams had come true. That my love summoned you."

"It probably did, but I was an asshole and didn't realize it."

She raised her head. Her eyes were red rimmed, but her expression serene. She scrunched her nose. "I don't know the exact meaning of that word."

"A jerk. An idiot. A brute, who hurt you out of his own insecurities."

"Yes. All of that. But you were hurt too. You lost eons of your life. We have so much catching up to do, and I plan on enjoying everything with you, both under the sea and on the surface."

And they could heal. Together.

He *could* love her more, and he did, with every moment that passed. He'd gladly show her again, but a knock on the door reminded him they weren't alone in the palace. "Hold on," he called out. Begrudgingly, he rolled Pherusa off his body. He stooped to snatch their robes from the floor, helped Pherusa with hers, and then pulled on his own.

Pherusa sat primly on the foot of the bed, but her meticulously closed neckline couldn't hide her messy hair, bee stung lips, and flush skin. "What?" she asked when she caught him looking.

"You might as well be wearing a *Thoroughly Debouched* sign around your neck."

He left her maniacally finger-combing her hair, and went to answer the door.

Nerites, Pherusa's only brother, stood outside, a sly smirk on his lips. "You're alive," he said. "We were worried when you missed breakfast."

From behind Prometheus, Pherusa asked, "Is it Eros again?"

Prometheus replied, "As if that little prick would ever knock. No, it's your brother."

Nerites arched both eyebrows. "*Little prick*?"

Taking a step back, Prometheus motioned him in. "Yeah. He's made a habit on dropping in unannounced."

"Who has?" Nerites asked with a frown.

"Eros."

The frown deepened for a heartbeat, and then disappeared. "Father would like you to join his council meeting," he told Prometheus. "I trust you remember where the council room is. I heard you made an appearance recently."

So Nereus still planned to prepare for war. An all-out offense might work against Kronos, but it would destroy much of the human world. They'd need a contingency plan. If the witch could turn Prometheus back to stone lest he unravel, why couldn't she do the same for his unhinged brother? "Won't you join us?" he asked Nerites.

The prince of Vythos shook his head. "I've been briefed in advance, as per usual. Besides, I'm a lover, not a fighter. *Was*, anyway." Pain darkened his gaze so briefly, Prometheus wasn't sure he saw it.

Right. Nerites had been head over heels for Aphrodite. Her loss must have cost him dearly.

"Don't mention her," Pherusa warned in his head. To her brother, she said, "What about me?"

"You, my dear, can come fill our sisters in on your revived romance, before they drive me crazy with questions I have no answers to."

# CHAPTER SEVENTEEN

Thirty of Pherusa's forty-nine sisters still lived at the palace, and most of them were gathered in the ball room. Large cushions were arranged in one side of the expansive room, and the Nereids were sprawled on them, oohing and ahing at all the right places, while Pherusa relayed a sex-free version of her reunion with her Titan.

Nerites stood beside a coral pillar in a corner, smiling at her, but Pherusa saw the sadness lurking in her brother's beautiful deep-blue eyes. Her one true love had been returned to her, while his was gone forever. The Titans wouldn't be waking if all the Olympians hadn't faded away, which meant all hope he had of winning Aphrodite's heart again was lost.

She tried to wrap up the remainder of her story and save him more torture, but the rest of the Nereids would have none of that.

"So he would destroy the entire world if the two of you didn't bond? That a whole new level of screwed up," Halie said. "And I thought ignoring Circe's prophecy came with dire consequences."

Pherusa rolled her eyes. "I know. And would you believe it? Before Prometheus came to accept I'd never hand him to Zeus, he was determined to go through with the unraveling. If it weren't for Eros' persistence, I wouldn't have found out, either, until it was too late."

Nerites' posture went as stiff as if a stingray had grazed him. "What did you say?"

Pherusa studied his furrowed brow. It didn't take away from the beauty of his face, though it aged him. "That I wouldn't know—"

He gestured impatiently. "No, before that."

"That Eros was the one who kept urging him to bond with me?"

"Yes." Nerites seemed confused. "Who is that?"

"Who's Eros?" Galene asked. "He's…" She shot Pherusa a panicked glance. They didn't mention Aphrodite's name in Nerite's presence when it could be avoided.

"The god of love," Pherusa supplied for her. No reason to remind her brother that Aphrodite had had a life after him, while he'd condemned himself to solitude.

Frowning, Nerites rubbed his temples. "How come I've never heard of him?"

Impossible. Nerites might have spent his entire life in Vythos, but you couldn't not have heard of Eros. "Perhaps you know him as Cupid?" Pherusa suggested.

He waved his hand in front of his face, as if to shoo away an annoying school of sardines. "Know whom as Cupid?"

For the second time, it was like Eros slipped her brother's mind. Or this was his way of letting them know he didn't want to hear about the god.

"Anyway, with some nudging, we performed the bonding." Pherusa let a naughty smile play on her lips. "A few times."

Halie laughed. "To make sure it took, of course." She was always quick to laugh since she and Delphinos bonded, and the sparkle of happiness suited her.

Pherusa knew the feeling of being so ecstatically blissful nothing could bring her down.

Except for her brother's lost expression.

"Are you done gossiping about me, ladies?" Prometheus' voice made her lift her gaze.

He leaned against the door frame, arms crossed over his wide chest, the seaweed struggling to contain his muscles. Imposing and regal in a dark-green robe wasn't an easy look to pull off, but he managed it impeccably.

Pherusa was on her feet and hurrying to him before she realized she moved.

"Hey! We didn't hear the juicy parts." Seemingly unperturbed by Prometheus' dirty look, Thalia added, "Whatever. Pherusa can fill us in later."

"How did the meeting go?" Pherusa asked when Prometheus whisked her out of the room. It was surreal, walking around her father's palace with her arm looped around her Titan's. So normal, and yet it had been out of her grasp even yesterday.

He nuzzled her hair. "As expected. We know Hyperion is awake, and according to Circe, he'll be on our side once he's bonded. Not that I'd ever expect him to join Kronos. Kronos has been quiet since you and I bonded"—he snorted—"for which your father congratulated me, though he wouldn't look me in the eye. We don't know how long this will last, so Nereus has patrols in all the seas, listening for signs of unusual activity."

Since the world was safe for now, Pherusa braved asking about matters closer to home. "And did everyone behave?" Through their mental link, she sent him, "Did you?"

His lips twitched. "There was some hero-worshiping, now that I didn't want to kill them. I got to know *your daimon friend* a little better too. He has a crush on you."

"You must be mistaken." Palaemon had been her escort to the surface since he was a young boy. She'd never seen him as more than a friend, and his behavior toward her betrayed no romantic feelings.

Prometheus shrugged. "Not like he told me he'll crush every bone in my body if I mistreat you. Twice."

"He *didn't*." She searched his thoughts. No hint of a lie. "You weren't uncivil to him, were you? I care about him deeply."

"And platonically, luckily for him and me both." Under the watchful gaze of two palace servants carrying linens, Prometheus brought her to a stop, folded an arm around her waist, and smashed his lips to hers in a kiss clearly meant to stake his claim. "Don't worry. I like the little guppy. He's loyal." He hummed and twirled her, before gathering her back in his embrace. "Was properly introduced to your sister's boy too. He's funny."

Pherusa laughed. If anyone would call hundreds-years-old sea daimons *guppy* and *boy*, it'd be Prometheus.

"What now?" she asked. "Can I have you to myself, or will you run off to play with your new friends?"

His gaze burned through her, the desire in his eyes making her feel as naked as ever. "I thought we'd stop by my cave first. Then, in a couple hours"—he waggled his eyebrows—"we could get dressed and go house shopping."

She licked her lips. "I hear house-shopping is best done in the afternoon, so we don't need to hurry."

"Then let's go to my cave and rut like beasts in heat."

# CHAPTER EIGHTEEN

"One last signature here, and the place is yours." The realtor, Magda, tapped one red-lacquered nail on the dotted lines at the bottom of the contract, her red lips stretched in a shark-like grin.

Prometheus took the fountain pen she handed him, careful not to break it. *P. Titanas*, he scrawled. The deeds would be in his name only, because Pherusa didn't yet have any identification papers. He'd have to talk to Eros about those too. He'd seen the god's name in the contacts list of the cell phone Eros had given him.

Magda took the signed documents with a smile, sat back, and crossed her legs. She looked very pleased with herself, which made sense, since she'd no doubt be getting a hefty commission on the six-bedroom villa Prometheus and Pherusa bought.

Magda had shown them several houses in Santorini that were *almost* what they wanted, but the moment they set foot in that one, he and Pherusa both knew they had to have it. They fell in love with the ample space, the white walls carved into the stone, and the magnificent view of the Caldera. *And* it came furnished. It was the perfect home, and Prometheus looked forward to filling it with memories—and making love to his soulmate on every available surface.

Magda snapped her fingers, and her assistant, whose name Prometheus didn't remember, appeared at the door separating her office from the waiting room. "Yes, ma'am?"

His searing glower would put a Titan to shame, but Magda was unfazed. "Boy, get us a bottle of champagne. Mr. and Mrs. Titanas have gotten themselves the most gorgeous villa in all of Santorini, and we must celebrate it."

Pherusa glanced at Prometheus, a question in her eyes. "Champagne?" she asked.

He flipped through his new memories. Alcohol. Fizzy. *Nice.* "You'll like it." He patted her hand and looked at Magda. "Now what?" When he called to say they were serious about buying and would like everything done as soon as possible, she'd let him know Greek bureaucracy didn't do *as soon as possible.* "How long do we have to wait?"

She waved her hand dismissively. "Waiting is for those who can't afford to oil the wheels. Once the wire transfer comes through tomorrow, you may come get the keys. Spyros will make sure all the paperwork goes through by the end of the day."

*Spyros.* Right. Prometheus hadn't seen the young man on their two previous meetings with Magda, but he probably held the fort while boss-lady took clients on-site.

Spyros glared at her as he half-filled the flutes with the bubbly golden liquid. His eyes reminded Prometheus of someone, but he couldn't put his finger to it. Then again, Magda's eyes seemed familiar too. Maybe all blue eyes looked the same.

Magda tutted. "Only three glasses, boy. This is above your paygrade."

Prometheus brought his glass to his lips, to hide his amusement. There was something going on with these two.

"Not before we toast," Magda raised her glass, and he and Pherusa mimicked her. "To the newlyweds and their great taste. May you be happy together, always." She stressed the last word.

"Do you think he's… fucking her?" Pherusa stumbled over the f-word even in her thoughts.

Prometheus squinted against the fizz that threatened to come out of his nostrils. "If he is, he mustn't be doing a very good job of it," he replied through their link. He stood and held out his hand to Magda. "Thank you so much for your help."

"You've made a wonderful choice," Spyros said. The way his gaze strayed to Pherusa, Prometheus wasn't sure he meant the villa, but he wouldn't go primitive on the boy's ass. Only a blind man wouldn't be awed by her.

Magda shook hands with him and Pherusa, and then said, "Spyros will show you out. Drop by tomorrow around noon for the keys."

"We have a house." Pherusa clapped and planted a noisy kiss on Prometheus' mouth when the realtor's door closed behind them. "I can't believe we can move in tomorrow."

He brushed a lock of hair back from her face and winked. "We'll have the keys tomorrow. No reason to wait till then to move in." He closed his arms around her, cast a wide mental net over onlookers, so their gazes would glide off him and his Siren, and blinked with her to their new bedroom.

# EPILOGUE

"Are they gone, *boy?*" Circe shouldn't be enjoying this charade so much, but Eros' discomfort at his role as assistant to her bitch-realtor persona was hilarious.

"You'd better be waiting for me naked," he hollered from the next room. He strode in her—well, *Magda's,* if she were to be technical about it—office and slammed the door behind him, his true facial features taking over the magic disguise. "*Boy?* You'll be lucky to only get away with a spanking."

"Oh, did I upset you, baby?" She batted her eyelashes, letting the realtor's pale skin deepen to her own golden tan, and the blond pixie cut give way to her chestnut locks. She might be kinky, but Eros' having sex with Magda's lookalike would be the wrong kind of *bad.*

"How long do we have?" he asked.

Circe looked at the clock hanging beside the door. "It's an hour and a half by car. Two, if they hit traffic. And that's after she decides he's a no-show." She'd intercepted Prometheus' last call and had sent the actual realtor, who had no assistant, to meet a nonexistent client in Nafplio, so she and Eros could make sure Prometheus and Pherusa got the perfect place with no legal hassle. Magda might not remember closing the deal, but she wouldn't mind getting the commission.

"Why couldn't we tell the big guy we were doing him a favor, intercepting for the realtor?" Eros grasped her skirt with both hands and pulled it higher, to expose her bare ass.

"Because this is more fun." And because Circe's visions told her to do so. If she hadn't reached into Magda's mind, to view her previous meetings with Prometheus and Pherusa, she wouldn't have recognized the latent—

Eros popped open the buttons of her pressed white shirt and dug his teeth in her flesh. "Where are you?" he asked.

She moaned and pulled at his hair, but they both knew she enjoyed a little pain.

"Right here, with you, my..." Instead of finishing that sentence, she flicked her tongue along the seam of his mouth, and bit his bottom lip when he pulled away.

"You and your secrets and your games…" With a wild laugh, Eros turned her and bent her over Magda's desk. "Now you've done it." His palm landed on her bare bottom with a loud *smack.*

Circe pushed all thoughts of Magda's reborn soul out of her mind. It wasn't *her* time yet, anyway.


# End of Book One

Book Two

# A Maid for the Titan

# CHAPTER ONE

It was too early for Olivia to be upright. She hadn't metabolized last night's alcohol in the mere two hours of sleep she'd managed before this morning's rude awakening. She didn't have a hangover; she was still drunk. And it was no fun, even without having to clean the largest room in the hotel.

She took in the spacious suite. Damn Katerina for calling in sick today, of all days. As if Olivia didn't have a spinning head and upset stomach to deal with.

*This* was why she didn't drink—didn't have more than a glass of wine with dinner, *ever*. Because one time was enough to screw things up. She never knew what awaited at the next corner, to demand a hundred percent of her attention. Or at least her ability to bend over without dry-heaving, like when she tried to pick up the remote someone had tossed on the floor by the front door.

Never mind. She'd get it later.

She huffed and twirled her feather duster. It slipped from her grip, to hit a vase. Olivia cursed under her breath, but stood frozen in place as the vase swayed and then thankfully righted itself. Stupid thing might cost her a week in wages she couldn't afford to waste.

Okay. Time to wash the too-little sleep off her eyes and get started. Manolis promised to pay her double for coming in on her day off, and if she was fast, she might manage to meet Christina and the guys from last night at the beach, as planned. Olivia bit back a wave of alcohol-soaked jealousy at the thought of her roommate sleeping in this morning, after last night's overindulgence.

She entered the enormous marble bathroom and gaped at the four-person Jacuzzi. She'd never been in one of these. Never would, either, because her chosen career path wouldn't make her that kind of money in a million years. And by *career path*, she meant archeology. The housekeeping thing was to cover this post-graduate summer vacation, before she leaped into her real life.

The sink in here was almost as big as the tub in her room, and had golden faucets. She turned on the tap and splashed copious amounts of water onto her face. It didn't help with the feeling like crap, but it did help her decide what to do next.

She'd dust, then vacuum, then make the beds, if she could stomach so much movement by that point. How many people did this suite sleep?

Boo. She'd never make it to the beach. She'd been on the island three weeks already and had yet to work on her tan. Or that general pinkness her pale skin boasted after a couple hours under the sun and copious amounts of sunblock.

When she'd seen the job opening online, it had seemed the perfect summer escape from her tiny New York apartment.

*Come visit the beautiful island of Crete, and work in the mornings in exchange for room and board.*

Plus tips, the manager, Manolis, promised when she talked to him on the phone.

This far, the tips didn't cover the disgusting things people did in hotel rooms that they'd never do at home.

At least this toilet had been flushed.

She returned to the main room. Things looked relatively tame here too. No used condoms in sight. No visible tears on the furniture or curtains. Nothing broken. Still, she had to sanitize everything before she left. She grabbed her duster and got started on the coffee table. *Ugh.* Every time she tilted her head, the world swam. Manolis said she had all morning. She could afford to put up her feet and snooze for fifteen minutes.

She dropped onto the leather sofa and let her gaze wander up the statue that stood on a pedestal in the middle of the living room. It depicted an enormous man with long hair and a beard down to his chest, his arms held above his head, fingertips touching the fifteen-foot tall ceiling.

Other than his size, he looked real, the level of detail incredible. Almost lifelike. The man might be Atlas, though if he were from the Classical period, as the style suggested, he'd be naked. Not like the statue could be an original. It was a tourist-y gimmick, and all wrong for the era. Ancient Greek statues reveled in the beauty of the human body, and genitals weren't covered until much later, when the Catholic Church decided they should be. Even then, penises were either broken off or covered by fig leaves, not loincloths.

Her eyelids were heavy. If she didn't get up soon, she'd drift off.

She groaned and stood. The sooner she started, the sooner she'd wrap this thing up. She no longer cared about making it to the beach. She just wanted to return to her bed and stretch out her tired body. And never drink raki again.

This work-vacation thing wasn't very restful or relaxing.

It took her an hour to dust and vacuum the bedrooms at a snail's pace. She pressed through the nausea and also did the beds. Was rather proud of it too.

Time to hit the living room.

Once she was done cleaning all horizontal surfaces, she looked up at the huge-ass statue. How on earth was she supposed to dust this? She didn't have a staircase handy.

Olivia planted her arms on her hips and inspected the room for something to step on. The dining chairs seemed flimsy. She should just clean what she could reach. Not many people would be able to see above that, anyway.

She swapped her duster for a piece of cloth, which she dipped in a mix of water and dish detergent. Better for the marble.

She ran it over the statue's toes, and she must still be drunk, because she thought one of them twitched. *Get a grip, Liv.* With quick strokes, she wiped up the man's calves and shins and along his thighs. When she reached the loincloth, she paused. From down here, it almost seemed like she could see part of a scrotum—hey, she might not have seen one in real life, but she had an Internet connection and normal urges. She just never found the time for a relationship and wasn't into casual hookups.

But why would a sculptor bother giving this guy genitals, if the loincloth was in place from when the statue was originally sculpted? She ran her hand over the sculpted cloth. It was warm. The window was at the statue's back, so this wasn't the side that got any sunlight. Were the lights in the room so hot?

A stain like oil from prying fingers on the part right over the statue's crotch drew her attention. She moistened her rag with more cleaning mixture and rubbed again.

The marble cloth moved.

No. What was beneath it moved.

She was still asleep on the sofa, wasn't she? She'd lose her job if she didn't wake up now and really clean the suite.

She pinched her arm and let out a little *yip*. That hurt. Not asleep.

She rubbed the loincloth again. Harder. It pushed against her palm, and she pulled it back in shock. A rock-hard shaft, perfectly visible from where she stood, formed a sizable tent. *Woah.* This thing was bigger than her forearm.

Someone groaned.

Olivia jumped around, but nobody was behind her.

She looked up again and saw the statue's arms were no longer reaching for the ceiling, because the enormous man was no longer a statue.

The tan man before her was obviously made of flesh and radiated heat. Golden eyes sparkled above his long, black beard, as he rubbed himself over the white piece of fabric wrapped around his hips. And he was still easily twelve feet tall.

Olivia stepped back, scared but unable to take her gaze off the ripping muscles of the man's chest and arms. She should be running for her life. She would, if this was real. But it couldn't be. She was sleeping off last night's buzz, in her own bed, never having set foot in the hotel suite.

But if this was a dream, the floor wouldn't shake when the man stepped down from the base of the statue he'd been moments earlier, his gaze locked on her.

Would it?

He held out his hand, and Olivia finally snapped out of her haze.

She spun on the ball of her foot and ran to the door. Thankfully, she hadn't locked it, and the handle turned at first try. Olivia threw the door open and sped to the elevator.

She jabbed the button with her thumb repeatedly, for all the good that did her. "Come on, come on, *come on.*"

A glance over her shoulder revealed the man was at the door of the suite, only now he stood no bigger than six foot four, and he looked at her with a mixture of confusion and lust in his eyes. He pointed at her and said what sounded like, "E.T."

No. He was saying *ithi. Come*, in ancient Greek.

Olivia felt a tug toward him. He was sexy, in a rough, primitive sort of way. And freaking ripped. Every muscle in his body stood out—especially the one under the towel or whatever was around his waist. The mental image of him, pressing her against the wall, lifting her skirt, and pushing into her made her head light. His hands would be rough against her breasts when he tore off her shirt, and his lips would taste of nectar.

*Nectar?* Where did that come from?

"*Ithi*," he said again, and the pull was almost tangible. Part of her wanted to go to him, take off her clothes, and let him do those deliciously wicked things to her body.

The elevator pinged, and she rushed in and pressed the *Close Doors* button, and then *R* for Reception. She'd send security up here, demand tomorrow off, and *nope* out of any more shifts at the suite.

Of course, she wouldn't tell anyone that the weirdo upstairs initially looked like a statue. That had been her imagination playing tricks on her, boosted by alcohol. Nothing a warm bath and a long nap wouldn't take care of. By the time she returned to work on Wednesday, the naked loon would be long gone, and she could get on with life as usual.

# CHAPTER TWO

How many centuries was Hyperion held in stasis, not asleep, yet not fully aware, and incapable of movement?

His last real memory was of Zeus' lightning bolt slicing through him. Whether out of cruelty or indifference, Zeus had trapped him with his eyes open, so in his lucid moments, he saw the seasons change before him, until he lost track of the years. He watched the Olympians act like petulant children and interfere with mortals' destinies.

When Zeus abandoned Olympus, Hyperion was sure he'd be left behind, but that wouldn't be punishment enough. From one conscious moment to the next, he no longer stood on green grass, but was surrounded by dark, still waters. He gave up. Stopped trying to see or hear. No light reached the depths of the sea that was to be his grave.

Then one day he awoke, and he was in this room, surrounded by noise and humans and lights. Voices spoke in tongues that made no sense, and a large opening on the wall across from him showed him images of war and famine and celebration. Of love and hate. After ages of feeling only cold, now warmth caressed his bare back for a while every few… hours? He chose to believe it was Helios, heralding the morning and shining down on him. Reminding him he wasn't alone.

But wasn't he? His brothers were lost to him, and the females of his generation were long gone. Hyperion couldn't begrudge his nephew the safety precautions. He'd warned Kronos not to eat his children, lest he share Uranus' fate, but did the giant pain in the glutes listen? No. And all Titans paid for it.

Hyperion didn't care whether the mortals that came and went were friends or foes; he could best any human. He yelled inside his head and raged against the unseen shackles holding him immobile. But Zeus' spell had enough of a hold over him that the void never failed to suck him back in.

Something brushed along his manhood and pulled him out of his spiraling thoughts. That he could feel it wasn't surprising. He hadn't lost sensation when he was turned into stone.

What *was* surprising was that he physically responded to the stimulus. The touch was feather light, but his body rose to the occasion.

Huh? His body had been locked in position for eons, and the one part that decided to move after all this time was what hung between his legs?

He looked down—*he looked down?*—and saw a dark-haired woman staring up, under his loincloth, her brown eyes wide and her lips parted. It had been a very long while since a woman looked at him with such open interest, let alone evoked a response.

The woman licked her lips, and his manhood grew to its fully erect position, which couldn't possibly fit inside a mortal female. Was this a new kind of torture—getting him ready to enter a female's body and leaving him incapable of sating his hunger? Another of Zeus' tricks? Hyperion groaned, and the woman gave a little jump and spun around.

*No.* She'd leave, and he'd be stuck here like a satyr, with desire burning in his loins.

He ached for her to finish what she started. He didn't realize when his hand moved, but he was no longer holding the ceiling. Delighted, he cupped himself. *Yes.* He could feel his palm on his shaft. Could feel the fabric between his grip and his erection. Was he turning into flesh again? Was his unjust punishment finally over? He rubbed his length over the loincloth and shivered with delight. This was real, not another wishful-thinking fantasy.

He looked at the woman again. Should he ask for her help?

First, use his mind-controlling power to compel her to forget what she saw. It would save him from having to explain how he'd gone from marble to flesh and blood, and she might be more willing to continue what she was doing when he awakened.

She turned back toward him, and shock and fear replaced the awe in her expression.

Yes, compulsion would be necessary. Good thing he was a master at reading and swaying the human mind.

"You never saw me as a statue," he said, compelling her to believe him. "I am a human male."

She looked perplexed. Like she didn't understand him.

*Right.* His mother tongue was dead to this world.

Luckily, thoughts didn't have to be words, and if he touched her, he could wipe her memory. *Come to me,* he thought at her, holding her gaze. A hint of seduction would do the trick. If she were attracted to him, she'd be more open to trusting him.

The woman took a step back, her eyes impossibly wide. But she wasn't leaving, so his planted suggestion was working.

Slowly, both to avoid losing his balance and so she wouldn't feel threatened, he stepped down from the plinth he'd been set on. He held out his hand, but she twirled around and ran for the exit.

*Wait*, Hyperion ordered in her head. *Come to me. Don't fear me.*

Yeah… That? Didn't work. She swung open a barrier and rushed outside.

Why didn't his mind-control work on her? Had his captivity rendered it useless? Surely it would return, even if it took some time.

He was about to chase her down, when he caught his reflection on the glistening surface of one wall. Of course she was afraid. Although Zeus' lightning had lessened Hyperion's size as it cast him in stone, he was still double the height and width of a mortal.

He could fix that. He hunched his shoulders and focused on reducing his mass. When he stretched again, he could pass for a tall human. Good thing he still had this power.

*The woman.* It was imperative he find her and figure out why he couldn't bend her to his will. And maybe then she'd let him bend her over an easily accessible horizontal surface and pound into her soft, writhing body.

He fumbled with the metal thing on the wood and pulled. It took a couple tries before the thing twisted in his grip and the vertical panel swung inward. The woman stood a handful of paces away, in front of a shiny wall that seemed as impenetrable as Tartarus' gates from the inside. She had her back to him and prodded a protrusion, tapping her foot on the floor.

Hyperion took the time to study her behind, which was clearly outlined by her tight, black… Argh. What was the word for this way-too-short chiton?

She turned to glance at him over her shoulder, and her warm brown eyes betrayed alarm, though nowhere near the panic he'd gleaned before.

*"Come to me,"* he mentally ordered her again. An opening appeared to his right, and a naked woman made to step outside. *"Not you,"* Hyperion thought at her and returned to *his* woman, who remained unaffected.

Why was she unaffected?

He didn't usually need his powers to make women desire him, but he'd do what it took to get her close. He focused on conjuring mental images of their bodies tangled together in ecstasy, and projected the thoughts to her. When he heard her breath hitch, he held out his hand and said aloud, "Come."

She frowned, and for a second, he was sure she would obey. Then a tiny bell sounded behind her, and the wall split in two. She entered the small room it revealed, and the wall slid in place again, concealing her.

Hyperion crossed the distance with a howl and banged at the wall, but it didn't yield. He was about to tap into his real strength and rip it into shreds, when he noticed the protrusion the woman had pressed with her finger. He pushed his thumb on it.

It glowed.

He jumped back.

The woman had to be a goddess, and until he knew more of her powers and why she'd turned him human, he should be careful of what he risked.

But if she had designs on him, why did she flee?

He stomped back into the halls he'd just vacated and stepped on something that crumbled under the sole of his foot. A loud voice made him spin around. A male was at the opening that gave him glimpses to the world, talking about the weather. Hyperion approached and looked closely at him. There was something covering the opening. Something clear, like water, that reflected his image back to him. He touched the surface, expecting it to ripple, but it was solid. Odd.

He tried to pull it off the wall, so he could talk to the man behind it, and when it wouldn't budge, he let his full strength flow through his arms and tore it in half. The male on the other side disappeared. *Coward.* Did he run to warn Zeus of Hyperion's return?

Something zapped Hyperion, like lightning but weaker. It made anger roil up his chest and pour out in a savage cry, as he pounded his fists into the thing that gave out sparks.

"Hold it right there."

The words meant nothing to Hyperion, but he turned toward the new voice. Another male, this one inside the room. He wore very constricting clothing and held something with both hands.

The man spoke again, and Hyperion made out some of the words. He was to follow without *something* and sleep *something else* off.

Hyperion had a better idea.

"Show me," he said, and let his compulsion engulf the man, who dropped his arms and spread his mind open, for Hyperion to soak up every piece of information it ever held, including things Vangelis—that was the man's name, and he was a *security guard*—didn't remember learning.

Vangelis wasn't the most learned man in Greece, or even Crete, but he was fluent in modern Greek and something called *English*. He also knew what Hyperion had trashed was a *television* and how *elevators* worked, and that the current Greek prime minister was a sellout and a liar, and that this was the year 2018, counting from the birth of Jesus Christ, son of the one God, in whose name atrocities were performed on a daily basis.

Gods in this era seemed more bloodthirsty than the Olympians, who were mostly interested in having a good time. Or rather, their followers thought them to be all for war and discrimination and hate.

Vangelis believed his God was about love, and he felt accepted by Him, though he wouldn't publicly admit his attraction to men while his mother was alive.

Ancient gods didn't care about things like *sexuality* either. Nor did they tell people how to live their lives, in the most part. They only punished direct insult, oath-breaking, and betrayal of familial bonds. Maybe that was why they were now forgotten. Nobody had feared them in a long time, and people had replaced doing the right thing with seeking profit.

Hyperion could use that. "Vangelis, I'm going to need you to bring me a lot of coal," he said in perfect Modern Greek. "Oh, and one last thing." He pushed past Vangelis' personal belief system and his knowledge of *mythology*, as people today thought of the stories pertaining the Olympians, and only skimmed through *Titanomachy*, the great Clash of Titans. He knew what version of it people were taught; he'd heard it from Zeus himself.

Hyperion scrolled—and this was a fun new concept—through the hotel personnel images and found the woman who'd tickled his fancy, among other things.

Olivia Johnson.

# CHAPTER THREE

"Here you are. Thought you were coming to the beach," Christina chirped.

Olivia raised her face from where it'd been pressed to the pillow and blinked bleary eyes at her roommate. "Hey. You're back. I was gonna meet you." She reached for her phone, but the nightstand was too far away and required her to move about five inches to the right, so she let her hand drop to the mattress. "What time is it?"

Christina tossed her beach bag on one of the only two chairs in the room and kicked off her flip flops. "Three. We had sandwiches at the beach, and the guys wanna take us to a small taverna by the sea tonight. They said the tables are literally *in* the water. Well, not submerged or anything. Just make sure to wear sandals. And nothing you don't want to get wet." Her bubbly disposition, usually pleasant and so fitting her lovely, heart-shaped face and innocent, wide, blue eyes, today grated on Olivia's nerves. As did the stupid cicada that had made its home on the windowsill but might as well be holding concert in Olivia's head.

"Got any aspirin? I'm still hungover from last night." Raki was not to be messed with. And it was not to be drunk on an empty stomach when you didn't know and trust the producer. All of which people had told her before she found herself with a group of locals, doing *koupes*, as they called the long shots of near-forty-percent alcohol.

Christina winced. "That bad?" she whispered.

"Worse." Olivia focused her entire being on rolling over and sitting up. She reached behind her, pulled the pillow out of the way, then scooted back until she met the headboard and leaned against it. Like all staff rooms, theirs was on the ground floor, which was below street level on the front but opened up to a small yard in the back, and Olivia was grateful for the relative darkness. She opened her mouth for the two aspirin Christina popped out of the blister pack and onto her tongue, and accepted a glass of water with a heartfelt *thank you.*

"Why didn't you call? I'd have come back sooner." Christina sat beside her on the bed and patted her shoulder.

"Oh, I'm okay now. You should have seen me this morning. I hallucinated an enormous naked guy."

Christina opened her big blue eyes even wider than usual. "Seriously?"

Olivia nodded. "The suite hadn't checked out after all. The guy came out in a bath towel, and I thought he was—like—a *giant.*" She wouldn't admit she also thought he was a statue, and especially not that she'd rubbed his penis like she expected a genie to come out and grant her three wishes.

*God.* She hid her face in her palms. First penis she'd touched in her twenty-three years on this earth, and she'd molested a stranger.

"I called security on him because he ran after me, but now I'm thinking maybe that was too hasty." Because he'd have every right to report her. Though he didn't seem to want to scold her when he chased her to the corridor. Rather to get her to come back inside and look under that towel. And when he called her, she'd been tempted to be impulsive and go to him and lose her stupid V-card.

But no. No more impulsiveness. She'd had one thoughtless night in her entire life, and she might lose her job over it. She'd never lost control before. Never got drunk. Never got carried away. Never did anything on a whim, until she came on this trip. And yes, her time here might have been a little underwhelming so far, but that didn't mean she wanted to be shipped back home and forced to face reality a couple months ahead of schedule.

"I should check in." She groaned as she made another try for her cell-phone, and Christina stretched out and got it for her.

The light at the top blinked ominously. She unlocked the screen and grimaced. "Three missed calls from Manolis. This can't be good." The man was friendly and easy going, unless the staff disrespected him or the hotel—and touching a guest's genitals might be seen as disrespectful.

"Want me to call him back? I can say you're violently sick or something," Christina said. She could probably talk him down—everyone loved Christina—but Olivia had to deal with this maturely. And hopefully keep her job.

She shook her head and immediately regretted it. The painkillers hadn't kicked in yet. She could do this, though. She slid her finger across the screen, over the contact name, and brought the phone to her ear, ready for a lot of yelling in a combo of Greek and English.

"Olivia. *Finally*. I was worried."

That didn't sound too bad. "I'm sorry. I wasn't feeling well."

"I hope you're better now. When do you think you could come by my office?"

This was it. She was going to get fired. "Manoli, I'm so sorry about this morning. I—"

"It's nothing bad. Just come see me. Say, in an hour?"

The interruption was welcome, since she wasn't sure how she'd explain her behavior, but she'd be more relieved at his words if his voice didn't sound… mechanical? Manolis was usually a hyper ball of energy. This was too subdued for him. "I'll be there," she said. "Is everything okay with you?" It was real concern. He might be demanding as hell, but he was a good guy.

"Everything is fine. Awesome. See you in an hour," he said in the same uninflected tone.

Olivia had a long shower to clean the cobwebs from her brain. She pulled her shoulder-length hair up in a high ponytail and let it air dry, while she threw on a pair of cropped jeans and a dark-green elastic crop top that kept her breasts in place without the stifling constriction of a bra. She glanced at herself in the mirror and added an oversized lightweight scarf. The top might be fine for the beach, like Christina insisted when she convinced Olivia to buy it, but the hotel manager might not appreciate seeing the outline of her nipples.

As she slid her feet into her comfiest sandals, she checked the time on her phone. She had half an hour to go, but now that she was ready, she wanted to get this out of the way.

She took the stairs up to the lobby, said *hi* to Kostas, who manned Reception most afternoons, and knocked on the door with the sign that read *Management* behind him.

"*Peraste*," said a deep male voice that couldn't possibly belong to Manolis.

Despite her rather good grasp on Ancient Greek, Olivia's Modern-Greek repertoire consisted of a few scattered words, other than *come in, housekeeping, should I come later*, and *let me call my manager*. Oh, and *aspro pato—bottoms up*—after last night, but she doubted she'd ever say that again. The man at the other side of the door had bid her enter, but her knees trembled without warning, so to buy some time, she called back, "I'm sorry, my Greek isn't that good. What was that?"

"Come in," the man said in accented English.

His voice made her want to run to him, and at the same time, far, far away. She steeled herself and pushed the door open.

And had to gather her jaw from the floor.

The man leaning against Manolis's desk was six-foot something of hotness, packed inside a tight pair of faded jeans and a white button-down shirt that stretched over corded muscle as far down as the open dark-blue blazer over it allowed her to see. His jet-black hair was pulled back in a ponytail, and the five-o-clock shadow on his tan face made his amber eyes pop.

*Amber eyes, almost golden.* She'd seen those eyes before. Had seen a whole lot of the man in front of her, too.

*Shit*, he cleaned up nice. Which was irrelevant when he was here to have her fired.

"Good to see you again," the man said. His voice wrapped around her like a caress, and she adjusted the scarf, to keep him from seeing her nipples tighten.

Manolis stood from behind the desk and approached her.  She hadn't realized he was here. "Olivia Johnson, meet the hotel's new owner, Mr. Titanas," he said.

The man gave a small nod. "Call me *Hyperion*."

She hid her surprise. What sort of parents decided that the best name for a boy whose last name meant *Titan* was that of an actual Titan?

The man smiled, and there was hunger and promise in his gaze. "Nice to have a name to go with the face, Olivia Johnson." His narrowed eyes said there was more than her face in his mind.

Did he expect her to do more of what she did this morning, when she thought he was statue?

*She thought he was a statue*—now there was a sentence that wouldn't land her in the loony bin.

"I'll leave you to it. I have a renovation to organize." Manolis practically skipped out of the room before she could ask what *it* was.

Maybe Hyperion expected an apology. She owed him one.

But he didn't seem offended, only curious.

She should apologize anyway. "About this morning—"

"I'm sorry I chased you. I didn't mean to make you uncomfortable." He didn't look sorry. He looked... about to eat her up.

"No, *I'm* sorry. I shouldn't have… I wasn't… I had too much to drink last night, and for some reason"—her forced chuckle sounded like a hiccup—"I thought I was dusting a statue when I… You know. I wasn't supposed to even be there. I'm usually off Mondays, but Katerina—"

He waved off the rest of her sentence. "No need to explain. It was a misunderstanding. That is not why I asked to speak to you."

"No? Then wha—?"

"I have a proposal for you."

She should be upset he'd interrupted her for the third time in a row, but her curiosity took over. "What kind?" If it had to do with sexual favors, she was out of here. Not that she'd mind sexing up this tall glass of—

What was the matter with her? Her hormones were usually way tamer than this. Her cheeks burned. *Damn.* Would she ever outgrow blushing?

A smirk played on his lips. "One I think will be mutually beneficial. How would you like to work for me?"

Wasn't she already? "You own the hotel. I work for the hotel. Ergo…" She trailed off.

"Cleaning for me is not what I had in mind."

All lustful thoughts were squashed by the fury that spilled through her veins. "I can't believe you just suggested that."

"What did I suggest?" He frowned, but the hint of a smile was still there.

"You know what you suggested."

He straightened and pushed a hand in his jeans' pocket, opening the jacket more and allowing her a glimpse of skin between his shirt and the waistband of his jeans.

"What I want from you is to help me adjust. I've been away for a long time, and I need someone to"—he scrunched his face—"teach me the ropes?"

"*Show me.*"

He arched an eyebrow. "Show you what?"

Olivia rolled her eyes, but she was glad for the change of subject. Not only had she accosted the guy, she'd also implied he tried to buy her or rent her or whatever. "The expression is *show me the ropes.*"

His lips split in a gorgeous smile. "And that was the second reason I chose you. You can help me practice my English."

But what was the first? "I'm not sure I'm what you need. I've only been in Crete for a month, and I've barely done any sightseeing."

"Perfect. We can do that together, and in the meantime, you can tell me about this world of yours."

Yeah, they had to work on his English, because what he just said didn't make much sense. "You said you've been away?"

"A forced exile, you might say." His face darkened. Had he been in jail?

"For how long?" she asked.

"As long as it takes."

Huh? Ah. "No, I mean, how long were you away?"

"Too long." So he wasn't going to talk about it.

"And what exactly would my job description be?"

Hyperion took a step toward her, and she bit her lip to keep from licking it at the whiff of his scent, earthy and spicy and entirely male. "You'll be my personal assistant. You'll assist me in fulfilling my needs."

She wrote off the double entendre as a language-barrier thing. How bad could being the guy's assistant be? "I'm only in the country till September. I won't do anything illegal for you, I'll need a day off a week, and you have to double my salary. Plus cover lodging." She really only wanted enough to get by. And maybe get a more PA-appropriate wardrobe.

"I'll triple it and throw in a clothing stipend." Did he read her mind, or was that a jibe for what she wore? She couldn't think about that when his eyes shone gold again and he was within licking distance.

She tried not to melt against him and used her most professional tone to say, "You're making it hard for me to say *no*."

# CHAPTER FOUR

The world was young, and humans weren't created yet, when those later named *Olympians*, led by Zeus, went to war with the Titans who ruled until then. The Olympians won, and Zeus sent those Titans who opposed him to Tartarus. For eternity.

Or so the story people knew went.

Hyperion had heard Zeus reiterate it while Hyperion and most of the other male Titans acted as lawn ornaments, outside the golden palace atop Olympus.

And it was all a lie.

Hyperion knew that, because he'd seen the world born, had fathered Sun and Moon and Dawn—Helios, Selene, and Eos back then—and had watched Prometheus and Thetis create man at Zeus' command, to be used as cannon fodder for when the *King of the Gods*—pfft—went after his own father, Kronos.

Hyperion had warned his brother history was about to repeat itself, but like most Titans refused to support his claim to the throne, and instead sought shelter among the humans.

Unfortunately, Zeus was an all-or-nothing kind of guy, and all male Titans were sentenced to be cast in living stone for eternity. Including poor Prometheus, by the way, in case anyone needed more proof of Zeus' loyal nature. Female Titans were stripped of their immortality and allowed to finish their lives as humans. Probably what passed for mercy, in Zeus' twisted mind.

But now Zeus and the rest of his ilk had faded into nothingness, and Hyperion was still here. And he was top of the fucking food chain, baby. *Fucking*—such a mouth-filling word, though Hyperion had different tastes than the images the word summoned in Vangelis's head.

Hyperion should look for those of his brothers he could tolerate, but there was time for that. First, he needed to fit in this era. And that had nothing to do with pursuing the female who brought him back to life this morning; it was a matter of staying out of the public eye.

He scanned what he'd absorbed of Vangelis' thoughts for today's *fashion icons* and selected the mental image of the sought-after GQ model. He should start by taming his hair and beard, and then get himself appropriate clothing. Shouldn't be too hard. Hyperion wasn't named the god of Watchfulness, Wisdom, and the Light for nothing.

A knock on the suite door brought him back to the future. Of course he'd stayed in the suite. The new living room TV was being delivered tomorrow, and by then, he'd be more than welcome here.

"Come in," he called out.

Vangelis entered, pulling a luggage trolley filled with bags of coal. "Where do you want these, sir?" he asked in Greek.

Hyperion answered him in the same language. "In the bathroom. It's going to make a mess anywhere else."

Vangelis shrugged and carried his purchases to the master bathroom. Hyperion liked the way the man took everything in stride. The only suggestion he'd needed once Hyperion had absorbed his knowledge of today's world was that Hyperion was a decent man who'd pay him handsomely for his services. Oh, and also that the hotel was secure without him for a few hours.

Hyperion followed him to the bathroom and waited for him to unload the trolley. "Thank you, Vangelis. Come back in two hours, and I will compensate you for today."

As soon as the mortal was gone, Hyperion tore open the first bag and emptied the coal in the bathtub. He selected a large piece and crushed it between his palms with his full strength, the magnitude of which could cause tectonic shifts. When he opened his hands again, in the place of the black, sooty piece of carbon lay a brilliant white gem. Mortals valued these above life. He stoppered the sink and laid the precious stone in there, before pressing and adding more gems, until the tub was empty and the bathroom light reflected on the bucketful of diamonds in the sink like the room was filled with rainbows.

When Vangelis returned, Hyperion handed him five stones, each as big as a walnut. "These are for your assistance so far. You are free to choose whether you want to keep working for me or not." He used no compulsion. Vangelis was a good man, and Hyperion wouldn't enslave him.

Vangelis arched an eyebrow as he looked from the diamonds in his palm to Hyperion. "Are these real?"

Hyperion nodded.

"Yeah, I'm working for you full-time, now on."

Hyperion chuckled. "Then take me to your leader." It was a phrase he'd picked up from the man's brain.

Vangelis laughed too. "You mean my boss?"

Hyperion searched through his newly acquired info and pursed his lips. "Would that be the owner of this establishment?"

"I'll have Manolis arrange it."

Manolis, the hotel manager, was as accommodating as Vangelis, though he was sad to let Vangelis go. He gave Hyperion the address of the owner and let him and Vangelis use his own car. Hyperion used his power to avert people's gazes from him as he entered the vehicle. This method of traveling made his head light. He'd stick to the astral plane, but even after picking Vangelis' brain, he couldn't project himself anyplace he hadn't physically visited before.

It didn't take more than a few handfuls of diamonds and a touch of compulsion, for the owner to sign over the hotel to a semi-naked stranger.

Since they were out already, Hyperion also used diamonds to pay for his haircut and beard trim, as well as for his new attire, though Vangelis protested that what he gave the barber and merchant was way above what their services were worth.

Hyperion assured him the result was worth it, and he'd been correct, judging by how Olivia raked her gaze down his body now. He tried again to compel her, sending her mental images of him pleasuring her, but she didn't react to his suggestions, though he heard her pulse ratchet up several notches. *What was she?* She didn't ping his immortaldar—*Uranus*, he was loving what people did with language—and she was apparently oblivious to his true nature.

Manolis had pulled up Olivia's personnel files for Hyperion on this marvelous device called a *Personal Computer*. She was from the opposite side of the globe, and her employment contract expired in September. She'd also studied archeology, which might mean she'd realized how old Hyperion's statue had been. Not that it mattered, after her panicked retreat.

But according to Vangelis, she'd reported a nude guest accosting her, not a giant statue turning to life. Was it possible this denial thing people were so into kept her from accepting what she'd seen with her own eyes? Hyperion couldn't count on that, though he hoped she wouldn't recognize him.

But she did. And against all odds, she apologized. Did she mean it? Did she honestly believe her inebriated state had made her *fondle* a normal mortal male?

Until this moment, he hadn't known what he was going to say to her—only that he had to see her again. The idea to employ her was a moment of pure genius, if he said so himself. And she said *yes*. Practically. He'd make her say the actual word, and then he'd take advantage of as much of her remaining time in Greece as possible, to get through to her and see what made her impervious to his power.

And woo her, if that was what it took, because he *would* lose himself between those shapely legs before she returned home and he went on to wake his brothers.

Speaking of those legs… She'd criminally hidden them inside trousers, but even covered from head to almost-toe, and with her hair in this austere updo, her body called to him with every minute movement. Was she part Siren and didn't know it?

Maybe he should stop pretending this had anything to do with figuring out her true nature, and acknowledge the lust driving his actions.

He looked into her deep-brown eyes and held out his hand. "So we have a deal?"

She bit her bottom lip again, and it took all he had to keep from claiming her mouth, but that would probably send her running again. She took his proffered hand, and something like lightning zipped through his veins. Maybe she felt it too, because her mouth formed a silent *O*, and she crossed her arms, like there was a chance he hadn't seen her nipples pucker through that flimsy top and the carefully arranged shawl she'd draped over her breasts. Like he couldn't smell her arousal.

"Deal," she said.

Hyperion was very pleased with himself. A deal with an immortal was binding. As long as he upheld his side of the agreement, which he would, she couldn't break hers. "First order of business—move you to the suite. You will have your own room, but I require access to you at all times." He projected an image of himself leaning against a doorway, this time without even a loincloth covering his nakedness. Was it his imagination, or did she shiver?

"I'm not sure about that. You said you'd cover lodgings. I expected my own place." Her pupils dilated, but her posture stiffened.

He meant to excite her, not make her feel threatened. "Your room will have a key, woman. I promise not to force myself on you, and my word is a contract. I won't touch you unless you come to me first."

Her eyes widened, and she shook her head. A lovely blush spread up her neck to her cheeks. "This isn't a good idea. You should find someone else." She turned and headed for the door, but he was faster and planted his hand on it, keeping it shut while she pulled on the handle.

When she turned to face him, her glare was fierce, but the scent of her desire for him was stronger than ever. "Let me go," she said.

Her chest heaved, inches from his, as he leaned closer so only a hairsbreadth separated their lips. She smelled even better up close. His mouth watered at the thought of tasting her. "You can't back out now," he whispered. "You'll miss out on a once-in-a-lifetime opportunity." The job would be good for her too. She'd see things she'd never afford on a housekeeper's salary. "Besides, we have a deal. I promised never to touch you without your consent, and I meant it. I won't rule out anything you initiate, because I won't pretend I am not drawn to you, but I can control myself." Could *she*?

He heard her breath hitch, as she splayed her palms on his chest. Her touch burned him and made his cock— another marvelous word—painfully hard. "This is just a job," she said in the same tone he used. "If you promise to only treat it as such, I'll stay."

He nodded and took another whiff of her delectable scent, before stepping back. "Bring your things to the suite, and you can have the rest of the afternoon off. Tomorrow morning, you will take me to"—what was that place with the currency?—"the bank. Unless you'd rather I paid you in diamonds?"

# CHAPTER FIVE

The guy was messing with her, no doubt. She should have guessed when he said he'd triple what she got now.

"Diamonds. Seriously." She leaned back against the door. She no longer felt threatened; he seemed sincere when he promised not to make any advances. Besides, if this was a fucked-up mind game, she was playing it cool. "Is the job offer even real?"

Hyperion shook his head. "So young, and yet so jaded. I told you, I'm a man of my word." He pushed his hand in his pocket again and fished out a small velvet pouch. "Here. Consider it a bonus."

Olivia uncrossed her arms to reluctantly accept it and empty its contents in her open palm. Six crystals, each as big as her thumbnail, glinted in the light that made it through the window.

Not crystals. Diamonds.

"*Holy fuck.*" She snapped her mouth shut and looked at him horrified. "I'm sorry, I don't usually talk like that, but... holy..."

Hyperion laughed, and the sound made her want to climb his body and feel it vibrate against her skin. "Is the holy version when you do it with a deity, or for when you call out for one?" he asked.

Her face burned, and her body hummed with feelings she'd never experienced to this degree till she met this man. Desire pooled between her thighs. Why was a virtual stranger, her new boss, turning her into a hornball?

With trembling hands, she put the stones back inside their pouch and held it out to him. "I can't take this. You don't know if I'll be any good as a PA, so no bonus yet."

"Women today are odd," he mumbled. "Used to be gems were accepted with gratitude."

She took a slow, deep breath, counted to ten, and let it out just as slowly. "Used to be women were bought and sold for less than that. *Thankfully*, times have changed."

He gave her another of those piercing looks, like she was a complex code he tried to decipher. "I have offended you again. I'm not sure how. In my time, women were different, but I want to learn how to be—how to act—better."

Again that disarming sincerity that had her weak in the knees. "Let's start with the easy stuff. You don't give women you just met extravagant gifts. It implies you want something from them."

When he frowned and opened his mouth, she held up a hand and said, "Sex. It implies you're paying them for sex, and that's degrading unless you know they're sex workers."

His frown deepened. "But it is okay to pay sex workers for sex, yes?"

"Yes."

He sighed, and the lines on his forehead smoothed out. "At least some things haven't changed."

If this was any indication of how working for him would go, she might want to rethink it. But she didn't need to change his antiquated view of women. Or even listen to it. She would tolerate him for the next couple months and go back home with an unexpected nest egg, new clothes, and a couple new experiences—like touching real diamonds.

"Go. Pack. Bring your luggage over, and we will talk more tomorrow." He leaned closer, and for a split second, Olivia thought he was about to kiss her. Not *kiss* kiss. A peck on the cheek. On both cheeks, like Greeks did too often for her liking. His arm brushed her breast, and she shivered, her body gravitating toward his.

"Let me get the door for you," he whispered, his warm breath tickling her ear. If she turned a fraction to her left, their lips would touch.

She gulped and stood stock still until he put enough distance between them for her to make a hurried exit.

There was no midway when he was around; she either wanted to jump him or flee from him.

* * * *

"You're shitting me." Christina perched up on the kitchenette counter and swung her legs. "Honest-to-God diamonds?"

Olivia stuffed the last of her meager belongings in her suitcase and leaned on it with one knee, so she could force the zipper shut. "I didn't have an appraiser handy, but they seemed like it." Maybe he'd been in Africa, and not in prison. Were the stones ethically sourced? Hyperion was a little rough around the edges, but she refused to see him as a possible smuggler of blood diamonds.

"But they looked real?" Christina asked.

"Yes."

"And you believe him when he says he'll pay you three times as much as what you make here?"

He seemed sincere. And a little too eager. And what he said… "I do."

Christina flipped back her hair. "Think Mr. Big Spender wants to add a spirited blonde to his staff?"

An irrational wave of possessiveness washed over Olivia. *Hyperion was hers.*

Where did that come from?

She gave Christina a watery smile. "I'll ask."

"Ooh, you like him." Christina hopped down and clapped her hands.

"No I don't." Olivia made a beeline to the bathroom, to gather her toiletries. "I mean, he's classically attractive—dark hair, caramel-colored eyes, tan, with the sort of body that's all about wide shoulders and narrow hips—but he knows it, and I don't do cocky."

Christina's snort came from right behind her, and she held a compact blush over Olivia's shoulder. "Here. Don't forget this. You can store it right next to your denial."

Olivia grabbed the blush and spun on her friend. "I don't see him that way, okay? He's hot, but he's also my boss. Yours too, since he owns the hotel. So can we not go there?"

"You *do* like him. This is so romantic. Like *The Maid* meets *Pretty Woman*."

Second person to call Olivia a prostitute today. "He's not buying my company. He wants someone to show him around and talk to him about Greece."

"Uh huh. And the market ran out of locals, so he asked for you. He is obviously into you. Or he's a Mafioso who flew in to take you to your real father. Who's a mob boss." Christina watched way too many action movies.

"My dad is back home with my mom, weirdo." Olivia shook her makeup bag, so things settled better inside it, and then closed it and took it to the bedroom. "All set."

Christina threw her arms around Olivia's neck and squished her. "I'll miss you."

Olivia squeezed her with one arm, then pulled back. "I'll literally be five floors up. And we're having dinner together tonight. By the sea, remember? I'll take these upstairs and be right back."

"Good," Christina said with a sigh. "And you remember who to call when you don't know how to spend all that money this guy's gonna throw at you."

Olivia shook her head, but she was laughing.

Her mirth dissolved when the elevator doors closed after her. As the elevator started up, her stomach sank to her feet. Was she in over her head? Maybe working for someone she was so attracted to despite herself wasn't a good idea. What worried her the most was that she couldn't tell if she was more afraid he'd break his word about hitting on her, or that he wouldn't.

Part of her expected him to open the door wearing nothing but a bathrobe. Or another towel.

The door was ajar, and tension stiffened her shoulders. Should she go in? Was he sprawled naked on the couch, waiting for her to suck him off?

Would she? It'd be a first, but maybe…

No. She was here to work. There would be no monkey business. Ready to slap him and leave, she pushed the door open with her knee. "Hello?"

Hyperion was indeed on the couch, but he was still in his button-down and jeans. He'd taken off his shoes and socks, and sat with his arms propped on his knees, the humongous new TV on the wall casting light and shadows across his beautiful face. His eyes were sad and his shoulders slumped, and he looked more real and sexier than ever.

His gaze was trained on the screen. "So much pain." The words were barely audible, like he was talking to himself.

Olivia looked at the TV. The news was on. Another bombing. More people crying and bleeding. More kids left orphan and homeless. She wanted to hug herself, but her arms were full. She swallowed past the lump in her throat and asked, "So which one's my room?"

He looked startled, like he hadn't realized she was here till she spoke. "Choose any one you like." He squared his shoulders, sat up straighter, and was again the self-assured bastard who thought he could have her just because he was rich. And hot. And she could totally see herself sitting in his lap and kissing him.

No. Bad Olivia.

"Which one's yours?" Because she wanted to keep her distance. No doubt he'd find company soon enough, once he got it through his thick skull that she wouldn't sleep with him.

He shrugged. "Haven't decided." He switched off the TV and slunk toward her, like a panther on the prowl.

She was losing patience. And control. Could she be irritated and turned on at the same time? "Well, where did you put your stuff?"

"Don't own anything other than this." He made a sweeping gesture down his body, and Olivia tried not to stare at his bulging muscles, and especially not the part of him she'd been kind of intimate with this morning.

She shook off her inner horndog and focused on his words. The plot thickened, and jail-time was back on top of her theory list. "I'll take that one." She pointed to the second room on the left. It was close to the exit and had a beautiful view of the sea.

"Let me help you with these." He pointed at her luggage.

"You don't have to."

He took the bags from her hands like she hadn't spoken. He definitely had boundary issues, but she'd pick her battles, so she let him lead the way and place her things by the large double bed.

And how cool was it that she wouldn't have to make it in the morning? "Thanks. I'll unpack, and then be out of your way," she said.

He shrugged again, but the cockiness had faded. "You can stay. We'll have food delivered. You could tell me about your family."

Olivia shook her head. "Not tonight. Sorry. I'm meeting a few friends at a taverna." And why didn't she say she and her friend were meeting a couple of cute guys? Because Hyperion had redefined *cute* for her? Nah, he wasn't cute. Scorching hot, maybe.

And when she met his sorrowful gaze, she thought maybe he was lonely too. Whatever his circumstances, a man who lived alone in a hotel suite couldn't have much family. And since he was new on the island, he probably had no friends either.

Shit. She'd regret this, but— "You could join us."

The smile that stretched his gorgeous, kissable mouth was brighter than the sun. "I'd love to. Vangelis will drive."

# CHAPTER SIX

Absorbing Vangelis' memories of food and tasting it for himself were two entirely different things.

"More of these." Hyperion lifted a plate that contained snails a few seconds ago and winked at the waitress. She was a pretty thing, curvy, with waist-length brown hair and deep-blue eyes.

And she didn't hold a candle to Olivia, who watched him with an amused twinkle in her eye.

"When was the last time you ate?" Olivia asked.

The guy beside her glowered, like he had since Olivia introduced them.

Hyperion scanned the guy's brain. It was only to recall his name—*Panos*—and not so he'd glean his intentions toward Olivia, which weren't all that noble. The man had a girlfriend studying in Athens, and was hoping to get some action till she was back in a couple weeks.

Hyperion arched an eyebrow at him and said, "Feels like forever ago." Which was true, but back when he last had a meal, it didn't taste this good. Not that he ate often. He didn't need mortal food to subsist. He didn't need *any* nutrition. He was made of the Earth and the Sky, and he was eternal.

Something clenched in his chest. Olivia wasn't eternal; her life would pass and end in a blink of his eye.

No matter. Their time might be limited, but they'd make the most of it once she stopped resisting the chemistry between them. Judging by how she squirmed during dinner every time he sent her provocative imagery of the two of them, he did access her mind to a point. He might not be able to sway her, but he got under her skin, and that would do for now.

He grabbed a fistful of humanity's greatest creation—fried potatoes—and shoved them in his mouth.

Olivia's female friend, Christina, watched with wide eyes. Or maybe her eyes were always like this. She was beautiful too, but like the waitress, she didn't make his blood sing. Because she wasn't Olivia.

"Pour me some more wine?" Christina held her glass out to the wimpy guy looking at her like a lovesick pup all evening. Michalis' intentions were pure. He wanted to be her boyfriend and hoped she wouldn't leave when summer was over.

And he almost dropped the bottle into the salad, in his hurry to fulfill her wish. Not that it'd be a great loss; with so much food on the table, who'd want to graze on lettuce?

"So, Hyperion, where are you from?" Panos asked.

Hyperion refused to look up from his food. "Here," he said and reached for a tiny cheese-pie dipped in honey.

"He's just been away for a while," Olivia supplied, piercing a piece of fried calamari with her mini-trident.

Panos asked something more, but Hyperion hummed with delight as he chewed, and pretended not to hear him. He had more meat and washed it down with raki, which gave him the tiniest buzz for a few minutes before wearing off. Damn his impeccable Titanesque constitution.

The flavors erupting in his mouth had been near-orgasmic during dinner, but the yogurt with rose jam was out of this world—and he'd tasted ambrosia. Who could have thought flowers were edible, let alone tasted this incredible? The tanginess of the yogurt should be jarring, contrasted with the sweetness of the jam, but instead they complemented each other in a combination that set his senses alight.

He'd wolfed down half of it before he noticed his four tablemates staring at him.

"I'll ask if we can take some with"—Olivia sounded amused—"but please refrain from licking the plate."

Christina brought her hand to her mouth, but her grin crinkled the corners of her eyes.

Hyperion's gut instinct was to feel insulted. They were laughing at him.

But there wasn't a mean thought in Christina's head, and he liked the way Olivia's gaze softened. She was less guarded toward him when he let loose.

He laughed with them, but his mirth dissipated when the fingers of his right hand twitched. What was this? His body wasn't mortal; he didn't do involuntary spasms. Did this have something to do with his punishment from Zeus? Was he turning human? His head was filled with an agonized cry. *Atlas?* He tried to mentally zoom in on the source of the sound, but there was nothing but darkness behind it.

A wave rolled toward them and crashed at their feet. The tables here were on a large slab of rock the water licked as it ebbed and flowed, but the sea had been quiet so far, and the wind hadn't picked up.

Odd.

Keeping his alarm from showing, Hyperion sat back and squared his shoulders. "You should try this," he said, as he filled his tiny spoon another time. Before he could bring it to his mouth, Olivia clasped his wrist and pulled it close, so she could wrap her full lips around his dessert.

He stared at her mouth, while she licked her lips clean. She'd taste like heaven, and he wanted to sample her. But he wouldn't until she asked him to.

"It's so good." She moaned in appreciation, and he gripped the table with his free hand, the one with the spoon still in her grasp.

Panos cleared his throat and pushed his chair back. "I'll pay, and then we can go." He was posturing like a peacock, but Hyperion was better at it. Plus, Panos thought Olivia was a bitch for being out with him and flirting with another guy, and that made Hyperion want to end him.

But she might not appreciate that.

"I will get it." Hyperion clicked his fingers at the beautiful waitress, and when she glanced their way, mimed writing on the air, like he'd picked up from Vangelis.

The woman came over with a smile and handed him a booklet. He opened it, barely glanced at the bill, and took out a handful of diamonds. He should create more of these.

The woman leaned closer and whispered in his ear, "Honey, those don't work here."

He expected her to be more impressed, but that was easily fixable. *"You'll take the diamonds and be happy,"* he thought at her. *"They are worth several meals in this establishment."*

"You don't understand. You cannot go around flashing precious stones. People will start asking questions, and we don't want them to know about certain things," she hissed.

Startled, he tried to pull away and look at her. Something held him in place, though. Like before. Like when he was stone. From the corner of his eye, he saw everything around him was still. He should have realized something was off, from the utter lack of sound other than her voice, but he'd been used to quiet his years under the sea, and didn't immediately notice.

He bit back the angry howl that clawed up his throat. "Who are you? What do you want from me?" he ground out.

When she tucked her long hair behind one ear, he caught a whiff of magic. Witch? "You may call me Circe, and I don't want anything more than payment for your dinner." She plucked the diamonds from his open palm and replaced them with something heavier, with a rough texture. "I believe you dropped this," she said in a conversational tone, as the world kicked back into gear.

Hyperion heaved a sigh of relief when he could move his head to look at what she'd given him. A leather wallet. He was surprised—though not really—to find it contained a plasticized Greek ID with the name *Hyperion Titanas* on it, as well as a number of credit cards he recognized from Vangelis' experience with them, and a couple he'd never seen before.

He held out a black card, and the woman smiled sweetly. "Perfect. Someone will be right back with your receipt."

"I'll get the tip," Christina said.

Hyperion shook his head. "I believe I covered that." The witch had kept the diamonds.

Olivia watched him with a tiny frown.

"What?" he asked, full of innocence. Had she heard what the witch told him?

Olivia tilted her head to the side and pursed her lips. "I thought you didn't have a bank account yet."

Hyperion forced out a chuckle, to stall for time. He *had* told her they should get him an account in the morning. He skimmed through the memories he'd gotten from Vangelis, and found the perfect reply in a TV series. "I thought my assets were frozen. Apparently, that's no longer the case."

Her frown deepened, but she didn't say anything more.

When a different waiter returned with Hyperion's card and his receipt, Panos stood and pulled back Olivia's chair. "It's still early, if you want to go for a drink," he said.

Olivia glanced at Hyperion, and if he read her correctly, she wasn't interested in spending more time with the mortal.

Hyperion could help with that. He stood and buttoned his jacket, like that guy, James Bond would. All women liked James Bond. Some men too, according to Vangelis. "We have an early morning tomorrow," he said.

"I'll take the girls back to the hotel, if they want." Well, Vangelis would be doing the driving, in the rental he arranged for them, while Hyperion sat in the back, pressed against Olivia's warm body.

Christina planted a too-quick kiss on her date's cheek. "Yeah, I'm tired," she said and rounded the table to stand by Hyperion, who felt a little bad for how happy the guy was over the light peck.

Olivia faced Panos, whose thoughts had turned to punching Hyperion repeatedly. "Thank you for showing us this place. It's lovely, and the food was amazing."

"My pleasure." Panos leaned in for what was obviously a kiss, but she averted her face and gave him a sideways hug.

Still, Panos got enough boob time to tide him over tonight when he was alone with his hand—and was Hyperion allowed to do a little smiting in this day and age?

Olivia broke the hug and looped her arm around Hyperion's. "Let's go, boss."

The warmth from where their bodies touched spread all the way to his groin. She was lust on legs, and every moment near her tested his self control.

Hyperion mentally called for Vangelis and led the women toward the front of the taverna, trying not to look at how Olivia's breasts bounced with every step.

As soon as they were outside, Olivia withdrew her arm. "Thanks for getting us out of there. The creep kept touching my leg."

That was why she flirted with Hyperion. To get Panos to leave her alone. "Do you want me to go back and kill him?" Hyperion asked.

She laughed. "Nah. I've dealt with his kind before. Hopefully he got the message that I'm not interested, and it's not like I have to see him again, anyway."

Christina pouted. "Michalis was cute."

Hyperion narrowed his eyes at her. "If you wanted *cute*, you'd have stayed behind, but you didn't. Because you want a man who will rock your world. Whose touch will send electricity sparking through you. Whose kiss will take away your breath and leave your legs weak. And who can make love to you for hours, before gathering your sated body close and letting you know you're safe with him for the rest of your life."

Christina's eyes glazed over, though he didn't use compulsion. He'd just told her the truth about what he believed she wanted.

Olivia gave him a heated gaze. "Maybe I should go back to Panos and leave the two of you alone?"

From the corner of his eye, he saw Christina nod. He turned to face her and said, "I'm not the man for you. I have my sights set on someone else, and I'm a one-woman man."

Let Olivia mull that over the rest of the night.

# CHAPTER SEVEN

Pretending the flirting was for Panos' sake seemed to convince Hyperion, but it didn't unjumble the clutter inside Olivia's head.

The covert glances Christina stole at Hyperion made Olivia territorial despite herself. She wasn't the jealous type, and Christina wasn't the man-eater type and would step back if Olivia asked her to.

But instead of asking, Olivia went and made googly eyes at her freaking boss. She laughed at his jokes, marveled at the appreciation he showed the food, and yes, got wet when he went to town on that yogurt.

It had to be the alcohol. She only had a glass of wine—not even a sip of Raki, despite everyone's protests—and she didn't feel dizzy, but maybe after yesterday's overindulgence…

Well, that was all over now. Or soon. When she was no longer pressed to him, from shoulder to knee, in the back of the rental BMW.

Hyperion seemed at ease, squished between her and Christina. He tapped his fingers on his leg to the rhythm of the music, and little shivers ran down Olivia's spine every time his knuckles grazed her thigh.

She took a deep breath and leaned her head back against the headrest, closing her eyes.

Bad idea.

The mental image of her sitting the exact same way but with her legs spread and Hyperion's head between them assaulted her. The sensations were so real, they overwhelmed her. She did her best not to squirm while she felt his fingers spreading her and his tongue swiping up her slit to brush her swollen clit.

A half-sigh, half-moan made it past her lips, and her eyes flew open.

"Are you all right?" Hyperion sounded concerned, but a hint of a smile danced in his eyes.

"Mm hmm." She faked a yawn. "Just sleepy."

He nodded and turned his attention to Christina, who was asking him where he grew up.

Olivia listened as he evaded the question with a *here and there*, and then closed her eyes again, this time trying to conjure him between her thighs, the backs of her knees propped on his wide shoulders.

Hyperion stopped tapping and adjusted his position, then dragged his palm up his thigh slowly, the edge of his hand gliding along her leg and setting her senses alight. Did he know what she was fantasizing? Could he?

Not possible.

In her head, he slid a long, thick finger inside her and touched her inner barrier.

His hesitation when he touched her hymen was a weirdly specific detail.

Fantasy-Hyperion met her gaze, as the one beside her groaned. She begrudgingly opened her eyes and faced him.

His gaze was heavy with lust and promise. Had she pulled the fantasy into reality?

He arched an eyebrow and whispered something she didn't catch in Greek.

"Huh?"

"I said, *delicious.*"

He meant dinner, right?

*Right?*

Vangelis pulled up in the hotel's parking lot and climbed from the car to get her door.

She exited shakily and waited for Hyperion and Christina to follow.

"Thank you again for the lovely meal," Christina said.

Hyperion smiled and gave her a curt nod. "Believe me, it was my pleasure." He touched his fingertips to the small of Olivia's back and leaned to whisper in her ear, "I think it's time we put you to bed. You don't look very steady on your feet."

She didn't have to close her eyes, to think of him lifting her and laying her on her double bed, then draping his body over hers. "I had a long day." She said *goodnight* to Christina and Vangelis, and lengthened her stride so Hyperion was no longer touching her when she reached the elevators.

Then why did she feel him on every inch of her skin?

Olivia led the way to the suite, but stepped aside and let him use his card key to open the door. He'd given her one too, but she still felt like a guest at his place, and probably would for the duration of her stay.

Hyperion motioned for her to go ahead, and she gingerly stepped inside, trying to calm her racing heart. What had her so on edge? Her daydream was over, and she could go to her room—alone—lock her door, and sleep. Just sleep. Maybe after she used… another relaxation technique.

Only, when she turned to say *goodnight* and thank him for dinner, he was standing much too close, and it felt natural to stand on her tiptoes, rest one hand on his chest, and touch her lips to his cheek.

His stubble grazed her skin like it had done her inner thigh in her mind. Her fingers itched to explore the hard planes of his chest, and every inch of her wanted to see how perfectly her body would fit his if she leaned closer.

He moved the tiniest fraction of an inch, so his breath caressed her lips. They felt dry, but if she licked them, her tongue would touch him. Her flesh broke out in goose bumps. Would he kiss her?

Did she want him to?

The tingling down her spine that made her nipples hard and moisture pool between her legs said she did. There was nothing she wanted more than for him to splay one large palm on her back and press her to him as he crushed his lips to hers.

She swallowed hard and waited, but he stood perfectly still, like the marble he'd resembled this morning.

Had it been less than a day since she first met him and ran out on him? What would have happened if she'd stayed instead? Would he have driven her to the heights of ecstasy his touch—hell, his tiniest smile—promised? And then what? She'd still be working as a housekeeper with the hotel, turning sheets for a man who pretended he hadn't been inside her.

Not fair. She knew nothing about how he treated his conquests, and he said he wasn't a player.

Which was what a player would say.

Anyway, he wasn't her type. Too tall, too dark, too handsome.

Even if her skin danced when it came to contact with his, and her nerve endings screamed, raw with need.

Slowly, she backed away and was stricken by the intensity of his gaze.

His eyes burned, and his nostrils flared over the hard line of his mouth.

"I'm sorry…" How many-eth time was this in the few hours she'd known him?

He shook his head, like he was shaking off her apology. "You'd better not come this close again if you don't want me to make you mine," he said through gritted teeth. His hands were fisted at his sides, the knuckles white.

She swayed, almost losing her footing. Something rattled behind her. Was it a mini earthquake, or was her body protesting the idea of keeping her distance?

"Goodnight, delicious Olivia." He gave her an obviously forced smile. "If you change your mind about this—about us—you need only say my name."

She didn't move until she heard his door latch shut. Then she ran to her room, kicked her door closed behind her, and threw herself on her bed.

She rolled onto her back, pulled her pillow over her head, and screamed into it. Her body was at war with her mind, begging her to invite Hyperion over and screw him and the consequences. Who cared that her first time would be with the man she worked for? Or that she'd never see him again after September? What did it matter that she was drawn to him with an all-consuming passion beyond reason, that might burn her to ashes if she allowed it to take over?

She unbuttoned her pants, tugged down the zipper, and slipped her hand inside her lace boy shorts. Her fingers slipped easily between her wet folds. Usually, it was a matter of a few strokes with the right pressure on her clit, but her touch wasn't enough tonight.

She squeezed her eyes shut and focused on recreating the mental image of Hyperion kneeling before her, but failed to achieve the same life-like quality. The sensations spilling through her veins in the ride over were now hazy, faded, and couldn't get her to climax.

"Hyperion." The whisper left her lips before she knew if she was calling the man or her memory of him.

The sound of her door scraping against the plush blue carpet made her open her eyes.

Hyperion stood at her doorway without a shirt, his jeans slung low on his hips. His body was as perfect as she remembered, with those impossibly broad shoulders and the abs no sculptor could do justice. His impressive erection was clearly defined beneath the denim. But it was those amber eyes of him, almost golden once more in this light, that spoke to her subconscious and made her quiver at the expectation of his touch.

"You called," he said in that sexy, rough accent.

Was she asleep?

No. She was awake and sober, except for the effect his intoxicating presence had on her. "You came."

He crossed his arms and stood his ground. "You want me. You cannot sleep because you're wondering just how good I could make you feel."

She did want him, but it wasn't as simple as that. They had to have rules, and not only because he knew exactly what kind of effect he had on her. If she didn't remain in control, he'd consume her like the flame did the moth.

"Only for tonight?" She hated that it came out as a question. It should be a statement; she was making the rules.

"No."

*No?* Annoyed and more than a little hurt by his rejection, she sat up and narrowed her eyes. "You were the one who—"

"I will not be your temporary relief."

He wanted more than tonight? Didn't he realize she was leaving after this summer? Why couldn't he just—

"But when you do decide you want to be mine, when you're ready for me, I'll make every second worth it," he said. "First I'll take my time undressing that beautiful body and kissing every inch of your skin."

His words held weight. They crossed the distance to the bed and fell on her body like a rain of touches and kisses that made her shiver with delight.

He smiled. "I'll bury my face in your pussy and run my tongue along your slit and taste your juices, until you cry out my name."

Even with her eyes open, and fully aware he hadn't moved from her doorway, she could see him kneeling at the foot of the bed. Fantasy-Hyperion clasped one ankle in each large hand and pulled her so her legs dangled to the floor. He gripped her pants and tugged, and they were torn in half, exposing her to his ravenous gaze. What was happening? She rubbed her eyes and looked again at the still man, feet away. At the same time, she felt his fingers make quick work of her underwear before separating her nether lips so his tongue could glide between them and tap her clit.

"How are you—?" She threw her head back and rocked her hips as the Hyperion that didn't exist sucked and licked and sent her need spiraling higher with every second. "Faster," she whispered, but the real Hyperion, the one who was her boss and who shouldn't be able to do whatever this was, shook his head. The tongue on her pussy kept its languid rhythm, sending jolts of electricity through her veins. She was a ball of energy, winding tighter with every long stroke. If she came now, she might pass out.

"I'll press my thumb to your button, and you're going to come apart," he said.

The pressure against her clit grew, until her body tingled and shook with the force of her release. Her head was light and her limbs heavy, and still she kept coming. She'd never managed an orgasm this hard by herself, and he… What? *Thought* one at her? She let her eyelids drift shut and gave into the sensations enveloping her body.

When she opened her eyes again, Hyperion smirked. "And when you believe you can't take more pleasure, I will enter you," he said.

It wasn't over?

She forced her body to relax, preparing for the unprecedented invasion, but her fantasy lover faded from existence.

"But not tonight." Hyperion backed out of the room and pulled the door shut between them.

The air in the room rippled, and the bed shook. Was it an aftershock of her orgasm?

More importantly—what the hell just happened?

# CHAPTER EIGHT

Hyperion was an imbecile.

He could have had her tonight. Was planning to, until he heard himself spout that nonsense about not being temporary relief.

What the *fuck*—he loved this word more by the minute—was up with that?

On the up side, it was obvious he *could* get through to her. He might not be able to read her mind or compel her into doing what he pleased, but he'd heard her heartrate accelerate as he sent her vivid thoughts that matched his promises. She responded to those thoughts like she would to his body when he made her his.

And why hadn't he?

He dropped on his bed. She'd been ripe for the plucking, ready to offer him her maidenhood, and he'd given her a fantasy instead.

He growled and pulled at his fly, meaning to free his erection. Instead, he ended up with his jeans torn in much the way he'd thought of tearing Olivia's.

His hand shook again, as he wrapped his fist around his shaft. A mental image of a male cast in marble flashed through his mind. A memory of his imprisonment? The image scattered and gave place to excitement and anticipation. And maybe anger at himself for not claiming Olivia's body tonight.

And what a divine body she had…

He squeezed and tugged on himself as he remembered her moans and how she shivered, her nipples visible under the thin fabric of her shirt. Vangelis hadn't thought much of female underwear, but Hyperion had seen those contraptions called brassieres in the man's memories, and had noticed them on most women around them tonight. Not on Olivia, though. Her perfect, perky breasts needed no support. If anything, tonight they were ready to escape the confines of her top. Eager to fill his palms, so he could roll the nipples between his fingers and suckle on them until she arched into his mouth, begging for more.

Close. He was close.

He twisted his hand on the down stroke, and when he drew it back up, he ran his thumb over the head and shivered. *This* was the first thing he'd wanted to do when he became flesh. Correction—sticking his cock in Olivia was the first thing he'd wanted, but that would have to wait, because a moronic part of him decided he desired more from her than one night of passion.

The thought of Olivia quivering beneath him made his hips buck off the mattress, and hot, sticky cum squirt all over his hand and chest.

She would be so beautiful, naked and sated, and marked with his spendings and his scent.

He padded naked to the shower and enjoyed the hot water washing the evidence of his release off his body.

He returned to his room and picked up his destroyed jeans. *Nope.* He had nothing to wear. Again.

Vangelis wouldn't appreciate a call in the middle of the night, and Hyperion doubted clothing-store owners would be eager to jump out of bed to dress him. Then again, he did have that black credit card…

He got the wallet Circe gave him out of his jacket pocket, tossed his destroyed jeans to the floor, and slipped under the covers, enjoying the feel of silk against his body. He flipped through the wallet idly, wondering how much of a fake life came with the accounts that matched these cards. Did he have a birth certificate? Vangelis' memories showed all males born in Greece were registered so the army could call on them when they reached adulthood. Was Hyperion in such a registry?

A flap he hadn't noticed fell open, and he saw a driver's license and a white business card that read in Greek, *Eros is here for your emergencies.*

*Eros.* Romantic love, and the name of the god responsible for it—if you believed in these things, which most people today didn't.

Hyperion flipped the card around, but there was no phone number or one of those website-address things that baffled him, despite the computer classes he'd absorbed from Vangelis.

"So much for being here," he mumbled and laughed.

A ball of white light appeared by the bed, and Hyperion rolled away from it. He wouldn't be caught in the line of Zeus' lightning again.

The ball grew arms and legs—as expected, when dealing with an immortal—but the head that topped the lean male body wasn't one Hyperion had seen before, and the power that emanated from the god was nowhere near that of an Olympian or a Titan.

"Who are you?" Hyperion demanded. "Did the witch send you?"

A smile made the man's rosy cheeks dimple and thin lines form at the corners of his pale-blue eyes. "You called me. You had an emergency?" He tossed back his shoulder-length curls and held out his hand. "I'm Eros. *Cupid.* I was born after you were taken away."

*Taken away.* Nice way for Aphrodite's brat to reframe millennia of isolation.

Hyperion searched inside himself for any traces of rage or the need to avenge himself and his brothers, but Zeus was long gone, and the kid in front of him was an innocent.

Eros rubbed his hands together. "So is it a girl you're after? A boy?"

Hyperion squinted. "Excuse me?"

"What's the emergency? You were playing with my card. What do you need? Am I to send an arrow through a fair maiden's heart for you?"

The thought wasn't tempting. Hyperion didn't need this guy's help to get his woman. *His woman?* What was wrong with him today? Olivia was the first female he saw after his punishment; she wasn't the only one left on Earth. And now that he knew his power worked on her—albeit in specific ways—she wasn't even a mystery.

Then why did every fiber of his being demand that he go to her room and take her?

Eros tapped his foot on the floor. "Any day now, big guy. Not like I have a life of my own."

Hyperion propped himself up on his elbows. "I have no clothes. Can you bring me clothes?"

Eros rolled his eyes and snapped his fingers. "Done. This is for you." A cell phone appeared in his hand, and he tossed it to Hyperion, who barely avoided crushing it in his palm. "I'm *2* on the speed dial. Circe is *3*," Eros said. "So you don't need any help with your romantic life? Got the tremors under control, yeah?"

"What do you know about that?" Clothing forgotten, Hyperion set the phone on his nightstand, sat up, and tossed the covers back. He wasn't ashamed of his nakedness, and it wasn't like Eros was covered with more than a loincloth that looked like a diaper.

Eros seemed taken aback. "You mean you don't know what's causing them? It's Zeus' failsafe."

"Speak, boy. Explain," Hyperion boomed. There was no reading a god's mind, even a lesser one's.

"The only thing that could revive one of you when Zeus decided your punishment was the proximity of your soulmate after the last of the Olympians had perished. In his infinite wisdom, he didn't foresee frakking or global warming, both of which have contributed to waking you up. In any case, the way his curse works, if you don't bond with your soulmate soon after rising, your powers will take over.

"The tremors will only get worse, messing with the elements, while you're unable to control them or yourself. Earthquakes, tsunamis, tornadoes—you name it—will wreak havoc to the world. And then, you'll erupt into stardust." Eros dropped his gaze to the floor. "It was why Zeus allowed the Titanesses to live and die as humans—so they wouldn't be around to bond with you if you woke up, and you'd unravel."

When the Titans and Titanesses were created, at the beginning of cosmos, they were created in pairs said to share a soul between them. Hyperion had bedded more than a couple of his line, but only felt a true, deep connection to Theia, the female who birthed him the sun and the moon and the dawn, and she'd been gone for nearly thirty thousand years when he was turned into a statue.

"So I'm going to destroy the world and die, no matter what?" And why could Hyperion think of nothing else but keeping Olivia safe from his unraveling?

Eros gave him a cryptic smile. "Nobody said Zeus was right about who your true soulmate was. She might even be next door. But she must become yours willingly, not to save creation. And until she does, you'd better stay away from the other unbonded Titans, or the devastation will be compounded."

Olivia could be his soulmate? Was that the reason for the insane attraction he felt toward her? Was it why he couldn't read her thoughts? The last thing Eros said sank in, and Hyperion narrowed his eyes. "Wait. You mean my brothers are awake? And some are already bonded?"

Eros lifted his left forearm and looked at his bare wrist. "Look at the time. I must go. Check out your new wardrobe and don't iron your jeans."

Hyperion grabbed for him—he'd hold him here until his questions were answered, Uranus be his witness— but the god shimmered out of existence, leaving him with a cell phone, a full closet, and a reeling mind.

# CHAPTER NINE

Olivia stirred toward consciousness. Was someone at her door?

Knocking, and then— "Are you up yet?"

Hyperion.

She sat up and called out, "Gimme ten." She was still in her clothes from last night. *Last night.* When Hyperion had given her the mother of all orgasms without touching her.

When her legs could lift her after the jellification that came with the crazy mind-fuck, she'd started packing to leave, but the need to know how he'd done it prevented her from fleeing. Well… that, and she'd handed in her resignation to the hotel and needed this job.

And there was the off chance he'd make her come like that again.

Not going there.

She crossed the living room to his door more than a couple times during the night, but the possibility that she dreamed up the whole thing kept her from knocking.

When she finally fell asleep, it was after four in the morning, and she hadn't set an alarm for today. Not that they'd discussed a schedule or anything, but her boss shouldn't be the one waking her up at—she glanced at the screen of her phone—11-fucking-AM.

She rummaged through her toiletries for her toothbrush and hurried to her bathroom. Brushing her teeth with one hand, she used the other to clean up the smudges from last night's makeup under her eyes with baby wipes.

A fresh layer of mascara made her lashes look like spider legs, but she couldn't delay more to remove it and start over. Deodorant on. A bit of blusher and lip gloss…

She threw on a fresh pair of underwear, different cropped jeans, and a white T-shirt. On second thought, she took off her top and secured her breasts in a plain nude bra, before putting it back on. She'd need that clothing stipend soon, if she was expected to be dressed more office-like.

Hair up in a ponytail, she rushed out of her room. "I'm so sorry I overslept. I'm usually more professional than this." Though that wasn't what had her shivering under his scrutiny.

"I didn't expect you to be up early, anyway. Room service will be here any moment now. I hope you're hungry." He smirked, looking yummy in his light-blue button-down and a pair of dark jeans. "Unless there's something you'd like me to do for you first."

She narrowed her eyes. "I thought we were keeping this *business only*."

"You didn't seem to mind last night." The intensity of his gaze belied his nonchalant tone.

So that wasn't a dream, and they were apparently talking about it. "About last night—"

She was cut off by another knock, this time at the main door.

Hyperion held up a finger. "We'll discuss after breakfast," he said to her, before calling out in Greek, "Come in."

Nikolas, one of the bell boys, entered, pushing ahead of him a cart laden with scrambled eggs and bacon, as well as butter, jams, fresh fruit, yogurt, and local honey. The smell of coffee mingled with that of freshly baked croissants, and a better look revealed a small plate of staka butter, made of goat's milk and packing a million calories per teaspoonful.

Did Hyperion plan on feeding her to death?

Olivia was reaching for a grape, when Hyperion's smile turned into a deep frown, and a growl rumbled up his throat.

Olivia dropped her hand and took a step back. "Okay. You can have all of it. *Jeez.*"

But Hyperion's attention was on Nikolas. "Leave. Now."

Nikolas arched a brow and looked at Olivia, who gave him a watery smile. "He's jet-lagged," she said, pretty sure that wasn't the case.

"Yeah, I bet." Nikolas's smile held an edge like a sneer. "I'll unload these, and—"

"You'll get out of this room immediately. And if you want to keep your job, you'll never cross my path again." Hyperion squeezed his fists, his knuckles white.

Nikolas looked stunned. "What did I do?"

"You didn't have to do anything. I know your heart." Hyperion's voice was full of gravel and menace. His shoulders were squared, and he leaned forward, like he was about to attack.

Olivia should be scared, but his wrath wasn't aimed at her, and something told her it never would be. She should also speak and defuse the situation, but she could only stand back and watch.

"I don't want you around her again. Ever," Hyperion said.

"What?" Olivia planted her hands on her hips. "This is ridiculous. Why are you being so rude?"

"*Now*," Hyperion roared at Nikolas, as if she hadn't spoken.

She bit back her ire long enough for Nikolas to scramble out the door. "What was that all about? Nikolas is my friend." Not really, but they'd worked the same shift since she got here, and he was fun.

"He thinks I only hired you because I'm fucking you. Wishes he could have fucked you first. Believes you owe him, for being *nice* to you." Hyperion rounded in on her, spitting the words out. "I could kick him out, or I could kill him. I went for the option I thought you'd prefer."

His face was inches from hers, his nostrils flaring. She should be asking how he knew what Nikolas thought. What rumors Nikolas was spreading. Why Hyperion was so casual, talking about killing a man.

She couldn't focus on anything beyond Hyperion's scent and his eyes and the warmth emanating from his body.

"Was I wrong?" Hyperion whispered. "Is the thought of me killing him what has you wet and panting for me?"

She should be upset. No man had the right to talk to her this way, least of all her boss. His protectiveness was sexy and made her feel safe, but she didn't need a knight in shining armor.

She opened her mouth to say so, but what came out was, "Kiss me."

Hyperion's eyes shone gold. He wrapped one arm around her waist, cupping her butt cheek. Too forward, but she couldn't complain, because he crushed his mouth to hers. His kiss was hungry. Primal. Raw. He bit her bottom lip, and when she moaned, pushed his tongue between her lips. There was no timidness in how it sought out her own. No hesitation, as he swallowed her groans, kneading her buttock. He grabbed her ponytail with his free hand and snapped off the tie holding her hair in place. Her shoulder-length tresses tumbled loose, and he buried his hand in it and tugged, tilting her head so he could deepen the kiss.

The wanton woman who'd taken over Olivia's body trapped his leg between hers and pressed her center against the hard muscle of his thigh. She needed… something. His erection dug into her stomach. He wasn't close enough. Clothes were in the way. They should disappear, so she'd feel more of him.

All of him.

Was this her, mewling? Hyperion got to her in a level no other man had. Her arms, slack at her sides till now, wrapped around his neck of their own accord. She bit his lips and humped his leg. She was feral in her desire.

What was she doing?

Not enough.

Hyperion slid his hand lower, pressing his fingers along the inside seam of her jeans.

She arched her back, wanting more of his touch. Offering more of herself to him.

He could lay her on top of the food cart and take her, and she wouldn't resist. Worse—she wanted him to.

This wasn't her. Whatever power this man held over her libido was out of her control.

But Hyperion let go of her hair to cup one needy breast, and she forgot to be worried.

Until the next knock on the door.

"Ignore it," Hyperion whispered against her mouth. He inched his palm under the hem of her shirt and paused briefly at her bra, before tearing it in half with a snap of his fingers.

Was she dreaming again?

The knock persisted. "Mr. Titanas? This is Manolis. I've had a complaint by a staff member."

"Not now," Hyperion yelled at the man.

"Very well. Please call me when you can talk."

But the spell was broken.

Olivia lowered her leg and used both hands to push against his—*wide, rock-hard, chiseled*—chest.

He let go, but fire burned in his eyes and stoked the flames between her legs. "I can make you come again. I don't have to touch you."

The dishes on the cart clattered, the sound tearing through her lustful haze. Hyperion made the cart move, like he made the earth shake and her body hurtle toward release last night—without contact.

"How? How would you do that?" she asked. She pointed to the cart. "How are you doing this?" Her voice reached her ears more shrill than she was going for, and she dialed it down. A new question nudged at the edges of her consciousness.

It took her a heartbeat to form the words. "What are you?"

He arched an eyebrow, and Olivia expected him to say she was crazy. That he was just a guy with a little too much testosterone.

Instead, he said, "Tomorrow. Give me today, no holds barred, and tomorrow I'll tell you all you wish to know." He didn't allow her time to answer, before he started unloading the cart onto the dining table.

She could have objected anyway—*no holds barred* was a huge concession—but she wasn't sure she wanted to.

Breakfast was awkward, with Olivia both wishing she were touching him and needing some distance.

Hyperion dug in the food with the same fervor he'd dived into their kiss. Was she jealous of bread and jam?

Yes. Yes, she was.

She focused on her eggs, had two cups of coffee, and watched amused, while he closed his eyes and savored a slice of bacon.

Wherever he was before must have had crappy food.

*Prison.* The word flashed in her head in neon yellow. He'd suggested he could kill Nikolas. Maybe in the past he hadn't held back.

A chill ran down her spine. She studied his hands as he tore a croissant in half. The large palms and long, thick fingers could no doubt pleasure a woman, if he used them in reality like he did in her fantasy. Could they take a life?

She'd know tomorrow, if he kept his word. For which there was no guarantee. How could she trust a man she only met yesterday?

No—*why* did she? Because she did, God help her. She believed every word that came out of his mouth. Was the crazy chemistry between them tricking her into it?

Done with her breakfast, she pushed back her plate. "What's the plan for today?"

Hyperion reached across the table for her hand and ran his thumb across her knuckles. "I was thinking I'd take you to my favorite place on this island. See if it bares any resemblance to how I remember it." His voice took on a wistful tone. "Imagine caves carved into lava rock, and nothing but the deep blue sea, as far as the eye can see."

It sounded so romantic. Which wasn't what their relationship was about. She cleared her throat and withdrew her hand under the pretense of tucking a loose strand of hair behind her ear. "You said you needed clothes?"

He shook his head and wiped his mouth. "Not anymore."

"Did clothes materialize in your closet during the night?" She laughed.

His expression was flat. "You could say that."

Another non-answer. *Neat.*

"Well, you said I'd get a clothing stipend. Do I?"

"Of course. We can go get you something right now. Preferably something red with a plunging neckline."

She pursed her lips. "I was thinking office clothes." Plus she wouldn't be dressing for him. Though she loved the way his eyes lit up…

Hyperion tilted his head. "You'll be using your room as your office, so *office clothes* could be lacy and skimpy."

"Nice leap of logic there." She batted his arm playfully, but electricity sparked along her skin at the thought of waiting for him in bed in sheer red lingerie.

Olivia stood, shaking off the mental image. "Well, it'll be more like proper slacks and a couple button-down shirts. You don't need to come with."

He stretched, and his shirt rose to reveal the taut muscles of his stomach. *Yum.* "I'm coming," he rumbled, causing another onslaught of sexy images. "You'll need my card."

Okay. If he didn't explain himself tomorrow, she was out of here, and Mister Sex-on-Legs could find someone else to pester with his stupid good looks and his amazing caress of a voice and his wicked orgasm-inducing powers.

* * * *

Though Heraklion was the largest city of Crete, Olivia preferred Chania on all counts. It wasn't the modern-day luxuries just blocks away from the old harbor that now served as a top tourist spot. It was the sea air and the beauty of another era—one of knights and princesses and the stuff fairy tales were made of—that were all pervasive and intoxicating.

She wasn't up for a stroll on the cobble-stone pathways today, so she led Vangelis and Hyperion to the commercial part of the city, where Vangelis double parked and promised to wait in the car.

Hyperion was rather tame during shopping. He kept his hands to himself and only nodded his approval, or shook his head when her choices weren't to his taste.

He also didn't complain when Olivia tried on the tenth pair of black pumps.

He was the perfect shopping companion, until the last saleswoman for the day was ringing up their purchases.

"That is a lovely necklace you're wearing," Hyperion said.

Olivia looked up, to see him holding the woman's gaze.

"Thank you." The woman caressed the three gems glinting in the artificial light. "They're rubies. It was a gift from my husband."

Hyperion smiled. "You should give it to my lady friend."

Shocked, Olivia turned to the woman, who unclasped her necklace and held it out to her with a sweet smile.

"No." Olivia pushed the woman's cupped hand back. "*No,*" she said again.

Hyperion frowned. "But it's a gift."

Olivia shook her head frantically. "No," she said a third time. "I'll be in the car." She stomped out of there and to where Vangelis waited in the BMW. She threw open the back door and dropped onto the seat, then slammed the door so hard, the car shook.

"What happened?" Vangelis asked.

"Hyperion is an asshole."

Vangelis laughed.

"Don't laugh. He asked a woman to give me the necklace she wore. And she did."

Vangelis shrugged. "That's kind of his thing. The mind-control. Not that he should need it with most women." He sighed wistfully. "Or some men."

Mind control? *Mind control?*

Hyperion showed up, carrying her purchases. He motioned for Vangelis to pop the trunk, stowed the bags inside, and came to sit next to her. To her relief, the necklace was nowhere in sight.

"Why are you upset?" he asked her.

"Why did the woman give you her necklace?" she said, in lieu of a reply.

Hyperion gave her a look so innocent, it had to be fake. "Because I asked nicely. People like indulging me."

"Did you… Did you force her to do it? With your mind?"

It took him a while to answer, but he said, "Tomorrow."

"In that case, we have nothing to talk about till then." She crossed her arms and sat back, not bothering with a safety belt as Vangelis revved the engine and took off for the hotel.

# CHAPTER TEN

The longer Hyperion sat beside Olivia, the harder it was for him to endure her silence. Why was she so upset? He'd meant to pay the mortal female for the necklace, and it would look better on Olivia than on her.

"Olivia…" He kept his tone calm. Reasoning. She had to see his point.

She made a show of turning away, to look outside the window.

He tried again, a little more forcefully, and let a hint of suggestion seep into his voice. "*Olivia.*"

"What?" she snapped. "What do you want? You said you'd explain everything tomorrow, so I'm waiting for stupid tomorrow. What more do you want? Should I give my watch to Vangelis?"

This was preposterous. "Why would I want you to give your watch to anyone, you insufferable woman?"

She hit her closed fist on the seat between them. "*I'm* insufferable? You're the one shopping with *freaking diamonds* one moment and a bunch of cards the next. You're the one who's only got a single pair of jeans in the evening but then needs no clothes because his closet is suddenly full in the morning. *You're* the one getting women to hand over their jewelry."

Should he tell her everything now? When he asked her for twenty-four hours, he meant for her to get to like him before he broke the I'm-an-eternal-being-who-may-lose-control-and-create-a-new-continent-or-send-Earth-out-of-orbit-unless-you're-my-soulmate-and-bond-with-me news. From what Vangelis, and therefore Hyperion, knew of the world, even people who worshiped a deity wouldn't believe they'd ever meet one, and Hyperion had no clue if Olivia was religious or agnostic or whatever, because he couldn't read her Zeus-blasted mind.

Olivia apparently wasn't done yet. "And you make me come from across the room? What the fuck was that about?"

Hyperion stole a glance at Vangelis, before he returned his gaze to Olivia's face that was a rapidly darkening shade of red. "I can explain everything, but you're not going to believe me." And if she did, she'd run away, unless he'd first gained her trust—and maybe her heart.

"You start talking, or I'm leaving." She lifted her chin, staring him down.

Irritation plucked at his nerves. He was done taking orders from a human. He wrapped his hand around her wrist and held her gaze. "No man can make you feel the way I can. You know it, and you're dying to find out what having me thrust between your legs will be like. You've been thinking of my naked body—*my cock*—since you first saw me on that pedestal, and it gets you wet.

"But most of all, you burn to know who I really am and what else I can do. So Vangelis can drop you off now wherever you'd like, or you can come back to the suite with me and let me sate at least one of your hungers." It was a risk, his guesses a shot in the dark, but she was making no move to go, and the fire in her eyes was no longer that of anger.

The car stopped, and Vangelis cleared his throat. "We're here. Should I park the car somewhere shady and come back for you in a couple hours?"

Hyperion arched an eyebrow.

Olivia shook free of his grip and opened her door. When he didn't immediately go after her, she ducked her head and gave him a flat look. "Well? Are you coming?"

Yeah, his words hit their mark.

Olivia walked stiffly across the lobby. Her prim-and-proper act made Hyperion lust after her even more than when she melted into his kiss this morning.

"Mr. Titanas, we need to talk." Manolis practically ran out of his office to intercept Hyperion as they approached Reception. "It's about Nikolas."

Hyperion barely slowed, to project to Manolis what he'd gleaned from that jerkoff this morning. "Fire him," he said. "If he complains, send him to me."

Manolis nodded. "Will do."

Olivia got in the elevator and cleared her throat, and Hyperion hurried to catch up.

Vangelis snickered. *Let him.* He was a good man, and if Manolis planned to do something about the thoughts Hyperion glimpsed from him, Vangelis would be getting his happy ending soon.

Hyperion slid into the waiting elevator seconds before the doors slid shut.

Olivia crossed her arms, staring ahead. "I'm still mad at you, okay?"

"Okay."

She faced him. "But this thing—I want to feel again like I did last night."

Hyperion took a step toward her. "I told you, I won't be your relief." But he no longer believed it. He didn't care about tomorrow or having a future. All that mattered was having *her*. Hearing her moan while her nails raised welts on his back. Getting drenched by her juices.

She stepped back, but he grabbed her and turned her so her back was to him. Pressing her body between his and the wall of the elevator, he whispered, "And I won't just be using my mind, this time." He rubbed his erection against her and wedged a hand to her front, to knead one perfect breast. "If you want me to stop, better say so now, before we enter that room."

She arched her back and wiggled her magnificent ass. "Are you worried you've oversold your abilities?"

Hyperion buried his face in her hair and let out a chuckle. "Such big words, from such a small girl. I'm only worried you can't take me." The elevator pinged their arrival to the top floor, and the doors opened. "Every cell of your body calls to me. Every nerve ending thrums when you're near, and my mind spins when you're out of sight. I need to make you mine." He let her turn to face him, but gave her no room to move away.

Olivia licked her lips and looked up at him with those gorgeous dark eyes of hers. Her breath came out in short puffs.

He studied her dilated irises. The thick lashes. The way the tip of her nose tilted up the slightest bit. "If you don't want the same thing, you must tell me now." He watched her throat work as she swallowed and shook her head. "I need to hear the words, Olivia."

"I want it. You." Her voice was hoarse and low, but he heard her, and it was all he needed, to claim her lips.

She melted against him, tearing at the collar of his shirt until she could dig her fingers into his shoulders. One of his buttons gave way, and she giggled against his mouth. "Oops," she said, before sucking on his tongue.

*Chaos*, but he'd give anything to feel that tongue against his shaft.

His little mortal was on fire, and he'd made no effort to stoke her lust with compulsion. This was her true desire for him. She wanted him with an urgency that matched his own. His cock was as hard as when he was made of marble, but now it throbbed with the pressing need to be buried inside her. If he hadn't felt her maidenhead the first time he projected himself pleasuring her orally, he would tear off her clothes and take her where she stood.

But he'd hold off until her body was ready for him. Gaia knew he'd waited for this long enough, but he'd make it as good for Olivia as a first time could be.

Hyperion could materialize them into the suite—command the matter of their bodies to dissolve and reform on his bed—but she'd panic, so he helped her wrap her legs around his hips and carried her to the door. There was no time to find his key card; he needed her naked as soon as possible. Holding her in place with one palm under her ass, he closed his free hand around the handle and tore that and the electronic lock free, then kicked the door open. He slanted his mouth over hers again, to distract her from the superhuman speed with which he crossed the floor to his bedroom and laid her on his crisp white sheets.

She looked gorgeous, all flushed and breathless, waiting for him to make the next step.

Hyperion stood at the foot of the bed and willed himself to calm down. Every muscle in his body was tense with the urge to pounce on her. He clenched his fists and forced his shoulders to relax. His turn would come soon, but first he had to make her writhe with pleasure.

"Is something wrong?" Olivia bit her lip, worry darkening her gaze.

He managed a smirk. "Just deciding where to start." He sent a soothing mental caress down her body, and she rolled her head back. When he was in control again, he lay down beside her propped up one arm, and leaned in for another kiss while he skated his hand up her thigh. He longed to touch her skin, feel her nipples pucker against his palms, and taste the sweat between her breasts.

"I'm afraid this will have to go," he said, before shredding open her T-shirt from navel to neck with one hand.

She sucked in a breath, and goosebumps rose on the flesh above her bra. Why was she wearing one of these again?

A snap of his fingers, and the torture device split open, revealing creamy-white breasts that begged for his mouth. The tips were darker than he'd imagined. He pinched one, rolled it between his fingers, and savored the moan Olivia let out when he wrapped his lips around the other nipple. She twisted her fingers in his hair while he sucked on her perfect flesh and grazed his teeth over it. Out of the corner of his eye, Hyperion saw her squeeze her legs together. Circling her nipple with his tongue, he glided his hand down her side and then to the apex of her thighs, to rub her heated center over her jeans.

Olivia rocked her hips into his touch and clawed at his shirt until the hem was bunched under his armpits. He let go of her and sat up, to pull it over his head, before attacking her other beast and resuming his attentions between her legs.

"Want you… touch me…" she managed between gasps. She grasped his hand and led it to her waistband.

Hyperion tugged at her zipper, and it gave way. His fingertips brushed the elastic of her underwear. He pushed it aside, to cup her mound. She was wet and inviting, and his cock begged him to fuck her *now*.

Olivia arched her back and drew her jeans and undergarments down her hips. Hyperion helped her take them all the way off, until she lay naked before him, shivering under his gaze.

"Divine," he murmured, hovering his palm a hairsbreadth from her skin, from the slim column of her neck, down her breasts and belly, to her pussy. She opened her legs for him, and he ran his thumb along her bare labia. This modern fad of stripping one's body of hairs wasn't bad at all. He tapped on her clitoris, and she spread her legs wider. His cock was about to burst through his jeans, so he undid his fly and pushed his waistband down until his shaft jutted out, oozing precum.

He slipped a finger inside Olivia's pussy to the first knuckle. *So tight.* He pressed the heel of his palm against her clitoris, and when she angled her hips, added a second finger in her opening. One thrust, and he'd bleed her, but he wanted his cock to be the first thing to pierce her hymen.

She groaned and stilled. Did he hurt her?

He withdrew his fingers and rubbed her clit with the pad of his thumb. Her gaze was locked on his exposed cock.

"Do you want me to stop?" he asked. Could he, at this point?

Olivia shook her head, and then threw it back, covering her eyes with her arm. "I just… I haven't…"

"I know." He rolled on his back and pulled her to straddle him. He should eat her out. Should draw out her pleasure. But if he didn't enter her now, he'd spiral out of control. His body hummed, his heart thudding in his chest. The bed shook beneath them. "I need to be inside you. Now." Though it would be easier if he were on top, he wanted her to feel in control of the situation.

She nodded, but her eyes were squeezed shut.

"Look at me, my gorgeous nymph." He caressed her hipbone with his thumb until she did as he bade. "I'll make it good for you. Trust me."

"I do."

Those two tiny words made his chest warm. He pulled her down, so she draped her body on top of his, and positioned himself at her entrance. "Push back," he said. "Slow and easy."

She did, but tensed when he nudged at her opening.

"Shh… Don't worry, baby. It will only hurt for a moment, and then it's all pleasure." He tucked her hair behind her ear and cupped her cheek. He could help her relax, using mental images of him eating her pussy again. *No.* This needed to be real. Gaze locked on hers, he wrapped his free arm around her waist and held her in place as he drove his hips up.

His cockhead entered her, touching her inner barrier, and she squeezed so hard, his eyes almost crossed. Olivia lowered her long, dark eyelashes and bit her lip. It was time. Hyperion tilted her face closer, so he could seal her lips with his, and at the same time gave a single hard thrust, forcing his way through.

Olivia hissed and clenched around him. She bit his lip until he tasted blood. Only fair.

"This was it," he whispered when she let go. "The worst part is over. Now ride me."

She winced as she sat back, but he found her clit and circled it slowly, while she balanced her weight on her knees. She rose and slid back down on his cock, and with every pump of her hips, her movement became less pained. When he could tell she was used to his girth, he asked, "Can you take a little more?" He couldn't assume his real form, or he'd tear her apart, but an extra inch would add to his pleasure.

Eyes hooded, she nodded, and Hyperion let his body grow just a little, to stretch her more. Fill her more.

Olivia seemed to take it in her stride, as she impaled herself on his length again and again.

# CHAPTER ELEVEN

Olivia's thighs trembled with exertion as she fucked herself on Hyperion's cock.

He was huge and hit just the right spot inside her—fuck, did he grow even bigger?—while his magic touch on her clit sent jolts of white-hot fire through her veins.

Faster. She wanted to go faster, but her legs wouldn't cooperate.

Hyperion's eyes glowed gold, his gaze slicing through her. Lightning fast, he rolled them so she was on her back.

It was like he could read her mind.

He palmed her thigh and lifted one of her legs over his shoulder, before thrusting inside her. The bed shook with the force of their coupling, the nightstands rattling. And still it felt like he held back.

"Harder. Fuck me harder." Olivia couldn't believe the words that came out of her mouth, but Hyperion's feral grin said he appreciated them. He pistoned inside her like his life depended on it, and she threw back her head and gave in to the waves of pleasure overtaking her, as he angled his strokes to plunge deeper still.

Was this what sex was always like? What had she been waiting for?

Hyperion. She'd been waiting for him. Nobody else would be so perfectly matched to her.

He swiveled his hips and thrust, and she lost control of her body. Her muscles tensed and fluttered and relaxed, as pleasure unlike any she'd felt before washed over her and pulled her under. She let her eyes roll back, as her arms flopped on the mattress.

Fingers rubbed her clit, but that wasn't possible. Hyperion had one hand splayed on her belly, and the other on her thigh, pinning her in place. The fingers pinched. Circled. Pressed.

*Oh God.*

Her legs tingled, and her head swam, as she came undone beneath him in an orgasm that seemed to last forever and left her sore and sated and panting for breath.

Hyperion growled. "Open your eyes. See what you do to me." When she did, he pulled out of her and stroked his cock.

How had that thing fit inside her? It was humongous. She stopped thinking as the invisible fingers spread her and dipped inside, to drive her over the edge again.

Hyperion came with a roar, his thick, warm cum covering her belly and inner thigh. His eyes shone brighter than ever. He looked majestic. Fierce. And big—larger than life itself.

God. She'd just had sex. For the first time. With her boss.

Without a condom.

She scurried out from under him, and he collapsed on the mattress and pulled her into his body. "We didn't use protection," she whispered, swallowing the panic that threatened to choke her.

Hyperion kissed her neck and along her jaw. "No need. I can't procreate unless I want to."

That was a weird phrasing, but Olivia would take it at face value, because worry was overtaking her post-coital bliss, and she wanted to savor the sensations that came with her incredible first time.

Still, she had to ask, "What about—you know—disease?"

"I can't…" He shook his head. "I'm fine, and you… Well, there's nothing you could give me."

His orgasm must have messed with his English, but the point came across. They were safe. *If* she believed him. She turned to look at him over her shoulder. He watched her with awe. No way to fake that.

Plus everything in her insisted he was telling the truth.

"What is it about you?" Her release had drilled huge holes into her mind-to-mouth filter. "I trust you, and I barely know you."

"Maybe my soul calls to yours."

So very cheesy, but it made her smile.

"Shower?" he asked.

She ought to clean up. She was drenched in sweat and sticky with cum. "You go first." Her legs wouldn't carry her to the bathroom yet.

The mattress dipped and moved behind her, as Hyperion got out of bed.

She squished the pillow and tucked it under her head, more than happy to take a quick nap while he cleaned up, but he said, "I meant together."

Even better.

She rolled toward him, and he wedged both arms under her and lifted her to him.

A girl could get used to so much pampering.

Especially when he had her stand toward the wall and sponged her back before gently lathering her mound and inner thighs. He lingered at her pussy, and fresh desire sparked in her core.

"Naughty," she said. The huskiness in her voice surprised her. She liked this version of herself.

Hyperion nudged her to turn around. He was hard. Again? Still? "Just making sure you're clean for what comes next," he said.

She wanted to kiss the smirk off his face. "Next? Like sleep?" she asked. "Or maybe I should do some PA-ing, since that's what you're paying me for."

He pursed his lips and nodded, the thin laughter lines by his eyes belying his serious expression. "You can do that while I eat your pussy."

Her nipples stood at attention before the sponge reached them. Hyperion cupped and kneaded each breast, massaging the shower gel into them before proceeding to her belly and back to her pussy. He slid two fingers inside, and discomfort dampened her mood. She was still raw from before.

Hyperion took a step closer, so his thick cock glided against her stomach, and pumped his fingers inside her slowly. "Your body is divine," he said. "I could make love to you for the rest of eternity."

Olivia dug her nails into his shoulder, to keep from losing her balance as pleasure pushed pain aside.

"I want to make you come until you can't remember your own name. Want to feel you strangle my cock. I want to fill up all of your holes. Make you mine in every way imaginable." He kept fucking her with his hand, until she started meeting his thrusts. Then he added one more finger. "I can't wait to squeeze inside your tight ass. See you stretch to take in more of me."

Her ass? That was a bit mu—

Hyperion found that spot inside and rubbed, and she'd let him take her ass if only he kept doing this.

Her knees buckled, and now there were four fingers inside her, and they were the only things keeping her upright, because her grip on him faltered.

Could she come again? Was it healthy? Maybe there was something wrong with her. Hyperorgasmia or something.

Hyperion dropped to his knees in front of her and lifted her with his other hand on her ass. "Wrap your legs around my head."

"What? No. I can't—"

"*Now*." The word echoed and bounced off the marble walls.

She lifted one wobbly leg over his shoulder, and he helped her raise the other one too, his hand still inside her. He made a humming noise of approval and blew warm air over her mound.

Olivia let her head thud back against the marble tile, as Hyperion ran his tongue up her slit. He was even better at this than fantasy-Hyperion had been.

He chuckled, the sound reverberating inside her. Had she spoken aloud?

When he sucked on her clit, she no longer cared.

By the time Hyperion carried her back to bed, Olivia was perfectly clean and utterly exhausted.

"I still haven't done any Personal Assisting," she managed with a yawn, as she turned to her side.

He tapped her ass playfully and lay behind her. "Oh, I don't know. Personally, I feel very assisted." He draped an arm around her and squeezed one breast.

He was incorrigible. She couldn't believe they'd done *this*, when she'd been livid at him in the car.

How *did* they get here?

Had he messed with her will? She fought to remember their exchange in the car, but sleep muddled her brain.

Or was this Hyperion, too?

# CHAPTER TWELVE

Hyperion wasn't into naps, but one wouldn't hurt, and dozing off with a naked Olivia snuggled against him was pure bliss. He caressed her stomach. He should have fed her lunch first; she'd be starving by now. Eh. He'd arrange a feast when they woke up. He might not need to eat, but he enjoyed it. It was his second favorite pastime.

He slid his hand lower and cupped her pussy.

Olivia groaned.

If he played a bit, she might be up for one more time, but he didn't want to break her. She needed her rest.

"Sleep, my wanton Olivia," he murmured against her hair.

She shifted to look at him over her shoulder, but instead of the look of a well-loved woman, she wore an angry expression, eyes narrowed and lips pressed into a thin line. She dug her elbow into his chest hard enough it must have hurt her. Surprised, Hyperion jerked back, and Olivia hopped out of bed, clutching the silken top sheet.

"Did you do that to me?" she asked.

Did she mean… "Did I copulate with you? Of course I did. Who did you think it was?" Had her repeated orgasms impaired her mentally?

She shook her head frantically. "Did you make me want you? Make me want to… fuck you? Was it one of your mind tricks?" She'd gone pale, and her eyes looked haunted.

"Of course not," he boomed. It hurt that she'd think that, though he couldn't blame her. Not like he hadn't swayed people's minds before. He wanted to hold her, soothe her, but approaching her in this state would only scare her away.

"Sit down, and I'll explain everything," he said in a calm voice. He didn't dare send her a suggestion. If she caught on, she'd never trust him again.

"I'd rather stand." In a whisper, she added, "Though I'm not sure why I'm not running away." She met his gaze. "Is this you too?"

"No, this is all you, wanting to know what I am. And I'm a Titan." Because, really, there was no subtle way to break this to her.

"A titan?" Olivia snorted. "Like… in bed, or do you mean filthy rich? Like a titan of industry?"

Hyperion shook his head. "Like a giant that preceded god and man alike."

"Haha. Very funny."

He moved toward the foot of the bed. He could cross the distance between them in the blink of an eye, but he didn't want to alarm her more. "I am not trying to be funny. I was locked inside a statue for millennia, until you freed me." There was no doubt it was her proximity—her touch—that brought him back to life. Their lovemaking had done nothing to reduce his desire for her, and it was evident she was the one his very being craved.

Olivia arched an eyebrow, but she must have seen something on his face, because her expression turned wary. "Shit. You believe it." She took a step back and let go of the sheet with one hand, to push her hair out of her face. "You're crazy. Oh God. You weren't in jail; you were in an asylum or something."

"Olivia—"

"No. I have to go. You… Who is responsible for you? Does your family know you're out? *God.* I need to get out of here. I can't believe I went to bed with a hot stranger and woke up next to a nutcase." She was muttering, talking herself into a frenzy and hyperventilating, as she inched backward toward the door, her gaze never leaving him.

She was afraid of him, and what he'd do next wouldn't exactly put her at ease, but at least she wouldn't think he was crazy.

"Let me prove it to you," he said.

Olivia reached the door and pawed blindly at the handle behind her. "Sure. Yeah. But maybe we should get dressed first and continue this talk somewhere public."

Hyperion relaxed and let his power suffuse him. In his true size, he wouldn't fit in the building, but he let his body grow to the size he'd been as a statue. And okay, maybe he commanded his skin to glow a little bit, for effect.

"Oh my God." Olivia brought both hands to her mouth. "Oh my God." This time, it came out a whisper.

"Don't fear me. I would never harm you." His voice was a little louder than necessary, but it matched the image.

"Uh huh. Whatever you say." She squeezed her eyes shut and rubbed her temples. "I need to sit down." She'd gone beyond pale, to as white as the sheet wrapped around her.

Hyperion blinked to the door and caught her as her knees buckled. He willed himself to his human size again and helped her to one of the armchairs in the room. He knelt beside her and took her hand. "I've been trying to figure out how to tell you since last night."

"Twenty-something hours, and this was what you came up with?" She huffed and propped her head on one hand, her elbow on the arm of her seat.

Biting back his laugh, he brought the other armchair over and sat, facing her. "I know. I'm sorry. That's why I wanted to wait till tomorrow."

"Yeah, blame me because you're… you're…"

"A Titan."

She gave him a half-smile. "I was gonna say *a freak*, but okay."

She was joking. This was a good sign, right? "You're taking this better than I expected."

"Well, either you're a Titan, or I'm nuts. I'm opting for the scenario that doesn't land me in the loony bin." She gasped. "Or maybe I'm asleep. Yes. I'm asleep, and this is my subconscious, telling me to run."

"Olivia…"

She went on like he hadn't spoken. "I mean, you're amazing in bed—"

"And in the shower," Hyperion supplied.

Olivia nodded. "And in the shower. Whatever. But you come with baggage, and this is my sign not to get tangled with you. *More* tangled."

It was so very late for that, and Hyperion had heard enough. He leaned forward and took her free hand in both of his. "This is not a dream, Olivia. You are not asleep. I am a Titan. The diamonds I used as money, I forged with my own hands. My hands that have shaped mountains. And people do what I say because I can manipulate human minds."

She snatched away her hand. "So you did mess with my mind. That's why I gave in to your advances so easily."

He could get mad, or he could laugh at her. The second was safer for everyone involved. Hyperion laughed, and the room shook. "You gave in because you couldn't resist me. Because you wanted me and still do. Yesterday morning, when you ran out on me, I tried to compel you to come back."

Her eyes widened. "I heard it. I wanted to come to you. Considered having sex with you in the corridor."

"But then you left. My compulsion doesn't work on you. I can't probe or make you do what I want. All I can do is project suggestions to you or pick up your most intense thoughts, and that only seems to work if you are already aroused. By me." He focused on sending her a scene from when they were in the shower, with him savoring her juices, and was surprised to see her squirm. Even now, she was drawn to him. "See? You want me, so you saw what I sent you."

Olivia stood so fast, her knees hit his. "I need to get out of here." She looked at him pointedly.

He was between her and the door. He stood and moved his chair out of the way. "Please don't leave," he said. "This changes nothing. I still want you, and I still need you." He hurried to add, "To help me acclimate. I haven't lived in a society since the Olympians were in power."

She looked at the ceiling. The floor. The bed. When her gaze returned to him, her posture was no longer subdued. She crossed her arms, the sheet still magically in place. "I can't trust myself around you. I need to not be here tonight."

Hyperion's heart constricted at the wide berth she gave him as she scurried out the door. Why couldn't she see she was safe with him? That he—

"*Olivia*," he bellowed, and the windows rattled until one of the glass panes erupted inward.

*Was* she safe, when he could barely contain his powers? A second window shattered. He couldn't run after her until he put a lid on his inner turmoil.

Squeezing his eyes shut, he focused on calming himself down. He could do this. He had to, if he ever wanted his woman back in his arms.

He no longer scoffed at the notion. Olivia was his.

The painting that hung over the bed fell. The shaking continued. Was it only this room, or was it spreading? Hyperion didn't dare leave, to check. Destruction would follow him until he had himself under control. If only Atlas were here. He could command the earth as well as Hyperion did, but had none of his quick temper and could balance him out.

Atlas was probably still in the dark depths of the Ocean. Along with the rest of their kind.

And Hyperion was chasing after a mortal, instead of trying to find them.

Not *any* mortal. His soulmate.

He knew in his gut that this woman was meant for him, and once he'd convinced her too, he could help his brothers rise. Besides, being near them wouldn't be safe until he had bonded with his soulmate, according to Eros.

*Eros.* He'd offered help.

Hyperion covered the distance to his nightstand in two strides and pressed *2* on the cell phone the god of love had given him. He brought it to his ear, and sighed when he heard Eros' voice.

"You've reached the God of Love. If I'm not picking up, I'm somewhere saving the known universe. Or getting laid. For emergencies, press *1*."

Oh for Chaos' sake! Hyperion pressed *1* and got a busy tone. Nice. Circe was supposed to be *3* on his phone. He kept the number pressed and waited.

"This is Circe. Please describe the exact nature of your issue after the *beep*."

"I can't stop," Hyperion yelled. "I need your help, before this gets out of control." He ended the call and stared at the phone, willing it to ring.

The tremors subsided. Was that Circe? How powerful a witch was she?

No time to think of that. He should find Olivia. If the damage spread, she could be hurt.

He pushed the door of his room, and when it didn't open, kicked it down. So what if it was made to swing inward? It was one more thing between him and Olivia. A glance around the suite living room showed no damage. The earthquake must have been localized. Good. She was safe.

"Olivia?" He blinked to her room, but she wasn't there.

Where had she gone, practically naked?

*Christina.* Where did Christina live?

Hyperion skimmed through Vangelis' memories, but he'd never been to the girl's room. He growled and tossed the phone on the couch, lest he throw it out the nearest window, and then blinked to the lobby. He stomped his bare feet to Reception, impervious to the looks he got from hotel guests and staff alike. "Olivia Johnson. Did you see her?" he asked the man behind the counter.

"I did, but I can't tell you where she went, sir. She seemed upset. And if I may say so, you're naked and scaring the guests." His loyalty would be admirable if it weren't annoying.

Hyperion glanced at the man's nametag. "Show me, Kostas," he ordered and entered the man's thoughts. Olivia had asked him for a key to her old room, where Christina now stayed alone. Thanks to Kostas, Hyperion knew where that was.

He took the stairs down one floor and hurried to Christina's door. He should rip it off its hinges and get his soulmate, but he'd done enough damage for one day, especially to his relationship with her.

# CHAPTER THIRTEEN

Olivia's chest heaved. She couldn't get her breathing under control, and it wasn't because she'd run the forty feet from the elevator to the room while trying not to step on the sheet she wore as a chiton.

Hyperion was a Titan. The real, actual kind that was the root for the adjective.

He *had* been a statue. He could move the earth. He made diamonds with his bare palms.

He made her come, repeatedly.

He was scary. Unstoppable.

She wanted him.

"Fuck," she said, not for the first time.

Christina sat on her heels, watching her. "Honey, please tell me what happened. Did Hyperion attack you? Should I call the police?"

Olivia shook her head. "No. No police."

"But he did attack you?" Christina's usually playful gaze turned murderous. "I can't believe I liked him. Where is he? I'm going to give him a piece of my mind." She dug into her purse and fished out a very illegal can of pepper spray. "Mr. Titanas is going down. I'll call Manolis, to keep you company, and then Hyperion's ass is mine."

This new, fierce side of Christina was thrilling, but also more than a little funny, considering her petite, curvy frame and large, innocent, blue eyes. Olivia was amazed to hear herself laugh. "Sit down, Rambo. You don't have to kick anyone's ass tonight. Anything I did with Hyperion was consensual. It was the talking, afterward, that screwed things up."

As she said the words, she knew them to be true. She hadn't been coerced into giving Hyperion her body. She'd wanted him since she'd met him. But had that all been her?

It must have. If he could control her, he'd have made her his that first morning. Hell, she'd still be in the suite with him now, unable to run away.

But just because he couldn't didn't mean he hadn't tried. And he'd had no compunction telling her so. *Ugh.* Was that good or bad? It made him honest, but not ethical.

Christina snapped her fingers in front of Olivia's face. "You still with me? Did he drug you?"

His lovemaking could be considered a drug. It was certainly addictive. "I'm fine. Honest," Olivia said. "He told me some things about his past, and I freaked out."

"Ooh, so he was in jail?" Christina hopped to her feet and planted her hands on her hips.

Olivia chewed on her bottom lip. "Sorta."

"You can't talk about it?" Christina clapped her hands. "Is he CIA? FBI?"

"Yeah, because he's so obviously American."

"Right. What's the name of the Greek secret service?"

Olivia rolled her eyes. "He isn't in any secret service, and I can't tell you more about it." Was that so Christina wouldn't think Olivia was crazy, or to protect Hyperion? And should she be hiding the true nature of a man who could destroy a city at a whim? Shouldn't she be turning him in to the authorities? But what authorities could contain him?

Heavy steps sounded outside the door, and after a moment, knuckles rapped against the wood. "Olivia? I know you're in there. Please open the door."

"Should I tell him to leave?" Christina asked in a hushed tone.

Olivia doubted that would stop him. "He'll probably huff and puff and tear the door down."

Christina arched an eyebrow. "If he's the big bad wolf, we could do with reinforcements. Are you sure I shouldn't call the cops?"

"Olivia, let me in. I need to talk to you," Hyperion called out. He sounded patient, but Olivia sensed his urgency.

"Come in," she said. He would anyway, if he decided to. No door could keep out this man. *This Titan.*

The door swung open hard enough to hit the wall, and Hyperion stepped inside the room, naked like a newborn and hung like a horse.

So *not* looking at that thing.

"You didn't have to run. I told you I would never hurt you," he said.

"Don't get any closer, mister." Christina stepped to Olivia's side and rested a hand on her shoulder.

"Is everyone hard of hearing today?" Hyperion asked the ceiling. "I do not wish to hurt Olivia. I love her."

Olivia felt her jaw go slack. "You what?"

"I love you. I was created to love you. You and I are supposed to be together, for my existence to make sense. If I'm not with you, I might as well be a slab of rock again."

His existence might make sense, but his words sure didn't.

Christina squeaked, "*Again?*"

Olivia narrowed her eyes at Hyperion. "You've only known me for a day."

He scowled. "You can't tell me you're not feeling this… this connection between us. I'm ancient, Olivia. Eternal. And yet I've never felt for a female, mortal or divine, the way I feel about you."

Christina's eyes were open impossibly wide. She looked as shocked as Olivia felt.

Olivia swallowed around the lump in her throat. "I… I can't…" Return his feelings? Say the words? Sleep with him again, when she knew he could be as big as a house and possibly crush her in one fist? "I just can't."

"Look into my eyes and tell me you don't want me." His voice brooked no argument.

She met his gaze, trying for defiant. His warm, amber-gold eyes melted her resistance, though. "I do, God help me."

"Then stop fighting it." Hyperion glowed with an ethereal light so bright, she had to shield her eyes.

When the light dimmed, she saw him look at Christina, his brow furrowed. "You will forget what you witnessed tonight," he said.

Christina snorted. "Yeah… That's not happening, dude. What are you?"

Olivia ran her tongue along her dry lips. "He's a Titan. Original version." Christina had heard enough; there was no hiding from her at this point.

"Huh." Christina crossed her arms over her chest. "And where can I get me one of those?"

Hyperion roared with laughter. "At the bottom of the sea, most likely, but I'll save you one if I find them."

This was too surreal. Olivia needed time and space, to process. She stood and held out an arm toward the door. "Hyperion—"

She didn't get to ask him to leave. He wrapped an arm around her legs, threw her over his shoulder, and turned to Christina. "I promise she'll be safe with me."

"You'd better keep that promise, if you don't want me going to the media with this."

He nodded and carried Olivia out of there.

Why wasn't she fighting him? Why wasn't she demanding to be let go?

Because deep down, she wanted nothing more than to have him inside her once more— filling her, stretching her to this side of pain, and driving her to ecstasy. And maybe his declaration of love spoke to something primal inside her. It wasn't hormones, drawing her to him. Oxytocin wasn't affecting her thoughts.

She was in love with him too.

# CHAPTER FOURTEEN

She didn't say she loved him, but she didn't deny it, either. She only said it was too soon—and wasn't it? They'd only been together a few hours.

But he'd waited for her five thousand years.

"Can you put me down? I'm getting lightheaded," she said.

"Hold on." Hyperion waited for the elevator doors to open and helped her to her feet inside the car. Now she wasn't going anywhere.

"I'm not going to run again," she said as if she read his mind. "Not like I can get far in this." She held up one end of the sheet covering her body. One of her breasts was exposed, and Hyperion reached for it without thinking about it.

Olivia followed his hand with her gaze but didn't move to cover herself or shy from his touch.

He rolled her nipple between his fingers and looked into her eyes. "I can't stop touching you." Cupping her breast with his palm, he leaned in to swipe his tongue over the hardened nipple.

She shivered visibly. "Tell me more."

Hyperion squared his shoulders. "What do you want to know?" If she asked about his imprisonment or what freed him, he'd tell her the truth.

"Everything."

He groaned and hit his head back against the wall. He didn't feel like talking about the loneliness and hopelessness that had been his existence for centuries, so he'd talk about his feelings for her. "You've taken over my thoughts. I should be roaming the seas, searching for my brothers, but instead I want to spend a lifetime between your legs. I want to hear you moan and know I pulled that sound out of you. I want to make you happy, and I want to possess you absolutely. I love you."

She sucked in her bottom lip. "We're almost at our floor." She slammed her open palm on the elevator controls, and the car came to an abrupt stop. "I don't know what you're doing to me," she said, "but I'm done trying to figure it out."

What was she saying? Was she giving in to him? Did she accept this undeniable attraction between them went beyond physical desire?

She dropped to her knees and wrapped her fingers around his shaft. Bewildered, Hyperion watched as she moistened her lips with her tongue and laid a wet kiss on the tip of his cock.

*Uranus.* Seeing Olivia on her knees like this, the submissiveness in her position, made the blood hammer in his temples.

She timidly pressed another kiss to his length. Did she know what to do, or was this a first for her?

"Have you done this before?" Hyperion fought to keep the jealousy from his voice.

Olivia shook her head and traced a circle with her tongue around the bell end.

He growled at the wet heat teasing him, and fisted both hands in her hair. "Open your mouth, sweet Olivia."

Her lips formed an *O*, and he pulled her so she pressed them to the head of his cock.

"Wider," he said.

She did as he ordered, lips stretched over her teeth, and Hyperion held her in place while he wedged his cock through them. *Ananke*, this was a tight fit.

Olivia tapped her tongue against the underside of his shaft. Rubbed it at the ridges the veins formed. Sucked so hard her cheeks hollowed.

He wanted to thrust all the way in, but he might choke her. "Suck," he barked.

She dug her nails in the backs of his thighs. The sheet had fallen off her body, allowing him a perfect view of her creamy breasts as she took more of his length in her mouth.

He pulled back and drove forward again, hitting the back of her throat. Her eyes watered, but she pressed at his ass, keeping him from withdrawing.

Hyperion let her dictate how deep he went this time.

Olivia swallowed around him. *Gaia*, she was taking him down her throat.

His loins were on fire. He ached to pump inside her mouth hard and fast, until he sated his need.

And then she stopped.

Hyperion looked at her, incredulous, as she stood, gave him a cheeky grin, and said, "The rest of that comes after we talk." She pressed the button to their floor.

The elevator started with a jerk, and Olivia leaned on the wall across from him, looking very satisfied with herself.

Let her. He'd answer her questions, and then they'd spend the night—or the rest of their days together—making love.

At her insistence, they got dressed and sat at the dining-room table, facing each other. As if Hyperion couldn't cover that distance in the blink of an eye, tear through a couple layers of clothing, and have her on his lap or bend her over the dark wood to ram into her from behind.

His cock, never fully relaxed since he met her, stirred again. He adjusted himself and met her gaze. "I don't know where to start," he said.

"At the beginning." Her warm brown eyes bored into him, daring him to lie. He wouldn't.

"I am of the first line of Titans, born by Gaia and Uranus. The stories told of our father are true. He was a tough, unfair ruler, and my brother Kronos sentenced him to Tartarus and took over his throne. But power and guilt drove him insane, and he started swallowing his children so none of them would imitate his treason. His wife saved the runt of the litter, you might say. She and Zeus asked help from those of us who didn't approve of Kronos' cruelty. I took neither side."

He looked down, at his hands. Would she consider him a coward for this? "Kronos was my brother, and I wanted no harm to befall him, but I saw his cruel nature. So I sat on the sidelines while Thetis and Prometheus created humans to worship Zeus and take his side against his father. After he freed his siblings, and the Olympians took down Kronos and the few Titans who supported him, Zeus turned all males of my kind to stone, including Prometheus. I don't know what became of my brothers after the Olympians cast me in the Aegean Sea, but I know the Titanesses were turned mortal, to—"

A splitting pain pierced his temple. He squeezed his eyes shut, and images of Atlas, Prometheus, Coeus, and Iapetus overlapped each other in his mind. Their screams of rage and torment filled his head, and the roaring of earth shifting beneath his feet almost threw him out of his chair. *No.* He had to hold on. Had to maintain control a little longer.

He forced his mind clear of the invasion and looked at Olivia again.

Her knuckles were white where she gripped the table. "Did you feel that?" she said.

"My brothers are screaming for me to release them." She might think he was changing the subject, but he didn't lie.

She let go of the table and steepled her fingers, but not before he saw her hands tremble. "Do you know where they are?" she asked.

Hyperion shook his head. "If their fates were similar to mine, they're underwater, waiting for someone to find them and their… destiny to awaken them." He couldn't tell her yet he believed she was his soulmate. It would be too heavy a burden for a mortal, especially if she didn't return his feelings. She desired him, no doubt, but did she love him? Could she?

"Why did you awaken?" she asked.

Because she touched him. Because his body couldn't remain motionless in her proximity. Because her soul called to his. He shrugged. "It was my time."

She pursed her lips. Her look of intense concentration gave way to shock. "Oh God. You were a statue for—"

"Five millennia, give or take a couple hundred years. I was lucky and outmaneuvered Zeus for eons before he finally found me. Atlas was captured first, almost thirty-five thousand years ago."

She sat back with an *oof*. "Zeus can certainly hold a grudge, if he hunted you for that long." She scrunched her adorable nose. "And you were cognizant throughout your captivity? I can't believe you didn't go crazy."

Didn't he? He saw and heard his brothers. He was spinning out of control and causing earthquakes. He gave her a sad smile. "I wasn't constantly aware. For a time, in the darkness, I was sure I'd lose my mind. Being brought to the suite was amazing and devastating at the same time. I caught glimpses of a world that had moved on and left gods and Titans behind, yet I was incapable of interacting with it."

"Is that how you know what you do about us? How you speak Modern Greek and English?"

He rubbed his face with both palms and met her gaze. She wasn't going to like this. "No. That was Vangelis. He let me in his subconscious, and I absorbed the knowledge he's acquired throughout his life. I can speak as well as he does, and I remember the feel of his mother's embrace when he was a newborn, though his conscious mind has lost that memory. It was not my intention to harm him, and my intrusion has left him unaffected."

Her eyes were as wide as the moon peeking in at them from the window. "Can you do that with any mortal?"

"I thought I could, but then there was you." And Christina, who'd sensed him and brushed his influence away, but he might have broken past her resistance if he tried harder.

Olivia blushed and ducked her head. Her innocence made his blood boil. Everything she did was alluring.

"Don't avert your face from me, sweet Olivia. I want you to look at me when I say again that I love you, with every fiber of my being."

She licked her lips, and he could hear her pulse speeding. He could have her again, this very moment, but what they were doing was important too. She was getting to know him, and now was his turn.

"Tell me about yourself," he urged. "Where were you born? How big is your family?"

"I'm from New York. United States of America. My mom and dad are still together, still stupidly in love, and I only have one younger sister. No drama." She smiled that smile humans got when they thought of home, and his heart skipped a beat. His home was lost to him, but he could build a new one with the mortal who had him wrapped around her finger.

"Do you miss them?" he asked.

She grimaced. "More than I thought I would. I mean, I spent the last four years in Boston, studying for my degree."

"In archeology." He nodded. She frowned, so he explained. "I saw it in your personnel file, when I bought the hotel."

"Less creepy than mind-reading, I guess."

He chuckled.

She grinned. "Anyway, as I was saying before you so rudely interrupted me"—she mock-glared, and he pressed his lips together, to show he wouldn't say another word—"after living away from home for so long, I thought coming here would be easy. But it's totally different, being on the other side of the planet from them."

Should he tell her he could blink her to New York for dinner? Or would it be lunch time there? He shook away the thought. Listen now, promise her the world later.

"Christina was a godsend," Olivia said. "She's so fun to be around, and she reminds me of Nina, my sister."

"It's good to find people you mesh with," Hyperion said. "They help you fit in." Would he ever fit in this world, outside his happy bubble with her? He'd have to. Olivia had actual ties she shouldn't have to give up to be with him. "How old is your sister?"

"Twenty. She's nothing like me. I was always the bookworm—always eager to learn more, get good grades, finish my studies in four years—and she's so easy going. The life of the party. I'd never admit this to her, but growing up, I envied her ease around people. Maybe she's the reason I took the chance to come here. All my life, I've done what I thought I should. Never what I wanted."

"The pressure of the parents' expectations usually falls on the first child."

She shook her head. "*I* was the one pressuring myself. My dad has this saying, that he'd rather be happy than successful, and it's worked out well for him. He's a high-school teacher at a private academy, and he loves his job. Mom is the breadwinner in the family. She works for a pharmaceutical company, as VP of sales. You'd think the power imbalance would mess with their relationship, but they complement each other."

# CHAPTER FIFTEEN

"You got your drive from your mother, then. Nothing wrong with wanting to be successful." Hyperion's smile was warm, inviting her to say more. Was there more?

"But I don't know if that's what I want. Since I was a little girl, I've wanted to become an archaeologist, but after graduation… I'm not sure that was even *my* goal, or if I was chasing a six-year-old's dreams." Apparently, there was more. More than she'd put into words before. "I told myself this summer would be my chance to let loose a little. Go out, drink, meet boys. Then I'd return to my life, build a career, and make the best of my degree. Be a success."

He tilted his head. His eyes, amber now, saw right to her very core. "But not happy."

"Not happy." She'd convinced herself *happy* wasn't good enough, but when she was in his arms, and he looked at her like she was his world, she'd been happy. Even when she was afraid of him, a little part of her reveled at the excitement of the unknown. "You know, I'd made contingency plans for everything"—including a summer fling—"except you."

"And now that you met me?"

She sighed. "Your existence is proof I can't be prepared. That plans aren't guarantees. And that maybe what I wanted out of life isn't what I need." She shouldn't have made him sit across the table. She wished she could pull his arms around her while she bared her soul like this. "But if I fought for the wrong thing so many years, where does that leave me? Who am I, if I'm not good-girl Olivia, soon to be archaeologist extraordinaire?"

"You're a woman in search of a new dream."

Was it possible she'd found one that combined her degree with the adventurous life she never allowed herself to experience? "I could help you look for your brothers," she said.

His expression was unreadable, his face more impassive than when he was made of marble. Was her suggestion too much of a commitment? Did he feel pressured?

She was done second-guessing herself. He was the one who talked about love, and *that* was a commitment.

Still, she whispered, "If you want me to, that is."

Hyperion stared at her, and the more he didn't speak, the faster the words spilled from her lips. "You obviously know more than I do about where they could be, and you can manipulate minds, so you don't *need* my help, but I could be your inside man. *Woman.* If you know where to look, and you fund an expedition, I can organize it." Did she sound desperate?

Why wasn't he saying anything?

She blinked, and he was beside her, pulling back her chair.

"What—?"

"I need to be inside you. Now." He picked her up like she weighed nothing, and tore open the fly of her pants.

No, wait. Yeah, he tore open her jeans, all the way. He had to stop destroying her clothes, damn it.

She'd yell about it later, because now he propped her ass on the dining-room table and shoved down his jeans so hard the seams popped.

He tugged her panties out of the way and pushed into her. She was still aching from this afternoon, but she urged him on with her heels on his buttocks. Who cared about the pain, when she knew the pleasure that would follow?

Her eyes rolled back in her head, as he ploughed her body. The vase that stood on the table rattled closer to the edge with each of Hyperion's thrusts, and then crashed to the floor. It would only take a pinch on her clit, for Olivia to chase it over the edge, but Hyperion kept driving her higher until she was a ball of desire, floating on air. She couldn't control her limbs. Her body was his now. And she was falling.

Hyperion took care of her again. He showered her, and then took her to his bed, and fed her room service. The energy was sapped out of her, and her ass was sore where the wood dug into it. She had bruises from his grip on her thighs and felt raw between them, but the sting was carried on euphoria at the memory of their time together.

A Titan had fucked her raw. A Titan chose her for his bed. *Her Titan.*

Her Titan had deflected with crazy sex when she implied she wanted a future with him.

"So did you like my idea about the expedition?" she asked, nuzzling his chest. The short curly hairs were still damp from the shower, and he smelled good enough to eat.

As if he heard her thoughts, he put his hand on the top of her head, and nudged her lower. His erection tapped her chin.

"Don't you ever go soft?" she asked, running a finger down his length.

"Not when you're around." His shaft bobbed in front of her eyes. "And I seem to remember a certain promise…"

After all they'd done, she suddenly felt bashful. In the elevator, she'd been driven by her need for answers and the illusion of power she held over him when she had him in her mouth. Now the angle was awkward, and she was too exhausted to move. Her inexperience would show.

"Kiss it." His voice had gone lower. Rougher.

She licked her lips and placed an open-mouthed kiss on the velvet tip.

"Deeper. Use your tongue."

He hissed when she tucked her lips over her teeth and pushed down on him. When the head was in her mouth, she swirled her tongue around it and along the tiny slit in the top. His hips flew off the mattress, and when she looked at him, his head was thrown back, the tendons in his neck bulging with strain. She circled his girth with her hand and tugged.

Hyperion groaned, and so did the headboard, where he gripped it.

*She* did this. To an immortal being.

Olivia closed her lips over him again and sucked, then used her tongue to trace the thick vein on the underside.

"You're killing me, woman," he roared.

She laughed, and one of his hands flew to her hair, holding her still.

"That tickles," he ground out.

She took more of him in and swallowed. Having her tonsils taken out finally paid off when he nudged the back of her throat and kept going. Her eyes teared up, but she fought her gag reflex and swallowed again.

"I'm not going to last long." He gathered her hair in his fist and pulled, but she wasn't done with him.

She pumped him with her hand and slid her mouth up and down his length until his thigh trembled.

"Olivia, I'm going to come."

She couldn't speak with her mouth full, so she tightened her lips around the head of his cock and sucked, pumping her fist faster.

He twitched, and then his cum spurted on her tongue and the back of her throat. It was salty and tangy. Not unpleasant. She swallowed, and then laughed when he dragged her up his body for a searing kiss. More questions could wait till morning.

# CHAPTER SIXTEEN

Hyperion felt rested. Rejuvenated. Restored.

Sleeping through the night with her in his arms was incredible.

And then Eros popped in, and Hyperion was a bunch of nerves again.

"You've got the physical thing down pat, I see," Eros said.

Hyperion wanted to wipe the smug grin off the god's face. With his foot. "You'll wake her."

"Nah. I'm not really here. You're dreaming of me."

Hyperion sat up, but didn't. He could see his body lying curled around Olivia's form, their breathing synchronized. They fit together like jigsaw pieces. She completed him, like that girl, from the movie that made Vangelis swoon.

"I have better things to dream of." Hyperion waved him away.

"Can't disagree with that, but remember—tick-tock."

Hyperion was woken by his own growl. The pesky god might have invaded his sleep, but what he said was true. Time was running out.

A look outside showed the sky was the light gray of predawn, and Hyperion knew how he wanted to greet the day.

His hand was around one of Olivia's breasts. He squeezed, and she moaned. His morning erection demanded taking care of, and this time they'd do things properly. He'd bond with her today.

Olivia stretched on her back, but he shook his head. "On your knees."

He didn't have to say it twice. She rolled over and brought her knees under her, her face pressed to her pillow.

Hyperion used more pillows under her body, to lift her hips. She looked so deliciously submissive, with her ass in the air, like this. He could think of a thing or two to do to this ass, but not now. Now, he'd claim her soul.

He moved behind her, draped his body over hers, and slipped his fingers between her folds. "So wet," he murmured, "and all mine."

Olivia let out a mewling sound and pushed back, but he withdrew his fingers and replaced them with the tip of his cock. Holding her hip with one hand, he slowly pushed forward until he was sheathed inside her. "Does it hurt?" he asked. It might, after last night's acrobatics.

"Nuh uh." That sounded like a *no*, so he slid out and thrust forward again.

She moaned and tightened around him, but he was beyond waiting for her to get used to his girth. He drove inside so hard, her body jerked. And again. Faster. Moving his grip to the back of her neck, he slid his other hand around her front, to rub her clit to the rhythm of his thrusts. "I love feeling you around me, strangling my cock."

In response, she rocked her hips faster, urging him on. Her fingers were buried in the pillow, and a rivulet of sweat trickled down her spine.

"Tell me you want me," he said.

"I want you." Her voice was muffled. "Want you so much."

"Tell me you love me."

She didn't speak, and he leaned forward, to place a kiss between her shoulder blades. "Talk to me, Olivia. Tell me you're mine."

"I…"

The ringing jarred him. What was that sound?

"Olivia, tell me you're mine." He slammed his hips against her ass, but her body stiffened, as the ringing continued.

"Your… phone…" she said between gasps.

Shit. His phone. Circe or Eros were the only ones who could be calling. Stopping at this point would require gargantuan effort, but if he didn't take the call, he risked destroying far more than a window or a door next time he lost control. Next time, Olivia might be in danger.

He looked around and spotted the flashing screen on the floor by his discarded jeans from last night. "Don't move. I have to get this."

Olivia glared at him over her shoulder. "Now? Seriously?"

"I promise to make it up to you." He got out of bed, already missing her wet heat, and snatched the phone. He pressed a button blindly and brought it to his ear.

"Hey, big guy. Glad you called. I was thinking about you," Circe said in Greek. Her voice almost deafened him, coming out in speaker mode.

He cursed under his breath and turned the speaker option off. Holding up a finger to Olivia, he took the phone to the bathroom. "I need your help," he said to Circe, in the same language. "The unraveling has begun. I was wrecking my bedroom when I called you, and I couldn't stop it."

She huffed. "Have you found your soulmate yet?"

"Yes." There was no doubt in his mind.

"Then you need to bond with her."

"I've already made love to her." Repeatedly.

"Not enough. She needs to give you her heart while you mate." Circe sounded like she tasted something sour.

Hyperion frowned at the phone. "Not literally, I hope."

She let out a throaty laugh. "No, gramps; it's a figure of speech. She only has to pledge her love and mean it. And soon, or the balance will be lost for good."

So he was on the right track. But— "What if she doesn't? Is there another option?"

The silence on the other end of the line dragged so long, he thought she'd ended the call. "The only one I can think of is to turn you back to stone."

Not an option, then. "I'll let you know how it goes."

He left the phone by the sink and returned to his room, ready to get his woman to admit she was his, but Olivia very much had moved. In fact, she stood fully dressed by the coffee table, arms crossed and her face a mask of fury.

"Mr. Titanas—"

"It's *Hyperion.*"

"*Mr. Titanas*," she said more pointedly, "you hired me to be your PA, not your whore."

"What are you—"

She raised her voice. "I'm not a warm body for you to fuck while you wait for other women to call."

She thought he wanted Circe? This was preposterous. He only had eyes for Olivia. He chuckled. "You're jealous."

"I'm glad you think it's funny, *big guy.* I'll be staying with Christina until I find a place of my own— which you'll pay for, as per our agreement—and I'll be here every morning at eight, for work. But you touch me or mind-fuck me or whatever again, and you'll be hearing from my lawyer." Chin raised defiantly, she made her way toward the exit.

"Olivia, I—"

"No." Her voice wavered. "You don't get to say you love me or that you're sorry, or anything to get me back into the sack."

What sack? What was she talking about? He blocked her path. "I do love you. The phone call wasn't what you think."

She slapped his chest with her open palms. "So you didn't leave me naked and dripping for you, to talk to another woman?" She pushed, but he didn't budge.

"Yes, but—"

"Let me go, or I swear you'll never see me again."

He stood aside, and she ran to the elevator. He knew where to find her, and he'd explain everything once she cooled off. Letting her simmer a little might make her more open to accepting the truth—that they were meant to be together.

This was what logic dictated, but with his dick still hard, Hyperion wasn't about logic. He was a tightly wound coil of raw hunger, ready to devour the world, to get to her.

The floor shook, and screams reached his ears. People in the neighboring rooms. The tremors weren't localized.

*Olivia.* He had to keep her safe.

# CHAPTER SEVENTEEN

Olivia smashed her thumb on the *-1* button, and then hugged herself.

He'd left her there, kneeling naked on his bed, wet and aching for him, so he could talk to whoever that woman on the phone was. *Megale.* Olivia knew enough Greek to recognize the word for *big guy*, and by the lilt in the woman's voice, she didn't mean Hyperion's height.

Hot tears ran down Olivia's cheeks, as the doors slid shut. She'd believed him, God damn it. When he'd said he was in love with her, she'd believed him. His eyes had been so honest, and that catch in his throat? Nice touch. Really sold it.

She wiped furiously at her eyes. Worst part? She was ready to say it back, when he left the room to whisper sweet nothings to his other mistress, while his cock was still drenched in Olivia's juices. Yes, after only forty-eight hours, she was in love with the big oaf. It was hard to believe she could fall so fast, but her body was in tune to his every move, without him even touching her, and when he looked at her with those big, gorgeous eyes of his, her heart melted. His voice felt like a caress, soothing her and making her feel safe.

She snorted. *Safe.* She'd worried about his superhuman strength, but it hadn't been his hands that broke her heart.

A sob wound around her lungs and slipped out of her lips. He'd left her, mid-sex. She'd been so humiliated, and yet she'd actually considered staying where she was and waiting for him to come back and finish what he'd started. Where was her self-respect?

Something jostled her. The floor trembled under her feet. She was dizzy. She hadn't eaten since last night, and the vigorous workout had left her weak.

"Olivia."

Was he speaking in her head? But she wasn't hot for him now. Or rather, she was blazing hot, but with anger, not lust.

"Olivia, we need to get out of here."

She spun on her heel and saw him standing there, still naked. "How did you—?"

He cut her off with an impatient wave of his hand. "I'll explain later. Need to get you to safety first." He held out both arms, like he meant to hug her.

Olivia took a step back. "No. I told you, you're never touching me again."

"You're in danger, woman."

The elevator shook, and she stumbled back but righted herself with a hand on the polished-wood wall. "Are you doing this?" she whispered.

Hyperion threw his head back and squeezed his eyes shut. "I don't mean to. I'm trying to stop, but we have to get you out of here." When he looked at her again, there was nothing human in his eyes. They were pure liquid gold. He reached for her, and she batted away his hand.

"I'll be fine if you leave." She didn't believe it, but her self-preservation instinct seemed more worried about his proximity than about being stuck in here during an earthquake.

The mirror on the wall behind him rattled and shattered in a million shards.

Seven years bad luck.

*Snap.*

And the countdown started now.

The car lurched, and then pivoted downward.

Olivia screamed, before logic kicked in. They'd be okay. Elevators had emergency brakes, for this kind of situation. It was compulsory.

Except, maybe they didn't work in cases of Titan-induced shaking, because their descent never slowed.

Time seemed to creep to a halt, as Hyperion closed the distance between them and wrapped an arm around her waist. The tendons in his neck stood out, and the muscles in his jaws bulged with effort. Was he going to fly them up? Up to where?

"*Chaos.*" It took a moment for Olivia to realize this was an exclamation, and not a description of their situation. "I can't blink us out of here," he said through clenched teeth.

The lights in the cabin flickered, as it picked up speed.

*God*, he'd come to save her. The world rocked and rolled, and Hyperion cared about saving *her*. He did love her, and now they were going to die, and she hadn't told him she loved him.

No. *She* was going to die, and he'd never know how she felt.

"Hyperion—"

She was silenced by his fist going through the wall beside her head. A loud screeching sound made her wince. Sparks came out of the hole he'd created.

He was using his hand as a brake, to slow their fall. The bit about being super strong hadn't been an exaggeration.

Olivia threw her arms around his neck and clung to him. If this didn't work, if she was going to die, she'd make the most of her final moments. "I love you," she said.

The car stopped, and Hyperion let go of her to wedge open the doors with his free hand. They were suspended between floors. "Go," he said.

She pressed her lips to his, and he responded with such ferocity, he destroyed any lingering doubt about his feelings.

"Go," he repeated when he broke the kiss.

"What about you?"

"I'll be okay. I'm immortal, remember?" He held the doors open while she climbed out.

Olivia turned to meet his gaze. The earthquake was over. They'd be okay.

His sad smile made her heart stutter. It wasn't the look of a man who just had his feelings reciprocated. "Hyperion," she cried out, as the doors slid shut between them. "*No.*"

A deafening sound rocked the bowels of the building.

The elevator had crashed.

She ran to the staircase and took it all the way down, two steps at a time. People scurried around, but other than plaster chaffing off the walls at points, she saw no damage.

Because the epicenter of the earthquake had been in the elevator. With her.

She made it to the bottom, and part of her didn't want to look. What if she saw Hyperion's body, broken and bloodied?

The elevator doors on the basement level were folded outward, the metal bent in places by what could be two giant sets of knuckles, like someone huge and powerful and timeless had punched his way out.

Hyperion wasn't here. He had to be okay.

Her breath came out in bursts, and her heart hammered in her chest as she took the stairs again, this time up. Her legs felt as sturdy as boiled spaghetti, but her heart soared. He'd be in the suite, and she'd run to him and tell him she was his until the end of her mortal life.

The lights were out on the top floor, but she made her way to the suite in the fading sunlight that made it through the window at the end of the corridor. The door stood ajar, and Olivia nudged her way in, searching the wall for the light switch. She found it and flicked it on, and a sole unbroken lamp came on. Pieces of the ceiling had landed on the furniture and smashed the coffee table. The flat-screen TV hung lopsided on the wall, and there was no vase or glass standing upright.

"Hyperion?" But she already knew he wasn't here.

A new bout of terror squeezed her insides as she went to his room, to find more devastation. Broken glass crunched underfoot, but amid the chaos, she saw his cell phone.

Maybe he'd gone to save that other woman…

Olivia squashed the pang of jealousy that threatened to rip through her insides and scrolled to last calls. She'd only check if the woman had heard from him. It was concern for his wellbeing, really.

She chose the top incoming call—Circe—pressed *Call*, and the same female voice from before picked up on the first ring, with, "Ola kala?" *Everything okay*, in Greek.

"Do you know where Hyperion is?" Olivia tried to keep her voice calm.

"You're her," the woman said.

He'd talked to her about Olivia?

"Yes." Olivia didn't know what she agreed to. "There was an earthquake. He was in the elevator when it crashed. I can't find him." A shrill edge crept into her words. "Is he with you?"

"No."

Then where was he?

His words from earlier came back to Olivia. *My favorite place…* Why hadn't she let him say more about it, like where the hell it was? "There's a secluded beach he used to love. Caves and volcanic rock."

"Aspes," the woman said. "I know the place. Stay where you are. I'm sending someone to get you."

Why did this woman know Hyperion's favorite place? A fresh wave of jealousy washed over Olivia, threatening to take her under. She resisted. "I can have a friend drive m—"

The line went dead. Awesome. Vangelis would take her there, if he wasn't off with Hyperion. If Aspes was in Chania, he'd know the place. Or they could look it up on a map.

A spot of blinding white light twirled in the air before her, gathering mass with every turn. Limbs elongated from it, and then a tall, gorgeous man about her age smiled down at her, his blue eyes sparkling. "Ready?" he asked.

"For what?"

He clasped her wrist, and the room dissolved around her.

# CHAPTER EIGHTEEN

Even after all these centuries, Hyperion recognized the place.

The sea had altered the waterline, and pollution and tourists had corroded the mouth of the cave, but he still felt like he ruled the world when he stood where the waves broke. The sky and the water and the earth met here, where his toes dug into the sand and were covered by sea foam. Gold and purple pushed out the blue of the skies, cradling the rising sun as it blossomed in the horizon.

This was where he once sought solace and peace. It'd make a fitting spot for him to spend the rest of eternity, as a statue. Wasn't that different from where Atlas had stood to support the sky, before the solar system was put into place to relieve him.

Hyperion had left his cell phone at the hotel—no clothes meant no pockets—but the witch could no doubt spot him, like she had at the restaurant. Her presence there hadn't been a coincidence.

As a rule, he wasn't the dramatic, self-sacrificing sort. He'd leave such grand gestures to Prometheus, *thank you very much*. No, Hyperion had always been of the live-and-let-live mentality. He wouldn't cause harm on purpose, but he put himself first. And then a slip of a human girl had come into his life and turned it upside down.

When he went after her in the elevator, he'd been determined to come clean. He'd save her and admit he was the reason for the destruction, but only because of his unfulfilled destiny. He was going to ask her to bond with him and keep him sane.

And when her lifespan was over…

Hyperion squeezed his eyes shut and pressed his knuckles to his temples. He'd tried so hard not to think about that, but mortals came with expiration dates, and when Olivia's was up… Well, he didn't mind unraveling then, the universe be damned.

He loved her, and she belonged with him until her dying breath.

That was what he'd meant to tell her.

And then she said she loved him, and he swore his heart would jump out of his chest. Until he caught a glimpse into her thoughts. She wasn't thinking of love and happiness. Her mind was filled with images of her body crushed to death and buried under what remained of the wrecked elevator. She'd kissed him, yes, but her lips tasted of fear and regret. She was afraid. *Of him.* His actions had scared away his true soulmate and sealed his fate. Olivia wouldn't be with him willingly. She'd seen the havoc he could wreak, and it terrified her.

This time he'd saved her, but he was the one who brought the danger to her to begin with, and there was no guarantee it would never happen again. Which was why he had to make this choice for them both.

He called Circe's visage to mind and focused his mental power on it. *"Witch,"* he bellowed in his mind. *"I need you. Show yourself."*

He expected a light show, but instead, the second time he summoned her, her head broke the surface of the sea. He crossed his arms and planted his feet in the sand, at shoulder width.

With every wave that swept over the shore, she came closer, as if she glided along the surf. When the water came up to her waist, she scrunched her nose and averted her face. "There is something you should know," she said.

"What? What other piece of existence-altering news have you for me?" Hyperion boomed. He turned on the glow too, as a reminder that she might be a witch, but he was a god before gods existed.

Still not looking at him, she said, "I'm kind of your granddaughter, and I *really* don't wanna see you like that."

"My granddaugh—?" Hyperion covered his cock with both hands. "How?"

She peeked through her fingers, and then faced him again. "I'm Helios' daughter, which makes you my grandpa." She made a little gesture with her fingers, and a loincloth was secured in place under his palms.

"I… don't know what to do with this information," he said. He hadn't heard from his children since his imprisonment, and with the old gods gone, he certainly didn't expect to find out he had more family. "Should we hug?"

Circe laughed. "Maybe later. First, tell me why you called me here." She came out of the water and stood before him, studying him with her brow furrowed.

"I am out of time," he said.

"Not yet. You still have a couple hours."

"I don't want to draw this out. There is no hope. Olivia is afraid of me. Love cannot blossom in fear." Especially not within an hour or two.

Circe rolled her eyes. "Olivia is in love with you."

"She said she loved me, but I read the fear in her mind." Hyperion's heart constricted at the memory.

A flash of light to his right made him turn. Eros had popped in. Beside him, Olivia swayed with her arms spread out. "You could have warned me," she said, righting herself.

"What is she doing here?" Hyperion funneled his worry into wrath. He'd fled from her so as not to hurt her anymore, and Eros delivered her to him like a lamb to the slaughter.

"*She* is looking for you, you... Titan." Olivia planted her palms on her hips and glared. "I was worried, and you were here. With *her*."

Hyperion followed her gaze to Circe, who held her hands up. "Hey, I literally just arrived," Circe said.

"I don't care." Olivia's eyes threw daggers at him. "He was with me, and he left me to come be with you."

Hyperion rubbed a palm down his face. His body buzzed with raw, barely contained energy. If they didn't do this soon, he'd sink the whole island. "I can't be with you," he told Olivia. "I almost killed you today, because I couldn't control myself. I won't be the reason you perish."

"You *saved* me today," she said.

"Olivia, this isn't up for debate. We cannot be together." To Eros, he said, "Get her out of here."

She stomped her foot, which might have had more of an effect if it were on hard soil, and not warm, golden sand. "No. You can't do this to me. This… hot-and-cold thing is driving me nuts. You can't say you love me one minute, and run away the next. This isn't how things are done in a relationship."

A relationship. If she'd said these words before, when they lay in bed, he'd be the happiest man in creation. Alas, it was too late. Even if she did love him, she was also afraid of him. She associated him with her bloody demise, for Chaos' sake. He lowered his voice and said the only thing guaranteed to keep her away. "I was wrong. I don't love you. It was my loneliness, forcing my words."

Her face crumbled, and her shoulders slumped. She wrapped her arms around herself. "No. You meant it. You love me. I saw it in your eyes." But her voice was small and weak.

And it broke him that he had to hurt her more, to save her later. "I'm sorry. I just don't feel the way I thought I did." It took everything he had, to give her a nonchalant shrug.

Olivia turned to Eros. "Can you please take me home? To New York?"

Hyperion swallowed his pain and nodded. She'd be safe there, and she'd never find out what became of him.

# CHAPTER NINETEEN

Funny, how two days ago her worst problem was too much alcohol in her blood system and a statue coming to life, and yet her life made more sense then than it did tonight.

Within that time frame, she'd found the perfect man, had him declare his love, offered herself up to him, and lost him. Probably to the stunning brunette with the bedroom eyes, who for some reason wore a soaked evening gown.

How could Olivia think he meant it when he said he loved her? He was immortal, and she only had decades to live. Of course he didn't want to be with her. He probably only said what he had to, to get her into bed. Stupid, *stupid* Olivia. Her pulse thudded in her ears. She had to get out of here before she dissolved into tears. If he could turn her away so easily, it shouldn't be that hard for her to forget him when she was back with the people who really cared about her.

And if she kept telling herself that, she might one day believe it.

Why wasn't Eros sweeping her out of here, so she never had to see Hyperion's face again? His beautiful face, with those hard angles and soft eyes that melted her determination even as he cast her out of his life…

"Forgive me, my love," Hyperion said. But his lips didn't move. She'd know; she stared at them, willing them to form proclamations of love instead of the words that tore through her heart.

"What was that?" she asked, taking a step closer to him.

Eros reached for her, but she pulled away. Another minute wouldn't hurt. "Hyperion, what did you say?"

He swallowed audibly. "I said I'm sorry. I misjudged my feelings." Why did he look so miserable, when he was the one calling the shots?

"After that. You called me your love."

Hyperion staggered, like he'd been socked in the gut. "I didn't say that." His eyes were wild. He whispered something after that, but she only caught the end of it. "—hear me?"

"Yes, I can hear you." Her hurt mingled with irritation. What fucking game was this?

Eros chuckled, and the corners of Circe's lips twitched. Were they all in on it?

But no. Hyperion looked as confused as ever. "How is this possible?" This time she saw him form the words.

"Oh I don't know… I have ears, I guess? What are you playing at? You said you don't want me. Why call me your love?" Why wouldn't he let her go, so she could start licking her wounds?

"This can't be. No mortal can hear a Titan's thoughts, unless the Titan projects them." Hyperion studied her face intently.

"Who knows what soulmates are capable of?" Eros stage whispered.

Soulmates? Olivia returned Hyperion's scrutiny, and now she heard more. *Love. Soulmate. Forever.* He wasn't saying the words aloud; she was plucking them from his head. She focused, and a wave of pain hit her chest and radiated throughout her body. It squeezed the air from her lungs and twisted like a knife in her belly. Not her pain. His. At the thought of losing her. *Can't hurt her again. Olivia. Witch can help. Stone. Must. Soon.*

The burst of thoughts was disjointed, but she probed more, until she made sense of them. He was afraid he'd somehow hurt her, and that was why he wanted to cut her loose. That was why Circe was here. She was a witch, who'd turn him back into a statue.

"You love me," Olivia said. "Everything else is bullshit."

He clenched his jaw. "You're afraid of me. I brought destruction into your life. My feelings aren't what matter, when all you see when you look at me is your death."

She ran to him, the warm sand propelling her feet forward, like even the earth wanted them together. She looped her arms around his neck and rose on her tiptoes to press her lips to his. "All I see when I look at you is the man I love," she whispered.

He tensed, not moving to embrace her or return her kiss. His body might as well already be marble. "It's too late. You must go. Forget about me. I am unraveling."

"And this is your chance not to," Circe said.

Eros laughed. "Ah, it's so good to see love conquer all."

They were talking nonsense, but Olivia couldn't be bothered with them. Hyperion's feelings of love washed over her, as tangible as his body in her embrace.

"There's still time." Circe faded into the breeze, the echo of her words trailing after her.

Hyperion finally brought his arms up around Olivia and nuzzled the crook of her neck. "I only wanted to protect you. Unless we're bonded, I am doomed to spiral out of control and destroy everything around me. I didn't want you to be in harm's way." That was what *unraveling* was about. And that was why he'd tried to drive her away.

Olivia wanted to be upset that he'd hide this from her and lie, but it was impossible when she'd glimpsed his pain at losing her. "Circe said there's still time." She bit her bottom lip. "What do we have to do?"

"Make love."

Her cheeks burned. "We did that. A lot."

He grazed his teeth over her shoulder and lowered the strap of her tank top. "You must offer me your heart when I'm inside you."

She wedged a hand between their bodies, to cup his shaft that hardened against her palm. "And your heart?"

"That's already yours."

Olivia molded her body to his and turned her face to him.

Hyperion slanted his mouth over hers. "I'm yours," he said in her head.

She opened her mouth and massaged his invading tongue with her own. "Whatever may come, I'll stay with you until the end of my days," she thought at him. Or until he no longer wanted her. Sadness marred her elation. Her lifespan wasn't a long time, by his standards.

Hyperion walked her backward, until they were inside the cave. "I love you." He swept his hand above the sand and rock and tiny flowers blossomed to form a bed for them.

Olivia allowed him to lay her down on the soft petals and helped him get rid of her top before peeling off her jeans. She hadn't taken the time to pull on underwear when she'd left his suite, so she was now spread before him naked. "Come to me." She'd never before felt so exposed or so safe.

She held out her hands, and he knelt between her parted legs.

Their previous times together, Olivia had been too preoccupied with the newness of everything and the intensity of her pleasure to really take him in.

She'd always found him gorgeous—even with the hair and the beard. Even as a statue. But now he was… She couldn't think of words strong enough to describe how stunning his eyes were when happiness mingled with the hunger in his gaze. She wanted to trace the hard planes of his chest and abs with her tongue, and feel his weight settle between her legs.

He squared his wide shoulders, preening under her scrutiny, and his long, hard shaft bobbed.

Olivia bit the inside of her cheek. How that thing fit in her would remain a mystery, but she couldn't wait to try it again.

"Say you love me," he said.

She snapped her head back up to look at his face. His solemn expression reined in her lustful thoughts. Her heart thudded in her chest. Why was she stalling? Maybe because despite his assurances, she was but a brief moment in his eternity.

Which didn't change how she felt. She smiled and arched an eyebrow. "You know I do."

"I need to hear it, Olivia."

She lifted her knees and swayed her hips. "I love you."

He glided his gaze down her body, heavy like a caress. "Say you're mine." He focused on her pussy and flared his nostrils, and fresh moisture pooled between her legs.

"Again?" she asked, and when he tickled her side, her laugh echoed in the cave.

"Say it," he ordered in her head.

"I'm yours," she replied the same way.

Hyperion splayed his fingers on her inner thighs and separated her nether lips with his thumbs.

"This is mine," he whispered.

Olivia pushed into his touch. "Then take it."

"Impatient." He gave her clitoris a little twist. "I was thinking of taking my time. Tasting you."

She snorted. "Not like the world may end if we don't hurry up, or whatever."

Hyperion's mouth found the apex of her thighs, without him moving. He held her gaze, while he made her feel his tongue slide inside her and then lick a trail to her clit. In her head, he wrapped his lips around the sensitive button and sucked, and her hips bucked. The sensation was incredible, but not as thrilling as the hunger the real Hyperion watched her with.

Could she return the favor?

She closed her eyes and thought of having him on his back as she sucked on the tender flesh of his throat, beneath his ear.

Real-Hyperion whooshed out a breath and sat back on his haunches. "How did you—?"

This was fun. She brought one finger to her lips, to shush him, and thought of curling her fist over his length. Her fingers wouldn't close around his girth, but she squeezed and tugged.

His cock jumped in her fantasy, and she ran the pad of her thumb over the head, to spread the bead of precum. She slipped her fist from the tip of his cock to the base and back up, tightening her grip on every upstroke.

The Hyperion kneeling before her panted, and his mental ministrations had stopped.

Olivia thought of climbing in his lap and positioning herself above his cock. The head nudged at her opening, and she tilted her hips so it bumped her clit. She conjured her memories from earlier today and felt herself taking in the first inch of his length.

"Ah *Hades*." The real Hyperion grabbed her by the ankles and pulled her to him.

Olivia fluttered her eyes open, as he settled her legs on his shoulders. He clasped her buttocks and lifted her, aligning her with his shaft.

She pumped her hips, letting him glide along her sleekness.

Hyperion growled and dug his fingers in her flesh, and Olivia barely had time to brace herself, before he drove inside her in a single, quick thrust.

*God in Heaven*, he was huge.

He was big yesterday too, but then she'd expected her first time to hurt. This position allowed him to go deeper, and he stretched her to the point of pain.

And she fucking loved it.

Hyperion used his grip on her ass to propel her to him again and again, hitting deeper with each lunge, and pleasure built inside until it overtook the pain. It overtook the fear over what came next. It overtook reason. She was being taken by a Titan—a primordial being, a god that predated the continents.

She was going to come.

"I'm close," she managed.

He let her legs flop to the crooks of his elbows, and pummeled inside her faster, as incorporeal hands kneaded her breasts and pinched her nipples into hardened peaks.

Olivia needed just a little more. More friction.

She tried to wedge a hand between their bodies, and Hyperion stopped her with a growl.

Two invisible fingers tweaked her clit, and a third one prodded her ass. She clenched reflexively, but Hyperion rolled his hips and hit that bundle of nerves he had such ease locating, and she gave herself over to him completely, as her orgasm crashed over her in a wave that had her grasping for purchase and gasping for breath.

# CHAPTER TWENTY

Hyperion tasted Olivia's release at the same time she squeezed his seed out of him.

He'd meant for this to last—at least long enough to save creation—but lost control when she'd gripped him like a velvet vice. He'd satisfied his soulmate, though. And since he was a Titan, he needed no recovery time.

He draped both of her legs over one arm and caressed her hip with his free hand.

*So beautiful.*

Her skin held a faint tan, except for the pale bikini lines. Her perfect breasts were perky, the nipples straining toward his touch. He cupped one and rolled the nipple under his thumb, then squeezed till a groan escaped Olivia's lips.

"Okay?" he asked.

She nodded and lowered her eyelids, her expression one of bliss.

Her nether lips were swollen and ripe like a peach, as he pulled out of her and slowly pushed back inside. With her legs pressed together like this, the added pressure threatened to unravel him faster than Zeus' failsafe, but the position allowed him to give her more of his length. And it provided him a perfect view of her dazed smile and the curve of a buttock at the same time.

Olivia moaned something incoherent, and he ached to kiss her mouth, but that would mean adding several inches to his height, and his cock would grow accordingly. Could she take more?

A couple inches wouldn't hurt. "You look incredible, taking all I can give you," he murmured, as he let his body grow just enough for his lips to reach hers. Olivia bowed her back, and he paused, but she buried her hands in his hair and sucked on his tongue greedily, her inner walls convulsing around him.

He drove into her like this, her body folded into his, while he drew out their pleasure, until he felt her tremble with another release.

"My heart is yours," he whispered against her lips, sending his spendings deep into her core.

"My heart is yours," Olivia replied. "Forever."

But she was mortal.

He clenched his teeth against the unwelcome thought and clung to her reply and Eros' words. *Who knows what soulmates are capable of?* Besides, lesser gods had granted mortals eternity. No reason he couldn't do the same. He'd find a way.

He brushed Olivia's hair out of her face, to meet her hooded eyes.

"Was this all?" she asked.

Hyperion pursed his lips. "I can keep going, but I may damage you."

She laughed, and his cock stirred back to life, but he let it lie wedged between her thighs. "Is my endurance funny to you?" he asked with a fake scowl.

"I didn't mean the sex—I already can't feel my legs, so yes, let's take a break for a few. Maybe grab a bite." She laughed again when he nibbled on the taut flesh of her breast. "*Stop it.* I meant, shouldn't there be some sign that we prevented your unraveling? Another light show or something?"

"Deus-ex-machina time." Eros' voice made Hyperion blink to the entrance of the cave. Only he was allowed to eye his soulmate naked and disheveled.

"Oh, relax, big guy. Not like I haven't witnessed every sex scene *ever,*" Eros said from behind him.

Hyperion spun and saw Eros handing Olivia her clothes.

"Still wanna leave?" Eros waggled his eyebrows at her.

Olivia sat up and held her shirt in front of her. Her glare looked murderous, but a grin tugged at her lips. "Now I want *you* to leave," she said. "Go somewhere far, far away, and leave us alone."

Eros blinked to the opposite side of the cave when Hyperion sent a fist flying his way. He huffed and crossed his arms. "Hey, I'm only here because someone requested a light show." He snapped his fingers, and drops of liquid light in all possible hues rained down on them. "*Tah dah.*"

Hyperion bit down his irritation in favor of more urgent matters. "So it's done? I'm safe to be around?"

"Yes, yes. You are. You'll be glad to know that your life forces' merging means Olivia will live for as long as you do. And since your big ass is virtually indestructible… I'd start making long-term plans."

This was the best news he could ever hope for. Unless Olivia objected.

One look at her beaming smile set Hyperion at ease. She was his forever, because she wanted to be.

Eros leaned back against the stone and sighed. "Now we have to figure out what to do about Atlas. Last I heard, he was in the sea, but Circe said—"

"Has he awoken?" Now he was in no danger of creating a hole in the world, Hyperion was ready to throw another punch at Eros for procrastinating and *still* looking at his soulmate.

Eros frowned. "Well, no, but—"

"Leave," Olivia said, pointing at Eros.

"Now." Hyperion took a menacing step his way.

There would be time to save the world again later, though he doubted Atlas would have trouble reining himself in. He was always the most self-composed of their bunch.

For now, Hyperion's first priority was spending quality time with his soulmate.

"What does your heart desire?" he asked her when the god of love popped out of their cave.

"I'm still hungry. I could go for Chinese."

"Done." He gathered her in his arms and blinked them across the world. They'd have to find clothes before he could feed her.

# CHAPTER TWENTY-ONE

"So you spent this morning saving the world *on your back*, and then Tall Dark and Stupid-Hot flew you to China?" Christina gaped.

"He calls it *blinking*. It's like you disappear from one place and appear at another the next moment. Very disorienting." Add in the time difference and the fact that he landed them naked smack-dab in the middle of a market in Shanghai, in the early afternoon, and he'd had to do *a lot* of compulsion before she was dressed in silk and sat in front of a plate of fried dumplings.

Christina nodded. "I bet. So what's the plan now?"

Olivia chewed on her bottom lip. "He wants to meet my parents." He wanted to do things properly—ask for her hand in marriage—since she told him they would appreciate it. Truth was she was torn between showing him off and keeping him to herself. Not that she planned on telling anyone else the truth about him anytime soon. After a few years, her family and friends were bound to notice she and Hyperion didn't age, but by then, she hoped they'd love him as much as she did and would accept him.

"And then?" Christina asked.

"Then… since we're now bonded, we'll go see his brother Prometheus—"

"Taken?"

"Very. By a mermaid, if I got that right. Eros and Circe showed up before I came to see you, and we got an info dump. The gist of it is Prometheus and his soulmate will help us get Atlas out of the Acropolis museum before he awakens and shocks a poor tourist to death." Or get the Greek and NATO military forces after him, if he decided to unfold to his full size.

Christina pulled out a duffel bag from under her bed and went to the closet. She opened the door and started taking her clothes off the hangers.

"What are you doing?" Olivia asked.

Christina shoved an armful of clothes into the bag and kept going. "Atlas is single, right?"

"Yes."

"And huge and gorgeous?"

Olivia grinned. "Probably."

"Well, I want me one of those." Christina opened a drawer, grimaced, and then slid it all the way out and emptied its contents on top of her clothes.

"It doesn't work that way. Soulmates are predestined."

Christina went on, as if Olivia hadn't spoken. "I guess I can leave cosmetics behind, but I'll need shoes." She pulled the edges of the bag together, but it took some effort to make them meet. She looked at Olivia over her shoulder. "Can we get shoes?"

There was no winning when Christina was this determined.

Olivia pursed her lips, to hide her smile. "We can get shoes."

"Good. Then I'm ready." Christina slung the bag over her shoulder. "When are we leaving?"

# EPILOGUE

"Two down, and how many more to go?" Eros lounged on the chaise longue in Circe's bedroom, watching as she brushed her long, brown hair. The sea world might see her as a withered hag, but she always appeared gorgeous and young and sexy as all hell to him.

"I can't see beyond the next one, but at least it's not Kronos." She met his gaze in the mirror. "Could you not look at my ass when we're talking business?"

He blew her a kiss. "It's always business with you these days."

Circe placed her brush on her dresser and turned to look at him. "Poor baby is feeling so neglected that his lover puts saving the world above sexy fun times." She dropped to her knees and crawled to him, swishing her rounded bottom.

Eros sat up and held out a hand, to help her climb in his lap. "I just don't understand why we can't tell all of them the truth, find the souls of the Titanesses and… I don't know—allocate them to their destined mates?"

"You know, for being the god of love, you're not very romantic." Circe laughed and tossed back her hair. "Don't you know people want to fight for love, to appreciate it?"

He kissed up the golden skin of her neck to the spot under her ear, and inched his palms beneath her silken skirt. "You're wicked."

"Just wait till you see what happens with Atlas." She kissed him and arched her back, so his fingers found her folds.

She'd keep the news about his mother to herself, until… after.

# End of Book Two

# Breathe

a novella

# CHAPTER ONE

"Are you sure someone's coming?" Christina wrapped her arms around her waist and dipped her toes into the cool water. With the sun dipping lower in the sky, her fuchsia bikini no longer seemed like the best choice of outfit, but it wasn't like she could look online for what would be considered appropriate attire for this evening. It wasn't every day your roommate-for-the-summer-turned-BFF took you to an underwater kingdom, to meet her soulmate's Titan brother, who was mated to a mermaid, who happened to be the daughter of the king of the freaking sea.

And Christina couldn't repeat that sentence out loud in front of anyone but the present company.

Olivia looked to Hyperion, who nodded. They weren't in swimwear, because they'd be *blinking* to Vythos, unlike Christina, who would apparently take an underwater cab of some sort.

A head poked out of the water in the distance, and Hyperion barely squinted in that direction, before saying, "That's him. I'll introduce you, and we'll meet the two of you at the palace." He waved at the man, who swam toward them, no sign of a submarine in sight.

"How exactly will he take me there?" Christina had asked before too, but Hyperion had glossed over that part.

"Magic," he said now.

The man stopped when the water reached his waist.

His eyes sparkled like sapphires under the perfect dark arches of his brows, and his long, blue tresses clung to his chiseled cheekbones and down the corded muscles of his neck, to his broad shoulders.

"*Holly fuck*, he looks like Aquaman with blue hair," Christina whispered. "Why didn't you tell me?" She elbowed Olivia in the ribs. Not that it'd hurt, now that Olivia was all new and improved and immortal.

"Good evening," the man said in Greek.

Christina knew enough of the language to introduce herself and order food at a taverna, but anything more was a stretch. "Hello. I'm Christina."

"Palaemon." He tapped his chest with his open palm.

"Hey." Olivia waved at him and said something in Greek that Christina didn't catch. It was unfair that Olivia now spoke a gazillion foreign languages.

Palaemon smiled, nodded, and replied in the same language. He motioned for Christina to approach. "Come."

She looked at Olivia, who nudged her forward. "Go. I'll see you in a few."

Christina trusted her. She reluctantly put one foot in front of the other and walked toward Palaemon. The water chilled her legs and made her shiver. It wasn't that bad, but it'd take a couple minutes to get used to. Her nipples didn't take the memo. They were so hard, they hurt. She looked from where they pushed against her bikini top to Palaemon's half-smirk. Was he staring at her? He was. His gaze felt heavy on her body, caressing her more languidly than the waves did. The water had covered her breasts by the time she reached him, and she felt hot. It had nothing to do with the temperature, and everything to do with the man in front of her.

She gave him her sweetest smile. "What now?"

Palaemon turned his back to her. *Rude.*

"Hey. What am I supposed to do?" she asked.

He reached behind him, found her arms, and wrapped them around him. They wouldn't meet across his wide chest. He kept his grip on her wrists as he dove underwater.

What was he doing? She kicked her legs and felt his between them. No, not legs. He had a freaking tail. *Damn.* He was a mermaid? Disappointment that such a gorgeous man was part fish almost overshadowed her panic when she realized they weren't coming up for air. She was going to drown. And then she'd come back as a ghost and haunt Olivia forever for doing this to her.

"Breathe." His voice, as masculine and sexy as the rest of him, startled her.

"What?" she asked, but no sound reached her ears.

"You won't drown. There's an air bubble around your head. Sound doesn't travel through it, though."

Then how was he speaking to her? And hey—she understood him. Did he speak English? Not like she could ask.

"I can hear your thoughts underwater. Language doesn't matter." He kicked his tail—she still couldn't wrap her mind around that—and took them deeper, as their surroundings darkened.

"What are you?" she thought at him.

"A sea daimon. King Nereus trusts us with transporting his daughters, so you're safe with me."

If all sea daimons were as hot as this one, King Nereus' daughters must be really bummed out about the tail part.

"So you think I'm hot, huh?"

Shit shit shit shit shit. Now he knew she found him hot. Could he also tell she was wet, and not because of the water surrounding them?

His laugh made no sound, but his back and scaled hips vibrated against her, and she pressed herself to him, partly to hide her embarrassment but mostly because it felt good.

"Wrap your legs around my waist," he said. "It'll be more comfortable."

Christina folded her legs around him, the scrape of scales against her skin oddly arousing. She wouldn't think of what a pity it was the clung to his back instead of being wrapped in his arms. Or what a pity it was he didn't have a cock. How did fish… copulate?

His grip on her tightened, and she felt his *hips*—it was the only word that worked, even if tails didn't come with those—swish harder. "We're almost there." His voice in her head was raspier. Darker. It promised things he couldn't deliver.

Damn it.

Palaemon laughed again. She needed to learn to keep her thoughts to herself. At least he wasn't touchy about his cock, or lack thereof, like human males were. And she really need to stop thinking. Now. *La la la.* Think of something other than how hot the man between her legs made her.

"See that light up ahead?" he asked.

She did indeed. A pale golden glow spread out beneath them, and as they closed in on it, she made out shapes that looked like buildings, inside crystal domes. This was the underwater kingdom, and in its middle, in the largest dome, stood a magnificent castle that seemed carved into coral and encased in gold.

"Hold on tight." Palaemon headed straight for the dome.

This would hurt. She squeezed her eyes shut, ducked her head behind his back, and… For a second, there was nothing around her. No water. Just air. And then, Palaemon hit something and rolled. Her back smashed into something soft that absorbed her fall, and he slipped out of her arms.

And stood.

On legs.

Between which, from a thatch of blue curls, hung a glorious, big cock.

It jumped under her scrutiny, and she jerked her gaze up to Palaemon's face. He was staring at her, expressionless but for the clenching of his law.

Christina licked her lips. "Thank you for the ride," she said. Could he read her thoughts now that they weren't technically in water? She tapped her chest over her heart and said in Greek, "Thank you."

Palaemon gave a curt nod, climbed on the pillows, and jumped through the dome and into the water, his legs giving way to a tail the same color as his hair.

A door Christina hadn't even noticed opened, and Olivia poked her head out. "There you are. I thought Palaemon would deliver you to the front door, but King Nereus said this is where he always dropped off Pherusa." She held out a green robe. "You need to put this on for dinner."

Pherusa was Prometheus' soulmate. Christina had heard all about her from Olivia and Hyperion. She'd also heard how Prometheus had been jealous of a sea daimon before he finally believed Pherusa loved only him. Pieces clicked together. Palaemon was Pherusa's daimon. The one who might still be hung up on her.

Christina found her footing and slipped her arms in the sleeves of the robe, then tied it around her waist. "King Nereus just let you roam around the castle?" she asked.

Olivia shrugged. "He said he likes my inquisitive mind. He's rather casual, for a god king." She looped one arm around Christina's and tugged. "Come. Let's meet everyone. King Nereus asked his witch to help you with your Greek, to make communication easier. Still, don't expect to remember everybody's names."

# CHAPTER TWO

He smiled to himself as he navigated through the water toward his cave at the outskirts of Vythos. The human—*Christina*—was fun. Obsessed with penises, but fun. And cute, if you went for bubbly blondes with huge, blue eyes and large breasts. He didn't have a type, but if he did, it'd be someone with eyes green like the sea and a leaner frame. Someone like Pherusa. Who was just his friend and happily bonded to her male. He wasn't pining over her. Hadn't avoided the palace because he couldn't witness her happiness. If anything, he was happy for his friend and giving her space while she and her soulmate got reacquainted.

And the thought didn't taste as bitter as he expected it to. Maybe because he still felt the warmth of Christina's breasts pressed to his back. She blushed the most delightful pink when he caught her gazing at him. And her lips… Rosy and full, they seemed made for laughing. And kissing. And sucking.

Luckily, his half-fish form didn't let his anatomy betray his thoughts, and with everyone who knew Christina safely inside the palace bubble, he was in no danger of being overheard.

Unlike merpeople and Nereus' family, Palaemon didn't automatically change into this form underwater. He could shift into any living creature at will. In fact, he'd looked fully human when he first laid eyes on Christina, but opted for the tail before she reached him, because it made swimming easier—as well as hiding unsolicited erections from innocent human eyes.

With his cave in sight, he ordered his body to reshape into his human form and strode the rest of the distance to the bubble surrounding the cavern, and then through it.

He lay atop his coral bed. He should be back at the palace for dinner, but someone would fetch him, and in the meantime, he could take a nap. It had been a long day, with patrolling the Aegean for signs of Titan activity, and he'd been moody when Circe suggested he go bring the human below.

Christina's smile when she introduced herself had made his weariness evaporate though, and then, when she wrapped her arms and legs around him, every curve of her supple form pressed against him…

He closed his fist around his erection and tugged. He didn't make a habit of this. Pleasuring himself while thinking of an unattainable female wasn't his style. He could have a woman if he wanted, but he wasn't interested. His duty to Vythos, as one of King Nereus' generals was his *raison d'être*. It fulfilled him.

Yet he kept tugging. And thinking of the line of Christina's mouth. And the waves of her blond hair. And the hint of a nipple almost slipping out of her top.

He spilled all over his lap, his mind painting a vivid picture of Christina licking him clean that threatened to make him hard again.

In the distance, he heard the horn calling the generals to the palace. No time for a nap, then. No matter. He felt more refreshed than he'd been in ages. He hurried outside and cleaned up, then brought his armor out of the treasure chest he'd salvaged and put it on one piece at a time. The blue steel glinted in the pale glow coming from outside, as he secured it in place. It covered him from his neck to the middle of his thighs, allowing his tail full movement, and keeping him reasonably decent while he walked on human legs. He was expected to wear it at official gatherings. Dinner at the palace wasn't *that* official, but he refused to make it through the night in one of the seaweed robes Queen Doris loved so much.

The robes hadn't bothered him before, but Christina hadn't been around to see him in one before. Besides, blue was much more his color than green was.

By the time he was shown inside the ballroom, everyone was seated at the long semicircular table that span half the great hall.

"Finally." Nereus nodded. "I was about to send Delphinos after you."

"My king, I apologize. Time slipped by me." Palaemon gave a sweeping bow. Nereus demanded no such shows of reverence, but they had guests, and some formalities were necessary.

"Come sit with us. We saved you a seat," Olivia said in Greek. She pointed at the empty chair between her and Christina, whose gaze was trained to her plate.

"Thank you." Palaemon took the seat and winced when the chair screeched as he pulled it back in place.

Olivia smiled. "Christina and I were actually just talking about you. Tell us, what do sea daimons do, exactly?"

The way she phrased it made him sound like a utensil. "We basically keep the world safe," he said as non-smugly as he could.

Christina snorted. Had she understood?

"And how do you do that?" Olivia asked.

"What is this? Twenty questions?" Christina said. So she did speak Greek now? The sea witch must have had something to do with it.

"What? I'm curious," Olivia said.

"I get it, but let him take a bite first. The poor man literally just sat down." Christina gasped and brought her dainty hand to her mouth. "Oh my God. Is that specieist?"

Palaemon laughed. From the other side of the table, Delphinos arched an eyebrow at him and whispered something in his soulmate's ear. Halie nodded and looked at Palaemon through lowered eyelashes.

"What?" Palaemon asked.

"You're laughing," Pherusa said from Halie's other side. "I don't think I've ever heard you laugh before."

Thankfully, Queen Doris chose that moment to make a toast to their guests, and soon the sounds of silverware clanking against china rivaled the light chatter filling the room. Palaemon was off the hook.

Christina trailed her fork across her plate, not touching her crispy seaweed salad.

"You don't like it?" he asked her.

"You could have said *no*. Didn't have to laugh at me." Her words were hushed, but they found their way to his ears and down to his chest, to wind around his heart. She thought he was mocking her?

He covered her hand with his and tried to ignore the jolt of desire that raced along his skin at the contact. "Forgive me. I meant no offense. Your question surprised me. I very much think of myself as a man." Leaning closer, he whispered, "One with a cock."

The blush that creeped up her neck and to her cheeks clashed with the green of the robe that had never looked more appealing. She tucked her hair behind her ear and whispered back, "Really? I didn't notice."

He should pull her in his lap and let her feel his cock and the fact that it was rock hard, but he had an inkling the king might not appreciate the initiative. Instead, he pretended to wipe his mouth with his napkin. "I'll have to show you after dinner," he said, relying on the piece of cloth to muffle his words.

"Show her what? I want to see too," Olivia said.

Christina let out a snort and choked, her bosom heaving with the effort to breathe. No, wait. She was laughing and trying to mask it. And the sliver of skin revealed at the opening of her robe called for his fingers to trace it.

"So what are we seeing?" Olivia asked.

All talk ceased, and everyone's gazes were on Palaemon, waiting for his answer.

"His seashell collection," Christina said.

Palaemon sent a quick prayer to Oceanus, wherever he was, that Olivia didn't care to see those, *since he didn't have any*.

And… prayer answered. "Oh," she said. "Oh, okay. I was thinking maybe you'd show her around the city."

"*Kingdom*, not city," Prometheus interjected, not looking up from his dish. "I'm sure Palaemon would love to show you around tonight. After he shows Christina his shells. I hear he has a large cephalopod he's rather proud of."

Hyperion chuckled.

Damned Titans and their super-sensitive hearing. Palaemon had no doubt they'd made out his private conversation with Christina loud and clear.

"Not sure I wanna see that. I hear those things can be icky." Christina arched an eyebrow Palaemon's way.

He gave her a smug smile. "You can judge for yourself. Unless you're scared it might bite."

"How could a husk bite her?" Queen Doris sounded perplexed.

Prometheus laughed heartily, and Hyperion joined in, while Pherusa and Olivia exchanged knowing glances. Lovely. The protogod bastards had shared what they heard with their soulmates through their mental link. Palaemon should drop this.

He glanced at Christina, but she was diligently avoiding his gaze, as she tried a mouthful of sea anemone. "This is incredible." She moaned.

Matter closed, then. She was obviously not interested. And someone should tell his cock that.

# CHAPTER THREE

Sitting so close to him made it impossible not to touch him. God knew she tried. But every so often, his arm would brush hers or his thigh would press into her leg, and her body would tingle with anticipation. *Of what?*

Had he actually offered to show her his penis? Or were they really talking about shells? Oh—or was he offering to show her his penis because Pherusa was close enough to hear and he hoped to make her jealous?

Christina's food went from spicy to bland in the time it took that thought to form. She pressed her legs together, so she wouldn't feel the warmth of his skin through the robe, and tucked in her elbows. The thought of being used as a prop for him to show off to another woman—a very taken woman—raised her hackles.

She managed to make it through the rest of the meal with minimum contact. Thankfully, with so many people at the table, she could socialize without talking to him. The Nereid beside her was full of questions about life ashore. King Nereus would have trouble keeping this one in Vythos, if he didn't already.

Christina tried to keep her sigh of relief inaudible when the king rose from his seat, signaling the end of dinner. Christina hurried to stand and bow her head along with the others.

"Thank you all for joining us tonight." Nereus nodded toward the double doors of the ballroom, and two servants hurried to the table. "Please show our guests to their rooms." To Christina, he said, "It was a pleasure meeting you. I will see you at breakfast."

Christina bit back her questions until he and Queen Doris were out of the room, and then turned to Olivia. "*Rooms? Breakfast?* You said it was just a visit," she hissed.

Olivia grimaced. "I thought it was. Apparently, Prometheus and Hyperion need to talk strategy with Nereus tomorrow, so we have to stick around. I guess Palaemon could take you back tonight, if you're set on it, but really"—her eyes glowed—"when will you get another chance to be in a freaking *underwater palace*?"

Christina couldn't handle being alone with Palaemon again this soon. Besides, Olivia was right. This was a once-in-a-lifetime opportunity. She wouldn't waste it because a hot guy was messing with her head and her hormones. "Okay. One night. But we're leaving tomorrow after breakfast."

The servant girls—one with purple hair and matching eyes, and one whose hair was a light-teal color and her eyes the orange of corals—led Hyperion, Olivia, and Christina out the gilded double doors of the ballroom and across a shiny hallway to a winding staircase. The banisters on both sides were carved into intricate scenes of… orgies? Yes, those were no doubt bodies, twisted together. Cheeks burning, Christina turned her gaze ahead and hurried after Olivia and Hyperion, who seemed to know the way.

Christina was the only one panting after the second set of stairs, and wasn't too shy about clutching her side and heaving for breath. "Give me a minute, and I'll be right with you."

"We've arrived." The teal-haired servant—mermaid?—unlocked the first door on the wide corridor and handed Christina the key. "This is your room. The guest wing was built to accommodate humans, so it ought to cater to all your needs. Should you require anything else, pull the cord by the bed. Your friends will be at the end of the hallway. The king said you might want a few sets of walls between you, to assure a quiet night." With a beaming smile, she spun on her heel and made her way back to the stairs.

"Wait," Christina called out. "What's your name?" But the young woman was gone. The other servant led a giggling Olivia down the corridor, Hyperion scowling at their backs.

"Goodnight," Olivia managed. "We'll try to be quiet."

Sure they would. Christina waved her off and cautiously pushed the door all the way open. Judging by the opulent ballroom, she expected the furniture to be carved out of coral, with gold liberally strewn across most available surfaces, but the humongous bed seemed made of driftwood, and the bright-blue throw pillows were the only color in the stark-white room. Despite the open space and sparse furniture—two nightstands, a vanity table with its mirror and stool, and an armchair at the far corner—it felt clean and welcoming, not sterile and faceless.

She padded to the bed, the floor cool beneath her bare feet, and took off her robe. The servant girl said this part of the palace was built with humans in mind. Did that mean it included indoor plumbing? The door to her left would hopefully lead to a bathroom, where she could shower. Did merpeople shower? Did people who lived underwater need to?

Did Palaemon? She wouldn't mind sharing a shower with him.

No. *Bad Christina.* She should be thinking about the awesomeness of this place and how unbelievable it was that much of mythology was true and how it only took a touch by a witch for her to be fluent in Greek now. Not pining over someone else's castoffs, especially when there could be no future between her and the—dreamy, incredible, magic—daimon.

Like, what would happen if they did hook up, and she fell for him? She couldn't leave her whole life ashore to come live down here. And could Palaemon even survive on land?

She was overthinking this. Not like she'd see him again. Except maybe at breakfast. And when he took her back to shore. *If* he did. She was introduced to other daimons at dinner. One of them might be providing underwater-taxi services tomorrow.

A knock at the door snapped her out of her Palaemon-shaped musings. She haphazardly threw the robe over her shoulders and hurried to get it. It would probably be Olivia, come to gossip about dinner.

It wasn't. Blue eyes that sparkled like sapphires looked down at her beneath a blue mane.

"Palaemon?" she whispered. Was he here to show her his… cephalopod?

He nodded. "I wanted to apologize for embarrassing you. It was not my intention."

His gaze challenged her, and she never backed down from a challenge. "I wasn't embarrassed for me. I just wasn't sure you'd want everyone at the table—especially Pherusa—to know what you'd said." She watched him for signs of discomfort at the Nereid's name, and her gut soured when she caught his tiny flinch.

"Pherusa has nothing to do with this," he said after too long a pause.

So what was *this*? A one-time fuck with a human chick? "There is no *this*. Apology accepted. Goodnight." She made to close the door, but he stuck his foot at the opening and shouldered his way in.

"If there is no *this*, why are your cheeks scarlet? Why is your breathing shallow?" he asked. "I can hear the blood rushing in your veins, and I don't even have amplified hearing. You want me, and I want you, and Pherusa has nothing to do with this."

Her traitorous gaze traveled down the glinting metal of his armor to the muscular thighs beneath it. Was he hard now? It must be painful, pressing against the unyielding plate that encased his pelvis and hips. She licked her lips, feeling parched, and backstepped inside the room to let him enter. "Show me."

# CHAPTER FOUR

This was insane. He'd only come over to apologize for being presumptuous. Christina was his king's guest, and Palaemon had insulted her. He was here to fix this, because keeping the peace was part of his duty to the kingdom of Vythos.

Instead he'd all but told the human he wanted to rut with her. And she was willing.

She swept her tongue across her bottom lip again, and he forgot all about duty, as his cock strained to break through his armor. "If I show you, you'll have to show me," he heard himself say. It was only fair.

Christina gulped and nodded.

"Take off that robe." Issuing orders came easily to him; he'd been a general for centuries.

It should come as no surprise that Christina let the robe glide down her body and pool to the floor without hesitation. "Now you," she said. Her nipples stretched the material covering her breasts—a material so thin, he made out the outline of her areolas.

He shook his head, forcing his gaze back to her face. "Take off your top."

She hugged herself. "It's your turn."

"Take off your top. Don't make me say it again." He expected her to ask, *or what?* or tell him to leave her room, but she dropped her arms and heaved a sigh before reaching behind her and undoing the straps holding the thing in place. It still clung to her, and he watched mesmerized as she peeled it off, leaving her creamy flesh uncovered.

He wanted to taste her skin. Trap a nipple between his teeth and feel the hard peak with his tongue. Graze it with his palm before kneading her supple flesh.

He wanted to own her.

The need to claim her was overwhelming, let alone surprising. For years, he'd believed his feelings for Pherusa went beyond friendship; she'd been his responsibility and should therefore belong to him. Those feelings were tame, compared to the ferocity of his desire for Christina. He didn't even know this human, but she was for him.

She would be his. Tonight.

"Still too many clothes," he told her.

She gave him a defiant look, the squaring of her shoulders pushing out her breasts. "Not until you take off that armor."

His hands tingled. He ached to cup her face and kiss her and spank her bottom for her insolence. "You've seen me fully naked. I won't shed my armor until we're even."

She turned her back to him, and for a second he thought she'd dismissed him, but then she leaned forward, hooked her thumbs in the elastic of her bottoms, and glided the scrap of fabric down her perfect legs. The curve of her ass arched toward him, and it was all he could do not to cross the distance between them and grab one cheek in each hand.

Her panties on the floor, Christina straightened, stepped out of them, and turned toward him. The scarlet of her cheeks had spread down her neck and chest, but she held his gaze. "Well?" She spread her arms to the sides with the grace of an anemone. He'd known her breasts were perfect for his hands even before she was undressed, but he hadn't imagined she'd be smooth and hairless between her legs.

He trailed his gaze back to her face and her gorgeous blue eyes, such a different, paler hue than his. "You're beautiful." He didn't mean it as a compliment; he was stating a fact.

Her watery smile belied the confidence in her stance. "And you're still dressed."

Her gaze followed his every move, as he undid the straps holding his breastplate in place, and bared first his chest and then his loins to her. His cock oozed a clear drop of precum and jerked toward her, as determined to be buried in her body as Palaemon was.

Christina swallowed audibly, making no effort to look up from his shaft. "You're hard."

"Have been since I met you." He grinned. "While I was in human form, that is. You know—the one with a cock."

Her startled laugh sounded like music to his ears, but the silence that followed was awkward. The couple meters between them felt vast, and with every second that passed, crossing it became more difficult.

"Now what?" Christina asked.

There was only one possible answer to that. "Now, I take you."

She shivered, and her nipples puckered further.

Palaemon didn't wait for more of an invitation. He strode to her, buried one hand in her golden mane, and swept in for a kiss. She moaned the moment he touched his lips to hers, and opened up, her warm mouth inviting. He thrust his tongue between her lips, and she timidly massaged it with hers. His erection dug into her stomach, as she clutched his shoulders and pressed into him.

She tasted of the sea anemone and sugar, and he wanted to savor all of her. Pulling on her hair, he arched her neck so he could nibble on her earlobe. "Remember my name. I want you to scream it when you come on my tongue."

She jerked back to look at him, and he waggled his eyebrows before grabbing her ass with both hands, lifting her, and tossing her back on the bed. Her hair fanned on the white bedsheets, and her skin was flushed, and she was more gorgeous than any nymph or Nereid or even goddess he'd ever laid eyes on. It made sense that he'd fall on his knees to worship her.

He crawled on the mattress between her legs and used his arms to pin her thighs open while he brushed his lips across her naked mound. "So smooth." Pointing his tongue into a spear, he drew a line up her slit.

Christina pushed down against him, and he bit her inner thigh, making her squeal. He laved the tender flesh with his lips and tongue, and then returned to the part of her that had him drooling—her bare pussy. He lapped at her juices like they were nectar. Her sweetness sparked on his taste buds as he pushed his tongue inside her, augmenting his desire. He sucked on her clitoris, and Christina fisted handfuls of his hair and ground into his mouth.

"You're so good at this," she muttered. "So good…"

He'd meant to make her orgasm with his mouth, but he needed to be sheathed inside her tight pussy. *Now.* "Don't come until I tell you to," he said.

"Typical male. Like these things happen on demand." Christina's eyeroll gave way to a naughty smirk, as he climbed up her body to give her another kiss. His cock nudged her entrance, and she tilted her hips.

"I owe you an oral release," he whispered against her lips.

She smiled and pressed down against him. *Oceanus,* she was wet. Unwilling to restrain himself a moment longer, Palaemon drove forward, burying himself inside her in one hard push. Her walls closed around his length like a velvet fist, threatening to undo him.

"I'll hold you to that." She scraped her fingernails down his arms hard enough to raise welts, and thrust her hips up to meet his next thrust. "Now fuck me."

Oh, his little mortal was a hellion. He smacked her thigh. "You don't tell me what to do, female."

Christina growled and rocked her hips faster. She liked it hard. Good. He pounded into her, and almost came undone when she lifted her leg to wrap her arm around it. She was spread out beneath him, allowing him to go deeper.

Her grin was feral, as she locked her gaze on his. He could get lost in the blue of her eyes.

But the blue faded under a bright green that overtook her irises and spread to the whites.

# CHAPTER FIVE

Palaemon froze on top of her. "What are you?" His wide eyes matched his bewildered tone.

Huh? Ah—the leg thing. "Cheerleader. Was. In high school." Why did he stop moving? She was hovering on the precipice of climax for the second time. Just a nudge would send her over. She clenched around him and felt his cock jerk, but except for that and the muscle ticking on his jaw, he was perfectly still.

"Not what I mean. Your eyes…" He trailed off.

Christina blinked rapidly. "What about them?"

"What are you?" he asked again. His dark brows came together in a scowl that scared her.

*Ha! Now* she was scared. An ancient deity who could sprout a tail had her pinned beneath him. He was deep inside her, *without protection*—that last part would be more worrisome if Olivia hadn't told her Titans procreated at will. Christina assumed the same went for other gods. But was she right?

And lying here, hugging her leg to her chest, a huge supernatural dick inside her, wasn't the time to freak out.

"I am me," she muttered.

Palaemon lifted his palm and brought it down on her thigh with a *crack*. The sharp sting shot straight to her core, and she moaned. She needed him to move. To do something for the throbbing in her pussy.

"You're not human." Palaemon landed another slap, this one closer to her ass, and she arched her back, seeking friction where she craved it the most.

His words registered but made no sense. "Of course I am. My whole family is human."

*Crack.* This time he pulled out and plunged inside her again before the pain from the slap had faded. "Don't lie to me."

"I'm not lying." Lightheaded with this seesaw between pleasure and pain, she was a ball of need. She consisted of raw desire. She couldn't lie to him even if she wanted to.

He flexed his hips again and sneaked a hand between their bodies, to pinch her clit and make her moan. "Mortals' eyes don't change color. What are you?"

"Must be the light." Her eyes didn't change color. If they did, someone would have noticed before now. And why were they talking about her eyes, when the most amazing man she'd ever met was balls-deep inside her?

This was the worst possible moment to be thinking about Hyperion, but his words from weeks ago echoed in her head.

*You want a man who will rock your world. Whose touch will send electricity sparking through you. Whose kiss will take away your breath and leave your legs weak. And who can make love to you for hours, before gathering your sated body close and letting you know you're safe with him for the rest of your life.*

Palaemon was that kind of man. The kind that could break her heart.

No. This wasn't about her heart. It was about something located much lower on her body. Something that couldn't get enough of Palaemon.

"Human," she panted, clinging to him as he upped the tempo of his thrusts. "I'm only human." And she might fall apart if he kept this up, but it felt so good… His every stroke hit a spot inside that made her body tingle, and his fingers on her clit sent jolts of pleasure to her womb. She was close…

"Don't come." He ducked his head to close his teeth around her nipple. Not nibble on it—bite. The pain was sharp but turned into liquid heat, pooling between her legs. She didn't know she was into kink, but he could pinch and slap and bite her flesh if he kept stoking the fire in her belly.

He licked the hardened peak and rubbed her thigh that still pulsed with the memory of his palm.

"I need to… *Please.*" Was she whimpering? Palaemon was turning her into a bumbling mess.

He pinched her clit and twisted, pistoning into her until the bed creaked. "Come. Now."

His throaty whisper triggered a release that had her body shaking with its force. Her eyes drifted shut, and a keening wail—his name—tore up her throat, as the flames in her core rose to engulf her. She felt weightless, and at the same time fuller than ever, as he kept pumping inside her, then pulled out to cover her belly and thighs with his seed.

He didn't fuck like a man hung up on another woman.

Palaemon ran his tongue along the seam of her lips, and she sucked on it hungrily. Her eyes were still closed when he whispered, "Whatever you may be, you're mine now."

And there went her postorgasmic buzz.

She lowered her leg, pried her eyes open, and batted playfully at his shoulder. "That's pretty caveman of you." Wait. Did he predate those?

"Caveman?" He frowned and rolled to the side, watching her face.

Sitting up took too much effort, so Christina stayed where she was. Her toes and fingers still tingled, and her brain was foggy, but she had to make things clear. "Yeah. The whole *mine* thing is rather primitive. We just had sex. It's not like we got married."

He flicked a finger over her nipple, which strained into his touch. "I see you'll need more persuasion."

"To what?"

He shrugged and pinched her nipple. Hard. "Accept that you belong with me."

Christina's heart jumped, and a fresh wave of desire coiled in her stomach. She wouldn't let her primal instincts dictate her life, though. "I just met you. I'm only here till tomorrow."

But Olivia belonged with Hyperion from the moment they met.

That was different. Olivia and Hyperion were destined soulmates. Christina and Palaemon were simply freakishly compatible in sex.

Palaemon ducked to lick a trail between her breasts. "You're not leaving."

*Unf.* Why did she hold his head to her, instead of pushing him away? Why was she reacting to him so viscerally?

"Because you're mine," he murmured against her skin and blew a breath down the wet path he'd drawn with his tongue. His fingers slid between her legs. She was sore, but she opened for his touch, and he slipped two fingers inside her. "I feel it. I *know* it. My hearts beat for you."

*Hearts?* "How many…?"

He pumped his fingers lazily. "Two."

She knew from the start that he wasn't human, but the reminder startled her back to her senses. She took hold of his hand with both of hers and pushed him back. "This was fun, but I need to shower and get some sleep. Early day tomorrow. Breakfast with the king, and all."

Palaemon stretched out on his back. "Go clean up. I'll be here."

She sat up and bit her lip. "Umm… I kind of meant *sleep alone*."

A grin tugged at one corner of his mouth. "I don't think you realize what happened here. You're mine, and I plan on fucking some sense into you."

That shouldn't be so appealing, damn it.

# CHAPTER SIX

Palaemon didn't recognize himself, but he liked who he became when he was with her. He'd always been assertive in his life, except when it came to women. Intense relationships were unstable relationships and could lead to broken hearts—or killing tendencies, like when his father, driven mad by the gods, tried to kill him and his mother. It was why Palaemon didn't listen to his instincts when it came to females.

He was all about compatibility. A good relationship wasn't one based on passion, but one that revolved around common interests and goals. Yes, he wanted genuine affection, but not the kind that came with wanting to touch the other person every chance he got.

Which was why this intense hunger he felt for Christina couldn't possibly lead to anything good. She was human. Mortal. She had a life on land. She was mouthy and opinionated.

She was also gorgeous and witty and funny.

She was his.

Everything else paled and faded into oblivion. He had her, and he would keep her.

His cock stirred at the memory of her lithe form pressed to his body. Why did he ever let her get out of bed?

Well, no reason not to join her under the shower.

He jumped out of bed and made his way to the bathroom. The handle turned easily, and he let himself in and took a moment to watch as Christina lathered her hair. Her head was thrown back, allowing him a wonderful view of her full breasts, taut stomach, and round hips. And at their apex, that perfect, smooth triangle he wanted to get lost in. But what made his hearts beat faster was the sweet, satisfied smile curving her lips. He'd put that smile there.

"Mind if I join you?" he asked. He'd done enough telling for now. He didn't want to scare her by accosting her in the shower.

Christina batted her long eyelashes, and then widened her eyes comically when she dropped her gaze from his face. "Don't you have a not-hard version in this form?"

Palaemon took that as a *yes* and stepped under the water spray. "Not when you're within a couple kilometers' range." He moved behind her and took over soaping her up, enjoying the opportunity to massage every square centimeter of her incredible body. She moaned as he dug his thumbs into the knots at her shoulders, and sighed when he cupped her breasts, working the lather into them.

As he circled from her hips to the small of her back, she leaned forward and pressed her palms flat on the mother-of-pearl wall. She waggled her bottom and looked at him over her shoulder. "I'm especially dirty down there."

The faint red mark of his palm on her skin mesmerized him. He wanted to spank that round ass till it glowed like a Pacific spiny lumpsucker, but he'd save that for later. For now, he massaged each cheek slowly, before running his thumbs forward between her legs, along her labia.

His cock throbbed painfully, and her pushing back into him made it harder to resist, but he wanted to drive her dizzy with desire before he impaled her on his shaft. He glided the edge of his palm along her slit, wedging his fingers between her nether lips, to rub her clitoris, but withdrew it when she bucked her hips. "Hold still, and I'll make sure to clean you properly," he said.

Christina's grumbles were silenced when he turned her to face him and dropped to his knees on the wet floor. Hands on her hips, he helped her lift one leg over his shoulder, so he could bury his face in her pussy. Partial shifting was part of his skill set. All it took was half a second of intense focus, and he was pushing a long, raspy tongue inside her. Christina dug her nails in the back of his neck and shook so hard, he had to still her trembling leg with his palm before she collapsed.

"How are you doing this?" she asked. "No. Don't tell me. Keep doing it." The words drifted into a moan.

He replaced his tongue inside her with his fingers, and licked her sensitive button.

Christina shivered. "Again. More."

*Insatiable little thing.* Not that he complained; he could feast on her forever.

"Less talking, more eating me out," she said.

What? He hadn't talked. He slid his fingers out of her, to give her clit a hard pinch. He wouldn't be talked to like that by his mate.

Christina rocked into his mouth until he plunged his elongated tongue back inside. "I'm sorry. Do your thing. Won't talk again," she managed between panted breaths.

Could she hear him, like when they were underwater? Impossible. He shielded his thoughts, just in case, as he clasped her ass with both hands and lost himself in the sleek smoothness of her pussy.

The way she moved her hips, his ring finger brushed the starfish of her ass hole. She stiffened for the briefest of seconds, and then pushed back against it.

Oh, she was wicked, and he should fuck her every hole until she didn't have the energy or the inclination to ever leave his side. But first, he owed her an oral release. He twisted and flicked his tongue, grazing the spot inside her that made her tense and clench and shudder.

"God," Christina muttered, pumping her hips wildly, fucking herself on his tongue.

No, not God. "Palaemon," he thought at her as he pressed the first knuckle of his middle finger past the tight ring of muscle.

Christina jerked.

"Relax," Palaemon sent her, inching his finger deeper inside her ass, while his tongue mapped every inch of her pussy. "Trust me."

# CHAPTER SEVEN

Trust him? She didn't *know* him. And yet when he wedged a second finger *back there*, where she'd never allowed a touch before, she clenched her teeth against the pain and focused on relaxing her muscles. After his first few careful thrusts, the pain lessened into a throbbing that added to the pleasure building up in her belly. Could she be enjoying this? She'd been brought up to think of anything anal as taboo. This was wrong. *So* wrong. But it felt incredible.

"Should I stop?" She heard Palaemon's question clearly, though his mouth was pretty full.

"Don't you dare," she hissed.

He kept fucking her with his impossible tongue and his long, thick fingers, until pleasure overtook every other sensation. She *was* the ball of fire in her belly. She was his.

Palaemon withdrew his tongue and closed his lips around her clit. One hard suck, a grazing of his teeth, and he sent her hurtling into an orgasm that had her head thudding against the wall and her body jerking.

Palaemon held her upright while he stood. He rinsed both of them, and then gathered her in his arms, to carry her to bed, sated and soaking wet.

"Why could I hear you in my head?" she asked. Her lips were numb, and she felt drowsy, but she had to know. "Is it because we're underwater?"

Palaemon lay down beside her and wrapped an arm around her waist, to tuck her into his side. "That only works inside the water. This is because you're mine."

He sounded so certain, for a heartbeat she could accept the idea. What would she leave behind, if she stayed with him? Her parents were on the other side of the freaking world, and her best friend was busy living her own impossible whirlwind romance. Christina had no place of her own and no career to speak of. Could she stay here?

No. That was crazy. She'd miss the mall and the movies and moonlit strolls on the beach and eating fried calamari or anything not based on sea flora.

But if she left—*when* she left—she wouldn't have this, possibly ever again.

"Sleep," Palaemon whispered against her temple. "I have more in store for you before breakfast."

Using his broad, hard chest as a pillow, his twin heartbeats thundering under her ear, she gave into her exhaustion.

Something tickled her lips. She averted her face, but the smooth thing nudging at her mouth followed.

Christina opened her eyes, to get an eyeful of Palaemon's huge cock hovering in front of her face. He half-knelt on the tall bed, fist around his shaft, and waggled his eyebrows at her when she sought his gaze. Part of her wanted to be upset that he'd wake her up to suck him off, but she wouldn't pass up the opportunity to taste him. This would be her last chance. She parted her lips and flicked her tongue across the bulging head of his erection.

"Take it in your mouth," he said.

*Gladly.* She stretched her lips around his girth and sucked tentatively. He tasted like the ocean, and she ached to drown in him. She rubbed her tongue along the underside, as she took in more of him. He filled her mouth until her jaw ached. If he went any further, she'd choke. But she was hungry—ravenous—for him. Letting her teeth graze his length, she pulled back and then sucked him in again. He felt like barely controlled power, encased in satin.

She wanted to snap his control.

With a growl she couldn't believe came from her chest, she closed her hand as far as it could go around him and sucked harder, twisting her grip on every downstroke. Palaemon groaned and thrust inside her mouth, her hand keeping him from bottoming out. "You're incredible." He fisted his hand in her hair and forced her to look up at him as he drove forward. "What have you done to me?" His blue eyes glowed, and the words came out choked.

*She* was doing this. And she would make him come apart, like he did her. She sucked for all she could, bobbing her head faster, stroking him harder.

She tugged on his balls and felt them tighten.

"I am going to come," he said through gritted teeth.

Good. She sucked for all she had, pumping him so fast her forearm ached with the effort, until he spilled in her mouth. Thick, hot, salty cum coated her tongue and slid down her throat, and Christina swallowed greedily.

She'd done this. She'd made him come. And all before she even got out of bed. A giggle escaped her lips, and he draped his body over her and kissed her so thoroughly, laughing was the furthest thing from her mind.

He made love to her, slow and gentle, introducing her body to more pleasure than she could ever fathom. By the time they lay facing each other, his fingers tracing patterns on her breast, she felt severely dehydrated, and her stomach grumbled.

"You're lucky it's time for breakfast." Palaemon kissed the tip of her nose and sat up.

He'd leave. They couldn't show up together for breakfast with the royal family. Nereus wouldn't allow one of his generals to be with a mortal. Besides, Palaemon might not want Pherusa to know what he and Christina did last night. The thought felt like a punch to the gut.

Palaemon held out his hand. "Aren't you coming? We need to put some food inside you before I ravish you again. I don't want you fainting on me." He gave her a feral grin. "Or under me."

She took his hand and stood, trying to ignore her heart thundering behind her ribs. They *were* going together? What would he tell the king and queen? Or Pherusa?

"That you're mine." His voice rattled in her head. "And I'm keeping you."

"Don't I get a say in that?" She should have sounded more assertive, damn it.

"You'll get your chance to dispute my claim before King Nereus. He's a fair man. I'm sure he'll see how you cannot stand me, and order me to stay away from you." Was he mocking her? He was mocking her.

She slapped his perfect ass—*God*, she'd miss this ass— and squealed when he returned the favor leaving her ass cheek stinging. Her lower body still throbbed from his attentions, and the seaweed robe scraped her skin as if it were made of rawhide, but she enjoyed the prickling. She tied the sash tightly. Would everyone be able to tell how she and Palaemon spent the night? Could they smell him on her? Her cheeks burned. "Do we have time for another shower?"

Palaemon shook his head as he put his breastplate in place and secured it. "The horn has sounded."

It had? "I didn't hear anything."

"The witch has bespelled it so only the ones it's meant for do." As if that explained everything. Then again, the witch had made her speak fluent Greek within seconds, so everything was possible.

Palaemon buckled the bottom half of his armor. "Ready?"

Christina nodded and looped her arm through his. Let this surreal scenario continue for another couple hours. Soon, she'd be heading home.

# CHAPTER EIGHT

He rolled his eyes. She wanted to go? Fine. She'd be back. He'd make sure of it.

He led her to the ballroom, their fingers tangled together. *Carp*, they were the last ones here.

Palaemon pretended not to feel the weight of everyone's gaze on them, especially when he pulled out a chair for Christina and she winced as she sat. Feeling proud for his lingering effect was inevitable.

Pherusa nudged Prometheus, and they exchanged a funny look. Beside her, Halie tried to hide a smile, but her mirth was reflected in her eyes. Delphinos studiously avoided Palaemon's gaze. So much for male solidarity. Palaemon sought out Nerites with his gaze. The prince of Vythos wasn't at his mother's side, like he usually sat, but at the far end of the table, laughing with a gaggle of his sisters—Palaemon still mixed up most of the Nereids' names when they were all together. Technically, *they* were laughing. Nerites wore that half-smirk of his that had replaced more joyful expressions in the long centuries since he lost Aphrodite.

Palaemon clasped Christina's shoulder as he sank in the chair beside hers. He'd seen what losing true love did to a male. He refused to suffer through it.

Olivia patted Christina's back. "Nice," she whispered, but not so low he didn't catch it.

Christina didn't react. She looked at the plate in front of her, twisted it a half-circle, and dug in. "Mmmm… This is incredible. What is it?"

Nerites studied Palaemon's face with an amused expression. "Unferitilized roe with seaweed. It's good for building stamina."

Christina coughed, and Palaemon passed her a glass of seaweed juice.

"I'm okay." She held up her hand. "It just went down the wrong way."

The memory of her swallowing his seed made him choke on his saliva. He thumped his chest with his fist, not that it did much good through the steel of his breastplate. He cleared his throat and leveled his gaze on the king. No reason to delay this.

"King Nereus, if I may." Palaemon watched as Nereus' chin lifted imperceptibly, the smile fading from his lips. This was the king's holding-court face. "I would like to…" Palaemon's self-assurance wavered, but he focused on his goal. "I would like to stake my claim on the human female, Christina."

"What?" Christina sputtered, flakes of dried seaweed flying out of her mouth to land on the pristine white tablecloth.

Olivia didn't take it much better. Her eyes threw light-bolts when she leaned on the table to glare at him from Christina's other side. "Excuse you? There will be no claiming my friend."

"Yeah, there will be no claiming me." Christina's protest sounded marginally less fiery and was easily squashed when he closed his mouth over hers.

King Nereus cleared his throat, and Palaemon pulled back from the kiss, bolstered by the fervor Christina returned it with.

"You do realize I cannot condone a forceful claim." Nereus' tone was grave. "Even if I didn't have fifty daughters and a wife—a lovely, patient wife—who'd have my gills for it, I will not sanction a union unless both parties are willing."

Palaemon smiled. "Forgive me, my liege, but our union isn't what I seek permission for."

Behind the king, the ever-present crone let out a chuckle that sounded like grinding gravel. "The half-human has already accepted his claim, my lord."

"Half-human?" Palaemon and Christina asked as one. They weren't the only ones surprised, judging by the hubbub that erupted around the table.

The king raised his fist, and all voices ceased. "Explain," he told the witch.

Circe's smile was beautiful and frightening. "A lot more than half, to be precise, but I do sense water-nymph blood in her, and I know the daimon's claim has been accepted."

Christina slammed her palm on the table. "I accepted nothing."

Palaemon blinked, and Circe was behind him, her voice in his ear while she caressed his cheek. "You do not think of him as yours, then?" she asked Christina.

"I... I..." Christina squeezed her eyes shut. When she opened them again, a spark of bright green flashed in the irises before disappearing in their depths. "What are you saying?"

"She's saying you're mine," Palaemon said.

A chair screeched against the floor, as Hyperion stood. The Titan squared his shoulders, and his body stretched until he was twice the king's size. There was no mistaking the element-controlling power emanating from him, or the threat in his stance. "King Nereus, the mortal is under my protection. I will not allow her to enter any agreement against her will."

"Will you people let me finish?" Palaemon knew better than to raise his voice, but he needed this out and approved, so he could start planning a future with his mate. It hurt that Christina had slid closer to Olivia and looked at him with a mix of fear and disappointment. "What I'm requesting, my liege, is your permission to spend half the year on shore, with Christina, once we've secured the"—*world*—"kingdom of Vythos. And if she agrees, I would have her by my side, here, the rest of the time."

Christina's mouth formed an *O*, her blue eyes wide. "I can do this," she thought at him. Or to herself. Aloud, she said, "We'll need to talk things out first. This is so sudden," but Palaemon heard the resounding *yes* in her head.

"King Nereus?" he asked.

The king's stark-white mustache and beard twitched, as a smile blossomed on his lips. "Granted."

Hyperion shrunk back down and retook his seat, as if he hadn't been ready to bring down the palace moments ago. "Congratulations, Christina. I believe you just got engaged."

The witch blinked back to behind Nereus. "There is one more thing the mortal should know about the bonding. While she's under the sea, she will age at the same rate as the sea daimon does."

Which was a day for every human year. If he convinced her to move here, she'd be practically immortal.

Christina pinned him with her big blue eyes. "How old are you?"

"A few millennia older than I look."

She swallowed hard and let out a forced laugh. "Guess I can stop wasting money on eye cream, then."

# CHAPTER NINE

"You okay?" Olivia leaned against the bedroom doorway, watching Christina pace from one side of the spacious room to the other.

Christina threw her arms up. "Yes. No. I don't know."

Olivia stepped into her path. "Hey. *Hey.*" She wrapped her arms around Christina and held her close. "I know how you feel."

Did she? Because Christina wasn't all that sure *she* did.

"You like Palaemon. More than *like* him. You're falling for him at a rate your logic cannot accept. Right?"

Christina nodded against Olivia's shoulder. "It's like I can't think when he touches me."

Brushing her hair back from her face, Olivia pulled back to look into her eyes. "That's your soul and your body recognizing your connection before your mind has caught up. I know Circe is scary, especially when she looks like this, but she's good, deep down. And she knows stuff. If she says you're meant to be with him, you are, but Hyperion and I won't let them force you into anything. If you don't want Palaemon to stay above—"

Christina huffed. "I do. That's what scares me. And practically being immortal when I'm down here? That's so *weird.*"

"I'm immortal." Olivia shrugged. "Won't affect you for a couple decades. The neighbors will be whispering shit about you getting plastic surgery, but they won't exactly be able to guess what's up. And you can always stay here, if you decide to."

"You make it sound so simple."

"Because once you get rid of preconceptions about what should be, you see what is." Palaemon's voice came from the entrance. "I should have told you what I planned, but I had to see your gut reaction, before doubt settled in. And what you screamed in your head was *yes*."

He crossed the room to them, and Olivia stepped back, letting him embrace Christina.

"I didn't give you permission to read my thoughts," Christina said. But her traitorous hands were already running through his gorgeous blue hair. She had a freaking sea daimon, an ancient deity, a real-life Aquaman, all to herself.

He laid a tender kiss on the crown of her head. "I wasn't listening in; you projected the thought. The fact remains that your first instinct was to accept my proposal. You want to be with me."

She did. She nodded, and Palaemon tightened his hold as he crushed his mouth on hers.

"I'll leave you two alone." Olivia padded out of the room and closed the door with a quiet *snick*.

Palaemon broke the kiss but didn't let go. "I must take you ashore. You'll be safer far from all this until we know Kronos cannot come out of stasis. Hyperion and Prometheus plan on bringing Atlas' statue to Vythos before he awakens, so I must return immediately." His gem-blue eyes sparkled. "But I will be back for you. Do you want me to, Christina?"

There was only one answer to this. "I do."

*

Book Three

# A Guard for the Titan

# CHAPTER ONE

Mid-August in Athens was a drag. Well, not for other people. The city had much to offer when the crowds had fled to the islands, but Iphigenia wasn't among the lucky ones who got to experience it. No. She was spending the night in the Acropolis museum. Alone.

Why did she even have to be here? Who in their right mind would break into this place? To steal what? Archeological *stuff* went for millions, probably, but they were hard to carry unnoticed, and it wasn't like someone could rob the most prominent museum in Greece and get away with it.

But the job paid her rent, so she wouldn't complain about it. Much.

She looked from one monitor to the next—again—and sighed. It wasn't even midnight yet, and she barely kept her eyes open. The rest of the year, the night shift was taken by two people at a time, but nothing worked in Greece in August. She and Petros had flipped for who would stay back, and she lost. So she got to watch flickering screens and pray for morning.

Something caught her eye in the far-left feed. Movement in the Marble Conservation unit? She studied the image. Shifted the camera. Checked the other cameras in that room.

Nope. Nothing to see there, except for the incredibly lifelike oversize statue of her guy. The faint glow of the safety exit signs reflected off his eyes, making them shine.

*Her guy.* She had the hots for a statue. No wonder, when her sex life was nonexistent since she broke things off with Pavlos.

She checked the rest of the units, saw nothing, *as expected*—even crime seemed to go on vacation in August—and ducked to the mini fridge by the desk, for yesterday's meatball pasta. No food or drink was allowed near the equipment in the security department, which worked out fine, because she'd rather eat with her guy.

She needed a life.

Iphigenia took her food to the kitchen, blitzed it in the microwave oven, and skipped down the stairs. Her pulse sped up as she approached Marble Conservation. It was silly, but the highlight of her nights this week was eating and talking to what was believed to be the statue of a Titan.

She was at work when they first brought him in, four months ago, and couldn't tear her gaze away as they uncovered him.

Even down on one knee, he was larger than life, and he was gorgeous, despite the dirt, algae, barnacles, and marine debris clinging to him. The sculptor who carved him out of marble had done an amazing job. Iphigenia could see the tension in every corded muscle as he raised his head defiantly at an unknown enemy, and his eyes seemed to see right through her, though the irises were blank.

And she was in desperate need of an actual flesh-and-blood man to obsess over.

She pulled out a stool from the working bench and sat facing him, her dinner in her lap.

"So how was your day?" she asked, twirling her fork in the pasta. The camera would record her eating—

which was a no-no here too, so she'd be careful—but its position kept her face hidden, so nobody would see her talking to herself. "Mine was boring. Mom called, to tell me for the millionth time I should quit from any job that makes you come in on Dekapentavgoustos"—the fifteenth of August, the Assumption of the Virgin Mary, was a major holiday in largely Christian Orthodox Greece—"and go back home, to Ioannina. You know the drill. Find a nice guy, settle down, spawn a couple kids..." Certainly not work for a living, and especially not as a security guard. *Not what a woman should be doing with her life* was her father's mantra when her job was mentioned.

The flash of gold that brightened the statue's eyes was gone so fast, she must have imagined it. And his jaw seemed clenched a little tighter. Or it was the fact that the scientists working on him had cleaned his face and upper body, uncovering more details she'd missed before.

*Do you want to go back home?*

Where did that come from? As far as she was concerned, *back home* was only for Christmas and Easter. Summer was for Mykonos and Santorini and Milos, and any of the dozens of Greek islands with stretches of sandy beach.

The sense of relief that flooded her felt foreign.

She looked around, a nervous chuckle escaping her lips. She was alone. Of course she was alone. She and her Titan.

"Wish you were real," she said. "You don't seem like the kind of guy who'd be intimidated by a woman who speaks her mind." Or by anything, judging by the fierceness in his blind gaze.

*I'm not. I like a strong female.*

The answer came in a deep male voice. In her head. Lovely. Now her fantasy guy talked to her too.

She speared a meatball with her fork, securing the pasta, and brought it to her mouth. Not bad, though it could use more grated cheese. Her culinary skills were far from enviable, but she was improving. Mom would be proud.

"This is nice," she said with her mouth full. Not like her Titan would mind.

She studied his stiff shoulders and tight chest. He looked like he worked out, but not at a gym. It was easy to picture him building a house with his own large hands.

Was all of him big?

*Naughty.* She smirked to herself.

The crew hadn't fully uncovered him from the waist down. She'd heard he was found half buried in the bottom of the sea, near Rhodes. He could be a water deity— Poseidon himself—but a different name clung to her thoughts. *Atlas.* The Titan forced by Zeus to hold the sky in place.

*Zeus couldn't force me to do anything.*

Her breath caught, as the mental image of him naked filled her head. His feet were planted at shoulder width, legs slightly bent at the knee and muscular thighs straining. His stomach was ribbed, his pecs and biceps bulging as he raised his arms over his head, balancing his invisible precious cargo. Even half-erect, he was long and thick, and when Iphigenia licked her lips, it wasn't to taste the tomato sauce.

She shook off the thought and its effect, stuffed more pasta in her mouth, and swallowed it only half-chewed. "Petros is right. I need to get laid." Only her work-buddy meant with himself, and serial daters weren't her style.

She tilted her head at the statue she'd decided was Atlas—it had to be him; it felt right. "You're not a serial dater, are you? Of course you're not. You're... a hunter. A provider. You bring home the bacon, but you don't expect your *little woman* to be the one who cooks it. You like her to challenge you. To be smart and funny. And sexy. It doesn't scare you when she tells you what she likes." Even if it leaned a little toward *kinky*.

It was getting hot in here. The collar of her shirt felt constricting. If there were no cameras in the room, she'd pop a couple of buttons, but it wouldn't look professional if someone decided to browse through tonight's footage.

Neither would rubbing against Atlas' hard body.

Okay, she needed to eat and go back to her station, before she did something more stupid than talking to a piece of marble.

The statue's eyes shone again, and this time it was definitely not a reflection. Maybe there were gems or pieces of glass inset in the irises? Had glass been invented when the statue was sculpted?

She stood, placed her dinner on the stool, and approached to take a closer look. *God*, his face was breathtaking, with the square jawline and chiseled cheekbones. His lips looked generous even drawn in a snarl, and his wild, long hair was uncharacteristically unadorned, compared to the other statues she'd seen around the museum. He looked like a man ready to take on the world. And his eyes were now purely gold.

# CHAPTER TWO

Up close like this, she smelled even better than the food that had him pining for his sense of taste since she set foot inside this chamber. She carried with her the scent of flowers and ripe, plump fruit. And she was gorgeous. Her midnight-black curls were begging to be loosed from that tight bun, and for him to dig his fingers in them.

There were two problems with that fantasy—he was currently five meters tall, and he was encased in marble.

No matter. He shouldn't be having the urge to touch a female that didn't belong to him.

When the archeologists fished him out of his watery grave, he'd thought his punishment was over. That he'd finally be taken out of stasis and allowed to catch up on all he'd lost. He'd find his Pleione and be complete again.

But Pleione hadn't come to him, and he was still here, on a land that was the same yet different, listening daily to people speaking a mangled version of the Greek he once knew.

His mind-reading power had returned to a degree, and he'd absorbed the knowledge those who touched him had of the current world—a world for whom Titans and Olympians were creatures of myth. Still, he couldn't touch

Iphigenia's mind except for the few occasions she opened her thoughts to him.

Like now.

Iphigenia reached for him, and her small palm seared his cheek.

She found him as fascinating as he did her, and despite himself, he praised Zeus for freezing him in place in this position, so he was almost eye-level with her. Beneath the thick fringe of dark lashes, the green specks in her hazel eyes made a stark contrast with the pallor of her face, and her full, rosy lips were kissable.

But he couldn't kiss her. Because she was flesh, and he was marble. And his heart belonged to Pleione.

Pleione might have moved on in the eternity they'd been apart though, and when Iphigenia touched him like this, his soul felt complete.

"Wish you were real," Iphigenia said again.

"I *am* real," he wanted to scream.

She snatched back her hand and let out a startled laugh. "I'm going crazy. Not like you can talk in my head."

He could, but he didn't want to scare her away, so he tried hard not to project his thoughts. Her proximity tugged at every cell of his body. With the exception of Pleione, he'd never been so drawn to a female. Damn Zeus and damn Kronos. Atlas should never have stood by his brother's side in the fight against the Olympians, but Kronos had convinced him Zeus was a threat to Titans.

Kronos had been right.

Zeus no longer existed though, or if he did, he was powerless enough that humans weren't aware of his presence. And Atlas never felt so close to breaking free.

His still heart ached. If Zeus had faded away, perhaps so had the Titanesses. For all Atlas knew, Zeus might have gone after the females once he was done with the males. There was no mention of their fate in what Atlas had gleaned of the Greek Mythology in his rescuers' minds.

"Your eyes aren't glowing anymore." Iphigenia's voice pulled him back to the present. She rolled her eyes. "My mind's playing tricks on me."

He ached to ask her to stay, but it would get him nowhere. Her shift would end, and she'd leave. And in a few days, when the rest of the security guards were back, she'd no longer be able to come to him for their odd, one-sided chats.

The thought of losing this limited interaction with her tore a gash deep inside him.

It was because she was the only one who talked to him like she *saw* him. Not because she was special.

"It's the dark, kicking my imagination into overdrive. I was never fully weaned off my night-light," she mused, not moving away. "Pavlos hated it. We'd fight about it almost every night. He said he couldn't sleep with a light on, even if it was no brighter than a candle. I couldn't sleep without it, not because I was annoyed—unlike his grouchy ass—but because I was afraid. He never got that." The man never got much of her, from what she'd told Atlas, which was why she'd left him a week before they were to be wed.

Smart girl.

She worried her bottom lip with her teeth. "It's not uncomfortably dark in here. I mean, I can see all around the room. But knowing I'm alone and underground..." She laughed again, and the sound sunk through the marble, to soothe Atlas' aching soul. "Being alone is supposed to be a good thing in this case. Means no intruders, which makes my life easier."

Out of the corner of his eye, Atlas saw movement. He couldn't turn his head to see better, but there was definitely a dark shape at the other end of the room, closing in on them.

"Behind you," he yelled in Iphigenia's mind. The words struck the walls around them and bounced back to him. He'd spoken them aloud.

Her eyes widened. "You... You can talk?" She leaned in closer and placed two fingers on his lips.

Behind her, the shape was close enough for Atlas to see it was a male. And he held a weapon. A gun, according to the memories Atlas had absorbed.

Iphigenia was only armed with a Taser—she'd told him last time she came down here—and still studied Atlas' face instead of spinning toward the intruder.

She'd have no time to defend herself.

A second man sneaked up beside the first one, pointed at Iphigenia and mouthed something, and the first one nodded.

They would harm her, unless Atlas did something. Now.

Before he realized he was moving, he leapt upright, curled his body around hers, and blinked the two of them to the last place he remembered being at—Mount Othrys.

Hazel eyes impossibly wide, Iphigenia pushed at his chest and kicked her legs. "Let me go."

Atlas carefully set her on her feet, and after a moment's consideration focused on condensing his mass, to reduce his height to that of a tall human. He still towered over her, but he didn't want to intimidate her.

It worked, judging by how she glared at him. "What are you?" she asked. When he opened his mouth, she cut him off with a raised palm. "Never mind. I'm dreaming, and any moment now I'll slide off the stool and bust my head." She took a step back, looked around, and frowned. "Christ, my subconscious is a dark place. Wake up, Iphigenia. Come on, girl."

Atlas was surprised his lips could still form a smile. "You're not dreaming." The words came easy in Modern Greek, though maybe he should let her believe that. It'd certainly make things easier and keep her from panicking.

But she didn't seem anywhere near hysterics, as she glanced from side to side speculatively. He took in the scenery too. With the stars above as the only source of light, it wasn't easy for human sight to register the houses in the distance, but he saw them, and they were more or less the only thing that had changed since he called this place *home*. The terrain was still rocky, with sparse flora, and the air smelled clean and pure.

Atlas filled his lungs with unneeded oxygen. He was free. He could move again. He could search for his Titaness.

Though he felt anchored to this small human female... *No*. Not anchored. Responsible for her. He'd take her to safety, and then go off on his journey. First though, he'd tell her the truth. It felt like the right thing to do. If she didn't believe him, he'd erase the past few minutes from her memory. He was back to his true self; he had the power to do so.

"We are on Mount Othrys, where Zeus attacked us," he told Iphigenia.

"*Us?*" She arched a brow, but her gaze skipped all over the place.

He shrugged. "Us, Titans."

She nodded, too composed for a human who just found out Titans existed. "Huh. I didn't know I knew that," she muttered.

Her words didn't make sense. He tried to read her thoughts again, but it didn't work. "I don't understand."

A few curls had escaped her updo, and the wind swirled them around her head, much as it did his long tresses. She tilted her head and pursed her lips. "I can't dream up something I don't know, even if I'm not aware of it when I'm awake."

Ah. This explained her demeanor. "This is not a dream, Iphigenia." He took her hand and was glad she didn't pull away. "I *am* a Titan, and I've been trapped in statue form since Zeus fought my brother—his father—over this world."

She snorted. "So you just decided to wake up now and take me on a stroll to Mount What's-its-Name?"

"*Othrys*. And I didn't *decide* it. Two armed men were about to attack you. I reacted. I couldn't think of anywhere else to take you. This world hasn't been mine in eons."

She took a step back, and then another, her expression guarded. "You're telling me I'm alone, in the middle of nowhere, with a very naked *Titan*, who can change his size and teleport anywhere he pleases?"

*Teleport.* A much more descriptive term than *blinking.* "Only to places I've been before or seen in—" Humans' minds, but she didn't let him finish.

"Did you drug me? How did we get here? What are you planning to do to me?"

Atlas sighed at the note of fear in her voice. "*Nothing.* I mean you no harm. I was trying to save you." He saw she was about to flee, a second before she spun on her heel and took off. He didn't have to follow her. He blinked in front of her, and she landed on him with an *oof.*

Steadying her, he said, "I apologize for upsetting you. I will get you somewhere safe, and you can forget ever meeting me." No reason to mention he'd make sure of that or how. And why did the thought of never seeing her again make his chest hurt?

Iphigenia raised her chin defiantly. "Take me back to the museum."

Stubborn female. "You'll be in danger there. I can take you to"—what was that authority called?—"the police."

"The museum, or I scream."

Idle threat. There was nobody nearby, and Atlas could blink her out of here in a split second. "You're sleepy. Need to go to bed. Think of your home." He poured suggestion into his voice. Other Titans could only blink to places they'd visited, but he was able to pick up a destination from someone's mind. He'd get her to her home, and she could sleep till morning. She might lose her job, but she'd be away from men with guns.

She visibly wavered, her expression going slack far too briefly, before turning suspicious again. "No."

*Chaos.* Wasn't his power of compulsion back? The wind howled in his ears as he tried again. "Focus on your bedroom. I will take you there."

Iphigenia crossed her arms over her full breasts. "*Nah* uh."

# CHAPTER THREE

"Why are you so stubborn?" He scowled, his body radiating raw power.

"Oh, I don't know. Because you're asking me to let you take me to my bed, and I don't even know you? Because you brought me to a mountain in the middle of the night, without my consent?" She should be more frightened. They seemed to be miles from civilization, and it was dark. Plus the guy might be half the size he was a moment ago, but he was still huge and incredibly fast.

And muscular all over and tall and dark and—*woah*—extremely well hu—

She snapped her gaze back up to his gorgeous face, her cheeks heating. The corners of his wide mouth twitched, and his eyes were the same gold she'd first seen in the museum. Was this their actual color?

"I'm Atlas," he said. "Now you know me."

So she'd been right about who he was. Made sense, if she was conjuring up this whole situation in a dream, whether asleep or drugged.

If she was awake though, and he was telling the truth, he was an ancient god. Older than ancient.

When did the Titanomachy happen?

Never. It was a myth.

But if Titans were real… Man appeared on earth a couple hundred thousand years ago, according to that documentary she watched last week. Could Atlas have been around that long? How much of that was as a statue?

And was he really able to beam her to her bedroom if she brought it to mind? How? Could he read her thoughts?

"I only mean to help you," he said with a coaxing smile that made her heart beat faster.

"By taking me away from work, when there was a break-in, and not letting me go back to fix things? Gee, *thanks*. Who needs a job, anyway?" She could at least call in the robbery. Holding a finger out, for him to be quiet, she fished her phone from her back pocket. No signal. Fucking marvelous.

She could record him, though. She turned on the phone's camera, aimed it at him, and pressed the red circle. "You say you're a Titan. Prove it. Do something… Titanly." *Titanish?*

The deep line between his thick, golden brows reappeared. "I know what this is. I've seen people use them."

So he could see things when he was a statue? Had he heard her, when she talked about her life?  Before she could ask, he grabbed the phone from her hand and turned it off.

Her analytical skills kicked in. "How did you know how to do that, if you're not a dream? Someone came to stand in your line of sight, to switch their phones off?"

Atlas rolled his shoulders.

Mesmerized by the flexing of his muscles, Iphigenia forgot what she'd asked him.

"Don't turn it back on," he said, holding the cell phone out to her.

Iphigenia heard the *or else* in his tone and had no doubt he could crush it in his fist. She took it and put back in her pocket. They were only a meter apart, and she could see him now. All of him—from the top of his blond head, to his chiseled abs, to his muscular thighs and large, sexy feet. And yup, she'd glossed over something impressive and half-erect in between.

"You know, you're still very naked." She licked her lips, her mental capacity exhausted by her effort to keep her gaze from dipping below his navel.

"Ah. Forgive me. I forgot your culture doesn't approve of that." He raised his hand, twisted it, and made a pulling motion, and a cloud swept down from the sky, to wrap itself around his waist and down to mid-thigh.

What. The. Fuck?

No. It was too dark. What she thought was a cloud was... What? What else could the white, puffy *something* clinging to Atlas like a loincloth be?

"Is that a cloud?" Her voice trembled, and her hand wasn't much steadier when she pointed at him.

"Yes."

She bit her lip. "Can I touch it?" Part of her wanted to ensure it wasn't an illusion, but mostly, she wanted to have touched a cloud.

He nodded, his gaze on her face.

Holding her breath, Iphigenia took a step closer. Mere centimeters separated them. She reached for his hip, and gasped when her fingers passed through what felt like nothing more than thick air, to brush his bare skin.

Atlas hissed like she'd burned him, but when she tried to withdraw her hand, he wrapped his long fingers around her wrist and held it in place on his hipbone. "This is the first touch I've felt in an eternity. I was dumped in the sea, surrounded by cold for longer than I care to remember. Men found me, took me out, and moved me to the museum, but the cold was unyielding. Other than pressure where their hands grasped me, I felt nothing." His voice dropped to a gruff whisper, as he took her other hand and placed it splayed on his chest. "Nothing like this. You drive the cold away."

His heart thudded under her palm. She curved her fingers, trailing them through the sprinkle of golden hairs on his chest. He was warm. He was real.

She leaned closer. The weirdest urge to sniff his neck made her rise to her tiptoes. His grip on her hand tightened the tiniest bit, and he met her gaze. His eyes looked even more beautiful, the gold almost swirling in the irises, as he lowered his thick lashes and tilted his head closer. His breath was a warm caress on her face.

Iphigenia inhaled the dark male scent of his skin. He smelled of the night and the sky and the sea that had held him captive.

*If she believed him.*

But if he was a dream, this wouldn't be wrong. She closed the last of the distance between them and brushed her lips over his. They felt warm and smooth, and she wanted to taste them. Lick the salt off them. Nibble on the soft flesh. He had the perfect lips for kissing.

But he wasn't moving them. He wasn't moving anything at all. He might as well still be made of marble.

She stepped back and brought her hand to her mouth. "I'm sorry. I don't know what I was thinking." She was thinking she wanted him, which was so not her. She wasn't impulsive, except for when she canceled her wedding at the last minute last year, but that was because logic insisted she and Pavlos weren't a good match.

Atlas shook his head. "I'm sorry. I can't." His expression was closed, but she saw the pain in his eyes. They were a warm-honey color now. "I am attracted to you, but I am bonded to another, and I will not betray her."

He didn't have time to meet someone. Was there a woman waiting for him all this—immeasurably long—time? At least he was honest, when he could have taken advantage of the situation.

Or he was lying, there was nobody else, and he thought Iphigenia was beneath him. He was a Titan, after all.

Whatever his reason, he'd rejected her, and she could let it get to her or brush it off. It shouldn't sting as much as it did, anyway. He was either a figment of her imagination or something unfathomably scary, and neither case scenario spelled *relationship material*.

She'd ignore the masochistic implications of her subconscious making him turn her down, if he was a dream.

She nodded. "Let's pretend the last couple minutes never happened. Take me back to the museum, please. Now."

# CHAPTER FOUR

"You heard the lady." The voice came from Atlas' right.

He twirled, to put himself between Iphigenia and the speaker, but there was nobody there. It wasn't that the male who spoke was hidden; he wasn't there.

"I thought the Olympians were gone," Atlas muttered. None of the people who touched his statue form believed in their existence, but the disembodied voice had to belong to a god.

Zeus wasn't done with him, then? The vindictive little lightning-wielder granted Atlas this reprieve, only to exacerbate his torture when he encased him in marble once more?

Atlas wouldn't allow him the chance. "Stand down, nephew. I've learned my lesson, and the world has moved on. I will not fight you, unless you provoke me."

The unseen man chuckled, and the stars dimmed as a ball of light materialized between Atlas and Iphigenia. The light stretched and ebbed, until a semi-naked blond male stepped out of it. "Good to know, but I'm not my grandpa," he said. "I am Eros. Son of Aphrodite. God of love. And I'm here to save your immortal ass. But first—" He snapped his fingers, and Iphigenia disappeared.

"What did you do?" Atlas' roar seeped into the earth beneath their feet and made it rumble. An invisible fist squeezed his lungs, as an emotion he hadn't experienced before threatened to choke him. Was it… panic? No. He was above panic. He'd faced the strongest of the gods and survived. He feared nothing.

But the possibility of something happening to Iphigenia made his stomach churn and his head throb. "Where is she?" he growled.

"I returned her to the Acropolis museum."

The fist squeezed harder. "She could be hurt. There are armed—"

"I promise you she'll be okay, and I swear I'm on your side."

That calmed Atlas down. Gods might be a lot of things, but they weren't oath breakers. "Explain, and then take me to her."

Eros drew a rectangular shape in the air with one finger, and a thick… *envelope* was the word, dropped into his free hand. He held it out to Atlas, who didn't reach for it. "Take it," Eros said. "After Prometheus and Hyperion awoke, we decided to hand out a starter pack to new arrivals. Everything you need to build a new life is in here."

Starter pack? New life? "Hyperion and Prometheus?"

Eros nodded. "Your brothers are awake and well. They planned on taking you to Vythos before you awakened, but you beat them to the punch. I'll take you to them once you're stable."

They might not want to see him after he'd taken Kronos' side, but it had been the logical thing to do at the time. They'd understand. Besides, he missed them. "I'm stable now." But his hand trembled as he rubbed his chest, where he still felt the heat of Iphigenia's palm.

"No, you're not." He studied Atlas' face. "But I admit I expected you to be in a much less coherent state after being essentially locked in your head for this long. Longer than either of the other two, by far."

Atlas harrumphed. His head was the safest place to be, when Zeus was after you. "I'm of as sound a mind as ever. When I felt my reason tested, I'd force my thoughts to shut down." Though that often happened without him realizing it. The curse that took away his ability to move or speak kept him drifting in and out of consciousness.

Eros nodded. "That's fortunate. Bad news is you're still an unbonded Titan, and you'll spin out of control within days if not hours, unless you fix that. Being near your brothers will make matters worse."

"I have no patience for your cryptic talk." Though he didn't exactly have someplace to be until Eros told him where to find his mate.

Eros winced. "Okay, so the way dear Grandpa Zeus set this up, unless you bond with your soulmate shortly after you awaken, your powers take over. They cause major catastrophes, and you and the world explode. Being near your brothers before you're bonded will make things worse. It's really all explained in the handbook."

"Handbook?"

Eros shook the envelope at him, and Atlas finally took it, as realization sank in. "What about Pleione?" he asked. "I was bonded to her when Zeus put me in stasis." The dreadful thought that she might have perished while he was away had crossed his mind a lot during the conscious moments of the long, dark night that had become his life, but that didn't diminish his pain at what he knew he was about to hear.

Real sympathy glimmered in Eros' pale-blue eyes, and his teasing tone turned somber. "Zeus made the Titanesses mortal after you lost to him. They were allowed to spend their lives unharmed, but this was thirty-five thousand years ago. She's gone. I'm sorry."

Gone. Forever. *No Olympians* meant *no Hades*, which in turn meant *no Elysian Fields*. Atlas couldn't demand the god of death release her.

His chest felt hollow, his shoulders too heavy for him to stand upright—him, the Titan who'd once supported the sky on his own. "Part of me knew this all along. I just hoped…" He shouldn't have allowed himself the folly.

He'd never again see her smile or arch an eyebrow at his antics. He'd never sleep with her supple form pressed against him. Never breathe in her scent.

But when he tried to bring her face to mind, Iphigenia's eyes hazel overtook the image, her lips quirked in a wicked grin.

Guilt sliced through him, maybe more deeply than pain. He couldn't even remember his soulmate's visage. The envelope slipping from his fingers, he leaned over and grasped his knees, dragging air inside his lungs as if he needed to breathe. He ought to be rational about this. He knew the possibility was there, and memories were doomed to fade after this long.

Thinking things through did nothing to lessen the ache gnawing at his very soul. The stars flickered over his head, and a tremor went through the ground.

Eros approached him slowly and placed a hand on his arm. "I am so sorry for your loss." A heartbeat later, he added, "But—"

"*But?*" The single tiny word snapped Atlas' self-control, and his bark made Eros hop back. "There is no *but.* Pleione is gone, and my soul will never be complete again," Atlas bellowed, uncaring that his voice no doubt rolled down the hill to echo around the scattered houses. "*But* nothing, God of Love. My powers *will* take me over, and this world will soon see its last morning." As if to make his point for him, the tremor in the earth intensified, dislodging stones around them. The moon dipped lower, its light dimmed.

"Stop this." The god's voice had a hard quality it lacked till now. "Your soulmate had a good life. She mourned you, but she found the way to go on. She fell in love again and grew old with a mortal. Had children with him, and passed a few weeks after he did. *But* the part that interests you is that she has been reborn."

Atlas couldn't begrudge Pleione's eventually building a new life without him. He wanted her to be happy. But that she'd been reborn was… Could it be true? He suppressed the sense of loss digging a hole in his chest, and straightened to glare Eros down. "Pleione is back?"

For a heartbeat, he wondered if Eros would reply. The god chewed his bottom lip, lines furrowing his smooth brow.

"Circe will kill me for telling you this—she didn't want any of you to know till the time was right—but Pleione's soul is in Iphigenia. When my mother, along with Hephaestus and Hestia, asked Zeus not to make your punishment eternal, he agreed to allow your soulmates to awaken you after the Olympians had faded. He couldn't break his promise, so he made sure none of the Titanesses would be left alive when time was ripe. Fate had different plans, though.

"At least three of the Titanesses' souls have been reincarnated, including hers. Iphigenia may have no memory of her time as Pleione, but they're the same soul— the one that completes yours. And you need to bond with her in the next couple days, or you'll lose her again for good, and it will be the end for life on Earth."

This wasn't… He couldn't… "Iphigenia is the reincarnation of my Pleione? She freed me from the marble?" It explained why he felt drawn to her from the start.

Eros rolled his eyes. "Didn't I just say that?"

"Then I have to claim her." Atlas would blink back to the museum, explain the situation to her, and demand that they bond. Surely she'd see it was for the greater good.

"*Woah.* Hold your horses there, guy. She has to fall for you, for the bonding to work. Plus, there are two things we need to do first."

"What?" Atlas ground out. Now that he had a plan, he wanted to act on it.

"Find you some clothes. And second, this." Faster than his grandfather's lightning, Eros wrapped his fingers around Atlas' wrist, and an onslaught of images and sounds filled Atlas' head.

Within a few short seconds, Eros had him view—no, *experience*—the history of the world he'd missed out on. And it was bloody. Humans were worse than gods, when it came to pettiness, ego, and greed.

"Are you sure destroying the planet and starting over wouldn't be the right thing to do?" he asked when Eros let go and the last of the images faded. Not that Atlas would, knowing he had a second chance to the life stolen from him.

"Positive. It may not look it, but humans are learning to be better. The bad is just louder, but they'll fix things. And their little ones…" A wistful smile curved Eros' lips. "They hold the future in their chubby hands." He clapped his hands. "Now, clothes."

Atlas was suddenly encased in something marginally less constricting than the rock he'd been locked in. "What is this?"

"Leather." Eros scratched his smooth cheek. "Too hot for this time of the year, though." He clapped again, and a soft white T-shirt—*hey,* he was up to date with the current lingo—hugged Atlas' torso, while Atlas' legs were wrapped in what his brand new memories said was a pair of jeans. The oddest sensation ever was what was around his feet, though. He looked down, and searched for the image in his mental bank. *Sneakers.*

The god saw him looking and smiled. "Boots would give you more *oomph,* but it's hot tonight. Plus these are better for running." He ducked, picked up the envelope and slapped it to Atlas' chest. "Better hurry. If Circe's right—

and she usually is, though I won't admit that to her—they'll
be snatching Iphigenia about now."

# CHAPTER FIVE

The ground beneath Iphigenia transformed from dirt and rock to wide slabs of marble so abruptly, she swayed. She squeezed her eyes shut to ward off dizziness and reached out blindly for purchase. Her fingers tapped a solid, smooth horizontal surface, and she grasped it for all she had, then took three long, calming breaths before opening her eyes again. She knew where she was before looking. The change in the warm air smelled of car exhaust, and the sounds of the city—even as empty as it was this week—rushed in to replace the eerie quiet of the mountaintop.

She was at the museum. More specifically, outside its main entrance.

With trembling fingers, she straightened her watch on her wrist and checked the time. A little after one. If she'd indeed passed out, this was half an hour to forty-five minutes unaccounted for. If she hadn't... she'd met not one, but two mythological creatures, and traveled to a mountain she didn't know existed and back in the blink of an eye.

She pinched her arm hard enough to bruise before she had time to reconsider. *Ouch.* Definitely felt that, but all it proved was that she was awake *now*.

Then again, she'd felt Atlas' lips against hers, and her palm still tingled where it'd touched his chest. Doubt seeped into her core, numbing her senses. Her mind had been the one thing in life she could always depend on. What if she was losing it? What if she couldn't trust her senses?

*Think. Prioritize.*

Whether Titans were real or not, whether an actual Greek god had sent her from a random mountaintop to right outside the Acropolis museum with a snap of his fingers or she'd dreamed it up, Iphigenia had a job to do.

She drew on her training, to focus on the task at hand instead of the fear she was losing touch with reality and her own sanity.

Whatever else might or might not be true, the break-in at the museum was a fact. From where she stood, she saw through the glass the sweeping glare of a flashlight coming from the first-level landing. She should stop the intruders, but if they were armed like Atlas said, she had no chance against them with just the Taser gun that came with the job. Though she'd pick facing humans with guns over ancient deities with grudges. Most days.

No reason to do this alone. During training week, she'd been instructed to neutralize possible threats during opening hours, but not try to subdue intruders by herself. She reached into her back pocket and let out a relieved sigh when her fingers closed around her phone. It hadn't been dislodged on her… journey back from Mount Othrys. If she'd ever been there.

She switched it back on and checked the screen. Three bars. *Yes.* Though the twin circles of light on the other side of the glass doors were almost at ground level, and she had no time to waste, she opened her video gallery.

The preview of the latest video was a still shot of Atlas, naked and tall and droolworthy.

He *was* real. Though he might not be a Titan but a crazy naked guy, who somehow—

No. She couldn't rationalize away the darkness around him in the image, or the gold in his eyes.

Would she see him again? Did she want to?

He wasn't interested. And neither was she, except to satisfy her curiosity.

"Curiosity killed the cat," she muttered to herself, as the memory of his hard body pressed to hers made her cheeks burn. *God*, she'd kissed him. And he hadn't wanted her to.

And could she call in the robbery, go home, and sleep tonight off?

She dialed *100* and waited for the police dispatcher to answer. Then, keeping the waver from her voice, she said, "My name is Iphigenia Konstantinou. I'm the night guard at the Acropolis museum. We've had a break—" She couldn't say more, because something hard dug into her back. A gun?

"Hand me the phone," a man whispered in her ear. She always thought bad guys would exude evil, but his breath smelled of mint. He pressed the gun harder against her back and held out his free hand around her side, where she could see his gloved palm.

She did as he ordered, and he ended the call, dropped the phone to the ground, and stomped on it. Iphigenia grimaced at the sound of her screen giving way under the heavy sole of the man's boot. The phone had cost almost a month's salary. This guy would regret ruining what was hers.

The man grabbed her by the arm and spun her to face him. He wore a sleek black hood. How movie cliché.

Iphigenia pretended to stumble, and when he reached for her, grabbed his forearms and brought up her knee between his legs. It would have landed too, if the earth hadn't rippled under her feet to fling her backward, into the waiting arms of someone else. Another man, judging by the hard chest she slammed into. This one smelled less pleasant—like old sweat and stale cigarette smoke.

His hands gripped her arms like vices. She tried to stomp on his foot, but he lifted her in the air and shook her like a rag doll. "Quit it, or I *will* hurt you." The gravelly warning was given in Greek, but with an accent she couldn't place. She stopped fighting, to buy herself time.

A woman to Iphigenia's right said, "Is this her?"

"Yeah," the chest-owner half-said, half-growled. "He turned into flesh and disappeared with her."

"Then don't hurt the girl yet. We'll need the needle."

Panic clawed at Iphigenia's throat. Would they give her more of the hallucinogen that had her seeing statues come to life, or—

No. If they meant to kill her, they could easily snap her neck. They planned to take her with them, and she had to buy time. Get them to talk. Keep them here till the police arrived. She let her body go slack, as if the fight was sapped out of her. "Please, don't. I'm afraid of needles. *Please.* I'll cooperate," she said hurriedly, as a cold point pricked the skin on the side of her neck. "I haven't even seen your faces. I can't tell on you." But her gut insisted they didn't worry about getting caught. They knew about her Titan.

The woman stepped within her line of sight, but Iphigenia couldn't make out her features beyond the long, blond hair, because everything was going blurry. The woman placed a gentle hand on Iphigenia's cheek. "Sleep, child."

A sudden wave of exhaustion weighed down Iphigenia's limbs, and her eyelids drifted shut. The world tilted sideways, as she lost feeling in her legs. Her brain was barely conscious enough to form a single word, which she screamed with all her remaining strength, though it never made it past her lips.

*Atlas.*

# CHAPTER SIX

Atlas didn't ask *who* or *why*. *Grabbing* meant she was taken against her will. He'd stop that.

Without a word, he blinked from the mountain and materialized in the room that had been his cell the past few months. Iphigenia wasn't here, and neither were the robbers. Had they taken her already?

His name echoed in his head in an agonized scream. Iphigenia. He'd end whoever terrified her this way.

Eros' words came back to him, and he wanted to smack himself. She was *outside* the museum.

Calling to mind the way he was carried in, he blinked to the entrance. She wasn't here either, but the sign read *For Personnel Only*, so it couldn't be the main entrance. Should he circle the building?

No time for that.

He tried to reach her mind and see what she saw, but though he sensed her presence, it was weak, and he had no visual.

*Chaos*, he wouldn't have time to unravel, if someone hurt her. He'd rip this world apart on purpose.

Desperation threatening to cloud his logic, he clung on a possibility so small, he'd never consider it in a less dire situation.

He concentrated on the spark of her soul he could feel, and tugged on it with all he was. The ground beneath him trembled, and the mental image of Kronos raging against the dark pressure surrounding him threatened to snuff out his connection to Iphigenia. Atlas ground his teeth and held on, while at the same time ordering his body to find her. This should be impossible—he'd never been in this city before, nor was he seeing it through her eyes—but his soul answered the call of its other half.

His surroundings wavered, and then disappeared, for the lights outside the museum to be replaced by a flickering street lamp. The majestic building gave way to tall, gray apartment buildings that framed a narrow street, and the air thickened further, infused with car exhaust, dirt, and old trash.

Atlas spun on his heel but couldn't see Iphigenia. A car turned the corner, speeding toward him, and he hopped on the sidewalk at the last possible moment before he rendered it a pile of junk metal and possibly killed the people in it.

But wait. His connection to Iphigenia felt almost palpable while the car was into view. She was in there, with her captors.

He could grow to his full size and chase down the vehicle, but the risk would be great. People might see him, and he doubted they'd appreciate meeting a Titan.

His only other option was to keep following Iphigenia's signal, until the car reached its destination.

Taking care to stick to the shadows, he ran after the car until he lost it, and then blinked near it again when it stopped at a traffic light. The face of the woman on the passenger seat was illuminated for a split second by a beam of light. She leaned her forehead against the glass, looking out, but her gaze was unfocused. She wasn't Iphigenia, but Atlas knew her.

Rhea—Kronos' wife. Zeus' mother.

How could it be?

Her hair was a lighter shade of blond, but her green eyes and the stubborn line of her mouth were unmistakable. This wasn't a passing resemblance; it was her. Another reincarnation?

The car started again, and he made to run after it, but a cacophony of horns stopped him. He couldn't dematerialize in front of so many witnesses, so he waited for his light to change, and jogged to the nearest building entrance, where, hidden from view, he blinked to Iphigenia again.

He almost ran head first into a mountain of garbage, and barely had time to duck beneath it as the car came into view. Hidden, he ignored the stench and watched as the driver pulled up to the corner building and Rhea exited and opened the back door. A large male scooted out and leaned back into the cabin. When he straightened again, Iphigenia's limp body was in his arms. Even from across the street, Atlas saw her chest rise and fall with her breath, and the spark of her life connected to him hadn't faded, but seeing her unresponsive boosted his wrath.

Atlas' first instinct was to barrel into them and grab her, but he might injure her inadvertently. Should he make his presence known? Demand they hand her over?

The night darkened further, and two street lights flickered off at the same time. Atlas looked at his hands.

He'd fisted them, but the left one was shaking visibly. This was disconcerting. Before he was put into stasis, he always had full control of his movements. Was this what Eros warned him of?

He stretched and curled his fingers. He still controlled them, despite the shaking. He could grab Iphigenia and blink back to Othrys, where he'd explain about the bonding and make her his.

It was for the greater good.

But when he looked up again, the male carrying Iphigenia wasn't in sight.

Rhea stood at the entrance to a gray building, holding the door open. She looked Atlas straight in the eye and said, "Well? Are you coming?"

Then she disappeared inside.

Atlas blinked where she'd been, barely making it into the building before the door swung close. His rational mind screamed this was a trap—why else would Rhea have made it so easy for him to follow?—but he would fight his way out of any situation, as long as he had Iphigenia.

He looked at the two sets of stairs ahead of him. One led up, the other down. Focusing on Iphigenia's spark, he took the latter, to the basement. The door he came upon, spotless, shiny, and reinforced, was in stark contrast to the peeling paint on the walls around it.

It couldn't stop a Titan, though.

Atlas splayed one palm on its center and pushed, and the door caved in. A second shove ripped it from its hinges, and he found himself looking down a short corridor, framed by doors on both sides.

"Rhea?" he called out. No reason to keep things low key. She knew he was here.

"Come right in, big guy." Her voice came from the first door to his right.

Senses on alert, since he didn't know how many others were down here, he followed her voice and found her sitting behind a large desk. Her expression was placid, even friendly, but her yellow eyes sparked with something he couldn't place.

They'd never been friends before, or even allies since she was on the Olympians' side, but they shared a history, and for that, he'd be civil. For now.

"Where have you taken the human?" he asked.

Rhea motioned for him to take the empty chair across the desk from her. "Sit. Would you like something to drink?"

He didn't need drink or food to survive, but he'd never said *no* to nectar. Still, this wasn't the time to drop his guard. "No, thank you. You have a sordid history with potions." Afraid he'd share his own father's fate, Kronos had swallowed his offspring whole, as Rhea gave birth to them. She'd managed to hide Zeus from him and instead given Kronos a rock to swallow. Once Zeus was old enough to fight, Rhea had drugged her mate, for her son to free his siblings from their father's belly.

Rhea seemed undisturbed by Atlas' jibe. "I was trying to save my children. You would have done the same." She shrugged. "I must say, I'm glad it's you."

Atlas arched an eyebrow, squelching his impatience. Rhea wanted him here for a reason, and he couldn't deal with her properly until he knew what that was.

She kept talking, as if to herself. "I'd rather it were Kronos, of course. Would have made things easier." She trailed off, the sparkle in her eyes gone.

"What things? Why am I here, Rhea? And how are you alive?" This close, he sensed her power and had no doubt she was truly the Titaness.

She tilted her head to the side and gave him a wistful smile. "You didn't think my son would let me wither and die, like he did my sisters? No. I supported him for millennia, while he ruled over humans and gods alike. And once he faded…" The glint was back, and Atlas recognized it for what it was—insanity. "You have to help me find Kronos," she hissed. "When he awakens, I can have my golden boy again."

Atlas recoiled. She wanted Kronos *and* Zeus back? "I will not help you free Kronos. Last time he and Zeus had it out, the world suffered the consequences. Now, I'm going to find Iphigenia and get out of here, and you'll stay out of my way if you know what's best for you."

Her gaze turned shrewd. "You fought on your brother's side. Why turn against him?"

He got to his feet slowly and shook his head. "I stood with him because he told me Zeus meant to destroy us all, and he was correct. But this is a new world. The only threat to the few of us who've awakened would come from our power-crazed brother, and I have no intention of allowing that to happen."

Rhea blinked between him and the door. "You're not the only one." The terrifying smile stretching her lips said he shouldn't have mentioned the other Titans out of stasis, but she didn't know who or where they were. She couldn't harm them.

"I've been dreaming of him," she said conversationally. "He says he'll awaken if there's a strong enough earthquake. A Titan's unraveling could make that happen, if I harness it."

Of course she knew about the unraveling, but she was delusional if she thought she could harness the power it would unleash. "That would end the world," he said. He needed to keep her talking while he sought Iphigenia's signal again.

Rhea rocked on the balls of her feet. "Maybe that's for the best. Maybe the voices will stop, and I'll rest. We'll see what happens, once your time is up."

He'd heard enough. He dematerialized from the room and out into the corridor. "*Iphigenia*," he bellowed in his head. "Can you hear me?" She might not be awake yet, but if he reached her, he could mentally nudge her into consciousness.

Rhea came out to the corridor behind him. "Get him," she yelled.

A dozen men rushed him. They were large and built like brick walls, but they were mortal. They had no chance of besting him, as he tossed them aside like rag dolls on his way to the only other closed door within view.

"Look, child. See what he's capable of." Rhea's whisper reached him despite the distance between them and the shouted threats by the humans.

He spun on his heel, to see her holding Iphigenia upright, one arm around his woman's waist.

"What have you done to her?" he growled.

Rhea stared him down. "It's not me she should fear, but you. Destruction follows in your wake."

He took a step toward them, and one of the men punched him in the solar plexus. Atlas barely broke his stride, as he threw the man into the wall. "Your men can't stop me," he told Rhea, as he blinked a hair's breadth from her.

The grin she gave him bordered between playful and maniacal. "All I need to do is stall, Titan." She disappeared, and he barely had time to drape his arm over Iphigenia's shoulders before her knees gave way.

"Hold on, my Iphigenia. I'll take you home," he whispered, and back to Mount Othrys, they went.

# CHAPTER SEVEN

Atlas was pacing before her, rambling, but Iphigenia couldn't register the words. Her mind was suffering whiplash from tonight's events.

Or was it last night's?

A gray haze lightened the sky, as dawn approached. Would the sun wake her up?

*You're not dreaming.*

Why was her logic arguing with her? Didn't she realize dreaming all this up was the safest, sanest option? If she was awake, she had to accept that a statue had turned human—no, *Titan*—that mythology wasn't just a bunch of stories, and that the guy she had the hots for could travel with the speed of light. Oh, and he was strong enough to send men crashing through walls.

He was imposing, the way he stared at her, fists on his hips. Like Superman. Only he wasn't made of steel but marble. Her giggle sounded maniacal.

"Are you listening?" he demanded with a scowl. "Rhea is dangerous. She will come after you." His eyes were the color of honey. Pretty eyes. Pretty mouth too, even drawn into a hard line, as it was. And he was dressed now, which should make it easier for her to think, but his T-shirt was about to rip over his bulging muscles, and his jeans fit him like a glove, leaving little to the imagination.

And she'd been kidnapped tonight. Three times, if she were technical about it. Was this Stockholm syndrome? Was she falling for her captor solely because of the power he held over her?

Nah. That took a while. This was insta-attraction, and she would get over it as easily as she got under it.

"You're not." He snapped his fingers in front of her face. "Has what they gave you not worn off yet?"

*What they gave you.* A syringe. The woman and her goons shot something into Iphigenia, and that was why she focused on the lust her Titan gave rise to, instead of the issue at hand. Which was multi-fold.

When the morning shift showed up at the museum, they'd find a Titan statue gone and her missing. Would they assume she stole Atlas? Security footage should prove her innocence, but even if that wasn't tampered with, they'd know she hadn't done a good job of protecting him.

Pfft. Like Atlas needed her protection. He was huge and strong and— Where did he find the clothes? He was almost as yummy in them as out of them.

*Focus.*

She'd need a story for the police. One that didn't involve the guy carved in stone walking out of there by himself.

The police. *Shit.* They'd be all over the museum by now. "You need to take me back to work. I must talk to the police. Give a description of the people who grabbed me." At least of the woman, since the men's faces were covered.

And maybe she could say she saw them load the statue in a van before she passed out.

Atlas shook his head. "We've been through this before. You can't go back. It's not safe. Especially now that Rhea knows… who you are."

Iphigenia sat on the ground with a *huff* and busied herself trying to uncover a piece of rock from the dirt. Anything, not to look him in the eye. "Is she your ex? The one you said you're bonded to?"

"No. She's my brother's…" He frowned. "His wife."

"*Brother?* As in, another Titan?" How many more were running around? Wait— "Which means she's…?"

He huffed. "A Titaness. Only, unlike my mate, she's been alive all this time."

Shit. So his mate was dead? Or in a museum somewhere?

She didn't have to ask.

"Eros told me my Pleione is long gone. Zeus turned all females of my kind mortal, after his lightning turned me to stone." His voice went gruffer, as if it hurt to utter the words.

His pain was so tangible, it squeezed inside her sternum. She suppressed the urge to go to him. He might mistake her offer of comfort for another pass at him, and that was the last thing he needed on the day he found out the love of his life was dead.

"I'm sorry," she muttered. "I can't imagine how you must be feeling."

He dropped to the ground, facing her, one leg bent at the knee, the other stretched out toward her. "It's odd," he said. "I'd given up on ever seeing her again, but for a while after you brought me back, I let myself believe..." He closed his palm into a white-knuckled fist, then splayed his fingers. Iphigenia saw them tremble, before he clasped both hands together and met her gaze. "When you kissed me—"

"I'm so sorry. I don't know what I was thinking..."

"I wanted to kiss you back. Not giving in to the feeling of your lips on mine was harder than you could ever know."

She licked her lips, self-conscious under his gaze. "I'm still here," she said. What was she doing? Part of her screamed that she was offering herself up as a consolation prize. She couldn't afford an emotional attachment to someone who'd just had his heart broken. But being this close to him made her feel alive for the first time. Her senses heightened, tuning in to every detail in his posture.

His breathing was shallow, the amber of his irises melting into gold as he shifted his position so he was on his knees. The pain in his eyes was replaced by something more primal. Raw. Hungry. And was that a hint of hope?

No. She was seeing things.

He crawled toward her slowly, his gaze boring into her. He emanated power, and she wanted nothing more than to yield to it. To him.

Atlas stopped centimeters from her and cupped her face with one hand. "I am going to kiss you again, Iphigenia. Properly this time."

Iphigenia swallowed hard. "Uh huh."

Despite his words, the first touch of his lips was soft, timid, as if he was giving her the chance to break away. When she parted her lips, the gentleness gave way to a breathtaking intensity. He nibbled on her lips and massaged her tongue with his, his free hand skating its way up her back to press her to him. He devoured her moans, slipping his palm from her jaw, to twist his fingers in her hair and let her curls loose from the band keeping them in place.

"Like silk," he muttered against her mouth. Did he mean her hair or her skin?

She didn't care. She dove back into the kiss, sucking on his tongue. Her body arched into him, as if of its own accord, and moisture pooled at the apex of her thighs. She knew he'd kiss like this. And when he lowered the palm on her back, to untuck her shirt and slide his fingers beneath it, she knew his touch would light a fire in her belly she would be unable to deny.

"I want you."

How did his words come out this clearly, when his teeth had her bottom lip trapped?

She groaned, and didn't resist when he used his body to urge her backward, until she was on her back, feeling the cool earth against her skin except where his palm burned her.

Never breaking the kiss, he cupped one of her breasts and pinched the nipple that throbbed against the lace of her bra. She wanted to lose that bra. The cotton of her uniform shirt suffocated her, and the slacks felt restrictive. She wanted to be naked, writhing under him.

Atlas pulled away and watched her face as he lowered his hand down her stomach, to undo her belt, and she arched her back, to drive him lower.

When he closed his large palm over her thigh and traced the seam at her crotch, she swore she was about to come.

He repeated the gesture with a little more pressure, making her pussy tingle. "Do you want me?" he asked.

Yes. *God*, yes. Right here, in the middle of nowhere, under the brightening sky and with the echoing bells of sheep in the distance, she wanted him inside her.

She nodded.

His grin was feral, as he slowly undid her pants. He blew down her front, and she watched mesmerized as the gust of air wrapped around each of her shirt's buttons and undid it, then spread the garment open.

"So beautiful. And all mine."

*My Pleione.* The chill in the air seeped into her bones, driving out the warmth in her belly, as the words came unbidden to mind.

Atlas didn't want her. Not so soon after his loss. He wanted his woman, his Pleione, and Iphigenia was just a warm body. A momentary distraction, after millennia of loneliness.

No no no. She should push him away. Only, when she rested her palm on his chest, fully planning to stop him, she found herself grabbing a fistful of the soft cotton and pulling him on top of her.

"Really? I make the effort to build you an entire life, and you can't bother not to lose it?" Eros' voice came from above them, and when Atlas rolled off her, Iphigenia saw the god looking at them disapprovingly. He shook the brown envelop he was holding. "Other than essential info about this world, like delivery numbers, this has credit cards, ID papers, a cell phone, and a key to Prometheus' house. Even if you ignore all my work, I doubt he'd appreciate you losing that."

Atlas plucked the envelope from Eros' fingers. "I'll make sure not to drop it next time I have to save someone from mortal danger," he said dryly. "Now if you don't mind, we're in the middle of something."

That snapped Iphigenia out of her shock at the god's arrival. With trembling fingers, she covered herself and buttoned her shirt over her breasts as she sat up. "No, that's okay. I should leave, anyway. The police will be looking for me. Museum people too."

Eros shook his head. "Fixed that. Only one looking for you is a semi-crazed Titaness. Sticking with this guy is your safest option for now."

"How? How did you... fix that? Did you make people forget about me?" She raised her voice, trying to control the tremble panic infused into her words. "Does anyone remember I even exist?"

Eros looked at her like she'd grown an extra head. "I simply changed your schedule so someone else had the night shifts this week, and moved that guy to the right place. I then erased the record of your call to the cops and arranged for an actual statue of a Titan to replace him." He hooked a thumb toward Atlas. "Though I had to convince a Nereid to give it up, so maybe it wasn't all that simple." He looked very satisfied with himself.

# CHAPTER EIGHT

"This is all... It's crazy." Minutes ago Iphigenia was offering herself to him, and now she crossed her arms over her breasts and glowered from him to Eros.

No world-saving activities would be enjoyed today, judging from her posture.

The nearest village was filling with early-morning life. Soon, they'd have an audience. "Can we move this someplace more private?" Atlas asked.

"I'll take you to Santorini. Prometheus said you can stay at his place till the bonding stabilizes you, and it's warded against Rhea." Eros pointed to the brown envelop he was so obsessed with. "Don't lose this again."

Iphigenia climbed to her feet, the flaps of her shirt billowing in the breeze when she planted her fists on her hips. "I'm not going anywhere until you explain. Why is he unstable? What is this bo—"

Eros grasped both their hands and blinked them out of there.

"—nding crap?" Her arms flew up and she stumbled back. "What the fuck?"

Atlas wrapped an arm around her waist and held her to him. It felt right, having her in his arms, but instead of melting into him like she did before, she stood stock still, tension rolling off her in waves. "I need to sit down," she said.

"You got this." Eros nodded at Atlas and disappeared.

Atlas led her to what looked like an outdoor lounge behind them and helped her into a wicker armchair, taking the chance to assess their surroundings.

They were on a spacious balcony, overlooking dark rocks that ended into the bluest sea. The stark white of the wall blended into the backdrop of bright-blue sky, and a wind chime and the sound of waves below them were all that disrupted the perfect quiet of the morning.

He turned to Iphigenia, who'd propped her elbows on the table and dropped her head in her palms. "Are you all right?" he asked.

When she raised her head, he expected an expression of despair, not the angry glare she shot his way.

"I don't know. Am I? Last night, my biggest problem was being stuck in Athens in the middle of August, with no boyfriend and nothing to do. Now I'm a runaway, hiding from a freaking Titaness and making out with a guy who's been around for—oh, I don't know—a few thousand years. And of course, a god has been tossing me from one place to the next without asking for permission."

Atlas sat across from her and placed the envelope on the table between them. "It was for your own good. You were in danger." And he should be more understanding and less focused on the no-boyfriend part. He already knew she was single.

She snorted. "Yeah, about that... Who put me in danger in the first place? I wouldn't be a bleep on your sister in law's radar if it weren't for you."

He fumbled for the right words, but only came up with, "I didn't choose for that to happen."

"Well, it happened anyway, didn't it? And then, instead of explaining things to me, you kissed me, and you were all over me, and I don't want to be a convenient distraction because you can't have the one you actually want."

He opened his mouth to protest and clear this up, but Iphigenia cut him off with a tired shake of her head.

"I—I can't process this." She looked tired now, the fight sapped out of her. "Please, take me home?"

"If you'd only hear me out—"

"I will. Honest. But I've been awake since yesterday afternoon. I'm hungry, and"—she sniffed her armpits and grimaced—"I stink. I need a shower and clean clothes. And maybe a couple hours of sleep. Then we can talk."

Freshening up and getting some rest would put her in a better mood. "I'll take you to get your things, but we can't stay long. We'll come back here, and you can sleep for as long as you need. When you're ready, I'll tell you everything." And hope she'd see reason.

For a moment, Iphigenia seemed about to argue, but then she sighed and nodded. "Do you need to touch me?"

Desperately. Was she offering? "What do you mean?"

"To read my mind. Get us to my place. Do you need to be touching me?"

He stood and rounded the table to pull out her chair. "Not necessarily, but it will ensure we don't end up in different parts of your house."

"Apartment." She held out her hand and let him pull her close. "So I just think of my bedroom?"

"Yes. Focus on your memories in that room." He regretted the words the moment they left his lips. What if she thought of herself naked with another man?

But when she opened her mind to him, he got a visual of her stretched out in bed, headphones blasting music in her ears, as she petted a shaggy blond dog lying with his head on her thigh. The dog's ears twitched, one raised and one flat to the side, and his tongue lolled happily out of his mouth.

"You have a dog." How come she hadn't mentioned him?

Sadness, thick and tangible, frayed the edges of the memory. "Ares isn't mine. My ex kept him when I— When we broke up. He said I owed him. I think he did it to hurt me."

Ah, her jilted lover was vengeful. Atlas would have to fix that. For now, he focused on the feel of the coverlet under her bare legs and the smell of jasmine wafting in from the plant outside her window. He ordered their bodies to dematerialize and take shape again on her mattress.

Or right next to it.

They tumbled to the floor, Iphigenia on top, and Atlas allowed himself to enjoy the weight of her body against his for a heartbeat, before hopping to his feet and helping her upright. "Get what you need, but stay within sight."

She snorted over her shoulder, as she headed for the closet. "What? Afraid I'll run away? Doubt I'll get very far, before you—"

"No, child. He's afraid I'll take you away." Rhea blinked to the door, and then behind Iphigenia. Her arm was around Iphigenia's throat before either she or Atlas could move a muscle.

"Let her go." He gritted his teeth. Could he blink to them before Rhea snapped his woman's neck?

Iphigenia threw back her elbow, that caught Rhea in the ribs, and stomped on the Titaness' foot with her booted heel.

Rhea was unfazed as she stared down Atlas. "Not unless you give yourself to us. And if I feel the slightest breeze, she's dead."

Us? *Chaos*, she wasn't here alone.

A red dot appeared on Iphigenia's chest—the end of a beam Atlas followed to a scary-looking weapon in the arms of a human male by the door.

"Drop that," Atlas ordered in the man's head.

Nothing.

Rhea cackled, the sound as crazed as her intention to awaken Kronos, and Atlas felt the walls tightening around them.

"Don't bother trying to influence Periandros. My men have sworn themselves to me. Only I can affect their thoughts." She fisted her free hand in Iphigenia's hair, stretching Iphigenia's neck backward.

Atlas watched, horrified, as his soulmate's eyes rolled back in their sockets and her body went slack. Her heartbeat still tattooed a steady rhythm to his ears, but she'd passed out.

"Let. Her. *Go.*" He squeezed his fists until his knuckles ached. The metal frame of the bed behind him creaked. No—wait. That was the closet doors, rattling on their hinges. Plaster fell on his head and shoulders. Got in his eyes. He didn't care. The building might rip in half, for all he cared. "*Now.*"

"Why should I, when keeping her from you will get me what I want?" The look Rhea spared him was almost kind. "You can't get to both me and Periandros in time. Yield, and I'll let you unravel as far from her as possible. Resist, and I'll wait till you spin out of control and kill her as well as yourself. Try to free her, and he"—she tilted her head toward the gunman—"will shoot her through the heart. Anyway, I win." There was no deception in her voice. She simply stated facts.

And she was right; she won in all scenarios. Except for the one that had Eros interfering. Atlas' best choice was to go along with her and hope the god of love would find him and help him out. To stall for time, he said, "How did you find us?"

"I asked her boss nicely for her address. He was happy to oblige." Rhea batted her long eyelashes, the epitome of innocence, before her expression hardened. "Enough chitchat. Are you coming, or do I rip her head off?"

"I'll come with you," he said. "Just leave her alone."

Rhea motioned with her head toward the door, and a second human male bypassed the armed guy and entered the room. The silver chain glimmering in his gloved hands made Atlas shiver even before the cold metal snapped shut around his wrists, locking them together. He tried to spread his arms, testing his restraints. No give. Worse, his thoughts felt muddled and his legs heavy.

"Don't waste your strength. Those were forged by my son's lightning bolt, to contain his father, if he awoke. You cannot break them." The pride shining in Rhea's crazed eyes added to the chill seeping inside him. Could he trust her to keep her word and leave Iphigenia alone?

"I did what you said. Now place her on the bed, and we can go."

Rhea let Iphigenia crumble to a heap at her feet. "You don't get to order me around. He does it too. Every day. Always there. In my head. *Shut up.*" Rhea's voice rose in pitch, as she gave Iphigenia a soft kick. "You know, I can kill her anyway, and there's nothing you can do." She turned her gaze to the man beside Atlas. "I could let Miltiades have his way with her while you watch."

Wrath spilled through Atlas' veins, potent and all consuming. It tore through the cobwebs muting his responses and pushed away reason that insisted Rhea's threat was meant to manipulate him. The floorboards beneath him vibrated, and a gust of wind smashed the door into the gunman's hand, making him drop his weapon.

"What are you doing?" Rhea shrieked. "You can't use your powers. The manacles—"

Atlas let his rage suffuse him, as he raised his arms and pulled. The manacles snapped apart, and their glow faded until they melted away.

He was going to end Rhea. Destroy her, for ever threatening Iphigenia.

The man who'd bound his wrists grabbed Atlas' arm, and Atlas let himself grow until his head touched the ceiling. One shake of his arm, and the man went flying behind him. He crashed on something, but Atlas didn't look.

His focus was on Rhea.

Bleed her.

Tear her heart out with his own hands, again and again.

Rhea leaned down, and time seemed to slow as reason took over his blood lust. If she touched Iphigenia, she could take her anywhere in the world. She could kill her or merely keep her and Atlas apart long enough for him to unravel.

Rhea's punishment for meaning his soulmate harm would have to wait.

He blinked between her and Iphigenia, gathered Iphigenia in his arms, and willed the two of them back to Santorini.

# CHAPTER NINE

Mmm… Soft.

Iphigenia rubbed her cheek against the silk and smiled. This pillow was fluffy like a cloud. Heavenly.

Shit. Was she dead? But she was breathing.

She wouldn't open her eyes. She was having a lovely dream. What was it?

Ah yes. Atlas. Naked, like he'd been when he first awoke. Kissing her.

*Rhea, choking her. Not budging when Iphigenia tried to free herself.*

No. She wanted the dream back. Titan-y goodness, not Titaness-y terror. Rhea could have killed her.

Had she?

"I know you're awake. Don't be afraid. She can't find you here." Atlas' smooth, deep bass glided down her body like a caress.

Iphigenia rolled toward his voice and cracked open an eyelid. He sat in a chair by the bed she lay in, elbows on his knees and fingers steepled. She looked at the room around him. Spacious and bright white, even in the dimming sun filtering in through the gauzy curtains. "We're in Santorini?"

"Yes." He studied her face.

His scrutiny made her self-conscious. She pulled the sheet higher, and when it slid up naked skin, raised it to look down her body. She was in her underwear.

Atlas pursed his lips. "I know you wanted a shower, but I didn't want to shock you with the water spray, so I… air-cleaned you."

She was surprised by the smile tugging at the corners of her lips. "Like a car?"

He grinned. "I guess. You can shower now. Bathe, if you'd prefer."

Would he offer to scrub her back?

His grin turned wicked. Did he read her thoughts? She imagined walls slamming down around her mind, and he sat back hard, as if pushed by an invisible force. Good. That'd teach him not to pry.

She should get out of bed, get dressed, and formulate a plan. She wasn't a wilting flower, staying huddled in a—gorgeous, sunbathed, comfortable—villa in Santorini, while an all-mighty ancient bitch searched for her.

A slew of questions flooded her. Why was Rhea after her? And what was the unraveling she and Eros had mentioned?

Atlas had promised to tell her everything, but in nothing but her briefs and bra, she felt too vulnerable to discuss a life-or-death situation.

*Her* life or death. Rhea wanted her dead. And could make it happen. The helplessness of being in the Titaness' mercy wasn't something Iphigenia cared to experience again. That same feeling was what first led her to martial arts, after a mugging sent her to the hospital with ten stitches in her right side and a mild concussion. She'd been taught self-defense, yet she'd frozen after her initial effort to free herself from Rhea.

Never again.

"Are you feeling well?" Atlas asked. "Eros said you weren't hurt. That's why I let you sleep. If you need medical attention, I can—"

"No. I'm fine." Once more, with feeling. "I'm *fine*. Really. I was just thinking we didn't get any of my clothes, after all." Better to focus on the practical than the terror of being at someone else's mercy.

He hopped upright and rushed to a sofa at the other end of the room, to gather up a stack of clothes. "Don't worry. Eros took care of that, too. He brought a few things, so you can choose what works for you."

"He did? When?" She sat up and scooted back, propping herself against the sun-bleached planks that acted as a headrest for the stone-built bed, the sheet clutched in front of her as a protective barrier. Against what? Atlas? Her lack of compulsion control when he was near?

"Yesterday," he said.

Huh? Before she and Atlas came to this place? Her brain stalled, and then kicked into gear. "How long was I out?"

"A day. And then some." He placed the clothes beside her and hurried to add, "But Eros assured me you'd be all right." His gaze begged her to confirm that she was.

It was tempting to let him worry, after what he'd put her through—Rhea wouldn't know Iphigenia existed if it weren't for this guy—but the only thing that hurt was her stomach. "I'm hungry." Her stomach growled its agreement.

"I can help with that." But he stayed where he was, watching as she flipped through her garment choices.

Iphigenia tugged at a corner of crisp, white, cotton fabric, and unfolded a short plain dress in her lap. Perfect for the weather and the time of year. Not so suitable for running for her life, though. More rummaging provided a red tank top and a pair of denim cutoffs. Perfect. She pulled the top on and squirmed into the bottoms under the covers.

Done.

And Atlas was still here, instead of bringing her something to eat.

"Um… so are we going out for lunch?" she asked. Was that safe?

"No. Of course not. I doubt Rhea will think of looking for us on the island, but we can't take any chances."

She pursed her lips and stared at him.

He stared back. "What?"

"Food. Need. Soon."

Someone knocked on the bedroom door, and Iphigenia's heart hammered in her chest. She forgot her hunger as her stomach plummeted to her feet. "Rhea?" she muttered with numb lips. Had she found them?

Atlas closed the distance to the bed and cupped her cheek. "No. You're safe here, with me. I swear it on my eternity. As long as I breathe, she won't lay a hand on you again."

She believed him, God help her. Despite the chaos he'd brought into her life, she felt safe with him. He anchored her. How was it possible, when she barely knew him?

Wind whistled in through the window, and Iphigenia thought she saw the air around the bedroom door ripple, before the handle twisted and the door swung open. The woman who entered pulling a cart backward into the room bore no resemblance to the Valkyrie-like Titaness. She was short and stout, with curly gray hair, and when she turned to smile at them over her shoulder, her wrinkled face was split by a warm smile. "Finally, you're up," she said. "Your man has been driving me crazy. With those large feet of his, his pacing can be heard throughout the villa."

Iphigenia salivated at the smell of bacon and eggs. Atlas stepped back, as the woman parked the cart by the bed. *God*, there was so much food, and Iphigenia wanted *all of it*. And were these tomatokeftedes? Santorini was famous for its cherry tomatoes, and these tomato fritters were a local delicacy.

And they went amazingly with feta, Iphigenia mused as she stuffed an entire fritter and a piece of cheese in her mouth. "These are delicious." She moaned in appreciation.

"I'm glad you like them, dear. Let me know if you need anything else." The woman glanced at Atlas. "Perhaps use the intercom next time?"

Iphigenia mumbled a *thanks* as the woman left, and then added a slice of bacon and some egg white to the perfect bite. She felt like a chipmunk, with both cheeks bulging, but if she didn't look at Atlas, she could pretend he wasn't seeing this.

Her stomach's protests quieted, but there was still a mountain of food left. She wiped her mouth and met his gaze. "Aren't you hungry?"

He shook his head. "I don't need food, though Marigo insisted I have a big breakfast this morning."

She gave him a blank look, and he elaborated. "The cook. The woman who brought this up?" He pointed at the cart. "Apparently she comes with the lodgings."

Right. "What was that about the intercom?"

"I reached to her mentally, to tell her you were up and required sustenance." He might as well have said he texted the woman, as impassively as he spoke.

Iphigenia washed down her last bite with a gulp of cooling coffee, before she spoke. "You *reached out to her* in another room? How long is your reach?"

He smirked and waggled his eyebrows. "Thought I'd given you some idea of its size. Before Eros interrupted us."

Her face burned, but she wouldn't be distracted. "You know what I mean."

He came to sit next to her, one leg folded at the knee on the mattress between them. "I haven't tested its extent, but the kitchen is two floors down."

Two freaking floors down? She gulped but kept her expression flat. "Okay. I'm fed, dressed, and mostly clean. I'm ready to hear why Rhea wants me dead."

He took a deep, slow breath, and let it out in a tortured sigh. Whatever he had to say was practically guaranteed to shock her, but unless she took it in stride, she'd drive herself nuts.

"Because of your connection to me. Because you're… Because you awakened me." He fell silent, drumming his fingers on his knee.

"But that's done now. You're up and running." He avoided her gaze. "What aren't you telling me?"

"It's not…" He scowled. "I'm trying to order my thoughts, so what comes out makes sense to you."

Huh. So they had this in common, other than intense chemistry. "Say it anyway, and we'll make sense of it after it's out."

With a snort, he said, "All right. Rhea wants to get rid of you because she knows you're my soulmate."

Her thoughts came to a screeching halt. "She knows *what*?"

"That you are my soulmate."

Iphigenia had heard the word the first time, but it made no sense. And some things couldn't be taken in stride. "We just met. I don't even know if I like you. I mean I *like* you, but we've barely spent any time together with both of us being flesh and bone and nobody trying to kill me."

He tilted his head back and scratched his wide chest with those long, thick fingers of his.

Yup. She definitely *liked* him.

But he was speaking. "—your reservations, yet it was fated." He seemed to wait for her response, but what could she say? She didn't believe in fate.

Then again, she didn't believe in Titans, either.

"You and I are meant to be together, and we are supposed to bond soon, or this planet and possibly the universe are doomed," he said.

*Bond?*

She didn't ask it aloud, but he explained anyway. "Claim each other's heart, while I make you mine." He shrugged and met her gaze. His eyes—gold now—pleaded with her to understand, and part of her wanted nothing more than to accept what he offered and lose herself into him.

Iphigenia slowly pushed aside the food cart and stood. She needed to move, to keep herself busy. She started making the bed, her back to him. If she met those eyes again, she'd give in to anything at all. "This is the lamest pickup line I've ever heard, and I've heard more than my fair share."

He appeared at her side before she realized he'd moved. He folded an arm around her waist and pulled her flush against him.

Were they being attacked again? She held on to his bicep, to steady herself, and not because it bulged through the smooth cotton of his T-shirt. "Hey. What—"

Atlas crushed his mouth to hers, and when she tried to protest, slipped his wicked tongue between her lips. It mapped every centimeter of her mouth, sending tingles spreading down her spine and making her toes curl. When she leaned into him, her body yielding to the intensity of his pull, his skin thrummed with power.

He buried his free hand in her hair and bunched it away from her throat, to nuzzle the spot under her ear. "Do I seem like I need pickup lines?"

"Nah uh." She sought his lips again, but his grip on her curls kept his face just out of her reach.

"You really are my soulmate, and we really need to bond."

The word Eros used clicked into place, and she reined in her desire. "To stabilize you?"

"Yes." The gold in his irises faded, his expression turning solemn.

"Or you'll… unravel?"

He touched his forehead to hers. "Correct."

"And the world will go *boom*."

He nodded. "Consider it Zeus' gift from beyond the grave."

Well, saving the world was as compelling a reason as any, to sleep with a guy who made her quiver with desire just by looking at her, but the *claim each other's heart* part stumped her. She'd spend years safeguarding her heart, and he expected her to hand it to him? "Can I think about it?"

# CHAPTER TEN

He couldn't blame her for needing to process things. He'd just ladened her with life-changing information that must have shaken her belief system to the core. In addition to coming to life in front of her when she thought he was a statue.

Anyone would need to think about it before being bound to another being for eternity. That didn't mean Atlas wasn't hurt by her reaction. Deep down, he'd expected her to jump at the chance to *be* with him.

And that expectation was irrational and sentimental. He wouldn't allow insecurity to take over. This wasn't a rejection.

The hollow feeling in his chest mocked his reasoning.

Waiting for her to shower felt like it took an eternity, but he'd hoped she'd be more amicable to seeing things his way now that she'd freshened up. Instead, she seemed set on rebuffing him.

"I understand." He tried to sound sincere. His hand shook, and he hid it in his jeans' pocket.

Iphigenia paced the length of the room, her arms folded over her chest. "I mean, we don't have anything in common. There is an undeniable pull between us, but you haven't been with anyone in way too long, and only last night, you expected to be rejoined with your wife. You must see why I have my reservations." Her voice was low, as if she was talking to herself.

The fingers of Atlas' other hand twitched. Was his unraveling drawing near? He should tell her. Pressure her to make a choice now.

No. She had to realize bonding with him was the best thing for both of them, as well as the only way to save creation as she knew it.

But he'd rather she offered him her heart because she ached for him like he ached for her. Because she couldn't draw breath without him.

He glided his gaze up her long legs, as she took step after step, and lingered on the curve of her buttocks, stretching the seat of her denim. The sliver of bare flesh that peeked between her waistband and her top invited him to touch it. Lick it. Make her shiver.

Iphigenia reached the door, spun on her heel, and started walking in the opposite direction. "And to be honest, I couldn't commit to a human fiancé, and he had decent odds of dying before I did. How can I commit to you?" She paused, hands on her hips. "Do you even age? Or will you stick around, looking like that, while I grow old and withered? What will stop you from having affairs?"

She looked incensed and ready to turn him down. His gut told him no words could change her mind. He'd have to show her why no other woman would ever measure up.

Instead of blinking to her, he took slow, deliberate strides to where she stood, close enough that she had to crane her neck to see his face. He heard her breath hitch. Heard her heart race. Saw the widening of her pupils. Her body reacted to his proximity, and he wasn't even touching her.

Then again, his body never ceased reacting to her.

He curled his fingers around her wrist and led her hand to cup his hard length. "You're arguing against our bonding, yet I can think of nothing else but burying myself inside you. The world is hanging at the precipice of doom, and I care more about tasting your divine pussy. You may not recognize this… *pull*"—he used the word she'd chosen—"between us for what it truly is, but it's a cord tethering our hearts together." If he could resist that when he thought he was still bound to Pleione, he could obviously refuse any other female's wiles because of it.

He had the sense to know that saying so, reminding her of Pleione, wouldn't help his case when she didn't realize she had Pleione's soul in her. And it definitely wasn't the time for him to disclose that.

He touched his forehead to hers, willing her to read the truth of his words in his mind. "I cannot deny that cord any more than I can resist it. Accept me, give yourself to me, and there will *never* be another." There wouldn't be anyone else even if Iphigenia wouldn't have him. Even if he didn't unravel. She was his other half.

"But—"

Like before, he swallowed her protest. He enjoyed this means of shutting her up immensely—doubly so when she fisted her hands in his T-shirt and pulled him closer, curling one leg around his thigh. Even through his jeans, her center scorched him where it pressed against him. He skated his palm up her bare thigh, to knead one buttock, and then pressed two fingers along the seam of her shorts, where her heat called to him. She rocked her hips into his touch, and he was done holding back.

He wedged his fingers under the thin strip of denim and the cotton of her briefs, and touched bare skin. She was smooth and soft and like a ripe apricot warmed by the sun, and he wanted to taste her more than ever before.

He turned and blinked across the stone floor, to lay her on the bed, then dropped on his knees before it.

She propped herself up on her elbows and blew a dark curl off her face. "What are you doing?"

In lieu of an answer, he clasped both sides of her shorts and tugged. They didn't give him more trouble than the thinnest lace would, as he tore them in half.

"Hey! Those were new." But she wriggled her ass to help him get those and her briefs down her hips.

He hadn't spotted any underwear in the clothes Eros gave him, so he didn't rip those, but slid them off and caressed his way up her legs.

Iphigenia dropped back with an *oof* when he used his thumbs to separate her labia and buried his face in her pussy. She felt like silk, and he wanted to rub his face in her slickness, but the scent of her arousal called to him. He groaned as he trailed his tongue up her slit, to find the pearl hidden there and close his lips around it. When he sucked on the tender flesh, she spread her legs wider and tilted her hips, grinding against his face.

Atlas let go of her clitoris to tease her entrance with the tip of his tongue. She was wet. For him.

She tugged at his hair with both hands, until his mouth was on her clit again, but he wanted to feel more of her heat. Feel it squeezing him.

He pushed two fingers inside her, and lifted his head to see her face as he slid them out and inside again.

She was biting her lip and watching him, those hazel eyes of her shining.

"Did I hurt you?" he asked as he pumped his fingers in and out of her.

She shook her head, her eyes wild, as she pushed him down again, to lick and nibble on her clitoris. He added a third finger in her and rubbed at the bundle of nerves inside, not picking up his pace when she moaned and mewled and rocked her hips faster.

"This is… too much," she managed between panted breaths.

It wasn't enough. Not until she came apart under his ministrations.

She tasted like nectar and felt like home. He wanted to take his pleasure of her now, but he held back. If he showed her what levels of ecstasy he could offer, she'd be more open to the bonding ritual.

Iphigenia's breathing came faster, the movement of her hips turning jerkier, as he sated her body. She was close, but he maintained the rhythm of his thrusts, as he teased her with his lips and tongue, to draw out her pleasure.

She thrashed on the bed, holding him pressed to her mons while she grinded against his face. She arched her back and clenched around his fingers, and still he made love to her with his mouth and his hand, until she collapsed back on the mattress.

He crawled up her body and kissed the smile forming on her lips.

"So that's one point in your favor." Her voice was throaty and laced with laughter.

He pushed up her top, to cup her breast, and rolled the hard tip of her nipple under his thumb. "I can add to that right now, if you feel up to it." He was painfully hard, the fly of his jeans digging into his erection.

"Give me a second to catch my breath. My legs are trembling."

"I *am* that good. You'd better lock me down." His smirk dropped from his face when he realized she wasn't the one trembling. The bed was. The ground shook, the sound of rock splintering filling the room.

*He* was causing this, and they were over a volcano. He had to get out of here. Away from Iphigenia. He couldn't risk her.

He tried to blink to Mount Othrys, but he was too consumed with emotion—desire and fear and so much more—to get a solid grip of his power.

He was spinning out of control.

He had to go outside, where he wouldn't risk bringing the place and possibly the island down, and focus on reining himself in.

"Stay here," he growled. "You'll be safe." Without a look back at her, he left the room.

# CHAPTER ELEVEN

Like hell, she'd stay here, the damsel in distress, while he ran into whatever not-safe situation he was hurrying to face.

Her logic argued that any such situation would be of a supernatural nature and she'd be risking herself without the means to fight back, but her heart—her entire body— screamed the Titan rushing into danger was hers. She should be by his side.

There might be something to that *soulmate* thing, after all.

Her top was intact, but she was far from dressed. She peeled it off, tossed it to the floor, and tugged on a long dress over her head, not bothering to look for her underwear. Not the best outfit for battle, if it came to it, but for now, she had to catch up to him.

She stopped outside the bedroom door, to orient herself in the unfamiliar setting. The corridor opened to a sprawling lower level that held a living room big enough to accommodate thirty people *chilling,* and a dining room to match, both managing to combine modern, clean lines with a comfortable, rustic feel.

She'd take more time getting the feel of the place if she didn't see Atlas through the floor-to-ceiling glass panes, standing before a large pool with his arms raised.

Slowly, she climbed down the three steps to the lower level and looked again. The pool was larger than Olympic size, and at the other end of the stretch of water stood Rhea, her arm around Marigo's throat. The Titaness was taller than before by at least half a meter, and the human looked tiny in comparison.

Iphigenia swallowed painfully at the memory of Rhea's choke hold. Atlas had to do something. He had to save the poor old woman.

No. *She* had to do something. Rhea was after her, and Iphigenia wouldn't allow anyone else to die in her stead.

She slid open the patio door behind Atlas. Stepping outside felt like walking through an invisible barrier. As if the air itself tried to keep her from leaving the safety of indoors. Eros had said the place was warded from Rhea. That obviously didn't include the pool area.

Eros also said this place belonged to Prometheus. Was it *the* Prometheus—the Titan punished by Zeus for giving humans fire? She hadn't thought of that at the time.

"And it's not what you should be thinking of now," she muttered to herself. *Focus.* But on what? How could she possibly help Marigo? She stood still. Atlas' hulking form should hide her from Rhea, and with his attention on the Titaness, he might not notice Iphigenia was here until she made her move.

"Go back inside," Atlas' barked without turning around.

Well, there went that. "No. Marigo is innocent. I can't let her die." She ducked under his arm, to have a better view of the situation.

"Wise choice." Rhea's voice sounded from right beside Iphigenia. Iphigenia turned, startled, but there was nobody there. The Titaness hadn't moved.

"Come any closer, and I swear to Chaos, I will end you," Atlas yelled.

Rhea narrowed her eyes. Power sparked around her, making her blond hair stand on end. "Try it."

He waved one hand, and a cyclone appeared over the pool, gaining bulk with every spin. "Don't make me use this. How did you even find us?"

Iphigenia was wondering the same thing. Much good the wards did.

"Unusual seismic activity. I'm crazy, not stupid." Rhea smirked. She blew, and the cyclone faded to a breeze. "Now, you or your soulmate will come with me, or this nice old lady will only be the first of many, *many* mortals who'll die because of you." A row of tiles ripped out from around the pool, to form sharp blades, aimed at Marigo.

"Ah fuck," the old woman said. Her voice sounded different, and her form stretched and twisted under Rhea's arms.

What was Rhea doing to her?

But the Titaness looked as shocked as Iphigenia felt, while Marigo reshaped herself into a taller, slimmer woman, until Rhea was holding her waist, not her neck. The lines faded from around her eyes, and her short gray curls elongated into waist-length chestnut locks.

"I didn't want to do this," not-Marigo thundered and made a shoving gesture toward Iphigenia, who found herself inside the glass, looking out. It wasn't as disorienting as when Eros or even Atlas *blinked* her, but her lack of a physical response made it all the more disconcerting. Her body hadn't even registered the movement.

Rhea let go of not-Marigo and blinked a couple meters away. "Who are you? *What* are you?" The words somehow reached Iphigenia's ears unaltered by the window and the distance.

"Call me *Circe*."

*The* Circe, from *The Odyssey*? What was next?

*Oh no no no. You never ask that.*

A ball of light appeared to Iphigenia's right, and she barely had time to panic, before it swirled and grew into Eros. At least he was on their side. Who was Circe rooting for? Not Rhea, judging by how Circe spun on her and sent water flying from the pool to wrap around Rhea in a tight column.

Rhea's arms appeared through the water, and twin balls of light hit Circe in the stomach.

Circe let out an *oof,* but she was smiling as she snapped her fingers. The water unrolled from around Rhea, sending her hurtling into a couple of sun chairs.

Rhea shrieked in fury. "Why can't I blink?"

"Because that would be no fun." Circe shrugged.

"Can't you do something?" Iphigenia asked Eros.

"No need. Circe's got it." He shook his head. "When she's like this, I remember why I shouldn't piss her off."

So he'd just stand here and watch the crazy?

Would Iphigenia?

She'd never felt for a man the way she did for Atlas within a mere few hours. He was a magnet, calling to her. An artist, who made her body sing. But that wasn't all. She felt at peace when she was with him. Which was admittedly insane, when this was the most stressful situation she'd been in. When she looked into his eyes, something she never knew was missing fell into place. Five minutes ago, after that mind-blowing orgasm, she'd been ready to throw caution to the wind and accept the bonding.

Now, though… She couldn't cope with his world. Her life was about logic and plans and a steady job—even if the plans sometimes didn't pan out and the job came with a Taser. A witch and a Titaness fighting it out in the middle of the day, while a Titan contributed with gusts of wind that couldn't exactly boast laser-point accuracy, and an ancient Greek god watched with lovestruck eyes, didn't belong in her reality.

She had to go. Immediately. While everyone else was busy.

But where to? And how?

She turned to ask Eros, but he was outside, on Atlas' side. She never saw him move.

Yeah, *that* was the weirdest part of the past thirty-six hours.

Circe threw a blast of what looked like liquid light at Rhea. It bound the Titaness' arms to her sides and launched her into the sky so fast, she was but a speck in the horizon in a heartbeat, gone in two. Without missing a beat,

Circe turned to Eros. "Did you come to divulge more sensitive information?"

Eros' body leaned toward her, as if he longed to go to her, but his voice was icy. "Nah. Just missed seeing your role-playing skills."

So Marigo wasn't Circe's first… What? Secret identity?

Circe's blue eyes blazed. "You realize this would have gone more smoothly if you'd stuck to the script, yes?"

"What script?" Atlas asked.

Eros ignored him. To Circe, he said, "I said I was sorry." His face was a stony mask when he turned back toward Iphigenia.

Atlas was looking from the god to the witch. "She's the one you mentioned before, who told you about…" Atlas trailed off.

Eros nodded.

"So she knows?"

"Everything."

Circe arched a perfect brow Eros' way. "You told him about me?"

The god grimaced. "Only mentioned you once. Twice tops. Honest."

She rolled her eyes. "Men. Can't keep their mouths shut to save the world."

Eros scowled.

Atlas' shoulders bunched with barely reined-in tension. "Children, focus. Please." When the other two stopped bickering, he went on. "Rhea won't give up that easily."

Circe scrunched her nose. "Our… skirmish brought down the wards, but it'll only take a couple days to set them back up."

"What if she comes back before you do?" Atlas' voice thrummed with his tension.

"Doubtful. I sent her into orbit."

Atlas threw his head back, and Iphigenia sensed his frustration even without seeing his face. "Still, at some point she'll be back. What do we do? Iphigenia is in danger," he said.

Eros clasped Atlas' shoulder. "If you don't get on with the bonding, we all are."

This was Iphigenia's cue.

"I'm sorry to disappoint, but I'm out of here," she called out. Being sneaky about it would only lead to three more immortals coming after her. She'd stand her ground, let them know bonding was out of the question, and then ask Eros for a magic ride, somewhere far, far away.

# CHAPTER TWELVE

Iphigenia wanted to leave, when moments ago she'd been so willing to give herself to him?

Anger, potent and hot and irrational, roiled up Atlas' chest. "You will go nowhere," he snapped and blinked in front of her.

Her pursed lips and arched dark eyebrow said she didn't appreciate being told what to do. Could he blame her? He'd thrust his world on her and expected her to take it in stride and like it?

He swallowed down the urge to bodily prevent her from walking away. "Please. You can't leave."

"So you'll keep me here against my will?" The way she tapped her foot betrayed her nervousness, despite her sneer.

He considered lying, but he wanted her trust as much as he craved her love. "I will, if I have to." He looked at Eros over his shoulder. "May we have some privacy?"

The witch—she had to be a witch; she wasn't a goddess or a Titaness, and no other could wield such power—pouted. "But I want to hear this."

Eros shook his head. "We'll go."

"Not together, we won't." Circe's scowl wasn't very convincing.

"I said. I'm. Sorry." Eros blinked to her and wrapped his arm around her waist in a manner that said they'd been this close before. A lot.

When they disappeared, Atlas turned back to Iphigenia. Her posture was even stiffer now, like she'd bolt at the first opportunity.

But she hadn't so far. If he found the right words, she wouldn't.

Words never failed him in the past; he could always express himself precisely and effectively. It should be easier now that he apparently spoke a few dozen languages, thanks to Eros. This time, though, he didn't need to put thoughts into words, but feelings. And this was new and frightening.

"You want me." He stared her down, challenging her to deny it.

Instead, she gave a small nod.

"Then I won't let you go," he said. "I can't. And it's not because I want to save this world I owe no allegiance to. It's because I need you. The centuries I spent surrounded by darkness melt away when you touch me. From the moment I first saw you—"

She snorted. "A whopping two days ago?"

He poured his sincerity into his gaze. "No. Four moons ago. You shone brighter than the sun that blinded me after being underwater so long, and I knew I had to have you." He'd felt he was betraying Pleione for being so drawn to this human, and he'd denied it with every fiber of his being. Now that was no longer the case.

"Fuck." Her voice was so tiny, he wasn't sure he heard right.

"Sorry?"

She huffed. "I said *fuck*. As in, *Fuck. Now I want to kiss you.*"

Like his anger before, the glee blossoming inside him was unprecedented. It made his heart beat faster and his fingertips tingle with a fresh wave of power.

No. He had to control this. Control his happiness. Control all emotion until they were bonded.

Which should be in an hour or so, if he had his way.

He clasped the back of her neck and crushed his mouth to hers. This kiss wasn't meant to seduce, nor was he trying to make a point. He was staking his claim, and he did so with all the passion and hunger Iphigenia ignited in him.

Her hands found their way beneath his T-shirt, and she clawed at his skin, trying to raise it over his head. Her palms scorched him, the scrape of her nails adding to the desire roaring inside him.

He pulled away and tore the shirt open, neck to navel.

The lust in Iphigenia's hazel eyes mirrored that stretching his jeans.

He tensed under her scrutiny, his pecs flexing as he hooked his thumbs in the loops of his belt.

She dropped her gaze below his waist, where his hands framed his erection, and licked her lips in a motion too natural to be intentional.

"Do that again, and I'll make you mine where you stand," he said.

"Promises, promises…" The smile quirking one corner of her lips was devilish, and then her tongue made another, more lingering appearance.

He needn't hear more of an invitation. He blinked behind her and pressed her body against the window. He ran his fingers down her arms, took hold of her wrists, and led her palms over her head, to splay on the glass.

"Don't move," he whispered in her ear, as he bunched up the hem of her dress. He made quick work of his fly and pulled himself free without bothering to peel off his jeans. He needed to be buried inside her. Now.

He slipped his shaft between her legs, rubbing against her moist heat. She was drenched with her arousal and the remnants of her last release, and she tilted her hips, inviting him.

With her body almost completely upright, the angle wasn't optimal for an average sized male, but Atlas was as far from average as they came. He used his hand to position himself at her entrance and pushed inside, centimeter by agonizing centimeter. It was like touching the sun again. Blazing hot and energizing and filling him with the desire to create. He would have children with this woman.

But not today.

Iphigenia's breath hitched, and she tried to push back, but he held her steady with his hold on her dress until he was fully seated inside her. She fit him like a glove, but it wasn't enough.

"Want more?" he asked.

Her answer was a breathless *yes*.

He focused on growing his length three more centimeters, and reveled on the shiver that rocked her frame.

It took all his effort not to pull back and slam into her again. Instead, he withdrew as slowly as he'd entered her, feeling her strangle his length.

Her breath fogged the glass at her irritated huff. "I won't break."

He drove forward with a hint more force, and she moaned, rocking against him.

He wanted to be gentle, wanted to make this sweet and slow, but his body was done holding back. His next thrust shook the frame of the window. He ordered the air to hold up her dress, and he grabbed her hips with both hands to plunge inside her faster… harder…

*God, yes.*

Her words were spoken inside his head, almost inaudible beneath her moans and his grunts. He could hear her again.

Other voices overtook hers for a heartbeat. Hushed cries and angry protests he couldn't exactly make out. The room darkened, and Kronos' angry scowl filled Atlas' sight, before he harnessed his emotions. As much as his lust could be harnessed, when Iphigenia was squeezing around his cock.

"Tell me what you need," he ordered mentally.

She gasped and turned to look at him over her shoulder, but a couple hard thrusts had her dropping her head forward again. "My nipples," she whispered.

He thought of his hands cupping her breasts and pinching the dusky-pink peaks through the fabric of her dress. Rolling them between his fingers. Tugging on them.

"How…?" The rest of her question was taken over by a keening sound when he imagined biting one nipple and twisting the other.

Iphigenia bucked her hips, and he had the undeniable urge to smack her round bottom. He let go of one ass cheek to bring down his palm on it with a *crack* that reverberated through the living room.

She clenched around him so hard, she could have Titan blood in her, as well as a Titaness' soul.

"Tell me you want me," he barked.

"Fuck… Am I being too subtle?"

Another hard smack. "Tell me," he said in her mind.

"I want you. Please make me come."

The last of his restrain snapped, and he amped the rhythm of his thrusts, as he sent her mental images of his fingers rubbing her clitoris.

Her hips bucked, and she met his strokes with a fervor that matched his. The red mark of a palm print was blossoming on her behind, and he wanted to kiss it. Lick it. So he used their mental connection to make her feel like he did.

"Yes." Panted breaths shook her body, and her heartbeat drummed in his ears. "More."

"Tell me what you want."

She whispered, "I can't."

"Then show me."

Confusion flowed through their connection, and then a fractured thought, draped in embarrassment, nudged at the edge of his consciousness.

Not slowing, he probed for more. Ah, his little human enjoyed an extra touch of kink.

Should he claim her ass, as he did her pussy? Tantalizing. Maybe next time. For now, he pressed his thumb to her asshole, as he fucked her harder and redoubled his mental ministrations on her clit.

She came with a violent shudder that almost made him slip out of her, but he held her in place with his grip and his thumb and his cock, and pistoned inside her until his release claimed him and he was spent inside her divine body.

He withdrew and helped her upright, but she wouldn't face him. When he cupped her chin and raised it to meet her gaze, her cheeks were wet.

"My love?" The words sounded right, though he hadn't intended them. Had he done something she didn't want? Had he forced her? Titans didn't have human afflictions, but the thought brought bile bubbling up his throat. "What's wrong? Did I hurt you?"

She shook her head, but fresh tears spilled from her beautiful eyes. "It was just so… perfect. I've never felt like that before." She sniffed. "I was overwhelmed. I'm sorry."

His heart expanding with joy, he gathered her to him and pressed a gentle kiss to her forehead, before picking her up in his arms. "Don't apologize for enjoying yourself. Let's wash up, and then we can work on overwhelming you some more."

The bowl of artificial fruit on the coffee table rattled as he passed by it, and the wind whistled through the sliding doors. He had to bond with her. Soon.

# CHAPTER THIRTEEN

"Mmm… more." Iphigenia arched her back into the probing touch between her legs. She thought he'd let her sleep after she sucked him off in the shower, but she *really* didn't mind this.

Atlas barely moved his fingers, but vibrations spread from her pussy to her womb, making her body buzz with his power. So. Much. Power. She'd felt horrible for turning into a mumbling mess after the orgasm he gave her in the living room, but it was impossible to hold back the flood of sensation rushing through her.

And he was apparently out to top that performance.

He trailed a finger soaked in her juices lower, to her second hole. "So you like to be teased here," he said. Without speaking. Because his tongue was busy with her clit.

*Don't think of how much you like it. Don't think of how much you like it. Don't think of how much you like it.* She'd told Pavlos once how she wanted to try… *this*, and he'd called her *filthy*. She wouldn't handle seeing Atlas regarding her with similar disgust.

Only, his eyes blazed gold when he looked up at her and gently pressed his finger through the tight ring of muscle. Because Atlas wasn't Pavlos. He wasn't any mortal man. He was hers, and he truly saw her. And he accepted her.

Her hips all but flew off the mattress. She'd anticipated this and more since he pressed his thumb there. She'd been curious before, but now she longed to know how it would feel if he—

Atlas nibbled on the sensitive bundle of nerves he'd been lapping at. "Come back to me," he thought at her.

"I'm here. I'm here." It felt weird, speaking out loud when he didn't, so in her head she added, "Just a little jittery."

"About…"

"What you're doing."

He pushed his tongue inside her pussy and withdrew his finger from her ass, only to probe at it again, this time with two fingers pressed together. Iphigenia clenched reflexively against the intrusion, and Atlas chuckled. "Relax, my glorious nymph. I'll make it good." He kept spearing her with his tongue and returned to inserting a single digit in her second hole.

Iphigenia forced herself to relax and push down into his mouth and his hand, as he slowly pumped his finger inside her. With every new thrust, she felt fuller, like his finger was somehow growing thicker. Could he do that? He could make her feel three—or was it four?—tongues and twice as many hands at the same time. Why would this be above him?

She stopped questioning what was happening when he filled her to this side of discomfort, but he latched his lips on her clit and tapped it with his tongue, and the pain gave place to the slow burn of impending release. An invisible cock slowly wedged itself in her pussy, stretching her and filling her up and making the ball of emotion and sensation in her belly swirl, gaining mass and heat.

She still felt Atlas' face between her legs, as he crawled up her body and claimed her mouth for a kiss. Tasting herself on his tongue amped her arousal, and she didn't protest when he lifted her legs, to drape them over his shoulders, folding her in half. Which of her holes would he enter? Having his finger inside her ass had been incredible, but would she manage his cock?

She was about to find out.

All mentally-induced ministrations ceased, as Atlas let go of her long enough to plunge his real cock in her pussy. "So wet," he whispered in her ear, then licked a trail to the hollow of her throat and withdrew from her body.

The bell-shaped head pressed against her tight entrance and then into it. She squeezed, her ass on fire, and he stilled long enough for her to relax the tiniest bit, before pushing forward. It hurt, but the burn mingled with pleasure and amplified it.

When he was fully seated inside her, his phantom second cock entered her again.

He took turns thrusting into both her holes, creating a seesaw of pleasure that bordered into the most delicious pain. This… This was too much. She would come apart. Spin out of control. She wasn't used to losing control and it happened too often when he was touching her.

It was as frightening as it was exhilarating. Was this what falling in love was like?

The mattress shook with his thrusts, and howling wind picked up around them, making the drapes dance and swirl. Her vision turned blurry with tears, as her limbs thrashed with each new push that rocked her body. Her hamstrings burned, her ass throbbed, and her pussy fluttered, her orgasm just out of reach.

She dug her nails into his strong, muscled arms, as he pistoned inside her. The headboard slammed rhythmically against the wall, and something snapped, but he kept fucking her, his barely restrained power humming just beneath his skin. Corded tendons roped down his neck, as he threw his head back and squeezed his eyes shut. "Bond with me," he roared. "Say you're mine."

Instinct made Iphigenia reach into his mind. If she gleaned a hint of the emotion burning in her heart, she'd pledge herself to him and not look back.

Her release crashed into her, but what she saw in Atlas' thoughts sent ice down her spine, to chase away the euphoria. Another woman's face was superimposed over her own. A woman with Iphigenia's coloring but higher cheekbones, thicker brows, and fuller lips.

No, not a woman. A Titaness. *His* Titaness. Pleione. Atlas was fucking Iphigenia, while thinking of his dead love.

"Stop." She slapped his chest with both hands, trying to get him out of her, needing to distance herself from the Titan who introduced her to a whole new world of pleasure, and at the same time broke her heart in a manner she hadn't believed possible.

Atlas froze and slipped out of her, letting her lower her legs. Aching inside and out, she scooted back gingerly, away from him, and he sat on his haunches and studied her with concern. She wanted to wipe that expression from his face. With her knuckles.

"Did I do something you didn't like?" He caressed her ankle.

Iphigenia snatched her leg from his touch and sat up. She felt lightheaded, which only added to her ire. How could someone who stomped all over her feelings make her body sing?

"Iphigenia? Talk to me, please."

"So you do remember who I am."

When he furrowed his brow in confusion, a fresh surge of anger bubbled in her gut. "Because a moment ago, you were thinking of being balls-deep inside your ex. While asking *me* to bond with you." She sounded furious. Good. It hid the pain that tore at her ribcage and stole her breath.

A gust of wind rippled around her and pushed her into him, as he moved beside her with the speed of light.

"You're jealous." His chest reverberated with his chuckle. He was laughing. At her.

She tried to push him away, but his thick arms were wrapped around her like steel bars. She tried to knee him in the groin, but the hit glanced off him. Damned Titan with his damned Titan abilities.

"Stop laughing," she said in as uninflected a tone as she could muster. "And stop touching me. I don't want anything to do with you. Find another stupid mortal to mindfuck into bonding with you." She needed to leave. Now. Go where he wouldn't see her break down and cry— this time because she was desperately, irrationally drawn to someone who'd never choose her over the ghost of the woman he truly longed for.

# CHAPTER FOURTEEN

The green flecks in Iphigenia's eyes sparkled, and her face was pale but for the red tinting her cheeks. Her full lips were pinched together, her breathing coming in short pants that made her chest heave. She was made of passion and fire, so beautiful when she was furious, it was almost worth trying to enrage her further.

He could sense the hurt beneath the rage, though, and nothing was worth hurting his soulmate.

"My Iphigenia"—Atlas coiled a dark curl around his finger and tucked it behind her ear, grateful when she didn't recoil—"it's not her face I see when I bed you. It's your face that overtakes my memories of her." It was true. When he'd tried to remember how it felt to be as intimately joined with Pleione as he was with Iphigenia moments ago, Iphigenia's presence had chased off the Titaness' ghost. For the briefest of moments, it had left his chest hollow, and then a slew of new emotions had crashed in, to fill the void. And they were all for Iphigenia.

Her lips parted, as if she was about to speak. The pinch of her brows foretold nothing he'd like to hear, so he hurried on.

"I loved Pleione for millennia, and then lost her for millennia. When you brought me back, I was horrified by the intensity of my attraction to you, because I saw it as a betrayal. But she's long gone, and you're here. She's my past, when I can see myself building a future with you. I'm yours. Can't you see it? Didn't you feel it when I was inside you?"

Her bottom lip trembled, but her eyes were softer as she said, "I won't be Pleione's substitute."

Now this, he could work with. "You're not."

"Because…?" There was pleading in her voice. What did she want him to say? He tried to touch her mind, but her thoughts were guarded. Should he admit that he was falling in love with her? Would she believe him?

He drew a long, unnecessary breath and met her gaze, pouring all his sincerity into his words. "You can't be a substitute for her, because you *are* her."

He leaned in for a kiss, but Iphigenia tensed in his arms. "What?" she asked.

He wasn't saying this right. He tried again. "My love for Pleione, our bond, transcends the ages. It transcends form and norm."

And that was the wrong way to go about it, because Iphigenia disentangled herself from his embrace and glared daggers at him. "What are you talking about?" Her hazel eyes were wild.

"Our souls found each other again, like they were meant to, and hers was reborn into you. This undeniable pull between you and me is not only because we belong together. It's because we were once bonded. Eros told me you are Pleione's reincarnation, like my bonded brothers' soulmates are reincarnations of their Titanesses. It explains—"

She pushed away from him and half-fell, half-got out of bed on the farther side, pulling the top sheet with her. "That's why you had sex with me? Because you thought I was *her*?" She spat out the last word.

This wasn't going well. Every time he opened his mouth, the distance between them grew. "I made love to you because I wanted you. I thought you felt the same."

"Don't turn this on me." Iphigenia looked around. Her dress was in a heap on the floor. She strode to it and manically turned it the right way, before pulling it over her head. "*You're* the one who pursued this," she said through the thin fabric. "You're the one who decided we should bond. And you're the one with all the information." The sentence came out shrill.

"My Iphigenia—"

"No. Not *your* Iphigenia." Her head cleared the neckline of the dress so hard, her curls seemed to hover midair before bouncing down to frame her face. Unshed tears glistened in her eyes, but her expression remained stony. "I'm no more yours than you are mine. *She* is your soulmate. I'm just— What? Her vessel? Will she take over? Will I lose myself, so you may have your precious Pleione back? Is that what the bonding is really about?"

Her wrath was palpable, squeezing his heart in a vice. She thought he'd lied to get her into bed? That he'd sacrifice her, to bring back Pleione? A small part of him wondered if there was a hint of truth in the accusation, but Pleione hadn't crossed his mind while he was with Iphigenia, and that was why he'd tried to invoke her image. Because guilt, utterly unreasonable yet undeniable, ate at him. Pleione was gone, and he was moving on, falling for someone else.

Yes, Iphigenia's soul—Pleione's soul—called to him, but it was in a new person. It came with new memories and a new past, and a whole new level of stubbornness.

He pinched the bridge of his nose. "If you'd just calm down…"

Iphigenia slapped her palm on the wall by the headboard. "Don't tell me what to do. You have no right. You lied to me and manipulated me."

"Hear me out, please."

She closed her eyes and took a deep breath, making a visible effort to compose herself. "I don't want to talk to you. I don't even want to look at you anymore. You and I are done. And put on some clothes, for fuck's sake."

He snatched his jeans from the foot of the bed and pulled them on, not bothering to button them up. "But we must bond. The world—"

"May die in a fire, as far as I'm concerned." She circled the bed with quick strides and headed for the door. She was leaving again. Running away from what they could have. From what they just shared. From him.

"No." His bellow was so loud, it shook the room. A whirlwind began forming by the coffee table, and the curtains were sucked toward its center, their dance mocking him. Atlas blinked between Iphigenia and the door. She couldn't leave. The world needed her, and so did he.

His powers pulled his body to all directions, urging him to unfold to his true size, but he didn't want to intimidate her. Just make her see reason.

*Screw reason.*

Was that his thought or hers?

*Don't hurt me. Please don't hurt me.* This was definitely hers. Though there was no hint of fear in the squaring of her shoulders or the clenching of her jaw, she was afraid of him. What kind of monster was he, to scare the woman he loved?

*Loved her.* He loved her. He wasn't *falling* for her. It wasn't a process; it was a done deal.

He matched her posture, but instead of fisting his hands, he dropped his arms loosely at his sides. "I swear to you by the sky and the stars I can bring down around us that you're not a means for me to have Pleione back," he said. "You are the one I desire. The one I wish to bond with. And I won't let you out of this room until you believe me." He ordered the wind to close the door, which slammed shut behind him.

When Iphigenia glanced at the window over her shoulder, he had it swing into its frame so hard, the casing rattled.

The whirlwind grew, sucking in the hem of her dress and exposing her legs. He'd be turned on if it weren't for the dismay in her expression. He had to stop this.

*Enough.*

But the wind didn't die down. It whistled and blew and ripped the sheets from the bed. Iphigenia's breathing turned labored. He was sucking the air from the room. *He* was doing this.

When he was trapped in stone, he could will his conscious mind into perfect stillness. He tried it now. It wasn't as easy, when Iphigenia seemed about to crumble in front of him and all he wanted was to take her in his arms and carry her to safety, but there was no safety to be had when he wasn't in control.

"*Stop it.*" Her hair whipped around her face, hiding her mouth, but her cry reached him easily.

He squeezed his eyes shut and thought of the night sky. Of the vast darkness. Of the pale curves of Iphigenia's body. He kept his mind away from what he wanted to do to her—what he'd already done with her—and on the moments between passion, when he just held her, their bodies curved around each other like their souls should be.

The wind died down, and he ran to her side as her legs gave way. Her eyes were closed when he tucked her against his chest and carried her to the bed. She'd listen to him. She had to. Or everything would be lost.

# CHAPTER FIFTEEN

Atlas' heart thundered against her ear, as he cradled her and whispered soothing words. He had her. He'd never hurt her.

And wasn't it ironic he was promising that seconds after he'd stolen the breath from her lungs?

As ironic as it was for her to feel safe in his arms, physically, while her soul cried for him not to break her heart.

"You're my everything," he whispered in her ear. "Pleione *is* in the past."

But how could that be, when Pleione was the original owner of the soul inhabiting Iphigenia's body? When that might be the only reason Atlas was with Iphigenia in the first place?

He'd sworn that wasn't the case—*could he bring down the stars, like he said?*—but should she believe him? What was the alternative? Sit back and watch the world burn? Moments ago, she'd felt ready to, but when she was in his arms, trapped and protected at the same time, bonding did seem like the better idea. She could stop thinking, and give in. Atlas would make love to her again, their souls would bond, and creation would be safe.

*God*, for a soul she hadn't realized she had, it had quite the itinerary.

Should she open her eyes?

No. Two more minutes. Opening them would mean she was ready to either talk things out or storm out of here despite his efforts to stop her, and she first had to decide what she wanted.

Armageddon or not, the possibility of not seeing Atlas again threatened to sour the meal in her gut, so she focused on the new info instead. She had a used soul. The soul of someone who'd loved him. Did it come with its own memories and feelings? Would getting closer to Atlas unlock them? Was her attraction to him an intense case of déjà vu?

She chanced a glance through lowered eyelashes. He was watching her intently, his thumb drawing circles on her shoulder. If she confessed to being aware, would she have to leave his warmth?

No. No sappy thoughts. She was upset. He knew something as big as the fact that she practically had no say in loving him, and he kept it from her.

"I love you. Honest to Chaos, I do. Pleione has nothing to do with it," he said.

Okay, she was done with this crap. She opened her eyes and rolled off him, catching herself before she toppled to the floor. He patted the mattress, for her to sit beside him, but she stood her ground.

"I practically have a beacon with her name on it up my ass, calling to you, and you think she has nothing to do with you having the hots for me? I'm a strong, independent woman. I make my own destiny." Though she had no trouble using clichés, apparently. "I've fought for my job, for the respect of my peers, for my family's acceptance. And then you come along, and you screw everything up. Because *we're meant to be*. And who cares about what *I* want, right? I have a destiny to fulfill. *With my pussy.*"

Was he biting back a grin? Ugh, she could slap him. Or kiss him.

But mostly slap him.

"Why aren't you saying anything?" she screeched. Was she being irrational? Maybe. But she needed him to put this all into order, force it to make sense, so she could *choose* it. Choose him.

His voice was low when he spoke, his gaze trained to her hair, instead of her face. "You know, when I was in the museum, the highlight of my day was the moment you passed by, when you were doing your rounds. I'd listen for the clacking of your sensible shoes on the corridor outside, and wait for a glimpse of your smile. Until this week, you were a gorgeous nymph I couldn't take my eyes off. When you started talking to me, though, telling me about your family and your dreams and your struggles with cooking"— he chuckled—"it was impossible not to fall for you."

Atlas looked into her eyes, molten gold swirling in his irises. "And I have, Chaos help me. I'm helplessly in love with you. The thought of being separated from you threatens to unravel me faster than Zeus' curse. I don't want this bond so Pleione can come back, if that were even possible. I want to mate with *you*. Bond with you for life. One day maybe have stubborn, curly-haired children with you. I want to tell your parents their daughter is incredible and fierce, and I want to find your ex and get your dog back for you. So no, this has nothing to do with Pleione. I need you, not because I'll unravel unless we bond, but because without you, I won't care if I end creation."

*Fuck.* A few words, what might be the world's most romantic-slash-threatening declaration, and all her anger and frustration evaporated in a pink cloud of hearts and roses. How the fuck did he manage that? "What you're saying is you're in love with me?" she asked, stalling for time, to regain control of the thoughts spinning her into a knot.

He tilted his head and narrowed his eyes, like he wanted to see inside her head. Like he was doubting her intelligence. "Yes. That *is* what I'm saying," he said in a slow, measured tone.

"I see."

Atlas raised his face to the ceiling and let out a tortured sigh. "That's what every male dreams of hearing from his soulmate when he declares his love." He met her gaze again. "Look again."

Iphigenia wanted to hold on to her anger from before or crack a joke or walk away—anything to diffuse the intensity of this moment—but the mental image of a woman blossomed in her mind, until it overtook her thoughts.

*Pleione again?* No. Not her. But who? Iphigenia should know the woman, but she couldn't place the gorgeous, sleek ringlets of her dark hair or the glow of her smooth skin. Those eyes, though…

"*Your* eyes," Atlas said. "You are on my mind. Always."

Now he'd said that, she saw the resemblance, but the woman was… livelier. More ethereal, maybe? More elegant, for sure. She was… *more.*

"This is how you see me?" The words came out breathy.

Atlas nodded and opened himself to her further, allowing her to feel what he felt. *Everything* he felt. His love and his need and his hope and his fear poured inside her, making her head light and sending butterflies fluttering in her stomach. He loved her with a ferocity that took her breath away. Her heart raced, and her palms were sweaty, and her chest ached like it had grown two sizes, to fit the swell of emotion inside.

*Her* emotion, not his—the realization hit her like a punch to the solar plexus.

She was in love with Atlas. There was no denying it.

Saying *no* to the bonding really wasn't an option, but not because of the magnitude of what was at stake. She couldn't refuse Atlas, because no man could possibly take his place in her heart or between the sheets after their short time together. He'd exposed her to a whole new reality that was terrifying and stimulating, and not even a little bit boring. Her life had changed irrevocably, and to pretend she could go back to the existence she had before she met him would be to fool herself.

Plus, she'd be saving everyone on the frigging planet. She was practically a superhero. She laughed. Her dad would totally freak out over that. Though he might be happy she finally found a guy to make an honest woman out of her.

"Iphigenia? Are you still with me? Did the oxygen deprivation damage you? It didn't last more than a couple seconds, but you never know." He frowned, but his eyes twinkled, and that secret smile danced on his lips.

She was with him, all right. And now that she'd made up her mind, there was no reason to delay things. "The world depends on my putting out again, huh?" She ghosted a finger down her neck and along her neckline, and a shiver ran down her spine at the growl that bubbled in Atlas' chest to vibrate through her skin. She gave him a lopsided grin. "Then I guess I'll do it. Sacrifice myself for the greater good…" She let out an exaggerated huff.

"The bonding won't work if you don't pledge your love to me." Atlas watched her, his body tense, no doubt ready to block her way again if she tried for another escape.

She was here to stay, though. His to keep. "I know."

His gaze caressed the path her hands drew, as she skated them along her thighs, pulling the dress up. He stood and swooped in for a kiss.

Iphigenia yielded to his claim over her mouth. *God,* he was magical when it came to kissing. And to anything else that had his body making contact with hers. Or his mind…

He closed one large palm over her ass, and she grasped his shoulders, clinging to him. She sucked on his tongue and locked a foot around his ankle, then pushed him back to land on the bed with an *oof.*

He arched one golden eyebrow. "So…?"

Did she have to spell it out for him? "Yes," she said with a smirk and straddled him. She'd landed herself a Titan, and now she was gonna ride one.

# CHAPTER SIXTEEN

She'd said *yes* to the bonding. To him.

Atlas had no doubt she lusted after him, and taking the step to stabilize him was the rational thing to do, but until she said the word, he still feared she wouldn't return his feelings. That she'd reject him. His worry had morphed to relief when her frown melted into that cheeky grin, and then to an overwhelming sense of pure happiness when she began undressing herself.

Now that she was in his lap, naked, both hands inside his open fly, Atlas was engulfed by feelings he couldn't put into words. How could he define the air and fire and sun swirling behind his ribs?

Iphigenia pulled him out of his jeans and waggled her eyebrows. He wanted to roar with laughter, and yet, this was the most serious thing to ever happen to him. Her touch burned him, but not as much as her bare, wet pussy did when she rose to her knees and positioned him at her entrance.

He ached to bathe himself in the intoxicating aroma of exotic fruits and flowers that wafted from her hair, but most of all, he wanted to slam her down on him. Impale her on his shaft. Bottom out in her and take his pleasure. Take her heart. Make her his.

He grasped her hips, but when he brushed her thoughts, he sensed her need to set the pace this one time, so he allowed her the illusion of having the upper hand. He let her slowly sink down around his cock, taking him in a centimeter at a time, squeezing and scorching and making him throb with the need for release, until she sat on him with a sigh of contentment.

"I could stay here forever," she murmured. "Feels like—"

"Home." Because it did. *She* did. She was his home—his center. And once they'd claimed each other, she'd be the one to ground him. Keep him from unraveling. Though when she rose and fell on him again, inner muscles clenching tight around him, he almost lost control.

Iphigenia withdrew until only the tip of his erection remained inside her, and then slowly took him in once more. And again. And again. She picked up speed with every down stroke, twisting her hips to rub her clitoris against his pelvis. Her skin was pale where their bodies came together, compared to his darker hue, and her thighs trembled with the strain of her movements.

Atlas roamed her body with his hands. He wanted to feel all of her. He palmed her breasts. Kneaded them and caressed the soft curve of her belly. Grazed his way up her creamy thighs. Skated his palms down her front and traced the white sliver of raised skin across her right side with his thumb. The scar was old, but he hated the thought of anything causing her pain, even years before he ever met her. She'd never be harmed again. He'd be here for her, always.

He looked up at her, his gorgeous amazon. Her face was pinched in concentration, dark brows drawn together, her breathing slow and deliberate.

"I love you," he thought at her, and her face relaxed.

"I love you," she thought back at him.

Atlas could no longer hold back. He fisted both hands in her curls, to bring her down to him and crash his mouth to hers, before rolling them so he was on top. "I'll love you till the end of time," he whispered and bit her bottom lip.

He nibbled along her jaw line, tasting the saltiness of her sweat, and then dove between her breasts, to lave the valley there with his tongue. He cupped a perfect handful and squeezed. It blushed a beautiful red that matched her flushed cheeks, but the color faded too soon. He wanted to emblazon his claim on the unblemished skin, so he closed his teeth on the yielding flesh and sucked.

Iphigenia bucked her hips beneath him and scratched furrows down his back. She was a lioness, feral and passionate and his. "Yes," she screamed in his head. She was wide open to him now. He could sense her fear of the future and her determination to face the unknown by his side. And he could see the golden glow of her love, binding her soul to his.

When he let go of her breast, it bore two rapidly darkening crescent-shaped marks surrounded by a purple bruise. *His* mark.

His orgasm closing in, Atlas thrust harder, pounding her into the mattress, which moved aside to reveal the stone beneath it. His shins chipped the paint off, but he felt no pain. There was only pleasure. Pleasure and love. "Say you're mine," he ordered Iphigenia mentally, and this time, there was nothing to stop her from answering.

"Yours. My heart, my soul, my body—yours forever."

He was more alive than ever. He was complete. Iphigenia was in him like he was in her. Through their mental link, he made her feel his fingers tweaking her hidden pearl and rubbing circles over it. Her panted breathing grew erratic, and she wrapped her legs around his hips. Pressing her heels in the backs of his thighs, she ground her mound against him, until her body shook with the force of her release.

A few quick, hard thrusts, and his balls tightened, his cock jerking as he shot his load deep inside her. He was tempted to make his seed potent, to start in on the curly-haired children immediately, but his soulmate wouldn't appreciate the initiative. He rolled to the side, holding her close, and laid a chaste kiss on her temple. "I love you."

"I don't think it took," she croaked against his chest. "We may have to do it again."

He laughed. "Better safe than sorry."

"But not yet. I'm oozing Titan." She pulled back and sat up, to mock-glower. "How many showers can I take in one day, before I start peeling?"

Atlas pretended to consider it. "You should be good with one more. I'll join you, to make sure." He started to get up, but she climbed from the bed and pushed him back down.

"Nah uh. You stay here. I can't trust you to behave yourself, and I need to clean up and eat." Her stomach growled, stressing her point. "Any chance Circe could turn into Marigo long enough to whip us something up?"

"I'll do you one better. I'll take you out for lunch." He looked toward the window. The sky outside was graying. "Dinner?"

Iphigenia narrowed her eyes and crossed her arms, which did delightful things to her naked breasts. "Do you even have any money?"

Huh. Good question. His gaze fell on the brown envelope Eros had given him. It was on the floor by the coffee table. He twirled his fingers, and the air slapped the envelope on Iphigenia's ass, earning him an indignant squeal, before delivering it to his waiting hand. "Eros said this has everything I need. Except you." He winked at her. "Go shower. I'll be here." He watched her ass wiggle as she walked gingerly out of the room, his spendings glistening down her thighs.

Wishing was watching her lather her body with foam and maybe helping her massage it properly into all the right places, he sat up and emptied the contents of the envelope on the bed beside him.

*One… two… three…* Huh. *Five* credit cards, a handful of takeout menus—for Athens, so useless here—a small black book that read *A Titan's Guide to the Modern World*, and a slim cell phone. Iphigenia could have this. She didn't have hers when he retrieved her from Rhea's hideout, and she should contact her family at some point. Tell them she was… getting married? He chuckled. Three days ago, he thought he was doomed for eternity, and now he had it all.

The sound of glass breaking had him doing up his jeans and blinking to the corridor. The bathroom door was closed, and he could make out Iphigenia's singing under the burble of running water. He plastered his back to the wall and walked sideways to the living room. Before he could duck his head in for a quick glance, Rhea stomped in his line of sight, five heavily armed men behind her.

"This time, I'm taking no chances," she hissed.

Atlas didn't lose his calm. He'd been to every room in the house and could blink to the bathroom, to get Iphigenia out of here with the speed of thought. Still, no need to run if he could talk his way out of this. "You're too late," he told Rhea. "Iphigenia and I are bonded. I'm stable. Go now, and I won't chase you down for what you tried to do to us."

Rhea shot him a withering glare, before shifting her gaze toward the sound of Iphigenia's singing. "The mortal can still be useful. You'd do anything for your soulmate, wouldn't you?"

Atlas had no warning, before all five men shot him. Their bullets shouldn't hurt, but they sliced through him, rendering him incapable of movement. What—?

"Forged of Zeus' lightening and imbued with my version of the stasis spell," she told him in a sugary voice. "You'll get out of it, but not in time." To the human males, she said, "Get her. And don't be too gentle. The bitch has given me enough trouble."

Atlas focused on moving even a single muscle in his body. On blinking to his soulmate. Nothing happened. He watched, helpless, as the men strode to the bathroom, and the first one kicked down the door.

"Don't hurt her," Atlas yelled at Rhea, though no words made it past his lips. "She's got your sister's soul. Pleione's soul."

Rhea snapped her head to him, eyes wide like twin full moons. "Pleione?"

He was about to confirm it, when Rhea's lips stretched into a frightening grin. "Oh, this is good. So much potential."

He searched her eyes for the gleam of madness, but she seemed perfectly in control as she called out, "What are you waiting for? Bring her to me."

*Fuck.* "Iphigenia, watch out," Atlas yelled in his mind. He hoped Rhea's spell, the distance, and the walls between them wouldn't prevent Iphigenia from hearing him.

# CHAPTER SEVENTEEN

Iphigenia smiled when she heard the door slam against the wall. "Thought you were feeding me first," she called out, eyes closed against the water and shampoo suds. She was sore and throbbing, but gooseflesh broke along her skin, and her nipples puckered at the thought of Atlas joining her in the shower. His enormous body would look even more incredible, glistening with water. She moaned at the thought of his large palms lathering every centimeter of her skin before sliding between her legs. And maybe she could take one more round—

"Iphigenia, watch out." His scream bounced in her head, slicing through her daydream.

She wiped her face and opened her eyes. Two dark shadows were visible through the fogged-up glass. *Shit.*

As they closed in, she looked around frantically for something to use as a weapon, but the gleaming white-marble surfaces were bare of anything but bathing products. She unhooked the showerhead and grabbed the faucet with her other hand. She might not get out of this, but at least one of these guys was getting blisters for his trouble.

The two figures stopped outside the shower, and the one on the right slid the glass pane open. "Out, or—" The rest of his threat was drowned in the scolding water jet Iphigenia shot straight into his face.

"You *bitch*." The second man raised the oddly angular bright-silver weapon—gun?—he was holding, and Iphigenia sent a short prayer to any deity paying attention, that she didn't slip and break her skull, as she spun and landed a kick on his forearm.

He lost his grip on the gun but managed a punch to her abdomen.

Iphigenia doubled over, though the pain was nowhere near as bad as she expected. Before she could straighten up, the first man grabbed her by the hair and pulled her out, head first.

His face was red, and his eyes wild with fury. "You'll pay for that. Rhea doesn't mind if we roughen you up a bit." He threw a punch at her face, but the moment before his knuckles made contact with her cheek, her fingers closed around his wrist, as if of their own accord, and twisted. And snapped. She actually felt bone give way beneath her grip.

What. The. Fuck?

The man roared in fury and let go, to nurse his broken arm. His buddy took a step back, allowing Iphigenia to straighten up.

A third man entered the bathroom. "They're bonded. She's got some of his strength." He pointed his gun at her from a safe distance.

And the surprises kept coming. How strong was she? Could she rip out a marble slab to throw at him? Could she order the wind around, like Atlas did?

"Won't do her much good," said a fourth one from the doorway. He too was aiming at her.

"Freakishly strong or not, we have enough juice to bring you down, so behave." The man who'd hit her in the stomach reached for a large fluffy towel that hung behind him, and tossed it at her. "Come on."

Iphigenia had forgotten she was naked in front of her attackers, and the reminder sapped the blossoming hope that she could make it out of this, as much as their guns did. She was naked and outnumbered. And they obviously had Atlas, or he'd be ripping their heads off for ever laying eyes on her.

She wrapped the towel around her body, and the man shoved her toward the door. The other two made way but kept their weird guns trained on her.

She exited to the corridor, and was relieved to see Atlas in one piece, though he seemed as solid as when she'd first seen him. "What did you do to him?" she asked the queen bitch.

Rhea smirked and motioned her closer, and the guy behind Iphigenia growled, "Move, or I'll shoot."

"How do we get out of this?" Iphigenia thought at Atlas. He had to be able to hear her, if she'd heard him in the shower.

"I don't know, but we will. Whatever happens, I'll find you. And if she's touched one hair on your head, I'll end her." His reply was growled in her head with finality, but Iphigenia sensed the doubt beneath it. The fear. For her.

"I am stronger than before. Maybe as strong as you," she told him the same way. "I can fight her."

"I know what you two are doing," Rhea sing-songed. "Your scheming won't help you much, since Atlas is staying here and you're coming with me." She narrowed her eyes at Iphigenia. "You know, I never liked you. You were always so sure of yourself. So convinced you were above the rest of us." She muttered something to herself, shook her head, and giggled like a kid.

The woman was nuts. "You don't even know me," Iphigenia said.

"Oh, I know you, *Pleione.*" Rhea sneered and turned to Atlas. "Once we're safely away, my boys will let you know what you need to do, to see your soulmate again."

She grabbed Iphigenia's arm, and… *nothing.*
"What—?"

"We're anchoring her." Circe appeared between them and Atlas, and blew a kiss at the nearest goon, who collapsed bonelessly to the floor. The other human men dropped too, as if a switch was turned.

A palm as large as Atlas' squeezed Iphigenia's free hand, not as if someone grasped it, but like it'd been there and she only now noticed. She tried to raise her elbow, to slam it in the man's solar plexus, but his hold was too firm. Besides, his solar plexus was much higher than she expected, since he towered over her. Another Titan?

"Prometheus." Atlas' mental cry was laced with relief.

"You can't take all of us on, Rhea." Eros materialized in the corridor, next to another huge-ass man. Another Titan? Was Iphigenia meeting her brothers in law in a towel? Her cheeks burning, she snatched her arm away from Rhea, who finally let go.

The Titaness hissed in frustration. "All I want is my son back. All you need to do is wake up Kronos. He's your brother. Why won't you help me?" She seemed to honestly not get it.

Since the others only exchanged glances and Atlas was still frozen, Iphigenia took it upon herself to reply. "Because from what I hear, he was an asshole who ate his own children." Under her breath, she added, "And considering he was your hubby, I don't find it hard to believe that he was batshit."

"*You, shut up*," Rhea shrieked. "It's all your fault." She grew, as she spoke, until her head grazed the high ceiling, and her shoulders crowded the corridor.

Iphigenia was too shocked to react, when Rhea's oversized palm closed around her neck, choking her. *Not again, damn it.*

"I think I'll snap your neck, just because I feel like it." Rhea squeezed and lifted, and black stars appeared before Iphigenia's eyelids.

No. Iphigenia wouldn't faint this time. She scratched at Rhea's wrist, but her fingers were too small to do any damage, despite her augmented strength. She looked at Circe. The witch would stop this. She'd done it before. Atlas raged in her head, threatening to skin Rhea alive and rip her beating heart from her chest as soon as he had control over his body again, but it would be too late.

Iphigenia couldn't believe the irony of finding her true love, her soulmate, only to lose him again.

"You can't," Eros said, as casually as if they were talking about dinner. "She's no longer mortal."

So Iphigenia was repeating herself, but— What. The. Fuck? Not mortal? Nobody checked with her on this. "If you knew, I swear I'll nag you into the next millennium," she muttered hoarsely at Atlas.

Prometheus chuckled, and Atlas' panicked thought came through loud and clear. "I swear I had no clue."

The third Titan rolled his eyes. "Will you let go, already? None of us is going to help you. I understand your pain, I really do, but this will get you nowhere. Leave the girl alone and go home. We promise not to come after you or your men," he told Rhea.

Rhea shook Iphigenia once, and then dropped her, to land not-so-elegantly on her knees. "I don't need your help or your promises. Thanks to Atlas, I know what to do." She blinked out of there without further warning.

Atlas hurried to help Iphigenia up, whatever spell held him back now broken. He looked her up and down, and then crushed her into a hug that squished the air out of her lungs. She didn't mind. The hard planes of his body pressing into her breasts and belly and thighs, his warmth enveloping her, made her feel safe. She belonged with him, and as much as the concept of immortality freaked her out, *forever* with Atlas wouldn't be long enough.

He tilted her chin up with his index finger and brushed his lips over hers. The fleeting contact sent heat speeding through her veins, her soreness forgotten in the face of her need for him. But she'd have to wait.

He stepped back and looked at Rhea's goons lying on the floor, before turning to Circe. "Wake them up. They'll tell us where she went."

"They're dead," Circe said.

Iphigenia gasped. "Dead?"

Eyes downcast, Circe said, "I didn't kill them. She did, before she left."

Eros clicked his fingers, and the bodies disappeared. "I'll make sure they're buried when we're done here. But we need a plan for when Rhea strikes next. She's unstable."

"*Fuck.*" Atlas squeezed his eyes shut.

"Lovely word," Prometheus said.

"Can't we celebrate this win, brother, now we're on the same side?" The Titan Iphigenia had no name for pulled Atlas into a bear hug, and the love and happiness that flowed through their mental bond overrode Iphigenia's shock and made tingle with delight. Her Titan didn't just have her; he also had his family back.

When they broke apart, Atlas motioned to him with his head. "This is Hyperion. He fathered the sun and the moon."

"And the dawn. Olivia made me swear any offspring I father with her will at least *look* human." Hyperion held out his hand, and Iphigenia shook it with a grin. Holy fuck.

Atlas wrapped one arm around Prometheus, who patted his back with a hearty laugh. "Good to have you back. Even better to see you haven't lost your mind, like Rhea," Prometheus told him.

"I came close a couple times, but Iphigenia put me back together."

"I know how that feels." Prometheus smiled at Iphigenia. "Pherusa, my soulmate, is dying to meet you since Eros told her about you. She wants to learn martial arts too." He snorted. "Like she doesn't kick my ass enough as it is."

"I'll be happy to help," Iphigenia said. "And thank you for putting us up. Your place is lovely, though I'm afraid you'll need a new bathroom door."

Atlas grimaced. "The living room may need some redecorating too."

Eros clapped his hands. "Circe will fix that. Let me get your ladies, and you can all catch up. Take a couple days off. Enjoy the island." He disappeared with a longing glance at Circe.

The witch came closer. "The damage is mended, at least in the building. Rest up. Then we can regroup with Nereus and his people, and make plans." She was out of sight before the last word was out.

Iphigenia was getting used to this now-you-see-'em, now-you-don't crap, and barely batted an eyelash. Judging by her track record, the witch would show up when she was needed. The name Circe mentioned rang a bell. "Nereus?" Where did she know that from?

"King of the sea," Atlas sent her.

"He rules the only supernatural army on Earth. Well, technically, it's in the sea," Hyperion said.

"He's my father in law," Prometheus added.

Wow. Information overload. And was she a thousand percent sure she wasn't still asleep in the museum?

The throbbing at the apex of her thighs and the pleasant ache radiating from the bite mark that peeked above the towel assured Iphigenia she wasn't. She was fully awake, and living the adventure she was born for.

And once she traded in the towel for a T-shirt and another pair of shorts, she was ready for anything.

Except for meeting the mermaid Eros brought with him when he reappeared. Correction—*Nereid*. Semantics, really, since Pherusa turned half-fish when she was submerged into water. And she invited Iphigenia to her father's palace at the bottom of the sea.

Iphigenia looked across the living room at Atlas, who joked with his brothers. Pherusa and Olivia were the only ones in the entire world who shared the experience of being bonded to a Titan. They were kind of like family.

Olivia was human. Or had been, before bonding with Hyperion. She was from New York, but had gotten a crash-course in Greek from Eros and could easily follow and contribute to the conversation. She didn't say much, though, mostly watching with an amused expression as Iphigenia rained questions on Pherusa about Vythos, her underwater kingdom.

"Wow." Iphigenia couldn't wrap her mind around any of it, but what really stretched the limits of her imagination was that Pherusa had fifty siblings. "Please tell me your parents didn't keep trying for the son." She slapped a hand over her mouth. "I'm sorry. That was rude," she mumbled behind her palm.

Pherusa laughed. "No, Nerites was the firstborn."

"And does he have to marry all of you off, in true Greek fashion, before he gets settled down?"

The Nereid's chuckle sounded forced. "No. None of that. We have… our own tradition. He just hasn't had much luck with love." There was a story there, but Iphigenia wouldn't pry.

Instead, she asked, "So do you have any memories from before?"

"Before?" Olivia tilted her head to the side.

Pherusa frowned. "What do you mean?"

Iphigenia took another sip of the martini Eros had served before making himself scarce for the night. "You know—*before*. When your souls belonged to the Titanesses? The originals? I freaked out when Atlas told me my soul initially belonged to Pleione."

The two women still gave her blank looks.

Iphigenia bit her lip. She ought to drop it, but she couldn't. They should know, shouldn't they? She'd want to, in their place. "The reason our guys awakened is that the souls of the Titanesses they were meant for were reborn. Into us."

On the other side of the room, Hyperion and Prometheus raised their heads, alarmed.

Oops?

# CHAPTER EIGHTEEN

"You sure know how to clear a room." Atlas tried not to laugh at Iphigenia's angry scowl. His brothers had swept their soulmates off to Vythos, to confront Circe. Neither of them had known about the reincarnated souls, and from what Atlas had seen of the witch, Eros would be in a lot of trouble for sharing that tidbit.

Iphigenia poked his chest with her index finger. "You could have told me they didn't know."

"I didn't imagine, *so how about those recycled souls of ours?* would be your icebreaker. I thought you'd discuss the weather, your families, the amazing Titan you're bonded to… You know."

She flared her nostrils, but inside, she was laughing. "I honestly didn't mean to upset them, but I had to tell them. I'm immortal now. Stronger. Who knows how else the bonding has affected me? Us?" Her thoughts shied away from him, but not before he brushed past her worry.

What was that about?

"The future," she answered his unasked question. "Anyway, now that our guests are gone—"

"Technically, we're the guests here." He licked his lips, still tasting traces of their last kiss. "Feel like taking greater advantage of my brother's hospitality? We could go back to bed. Or maybe try out the sofa. *Any* sofa?"

She looped her arm around his. "One-track mind. I swear, you men…" She shook her head. "No. You said we'd eat. Where's the food?"

Right. He'd meant to take her to her parents' for dinner. Should they drop in unannounced?

Well, why the hell not? "Put some shoes on, and we can go."

"Go where?"

"Home."

She scrunched her nose. "Mount Othrys?"

He let his amusement show. "*Your* home. I want to meet the parents."

"You know, I'm not that hungry after all." She sat on the arm of the couch and raised her shirt, exposing her perfect, creamy breasts to him. The reasons behind her reluctance to take him home were easy to read—she didn't want her family to mess up what she and Atlas had, and she hated having to lie to her folks about how the two of them hooked up.

Both issues were easily fixable, but there was no rush for him to meet her folks, so he didn't push for now. "Hold that thought," he said. "Actually, don't. Think of your ex's place."

"Pavlos? Why?" She didn't cover herself, but she might as well have, the way her posture hardened and closed up. It was an almost imperceptible change in how she held her shoulders, the tilt of her chin, the unyielding corners of her lips…

"Trust me."

He was surprised by how easily she gave in, and not a little annoyed by how detailed her memory of the spacious, well-lit apartment was. He focused on the black leather couch and dark wooden floor, and found himself leaning against Pavlos' armchair.

The place was empty, no sign of a dog in sight. Atlas frowned. What happened to the golden haired mutt Iphigenia loved?

A whining from outside reached his ears. The evening was warm, but it must have been scorching hot here earlier in the day. The bastard left his animal on the balcony in these temperatures?

Logic suggested the dog might not have been outside till mere moments ago, but Atlas was determined to hate this Pavlos guy, who wanted to shackle Iphigenia to a life that would break her beautiful, free spirit.

He only winced a little at the shrieking sound of a siren that tore through the apartment when he let himself outside.

The poor dog howled, not as capable of ignoring the sound. He twirled around himself, barking and whining, a blond blur of fluff.

Atlas had always been good with animals. He circled the dog to meet his gaze, and when the dog stopped moving, knelt in front of him. "Don't be afraid"—what was his name?—"Ares. Come. I'll take you to Iphigenia."

The dog bared his teeth but looked scared, not aggressive.

Atlas sent a soothing mental image of himself petting him and scratching his belly.

Ares quieted. He studied Atlas, swerving his head from left to right, then padded to him, ears and tail lowered in submission.

Atlas held out his hand for the dog to sniff. When the warm, wet tongue lapped at his palm, he closed his other fist around the dog's collar.

The shrill sound ceased, and a male voice asked. "What are you doing with Ares?"

Ah. The ex. Atlas gazed at the man behind him over his shoulder. He was tall, for a human. Classically handsome, though his eyes were too close together and his chin a little weak.

"Let go of the dog. You're scaring him." Pavlos patted his leg, and in an exaggeratedly upbeat tone said, "Here, boy. Come here."

Ares ignored him and licked Atlas' arm. He didn't seem to like his master much.

Atlas projected Iphigenia's image to the dog, who wagged his tail and yipped. Yeah, no contest there. "I'm taking Iphigenia her dog," he told Pavlos, using only the slightest hint of compulsion.

"Did she send you?" Pavlos scowled. "If she wanted to talk, she could have called me. You didn't have to break in."

The thought of her calling the guy had Atlas' hackles rising. "She lost her phone." He kept his tone conversational, as if that made absolute sense. He stood, lifting the mutt in his arms. "Do you even love this dog, or did you keep him out of spite?"

Pavlos didn't have to answer. Atlas picked up his thoughts about how he hated the dog's shedding and waking up early to walk him.

"That's what I thought," Atlas said.

"What…?" Pavlos shook his head and squared his shoulders, blocking the way back inside. "Let go of my dog and don't do anything stupid. The police are on the way. There's nowhere for you to go."

That was what *he* thought. "Try to stop me." It wasn't Atlas' proudest moment, but he focused on growing his body to double his human size—still a fraction of his true height and bulk.

Pavlos stepped back, but to his credit didn't shriek. "Who… *What are you?*" His calm took the fun out of intimidating him.

Atlas poured more compulsion into his voice, as he said, "It doesn't matter. You are going to forget you ever saw me, and not come after Iphigenia or Ares. He's her dog now."

Iphigenia's scowl when Atlas appeared in front of her in his five-meter glory melted into a beaming smile when she saw the dog he was cradling.

She held up her arms and snatched the animal as soon as Atlas shrunk back to a human-ish height. "*Ares.*" She kissed the dog's nose and laughed when he licked hers. "*Oh my God.* How…? Pavlos will be livid." She fell back on the couch, squealing with delight as Ares went on full-on attack mode with his doggy kisses and sniffs.

"Nah. He's okay with it." Damn, he'd forgotten the dog's leash.

Iphigenia held the dog aside with both hands and pursed her lips. "What did you do?"

"We'll need a leash for Ares." He backed toward the front door. "Maybe I could call Eros and ask him to drop one off."

She stood, and the dog hopped to the floor, where he proceeded to rise on two legs and paw at her. "What did you do?" she asked Atlas again.

"Shouldn't you be getting dressed? I thought you wanted to go for dinner."

"*Atlas.*"

He gave her puppy eyes. "I just wanted to make you happy."

She bit her lip but couldn't hide her grin. "I love you." Through their mental link, she added, "And after you feed me, I'll show you how much."

# RHEA

Rhea chewed on the inside of her cheek. She'd known the Titans could only be awakened by their soulmates—she was there when Zeus created the curse. She hadn't realized the souls calling to the Titans were those of their Titaness mates, reincarnated, though. Atlas said his human female had Pleione's soul. It made sense that would be the case for the rest of them.

If Zeus had included the same caveat in Kronos' curse, she'd only need to find him, but he was cloaked from her. The earth would have to shudder, to reveal and awaken him, and she couldn't cause a potent enough earthquake without knowing where its epicenter should be. Besides, her powers had weakened through the centuries of disuse; she hadn't been allowed to use them while the Olympians had ruled the world.

*It wasn't a natural deterioration.*

Nonsense. Her golden boy wouldn't do that to her, and Hera had gotten what she deserved for even implying it.

Rhea bit on a ragged nail and rummaged through her crystals. She had one that would do.

*Find the Titaness, raise the Titan, solve your problem.* If Atlas wouldn't help her, she'd have one of his brothers end existence as they knew it. She would survive, and she had ways of making sure Kronos did too. And then, they could start over. They'd bring her boy back to life and recreate the world.

She spotted the black crystal, colored with Pandora's life blood. The same crystal Zeus had used to imbue her with the curiosity that would be humanity's downfall. Pandora hadn't been a Titaness, but she was the one who'd held Epimetheus' heart. And if she'd been reborn and Rhea found her…

A lot of *ifs*, but her gut told her she was right. "It's all in place, my love," she murmured to the empty room, strewn with the dead bodies of her soldiers. They weren't the ones who disappointed her, but they'd been annoying with their questions about her failure and their fallen comrades. And maybe she'd been in a bit of a mood.

*Find me.*

She sighed. Her moods were getting worse. Her heart stammered at the memory of blinking from one man to the other with the speed of light and snapping their necks. She didn't have to do that. They'd been loyal.

She harrumphed. They were human. Of no consequence. They'd outlived their usefulness, and she'd taken care of them like any king of gods would.

Her moods scared her some times.

She blew on the crystal and ordered the air to find the soul that vibrated at the same frequency as the blood in its molecules.

Not long now…

# EPILOGUE

"Do you realize what you've done?" Circe glared at Eros, not for the first or even the tenth time since they returned to her palace.

He pulled at the ropes binding his wrists to the bed. "I said I'm sorry. I even let you tie me down." *Pfft*, as if he didn't like this. "You have to forgive me."

She slapped at his long, thick cock and watched it bounce, a drop of precum glistening on the tip. "I don't *have to* do anything. *You* had to keep your mouth shut. Do you know what will happen now?"

"Do you?" he asked in an unrepentant, challenging tone.

*No.* That was what irked her the most. He'd muddied the waters of her visions, by throwing in an extra factor. Rhea wasn't supposed to know who the Titans' soulmates were. Epimetheus wasn't supposed to be awakening. Areti was supposed to die in a car crash. "You've made a big mess." She let her irises darken, to show him she was seriously pissed off. Part of her was tempted to assume her façade, the appearance of the ancient crone, and kill the stupid god's libido once and for all.

But she couldn't. Because she—

"I just hate secrets," he whispered. He sounded so sincere and hurt, his gorgeous pale-blue eyes pleading with her to understand.

She sighed, her mind as far from sex as possible when he was around. Which wasn't all that far. "Breaking the rules has consequences."

Eros snapped his fingers, and the ropes around his wrists turned to seaweed ribbons which he broke free off with a tug. Before Circe could react, he was on top of her, her skirt lifted to her waist and his agile, long fingers tracing her slit. "Then punish me." He used his teeth to move aside the fabric covering her breast and wrapped his lips around her nipple. His erection nudged her thigh.

If she tilted her hips, he'd slide inside her with his fingers or his cock and they could put this behind them, but his telling Atlas about the Titanesses wasn't all that held her back. She pulled him to her by the hair and slanted her mouth against his, breathing in his power and the scent of rich, dark, delicious chocolate that was so exclusively his.

When he broke the kiss, he looked as dazed as she felt. *So easy to say nothing.* But he hated secrets, and if she held on to this one much longer, he'd end up hating her.

Not that she cared. Men—even supernatural, gorgeous, funny ones who could make her come like a rocket—weren't to be trusted. Definitely not to be loved. She and Eros were just having fun till they settled this thing with the Titans. So what if he hated her?

He positioned himself at her entrance, and she couldn't believe she was doing this, but she scooted back. "Not now." She tried to ignore his forlorn expression. "We have to talk."

Eros blew a long, blond curl out of his face. "I said I'm sorry. I vow never to betray your confidence again, and you know my promises are unbreakable."

"It's not that." *Ugh.* "It's your mother. She's back, in a mortal body." When he stared at her, she raised her gaze to the ceiling. "Remember the realtor who sold Prometheus his villa? Magda?"

# End of Book Three

# ABOUT THE AUTHOR

Sotia shares her life and living quarters with her husband, their son, and two rescue dogs, one of which may be part-pony. Sappy movies make her cry, and she wishes she could take in all the stray dogs in the world.

Sotia spent her formative years reading anything she could get her hands on, including steamy romances her grandma would frown upon—nah, Grandma would totally approve.

Hailing from the land of Olympians and Titans, Sotia could only resist writing about mythical immortals for so long. Her mythology romance boasts hot, powerful Alphas, who can handle sassy ladies and will stop at nothing to make them happy.

True love exists, and Sotia is determined to give her fated couples a happy ending!

*

To know more about Sotia, get your hands on freebies, and be the first to hear about new releases, check out her website!

*www.sotialazu.com*